WHEN THE WIND BLOWS

WHEN THE WIND BLOWS

BY LEON PHILLIPS

FARRAR, STRAUS AND CUDAHY

NEW YORK

Published simultaneously in Canada by
Ambassador Books, Ltd., Toronto
Manufactured in the United States of America

For

OLIVER G. SWAN

WHEN THE WIND BLOWS

CHAPTER ONE

A gust of raw wind swept across the Outer Drive, and Lake Michigan's angry spray pounded against the rocks of the breakwater and soared high in the air. The exposition halls and carnival buildings of the World's Fair, Chicago's pride but closed now for the winter, looked bleak, and the roof of the Globe Theatre was covered by several inches of soot-flecked snow. On the opposite side of the Drive beyond the shivering young saplings, the mass of slums was shrouded by fog and dusk, and the taller bulk of Michael Reese Hospital loomed grey and desolate.

A thin stream of cold air seeped in through the windows of the '32 Plymouth and a patch of icy slick under the left front wheel caused the car to skid slightly. But Paul Dawson, applying a slight pressure to the wheel, continued to hum the theme song of the "Easy Aces" program along with the organ that sounded through the speaker of the car radio. Timing his action with the practice of long experience, he snapped off the machine just as the voice of the announcer began to extol the virtues of the sponsor's product. Listening to "Easy Aces," Paul thought, was one of his minor secret vices; although he pretended to be contemptuous of almost everything on radio except the big evening shows like the Rudy Vallee hour and the

Fred Allen program, he had to admit, if only to himself, that he enjoyed the nonsensical adventures of Jane Ace. They reminded him of his mother in her more scatterbrained moments.

Remembering his mother he frowned, pulled off a glove with his teeth and fished in his pocket for a cigarette, then turned off the heater while he used the electric lighter. His battery was sometimes temperamental in weather like this, and he wanted no trouble with the car later tonight. Handling his mother was going to be enough of a problem.

It would be so easy if he could either say nothing at all about his date of this evening, and he certainly didn't want to lie, for there was nothing of which he was ashamed. But he knew there would be a certain strain at the family dinner table if he said, "I'm going dancing at the Balloon Room with a girl named Helga Bjornson. I don't know her family, I've never met them but I'm sure her father doesn't belong to either of Dad's clubs. All I do know about her is that she's a secretary, she seems to be very sweet and pleasant and by any standards she's quite pretty."

A car passed the Plymouth, kicked up a cloud of powdered snow and for an instant Paul's windshield was hazed; automatically he turned on the wiper, then just as automatically turned it off again when the glass cleared. If he spoke frankly to his mother, he could predict to the last word the turn that the conversation would take:

Surely he knew enough nice girls that he didn't have to date someone from a family they'd never heard of. Was it possible that his job as a reporter for the Express was coarsening him? When he had been at the University he certainly hadn't gone out of his way to have dates with such girls. Oh, there was nothing wrong with this particular one, of that she felt sure. But all the same, it seemed like such a waste of time when there were girls like Joan Adams who would just love to spend an evening with him. And it would be useless to explain that he already had a pending date with Joan for tomorrow night, that much as he thought she was a good kid he took her out principally to keep peace at home, and that he didn't intend to marry her, although the family—and probably Joan herself—thought that he would.

A passing car honked, and Paul glanced into his rear-vision mirror. Catching a fleeting glimpse of his own reflection, he grinned; only rarely did he think of his own appearance, and he guessed that the pending date with a new girl made him conscious of himself now. He was no Rudolph Valentino or Milton Sills, of course, but he had to admit he wasn't too bad-looking a guy. At least he was tall, just a quarter of an inch under six feet, to be precise.

His hair was dark brown, and his sisters always said they envied its wave, which they preferred to their own tighter curls. What he did not realize was that his eyes, which were hazel in color, were an indication of his character and that they had a dreamy expression, one that gave an illusion that his thoughts were far away, when he became serious.

The lights of the skyscraper apartment houses in the Hyde Park district made an uneven pattern in the growing darkness, and Paul pushed his foot against the gas pedal, then released it again when the car shivered. Dad wasn't going to find the roads any better, and maybe he wouldn't be home yet. Mother's insistence on dinner being served at six-thirty sharp was a nuisance sometimes, but Paul guessed that maybe her firmness was justified. She claimed that she couldn't keep a maid if the dinner hour was changed every night, and Delcie was a real treasure whose services weren't to be discarded lightly. Granted it was easy to find domestic help these days, even though the W.P.A. had taken up a lot of the employment slack, but there simply weren't many like Delcie.

Paul decided he was hungry and wondered what they'd have for dinner. He remembered that he'd eaten nothing for lunch but a small bowl of chili at the Thompson's cafeteria across the street from the office, and he hoped Delcie was cooking pot roast with potato pancakes. It had been two or three weeks since they'd last had it, and the dish was just about due again. If it wasn't served soon, Dad would begin to ask for it without ever saying in so many words that he wanted it. Grinning, Paul thought that in some ways he was very much like Dad; neither of them could ever come out in the open and say, "I want!" All they could bring themselves to do was to throw out subtle suggestions and intimations, and hope that the person on the receiving end was sensitive enough to understand their desires.

Jackson Park, desolate and bare under a patchy carpet of white, was on the right now, and the reproductions of Christopher Columbus' ships, their paint faded and their superstructures stripped, were held prisoner by thick blocks of ice that coated the surface of the lagoon. Paul swung the car onto South Shore Drive and saw the familiar lights of his family's house, which was set behind a low fence of matching chocolate-colored brick. Grandpa had built the place when he had made his first resounding success in business and had taken his only son into the company with him, and the house was bigger, more spacious than more modern dwellings. It had an air about it, an aura of stability and dignity and imperviousness to time or circumstance or change.

And that, Paul thought, as he brought his car to a halt in the front driveway, was one of the elements that so disturbed him these days. Most of the country was still suffering from hard times, but no one would know it judging by the scale on which the Dawsons lived; and his own parents' blindness to the unemployment and suffering that were universal increased his impatience and distress. It was almost as though they had no contact with the world, and Paul was convinced that they never looked past that brick wall of their own realm.

If most of the people with whom he worked realized that his

father regularly employed three servants, Paul knew they would regard him as something of a freak. And to be honest with himself, he felt a little like one at times. In addition to Delcie there was the chauffeur-gardener-handyman who had his own little apartment over the garage, and the five-full-days-per-week laundress who also did most of the heavy cleaning. It was fair enough, of course, for people who could afford servants to hire them, but the maddening aspect was that neither his mother nor his father seemed to be even remotely aware of how lucky they were, how vast was the gulf that separated them from the bulk of mankind.

Paul knew, of course, that he was not to blame for his parents' fault, but he felt responsible for them all the same. And it had occurred to him more than once that if nothing else woke them up, his own conscious rebellion against their callousness and indifference might shock them into opening their eyes. Mother spent more money on a clothes-shopping trip to New York than a great many people were able to scrape together for a year's food and rent. Only yesterday Paul had been sent out to cover the story of an attempted joint suicide, and when he remembered, painfully, the threadbare squalor in which that unemployed factory worker, his wife and two little children had lived, the big, sprawling house which he was now approaching seemed to belong to an era that was dead.

It crossed his mind as he slipped his key into the lock that perhaps he had made his date of this evening in order to break out of the confining pattern in which his parents were so determined to keep him. It was good, he told himself, for a man to know and appreciate people in every walk of life, and an attractive, intelligent girl was no less appealing, no less interesting because her parents were poor. They were people, and to Paul all people were important. His own mother and father could move around in their tight, select little circle if that was what they wanted, but he wasn't going to permit them to handcuff

[7]

him. That was one of the chief reasons he enjoyed his job at the newspaper.

The front hall light was burning and two or three lamps were lighted in the living room, but the downstairs portion of the house was deserted. Paul shed his outer garments and hung them in the front hall closet, then mounted the stairs two at a time, unthinkingly taking scrupulous care to observe the rules of a game he had invented in his childhood: under no circumstances could he touch the bannister. The second floor was warm and cheerful and cozy, and as he reached the landing he felt a sudden surge of comfortable happiness at being here. This part of the house was the real heart, the essence of home, and although he knew full well that his present reaction was a complete contradiction of the bitterness that had almost engulfed him when he had been parking the car, he felt a genuine sense of relaxation and pleasure at being here.

Some day, of course, he'd have to really make up his mind as to whether he wanted to continue to stay on here or take an apartment of his own somewhere. As a general rule, a young man didn't move out of his family's home unless there had been a sharp disagreement, and it occurred to him that it was strange that Chicago should frown on the idea of someone in his early twenties setting up a bachelor residence. New York and the other urban centers of the East attached no stigma to such a move; on the contrary, many families encouraged it. But Chicago had its own standards and lived by them. As a matter of fact, there was really only one section of the city in which a bachelor could even find a light-housekeeping dwelling, and that was on the near North Side, in the district just above the Chicago River. It was an area that had been considered disreputable for years, and Paul had to admit to himself that he had no desire to live in such unattractive surroundings.

Paul was aware that some day he would be forced to decide what he really wanted, but the end of a hard day of work when

[8]

all of the comforts of an orderly, extraordinarily pleasant home welcomed him was hardly the moment, and he shouted a general, "Hi, I'm home!" to anyone who might be within earshot. He heard a mutter of conversation from his parents' bedroom, realized that his father was already home and hurriedly started down the corridor to his own room. Lights were blazing in "the sorority house" as he passed it, and the door was ajar. He poked his head inside.

Marcia was sitting curled up in a small, curved backed easy chair that was a poor imitation of Louis XV furniture. There was something about that chair that had always made Paul somewhat uncomfortable; it was covered in blue satin, and it just didn't look as a chair should. Marcia, her immature figure covered by a shaggy yellow sweater and a full tweed skirt, lifted her curly brown head from her book.

"Well, if it isn't Richard Harding Davis."

"Hi, Goofy." Paul thought she seemed a little lost these days, that she'd been lonely ever since Betsy had gone off to college at Wellesley this past September. "Improving the mind with 'The Bobbsey Twins on Land and Sea' again?"

"I happen to be doing my homework, if it's all the same to you."

"It's all the same to me." He noted that she took care to cover the jacket of the book so he couldn't see it. "What a noble infant you are, doing homework on a Friday night." He entered the room, intending to pat her condescendingly on the top of the head, a teasing gesture that never failed to get a rise out of her.

But at that moment a clear, high voice floated down the corridor. "Is that you, Paul? Dinner's almost ready."

He shouted an inarticulate reply and dashed to his bathroom for a quick wash. When he came back into his own room to put on his jacket, it being a family rule that no gentleman ever sat down at the table in his shirtsleeves unless the weather was

[9]

insufferably hot, his mother was standing at his desk, idly looking at a pile of old textbooks which he had long intended to stash away somewhere.

Molly Dawson had once been a beautiful girl, and she was one of the few women Paul had ever seen who was still pretty in her fifties. Short, inclined toward plumpness but carrying her weight with dignity, she was usually either sweet or distracted and absent-minded. At the moment she was sweet, and Paul, feeling proud of her, wondered if his friends' mothers always looked that neat and trim. Molly was wearing a two-piece suit of dark grey wool, flecked with green, the jacket short and snug, the ample skirt extending an inch or two below the calves, as befitted her matronly status. Her jewelry was simple, too; she confined herself to tiny pearl earrings, an enameled lavalier hanging from a thin chain and, of course, the diamond wrist watch that had been her husband's twenty-fifth wedding anniversary gift last year.

She lifted her face and Paul kissed her on the cheek. "How are tricks, Toodles?"

Ordinarily she secretly enjoyed this kind of mock disrespect, though she would not admit it in so many words. At the moment, however, she seemed preoccupied. "I didn't know you were home until I heard you talking to Marcia."

"Sorry. I yelled from the top of the stairs, but I guess you and Dad were busy talking."

Molly studied him, but Paul could not be sure whether she was really looking at him or thinking of other matters.

As it happened, she was concentrating her full attention on him. He looked so strong, and yet so pitifully vulnerable and frail. Other women had told her that they worried more about their first-born than about their other children, but Molly thought that in Paul's case she had good and valid reasons for concern. She no longer understood him, although she could scarcely bring herself to admit it. Gordon said freely that he had absolutely no understanding of what went on inside the boy, but it was more difficult for a mother to be that blunt, particularly with herself.

Nevertheless it was incomprehensible to her that Paul should have rejected a place in a company which his grandfather had founded, a prosperous concern which his father now owned. It was Paul's duty to work there, a duty to his heritage, a duty to his sisters as well as to himself. And Molly felt, as she always did these days, that the blame was really her own. She had done everything possible from the time Paul had been a little boy to make him aware of the responsibility that would someday be his, but he hadn't been impressed, or he couldn't have accepted a position in the strange, not-quite-respectable profession of newspaper reporting.

Worst of all, in Molly's eyes, was the suffering Paul had caused his father. Gordon had been deeply hurt when the son on whom he had counted to follow in his footsteps had rejected him, and the sore had not healed. There were times when, as father looked at son, the pain in Gordon's eyes was so great that Molly wanted to scream aloud. It was so wrong, so evil to see this estrangement between the two whom she cherished most in this world, and she wanted desperately to achieve a reconciliation, but she felt powerless, helpless.

Gordon was more important to her than anyone she had ever known, and had been ever since the never-to-be-forgotten day twenty-seven years ago when she had met him at a stuffy musical recital given by her older, married sister. She had been introduced, he had smiled that patient, wise smile of his at her, and everyone else had faded into the background. No other man had ever really meant anything to her, although she had been more popular than the majority of her contemporaries. Gordon was her reason for being, and she couldn't help her reactions right up to this day: when he was happy, she rejoiced; when he was depressed, she wanted to weep.

[11]

It was unfair of Paul to worry and bewilder and upset his father. Of course all young people were insensitive, Molly felt; Paul's attitude and conduct went too far, however, and if there should ever be the need for a choice between husband and son, Molly would unhesitatingly side with Gordon. Fortunately that time had not come, and she prayed that it never would.

What mattered was now, and her sense of frustration increased because she felt so out of touch with Paul. But she could not fathom the reasons behind his antagonism. When she tried to question him, he became sullen, so she was left with no choice but to give him all the love a mother could offer her firstborn, to look after his wants and his needs as best she understood them, to make sure he was comfortable and warm and well-fed. It was her function as a woman, she thought, to act as buffer between Gordon and Paul; deep down, she was convinced that the tensions between them were only tempo-rary, and that the breach would be healed if she exercised enough tact and patience. She did not and could not doubt the end result. After all, they were of the same flesh and blood.

Paul was glancing down at her now with that faintly wistful, remote expression that always made her so ill at ease, and she repeated her question, which he apparently hadn't heard. "You look tired, Paul."

"I feel fine." This was absurd, he told himself, but his mother's over-anxiety for his welfare gave him a feeling of guilt he could not quite define, and he therefore became irrita-ble, even though realizing that his last intention was to slap at her or hurt her.

"Did you have a hard day today?" Understanding nothing about business and having no real interest in the world of men, she asked Dad this identical question every evening.

"No, Mother. No problems." Paul thought of the three hours he had spent in the Municipal courtroom of Judge Orbein, and of the three sordid, ugly little stories he had brought back to the city room. That seamy world had never touched Mother, and she literally wouldn't know what he was talking about if he tried to explain it to her. There was the gentle world of ladies and of men like Dad, and everything beyond its borders was vague and faintly distasteful.

"Did you have a good lunch? You ate something hot, I hope."

"Sure. You know me." He smiled reassuringly, took her arm and quietly led her into the hall, and together they strolled downstairs to the living room.

"What did you eat for lunch, dear?" When Molly settled her mind on a subject, she could be tenacious.

"Darned if I can remember," Paul lied gallantly, knowing she loathed chili.

Gordon was sitting in the green leather chair that no one else ever thought of using when he was at home. He was glancing through the evening newspapers and did not look up. And Paul tried to look at him for a moment, objectively. By any standards the head of the house of Dawson looked like what he was, an eminently successful American businessman. His greying hair was neatly parted, his hazel eyes were ever-alert, missing no subtlety, no nuance, and his chin was square and determined. The key to his character, in a sense, was his chin, for he jutted it forward at the slightest sign of dissension, as though daring anyone to take issue with him.

But he was sensitive, too, in spite of his pugnacious approach, and his mouth thinned into a compressed line at any hurt or insult directed toward him. His steel-rimmed glasses were so much a part of him that Paul could not imagine him without them, and in moments of stress he had acquired the habit of removing them, polishing them carefully and then settling them back on the bridge of his nose with an air of finality.

He always wore white shirts and subdued but expensive neckties, and his double-breasted suits were dark, conservative in cut and a tribute to his tailor, for they concealed a growing paunch, the penalty he had to pay for his long hours at his desk, six days out of every seven. He was a trifle concerned over his increasing girth, but liked food too much to watch his starches accordingly.

Now, still holding his newspaper in front of him, he became aware of the presence of his son. "How are things on the front page today?" he asked. It was his standard greeting.

"Not bad. How are groceries?" Paul could feel his father stiffen slightly and was sorry he had spoken.

The subject of "groceries" was a sore one, for it had been taken for granted that Paul would join his father after his graduation from the University. But Paul had spent two summers working at the company, and the atmosphere had stifled him. He had resented the careful smiles of the other employees, the ever-present sense of discretion that had pervaded every conversation in the presence of the boss' son. Worst of all had been the tension between his father and himself. Gordon had expected nothing less than perfection from him, yet had been reluctant to give him any real responsibilities, apparently feeling he was too callow to discharge them.

Of paramount importance in the reaching of his decision, of course, had been his lack of respect for the grocery business. Food purveyors had their place in the world, to be sure, and they were needed. But principles and ideas—and their application to day-to-day living—were of primary significance to a young man who felt that he had something to contribute to humanity.

And so Paul had quietly determined, at the end of his sophomore year, to build his career anywhere but at Whitmarket and Company. He had been working as University campus and neighborhood correspondent for the Express and had quietly arranged to be taken on the staff in a full-time reportorial position when he left school. He had considered himself lucky, for jobs were still hard to find, although everyone kept insisting that the worst of the Great Depression was over.

His mistake had been to keep silent for so long about his plans; someone in the advertising department of the Express who knew Gordon had mentioned something casual about Paul's future in a chance conversation at the Mid-Day Club, and Gordon had come home hurt and angry. Paul would never forget that night: Dad had first stormed, then retired in an aggrieved silence, and Mother had wept all evening. But, although tempted to succumb to parental desires, he had managed to show a strength of purpose he had never known he possessed, and he had clung grimly to his resolve. In retrospect, the most unpleasant part of the occasion had been the expressions on the faces of his sisters. Betsy had always looked up to him and to Marcia he had been something of a hero, but the disbelief in their eyes, the stricken looks on their faces had done more to convince him that he was guilty of family disloyalty than had Dad's rage or Mother's tears.

Even now it was difficult to explain to these people who felt he had wronged them that he took real pride in his work, that he was now a professional newspaperman, not a boy playing a romantic game. And this moment just before dinner, when Dad asked lightly sardonic questions in an indifferent voice was inevitably disagreeable. Tonight would be more disturbing than usual because Paul had been flippant.

"Any murders I don't know about yet? Any four-eleven fires that have turned the town upside down?" Gordon folded his newspaper carefully and placed it on a table of inlaid wood beside his chair. The table was littered with useless items of ornamental bric-a-brac, a delicate figured clock from Vienna that no longer ran, a dainty alabaster ash tray that was too pretty to use, a little marble statue of a girl's head. There was actually no space for the newspaper, but Gordon was never one to pay any heed to such details.

"We had a very routine day, Dad." Paul made sure that his reply was toneless, flat.

[15]

"Write any deathless prose on the views of some movie star who had a couple of hours to kill between arriving on the Twentieth Century and leaving on the Chief?"

"Nary an interview all day." Paul began to grow edgy, and ran the fingers of his right hand through his hair, an unconscious gesture he often performed when he was upset.

"Then there must have been some sort of spontaneous combustion at City Hall. Surely some ward heeler with the intellect of an ant gave you the inside story on who our next Senator is going to be—and why."

The tension was growing, and Molly cleared her throat nervously. She knew her husband, and he was apt to be most irritable just before dinner. Fortunately Delcie chose to appear in the open double doors of the dining room. She grinned at Paul and he winked at her in return; they understood each other, after ten years under the same roof, and Paul felt an immediate release of pressure.

"It's ready," Delcie said, wiping her hands on her apron and tucking a lock of greying hair behind an ear.

"Marcia! Dinner time!" Molly's relief was obvious, and she started at once toward the table.

Paul, out of long habit, allowed his father to precede him into the dining room; if anyone had ever accused him of following such an old-fashioned custom he would have felt a little ashamed and certainly would have denied it. But he was aware of it all the same, and so was Gordon, although neither had ever mentioned the matter aloud.

Molly was already in her chair by the time her two men arrived, and Gordon frowned as he sat and drew his napkin across his lap. "Must we shout ourselves hoarse at every meal before that child comes to the table?"

"She's reading, Dad," Paul said quickly. "And you know Marcia when she reads. A volcano could erupt right beside her chair and she wouldn't know it. Shall I get her?"

Marcia chose this moment to enter the room, and slid into her chair without moving it. Sure she was going to be rebuked, she chose to attack first herself, and Paul was the only target at whom she could strike with impunity. "I looked and looked for my good fountain pen when I came home from school this afternoon, and then Delcie told me you took it. You have no right to take other people's things without asking their permission."

After almost two decades of listening to various offspring squabble at the table, Molly handled the situation imperturbably. "Did you wash your hands, Marcia?"

"*Yes*, Mother." There was no dignity equal to that of a twelve-year-old who felt she was being treated like a smaller child. "And no potatoes for me, please."

Her mother continued to ladle out vegetables. "They're good for you, dear. You're still growing."

"But—"

"Eat what's put in front of you and don't argue." Gordon didn't miss a stroke as he continued to carve the roast veal. "When I was a boy I was glad to get good potatoes—or anything else I was served."

"All right, Daddy." Marcia knew better than to pursue a losing argument.

Paul wasn't particularly fond of veal, but thought he'd better eat all he could; otherwise he might be hungry later in the evening, and with dates both tonight and tomorrow night, he'd have to watch expenses. Joan always expected to be treated to the best, and accepted it as her due, so tomorrow wouldn't be cheap. Helga Bjornson was still an unknown quantity; it was possible she'd order steak. He'd been stuck like that before, and he'd learned not to take any chances. He accepted his plate in silence, and then frowned as Delcie appeared through the swinging doors of the kitchen with little saucers of stewed pears. Molly and Gordon liked stewed fruit with their main

[17]

course, and Paul emphatically did not, so he felt relieved when Delcie looked at him knowingly for an instant and served the others but deliberately gave him none.

Something was wrong with his nerves tonight, he thought. Ordinarily he wouldn't be bothered by the thought of one of Mother's set, stereotyped little speeches on the benefits of eating stewed fruit. He'd heard them all his life and he had never really minded in the least before. He wondered why he should be so tense, but his father broke in on his train of thought before he could find a satisfactory solution to his question.

"Paul, I ran into Ed MacAvity today. He said to give you his regards."

Ed MacAvity was a classmate who had dutifully gone into his father's business. Paul did not fail to miss the point. "Ed's a nice guy," he said vaguely, then remembered something that would help to ease his father's mind into other topics. "I bumped into an old friend of yours today, too, Dad. Sandy Smith. He was having trouble starting his car, and everybody within a full block of him knew it. I thought there was a riot going on from half a block away."

Gordon chuckled appreciatively; the hot temper and loud voice of Sanford Smith never failed to amuse him. Molly smiled to show that she, too, shared in the men's feelings toward Sandy, of whom she secretly disapproved. And Marcia, who had been occupied with thoughts of her own, suddenly launched into a long and involved account of a dispute that had taken place in the locker room of the school gym after a volleyball game.

Paul closed his ears and his father did likewise. Molly listened to the disconnected, rambling story with sympathy, and for a few minutes the men ate in silence. At last Gordon began to grow irritable, and Paul detected the signs: his father frowned, then pushed his glasses higher on the bridge of his nose. Finally he started to drum on the table lightly with the fingers of his

[18]

left hand, and, unable to tolerate the tale of his youngest any longer, he launched into an anecdote about Sandy Smith.

Paul devoted his full attention to his father's words, and they laughed heartily together when Gordon reached the climax. By this time Marcia had finished talking and had retreated into a dream world of her own. Her fork remained poised in the air for long moments between each bite, and she gazed absently into space. For all practical purposes she might have been alone at the table.

Molly, freed of the burdens of adolescence, helped herself to another portion of buttered broccoli and gazed fondly at her Limoges china and the delicately rainbow-hued Bohemian glassware, at the heavy, handsome silver which she had been collecting since the day of her marriage and at the rich, creamy linen of the tablecloth. Life seemed to be very good, her husband and son were in harmony, and she sighed contentedly.

"It's a wonderful night for being snug at home," she said.

Gordon smiled at her. "Maybe we can all call Betsy after dinner," he suggested.

Marcia was jealous and consequently flatly unsympathetic. "All she ever says when we talk to her is that she's having a wonderful time and she needs money. She thinks she's wonderful just because she's at college. Who wants to listen to her?"

Paul took a deep breath; he could not avoid mentioning his date forever, and this was perhaps the best moment to reveal his plans. "Give Bets my love," he said.

"Oh? Are you going out, dear?" Molly's fine, reddish-brown brows drew together and there was an expression of faint dismay on her face.

"Yes, Mother. I have a date."

"I'm always so nervous when you're out at night, driving in this weather."

Gordon tried to come to his son's rescue. "I think Paul can manage a car by now, Mother. He's never had a crack-up yet."

[19]

"I worry all the same." Molly was adamant, then a subtle change came over her face as she turned back to Paul. "Who are you taking out tonight, Paul?"

"Nobody you know, Mother." He was polite, but had no intention of saying any more.

"It's just possible that I might know her or her famil—"

Again Gordon intervened. "Paul's a big boy now, Mother."

It was a rare occasion when Molly dared to flout her husband's authority, and she subsided into silence now, though everyone else at the table knew that she would not be content to let the matter drop. Sooner or later during the course of the weekend she would contrive to question again, to pry gently but insistently into what she considered it her right and duty to know.

Marcia grinned impishly, and there was a gleam in her eyes. "Where you going, Romeo?"

Paul could have throttled her. "Out," he declared curtly.

Quickly noting that her parents were not looking at her, Marcia dipped a teaspoon into her water glass, flipped the spoon expertly, and a splash landed on Paul's cheek. He had taught her the trick years ago, he thought, so he had no one but himself to blame. Nevertheless the child needed to be taught a lesson, and in her own language, so she would understand. He picked up his butterknife, cut off a little piece of butter, then reached out and deftly smeared the grease on Marcia's hand. She giggled and surreptitiously licked off the butter. Gordon and Molly were chatting about a party they were to attend the following week, and were unaware that anything extraordinary had taken place.

Paul, recalling that he hadn't buttered anyone's hand in at least ten years, wondered if he was reverting to childhood. At least he had silenced Marcia, and that was something. Delcie cleared away the dishes and brought in dessert, and Paul glanced at his watch. There would be just time to change his clothes before leaving. He began to think about Helga Bjornson, and for no reason he could analyze, he felt a growing sense of excitement. He felt positive that she would not be just an ordinary date, nor would tonight be an ordinary evening. He couldn't remember when he had felt this strongly attracted to any girl.

CHAPTER TWO

Chicago boasted newer, richer and gaudier hotels than the Congress, but to all of the Middle West the faded elegance of the old establishment was the summit of genteel grandeur. It did not matter that the carpets that lined the corridor known as Peacock Alley were threadbare, that the furniture was slightly shabby or that the bigger than life portraits of ladies of the 1890's were smeared with a thin coat of grime. There was a faint scent of perfume in the air, renewed hourly by a bellboy armed with an atomizer, no gentleman dared to walk through the Alley until he had first removed his hat, and every lady paused to examine herself critically in a full-length, gilt-framed mirror before braving the length of what to the uninitiated was just another hallway on the lobby floor of a hotel that had once seen better days.

The glamor of the Balloon Room was deceptive, too. The bandstand was half-hidden behind pillars at the far end of a cavern that had been built in the days when diners had wanted elbow room, not intimacy, and the dance floor was partly concealed behind posts, too. A balloon motif predominated in the decor, of course, and was chiefly to be noted in the green, blue, yellow and red pastels of the round shades that covered clusters of wall and ceiling lights. An uninitiated visitor might have thought the room drab, but the Chicagoans who made reservations for tables several days in advance knew better, and so did mildly awed patrons from St. Louis and Kansas City and Pittsburgh.

The waiters were respectful but not servile, the maitre d'hotel was courteous but not haughty, and the bus boys, while forbidden to speak to the guests, were not above smiling in unabashed friendliness at anyone who happened to glance at them. The orchestra was lively but maintained an air of dignity, and confined itself to the scores of current and past musical comedies and to the more refined of the popular songs of the day. The conductor turned a deaf ear to an occasional request for a tango, for "Brother, Can You Spare a Dime" or for such novelty hits of the previous decade as "Boop-Boop-a-Doop" or "Don't Bring Lulu." Even the soloist who was the Balloon Room's concession to a floor show was a red-faced tenor who wore white tie and tails and who specialized in a repertoire ranging from "Night and Day" to "The Road to Mandalay."

Patrons, even the younger ones who elsewhere were inclined to be loud, were rarely vulgar, and the atmosphere was one of decorum. There were elderly couples celebrating anniversaries and birthdays here, as they had done for years; there were family groups who were served quickly and efficiently so the younger children could be hustled off to their beds; and of course, there were the young couples getting to know each other, falling in and out of love, romancing and quarreling and dreaming.

Paul was always slightly abashed and ill at ease when he first stepped into the Balloon Room, but this sensation gave way to one of joy that he was in a position to take advantage of the luxuries and delights that this quietly sumptuous place offered. He followed Helga Bjornson to their table behind the assistant maitre d'hotel, conscious of her beauty and gratified at the attention she was creating. At the same time he was a little annoyed

[23]

with himself for being something of a snob. He was aware that her sturdy, black wool coat was out of place in a room where most ladies wore furs or long evening cloaks, and although he knew that Helga could not afford a more expensive coat, he could not quite rid himself of a faintly uncomfortable feeling.

Her dress was not right for the Balloon Room, either. It was a scoop-necked, shiny peach satin with a ruffled skirt. It was too fussy, and her pumps of matching satin, a little sleazy and narrow-toed, had not been bought at Field's or Blum's Vogue, that was sure. Ordinarily Paul did not think much about what a girl wore; he expected her to look like a lady, and he knew either that her dress was pretty or it was not. It irritated him that he should be so sensitive over Helga's clothes, and the realization increased his discomfort.

He wondered if she was embarrassed or self-conscious, and thought that if she should be, the evening could not be successful. As he took the seat opposite her she smiled at him calmly, however, and his fears vanished. She really was attractive, even startling in her appearance, and he felt proud and rather cosmopolitan. At first glance Helga's hair was her most distinguishing characteristic, for she was a true Scandinavian blonde, and she disdained the current medium-length bob by wearing her hair parted in the middle, combed smoothly back into a soft bun at the nape of her neck. Her eyes, wide-set and large, were a deep blue, and while her nose and her full but firm mouth were too big to fit a classic pattern, they suited her and combined to make her one of the loveliest girls Paul had ever seen.

She was taller than anyone he had ever before taken out, and although he was not good at guessing someone's height, particularly when the hazard of high heels was added, the top of her head came up to the bridge of his nose; so she was probably around five feet seven or eight. She was big-boned, but fortunately slender; he'd always disliked plumpness.

Suddenly he froze. Helga had not draped her coat over the

[24]

back of her chair, but instead was folding it, inside out, with the meticulous, loving care of one who owned few physical possessions and was protecting those she had. He could not refrain from thinking that Joan Adams—or any other girl he dated—would never be guilty of such gauche behavior. His attitude, he knew, was snobbish, but at the same time he was forcibly reminded of one of his mother's favorite homilies, "Breeding will tell."

He was therefore guilty of the very qualities that he found so objectionable in his parents. They didn't know that their neat, ordered world was no more, and so perhaps their very ignorance partly excused them. But Paul realized that he himself was conscious of the sweeping changes that were taking place, that his own family was one of the very few that had not been forced by the Depression to retrench, and consequently he was more to blame than either his father or his mother.

What disturbed him the most was that he was convinced he cared nothing about social distinctions. Class distinctions were artificial barriers; the mere fact that he was spending the evening with Helga proved it. Why, then, should her ignorance of conventions upset him?

A waiter hurried forward and Paul thought he caught a note of condescension in the man's voice. "Would *Mademoiselle* wish me to check her coat for her?"

"No. Thank you very much." Helga was cool and unruffled as she looked for a place to put the coat.

The Balloon Room personnel was trained for any exigency. The waiter snapped his fingers and a bus boy approached with an extra chair; in a matter of seconds the coat was deposited on the seat, with a napkin neatly draped over it to protect it. Helga sat back, oblivious of the error she had made, and Paul, after a brief struggle with himself, felt ashamed of his own reaction to such a trivial incident. Here was an extraordinarily pretty and sweet girl with whom he was going to spend a pleasant evening, and he relaxed again, even though continuing to study Helga covertly.

It astonished him that she was so reposed, for he would have sworn that in all probability she had never before been to the Balloon Room, and he had actually brought her here in the hopes of impressing her. But judging by her quiet acceptance of her surroundings, it seemed more likely that she came here two or three nights a week. That was logical, of course; an attractive girl never lacked escorts who showed her off in the best places.

"Nice joint, don't you think?" He dropped the question casually.

"Oh, it's lovely." Helga's voice was rich and mature. "I always wondered what it was like, and it's every bit as handsome and plush as I'd imagined."

So she hadn't been here after all! Paul searched her face for an instant, marvelling. Most of the girls he knew invariably squealed and made a great fuss when they were taken somewhere new. Helga, plainly, was cut from a different mold. "What would you like?" he asked, handing her a menu.

She studied the tasseled card, then lowered it abruptly. "These prices are frightful!" she declared in a shocked voice.

It was hard to resist a grin. Young ladies were trained never, never to mention prices, but Helga was obviously too honest a person to concern herself with trivialities. Paul was tempted to shrug indifferently, to pretend that money meant nothing to him. But he could not reply to her frankness except in kind. "They make it as tough on you as they can," he admitted.

Helga dropped the card to the table, unwilling to cope with the problem. "You order."

"Okay." Here was a chance to show her that he was a worldly young man, and he beckoned to a waiter. The man looked through and beyond him, not budging, and Paul wondered, not for the first time, why it was that his father could summon a waiter with a single glance when he had to signal frantically. He waved his hand back and forth methodically, and at last the waiter hurried to the table.

"Yes, sir?"

"Two large ginger ales with the long twists of lemon peel. You know, the kind you always serve."

"Yes, sir. Two Congress Specials. Will you be ordering anything to eat?"

Paul looked at the girl, who smiled shyly and shook her head negatively. Relieved, he handed the menu to the waiter. "Not just now. A little later, perhaps."

The orchestra members were filing in, taking their places on the bandstand, and the tenor banjo player began to tune up his instrument. The room was perhaps half-filled now, and a steady trickle of new arrivals indicated that the evening would be a profitable one for the management. Perhaps the country had gone to the dogs, perhaps everybody was broke, but there were still enough people of substance left to pack the Balloon Room on a Friday night. It was an encouraging sign. Paul could neither accept his father's view that the New Deal was driving the United States straight toward ruin, nor could he agree with his friends that F.D.R. was the greatest of all Presidents. All he knew was that he was earning forty dollars per week, that he worked hard for his money and that he was doing as well if not better than the majority of his contemporaries.

And he certainly knew what his father did not—that there was insecurity everywhere, and that it was wrong. Poor people had as much right to be free of fear as people who had the protection of money and an established social background. One thing he liked about this unusual girl was that although she enjoyed the benefits of neither wealth nor family standing, she seemed to be at peace with herself.

He offered a cigarette to Helga, and when she refused it he lit one for himself. "Well," she said, leaning back in her chair.

"That's a pretty dress." Paul had been taught that a gentleman always complimented a lady on her appearance, but he felt slightly ashamed over his lack of sincerity right now. Helga didn't seem to be the sort of person for whom a glib approach was appropriate.

However, she accepted his remark at face value and smiled in quiet pride. "Thank you," she said. "I had some doubts about it while I was making it, but I'm glad you think it's all right."

"You actually made it yourself?"

"Oh, yes. I make all my own clothes."

"Is that so?" He knew he sounded inane, but could think of nothing else to say.

"My mother taught me to sew before I even started going to school."

"We're bound to start playing 'who do you know' sooner or later, so I suggest we start it sooner." Paul was relieved at the opportunity to move onto surer, more familiar ground. "Where did you go to school?"

Before she could reply, a male voice said, "This used to be a nice, exclusive room. Now they let anybody in here, even newspaper reporters."

Paul looked around, then rose to his feet as he saw Warren Palmer and Phyllis Drake, a couple who were members of his "crowd," and both of whom he knew well. His first reaction was one of dismay, for he felt acutely conscious of the off-beat, tinsel effect of Helga's dress. Phyllis, whose principal attraction was her vivacity rather than her beauty, was impeccably groomed, as always, in a sleek gown of flame-red chiffon. By comparison Helga looked shabby and more than a little out of place.

"Miss Bjornson," Paul said, "Miss Drake and Mr. Palmer."

To his horror, Helga stood as she held out her hand and said, "How do you do?" It had never occurred to Paul that any girl could be so abysmally unaware of correct manners. Surely she knew that a lady never, never stood when accepting an introduction.

The cool, studied appraisal by Phyllis, the faint but definite expression of incredulity in Warren's eyes didn't help. It wasn't quite enough for Paul to tell himself that his friends were narrow-minded and bigoted, particularly when he shared their sense of embarrassment and discomfort.

He could never quite remember later just what was said in the next three or four minutes. He and Warren exchanged inconsequential quips, Phyllis drank in every minute detail of Helga's appearance and did not bother to veil her rude curiosity with more than a tiny, polite smile. Only Helga herself was at ease. Perhaps she realized that Paul's friends regarded her at worst as something of a freak and at best as a person who was outside the pale. But their attitude in no way shook her composure; she was relaxed and there was no sign of tension in her face.

But it developed that more than her basic inner serenity was responsible for her control, for her disregard. When Phyllis and Warren murmured goodbyes and wandered off, a smile in her eyes indicated that she was sensitive to their views but found them amusing. It was her impersonal air of detachment that restored Paul's sense of balance. He found himself championing her cause.

He could dismiss Phyllis and Warren from his mind; they did not matter. What was important to him was that he had himself been betrayed again by the very attitudes he condemned. Had he sought the company of someone who knew the right fork from the wrong, he could have brought Joan to the Balloon Room. He was being inconsistent when he dated a working girl whose background he did not know and expected her to display the manners of a finishing-school graduate. It was confusing, after telling himself that social conventions were unimportant, to be disturbed by a minor breach of this code that was made up of trivia.

Either Helga was important for her own sake, because she had character and integrity and intelligence, or else she was not worth an evening of a young man's time. The color, cut and material of her dress either meant nothing—or else they were of paramount importance, as they obviously had been to Phyllis. Or, Paul thought, as they would be to his mother.

He had brought this particular girl to this particular place because he believed in certain principles. He felt sure, in spite of these inexplicable momentary lapses, that he did subscribe to them, too. If he did not, he'd be working for his father now instead of "throwing away his career." He'd have long ago asked Joan to marry him, and would have settled down with her to a comfortable life that would have followed the joint parental blueprint and would have enjoyed enthusiastic parental blessings.

But he had not done these things, and he was determined not to do them. Therefore he needed to act accordingly, right now. Correct dress or no correct dress, proper manners or crude manners, Helga was an exceptionally attractive and interesting girl. "We were saying something of vast inconsequence, I think, before we were interrupted," he said.

She smiled, and for an instant he felt that she knew everything that had gone through his mind; then, just as quickly, the notion passed away. "We were starting to play, 'who do you know,' and you had just asked me where I went to school."

It was rather remarkable that she had no desire to gossip about the couple who had stopped at the table. Almost every girl Paul had ever known would have found the urge to ask questions about them irresistible. Yet Helga seemed to be so self-contained that she could forget Warren and Phyllis as though they had never existed. If Paul chose to talk about them, her attitude seemed to indicate, she was willing, but if he did not, then she could drop them from her consciousness without effort.

"All right, then. Where *did* you?"

"Hyde Park High."

"Really? I knew a lot of Hyde Parkers. Did you ever know Ed Finley? He finished there back around '26 or '27."

Helga smiled broadly and shook her head. "I just got out two years ago."

"Then I'm afraid all my friends were before your time." Paul felt very old as he speculated on her age. She had been around eighteen or nineteen when she'd been graduated from high school, so that would make her twenty or twenty-one now. "You've been working for Inland Insurance ever since?"

"Yes. I'm a secretary. The usual sort of thing." She glanced down involuntarily at her finger nails, on which she wore only a clear lacquer. "Just for fun I'm going to let them grow long on my vacation."

"You sound," Paul said, hesitating slightly, "as though you don't care much for your job."

Helga raised her shapely shoulders and let them drop again. "It's a living, and I'm lucky to have a job. Half the kids I know can't find one. And the money helps at home," she added, then grew self-conscious because she thought she had said too much and started to finger the strap of her inexpensive patent leather handbag. "The day Dave introduced us, he said you're a reporter." Her momentary nervousness was gone. "That sounds very glamorous."

"Drop in at the Express some day and you'll see how glamorous it is." Paul grinned at her and discovered that he was beginning to enjoy himself. "Newspaper work is just plain hard labor. The trouble is, too many people have seen 'The Front Page.' If I ever talked to my boss that way, I'd be thrown out in two seconds. And believe it or not, being a reporter is a pretty lonely life, too, Helga." It required something of an effort to speak her name for the first time.

"Really? I'd think you'd see just dozens of people all day." The music had started and she unconsciously began to tap her slender but capable fingers.

"Sure, you see people, but you're just a machine asking questions, sucking information out of them. That isn't what I meant, though. It's a crazy sort of life. Do you know where I ate my Christmas and New Year's dinners? Do you know where I'll continue to eat them so long as I'm in this crazy business? By myself, at a one-arm hash joint." He hadn't opened up to anyone like this before, and it confused him when he realized that he was speaking so freely to a strange girl on his first date with her.

"You sound as though you're not very keen about your job." Coming from someone else the remark might have been snide, but Helga's voice was sympathetic and warm.

"I like it. Though a job on a metropolitan newspaper isn't an end in itself, at least not for me. In a manner of speaking, I'm still going to school. Some day, maybe in three or four years if I've absorbed enough in that time, I want to own a newspaper of my own. Somewhere in this part of the country—some small town in Michigan or Illinois or Wisconsin." He was about to add that he intended to use his inheritance from his grandfather for the purpose, but realized just in time that such a remark would be tactless. So he grinned, a trifle self-consciously, and leaned back in his chair. "Ever hear of William A. White of Kansas?"

"I think so. He owns a little newspaper out there, isn't that right?"

"It sure is. And he's made himself an international reputation by crusading for truth. There's lots of room for truth, and a big need for editors who are willing to express the courage of their convictions."

The blonde head nodded sagely. "You're very ambitious, Paul. That's good."

He glowed at her easy use of his name, but her words puzzled him. "I think every man is ambitious." This was serious talk for so early in the evening.

"Men like you. But there are many of the other kind. Like my father. His way is good, too, but it's a different way. He was a carpenter when he came over to this country from Sweden twenty-four years ago, and he's still a carpenter today. That's all he's ever wanted to be."

Paul quietly marvelled at her lack of embarrassment; he could never discuss his parents, particularly with someone who didn't know them. "So long as he's contented, that's the main thing. Though I must admit that if I had to choose between ambition and contentment, I'd take a mixture of both."

A distant look came into her blue eyes. "It was Robert Browning, wasn't it, who said, 'I go to prove my soul'?"

Paul gazed at her in admiration tinged with wonder. "You didn't study Paracelsus in senior English Lit at Hyde Park High."

"I like to read." She made the statement flatly, without affectation, and she was openly pleased that Paul had recognized the quotation.

Their eyes met for an instant, and Paul felt stirred by a force he didn't quite understand. The sound of the music insinuated itself into his consciousness for the first time, and he conceived what he considered at the moment to be a brilliant and original idea. "Care to dance?"

Helga replied with the automatic, "Love to," but she spoke the words as though she meant them.

Paul stood, crossed to the other side of the table and held Helga's chair as she arose. Again he was struck by a realization of her height, and he wondered how it had happened that he had never before taken out such a tall girl. As they reached the

[33]

polished floor they drifted into each other's arms and moved off in perfect synchronization. It was unusual for Paul to hit it off so well the first time he danced with a girl: he and Joan Adams had practiced together for weeks before they had achieved even a semblance of this smooth, flowing rhythm. And he liked the way Helga held herself, too. She didn't lean her face against a man and smear cosmetics all over his shirt collar and jacket lapel, nor did she consider a dance floor an appropriate arena for a wrestling match or for an adolescent display of agility. Her soft, gleaming hair barely touched Paul's cheek, her stance was dignified and she carried the weight of her own right arm with her hand firmly but lightly touching his.

Helga began to sing, softly but with a true voice, and Paul joined in, not quite realizing for a moment what he was doing, then enjoying the sensation. He was none too familiar with either the tune or the words and had to hum occasionally, but that didn't matter. Rarely had he felt such a sense of satisfaction, of completeness with any girl, and he gave himself up to the mood of the moment.

The orchestra slid smoothly into another song, and this time he felt more confident; the number was one of his favorites, and although his voice would never cause either Russ Columbo or Bing Crosby to spend any sleepless nights, he sang the lyrics with considerable feeling.

The clarinets finished with a sad flourish, and both Paul and Helga applauded spontaneously, enthusiastically. The floor had become crowded, and they noticed the press for the first time; with unspoken accord they moved back to their own table. And Paul was gratified that his companion neither took his hand nor slipped her arm through his. Too many girls made a practice of indulging in such gestures and he always resented their casual assumption that they could appropriate a man. Anyone who gave herself up to such little intimacies without meaning them was cheapening herself in the eyes of her escort, and

Helga's natural self-esteem was such that she seemed to know it.

Tall, frosted glasses of ginger ale with long twists of artfully cut lemon peel were waiting at the table, and Helga, who was thirsty, took a long swallow of the concoction. Paul thought that most of the girls he knew, like Joan, would never permit themselves the luxury of anything more than a tiny sip at a time. Once again he felt embarrassed by his companion's ignorance on the subject of good manners. But this time he deliberately squelched the feeling and told himself that it was novel and very pleasant to watch someone who felt free of false constraints, who acted naturally and made no attempt to be anything other than what she was.

"What in the world are you thinking?" She asked the question suddenly.

"About you," he replied, startled.

"That's all right then."

"What makes you say so, Helga?"

"Because you were looking very pleased." It was astonishing how she could be so personal without showing the slightest signs of coyness or flirtatiousness or cuteness. "You might have been thinking about your work or what you had for your dinner or even some book you read recently that you enjoyed."

"I didn't realize that I showed quite so much on my face." Paul achieved a grin but nevertheless felt self-conscious.

"Oh, I'm flattered." She was, too.

"You're really an unusual person." He knew he was saying too much, that he ought to guard his tongue or she'd be sure he was handing her a line, but he couldn't stop himself. "I've never met anyone quite like you. I really mean that." He paused, expecting her to respond with, "What *do* you think I'm like?"

But again she surprised him. "No two people are the same, you know." She laced her fingers and leaned forward slightly, deeply intent on what she was saying. "I'm not very bright, and

I've had only the beginnings of an education, but this much I understand—the better you come to know someone and to study that person, the more of an individual he is. Everybody has been so frightened about not finding jobs, the whole country has been so frightened that you'd almost imagine we were a nation of machines. But we aren't, we're people. And we're good, too. I think there's a great deal of good in every single one of us," she concluded, glancing at Paul defiantly, as though she expected him to contradict her.

"I guess you're right, though I spend the better part of my vocational life digging out the bad in people. I'm afraid that wickedness, sin and corruption is what sells daily newspapers."

"Of course." Helga was very serious, and her eyes seemed to grow darker. "It's so much easier to find the bad than it is the good. I have an uncle who—well, he's not too admirable in many ways. My mother says he's lazy and irresponsible and shiftless, and even I have to admit he puts on airs." She laughed, but she made it sound as though she were sympathizing with her uncle, not mocking him. "He's the janitor of an apartment building, and he loves to tell people he's the superintendent. My mother is so honest she can't stand that sort of fooling."

Paul nodded and waited for her to continue. The vague thought crossed his mind that his father would be almost as disturbed as his mother if they knew he was spending the evening with the niece of a janitor. However, that was their business. Right now he wanted to devote his full attention to Helga.

"I happen to know something about Uncle Sven that would—well, he'd just curdle up if he had any idea that I'm wise to him. He's a bachelor, you see, and I found out by accident one time that he goes over to the Swedish-American orphanage on his days off and takes the kids out. He spends every penny he can spare on them, too. Maybe that isn't a very good example." All at once she looked less sure of herself, very young and a little bewildered.

"I think it's a wonderful example!" Paul had the distinct sensation that he was beginning to fall in love with this unpredictable girl who fitted none of the conventional patterns he knew so well. It was absurd, romantic and adolescent even to entertain such a notion; this was real life, not a short story in one of the women's magazines or in the movies. Nevertheless he could not shake off the feeling, and most frightening of all, he didn't seem to want to rid himself of it.

The orchestra started playing again, and the muted strains of "Stardust" filled the Balloon Room. Paul and Helga looked at each other, and there was no need for words as they stood and started toward the floor. "Stardust" created a world all its own, and at this moment it was their world.

CHAPTER THREE

The hours between ten and twelve on Saturday morning were the most precious in the week, the one time when Paul felt completely free to indulge himself, to forget every responsibility. He could lie in bed, protected by a mound of covers from the penetrating, damp Chicago cold that whistled in through the open window, and he could day-dream, doze, wake up again or even drop off into a deep sleep if he wished. A cardinal rule was that he must not really open his eyes, for he knew that if he did he would awaken and there would be no choice left but to get up. However, by raising his left eyelid cautiously and squinting at his bedside clock he wasn't actually taking any chances of rousing himself.

He saw that it was eleven-thirty and that gave him another half-hour before it would be time to get up. He had a date to play tennis at the Meridian Club's indoor courts with Billy Wilson at one-thirty, so he'd just have time to dress, grab a quick bite of breakfast and drive downtown. He burrowed deeper under the blankets and settled down to a leisurely reconstruction of the previous evening. He wanted to savor everything he had shared with Helga, to recall everything she had said.

His reverie was interrupted abruptly, however. He heard the

door of his room open, but he did not move. It was probably either his mother or Delcie looking in to see if he had yet arrived in the land of the living, and if he remained very still the door would close again in a second or two. Instead he heard someone tip-toe toward him, and the next sensation he felt was the impact of an icy washrag as it landed full on his face. Outraged, he sat bolt upright and hurled the offending cloth at Marcia, who had retreated to the far side of the room, giggling.

"Play your schoolgirl tricks on somebody else!" he said, recovering his sense of humor but not daring to smile for fear of encouraging a repetition next Saturday.

"It wasn't so long ago that you used to do the selfsame thing to Betsy and me," she replied righteously.

"Oh, close the window and turn on the radiator. As long as you're here you might as well make yourself useful."

"Okay, helpless." Marcia became meek and complied obediently.

"Now get out of here. This is not a recreation hall for little children."

"I came in to tell you something."

"Really? I thought you were merely trying to prove that you're an unspeakable junior-sized monster."

"Very funny. Just listen to me for two seconds, even though you love the sound of your own voice more than anything in the world. Your office called you about ten minutes ago, Richard Harding Davis."

"What did they want?" Paul ran his fingers through his hair and frowned. The city desk had an unpleasant habit of forgetting that reporters had days off, especially when there was some minor fact that needed checking in the neighborhood.

"They just said to call right away. Mr. Austin wants to speak to you."

"Austin?" Paul swung his legs to the floor and jammed his

feet into his slippers. Harry Austin was the City Editor, and when he wanted words with a hireling, it was important. "Why didn't you say so in the first place?"

He brushed past Marcia, almost bowling her over in his haste, and he didn't hear her indignant, "You didn't give me a chance to tell you, that's why, clumsy." He started down the corridor toward the telephone in the downstairs front hall clothes closet, and as always he felt a faint stirring of annoyance that his parents had insisted on placing the instrument in such an inconvenient place. Were this his house, he'd install a phone in the living room, and if guests thought him less than fashionable because of it, that would be just too bad for them.

Molly was chatting vivaciously with one of her innumerable women's club friends on the extension in her bedroom, and Paul stopped as he heard her voice, then shouted, "I've got to make a call. Would you get off the wire, please?"

There was no reply, and he heard his mother's uninterrupted laughter. A sense of pique came over him, and he felt that she was being deliberately unfair, so he walked quickly to her room and stood in the door. "Please," he called, emphasizing each word distinctly, "I've got to call my office. It's urgent, so will you do your gossiping a little later?"

His mother looked abashed and faintly frightened, but Paul did not relent. Instead he remained in the frame, scowling, until she brought her conversation to an abrupt end. Then, as she started to say something to him in the way of an apology, he turned and stalked down the stairs to the hall closet and firmly closed the door behind him. He dialed the office number, asked for the city desk and then waited for a considerable time before he heard the familiar cacophony of typewriters and voices in the background.

"Desk," said a bored voice.

"Eddie, this is Paul Dawson—"

"Where you been, kid? The old man is fit to be tied. He's been calling you just about every name there is."

"What's up, Eddie?"

"Plenty. He'll tell you about it. Hang on, kid."

There was a click, a pause, and then Paul heard a familiar cold, rasping voice. "Dawson!"

"Yes, Mr. Austin?" The worst of all blunders would be to make excuses for not having called back more quickly.

"There's a four-eleven at the Yards—"

"The Stockyards?"

"Yes, you idiot. Looks like the biggest thing since Mrs. O'Leary's cow. Get over there fast. You should be able to make it in ten minutes—it's right in your neighborhood. Tony Mc-Closkey is in charge for us. Report to him." The City Editor hung up.

Paul raced up to his bathroom, bitterly condemning his superior for an astonishing ignorance of local geography. The huge meat-packing complex known under the collective name of the Stockyards was located on the southwest side of the city and in bad weather was a thirty to forty minute drive from the Dawson apartment near the lakefront. And there would be a major fire just today. Paul grudgingly wrote off his Saturday, but in spite of his resentment he felt a growing sense of excitement. Something of importance was taking place, and he was going to be in the center of it. The spirit of enthusiastic inquisitiveness that had prompted him to become a newspaperman in the first place overwhelmed him now, and he dashed into his bedroom from the bathroom and started to dress with feverish haste.

He was buttoning his shirt when his mother hurried in, carrying a tray of coffee, milk and toast; for the past four or five years he had drunk coffee, but still clung, unthinkingly, to the childhood habit of drinking milk, too. There were times, he thought, when he had to hand it to Mother. She always sensed an emergency and knew exactly what had to be done. And although she was nervous, she made a gallant attempt to hide her feelings. "You'd better have something to eat before you go, dear."

"Thanks." He gulped down half of the milk while reaching blindly with the other hand for a necktie.

"What is it this time, Paul?"

"A four-eleven at the Yards. Biggest thing since Mrs. O'Leary's cow. Do me a favor, will you, Mother? Call Billy Wilson down at the Meridian for me and tell him I can't keep our tennis date."

"Oh, what a shame. Are you sure—"

"Yes, Mother. I'm sure." He pulled a heavy sweater over his head, then donned a jacket. There was no experience more chilling than dancing attendance on a fire in midwinter. He had been sent to two minor blazes in the past couple of months, and this was one time when he didn't intend to freeze.

Molly watched him anxiously as he scooped a thick wad of yellow newspaper copy paper from a desk drawer and jammed it into his inner jacket pocket along with a handful of pencils. "Are you wearing wool socks, Paul?" She wasn't sure why she asked, but she knew that he must be dressing warmly for a purpose, and this was her way of showing sympathy and concern.

"You bet." He snatched up his wallet and removed his press card, which he'd need to carry him through the inevitable police cordon.

"Please have a little more breakfast, dear. You really shouldn't go out on an empty tummy." She nudged the tray toward him across the top of his dresser.

The mere idea of food made him irritable, and he started out of the room, into the corridor and down the stairs. His mother followed and observed him in apprehensive silence as he climbed into his overcoat and stuck his reporter's card in the band of his oldest hat. Battered headgear was a favorite movie device in portraying newspapermen, but Paul had learned that under certain circumstances the habit was valid and legitimate. Fires meant sprays from water hoses, ashes and carbon and perhaps an odd spark or two. There was no sense ruining a good hat.

"You will be careful, won't you, Paul?"

"Sure, sure," he replied ungraciously. "Be seeing you." He opened the front door.

Molly hesitated for an instant, then called after him. "Paul, dear. Don't forget—you have a date with Joan tonight."

*   *   *

Traffic in the vicinity of the Stockyards was so snarled that Paul was forced to park his car three blocks from the main entrance, and then wasted another ten minutes forcing his way through the dense crowds of curious onlookers, who had gathered in spite of the cold. Fire engines and trucks filled the streets and men in thick rubber coats and high boots were carrying hose lengths and long-handled axes toward the scene of the conflagration. A half block from the main gate to the Yards the police department had set up its line, and Paul, after shoving aside several men in lumberjackets who refused to move out of his path, climbed under the ropes.

A young police patrolman, red-faced and self-important, held out a detaining arm. "Here, you. Where do you think you're going?"

Paul enjoyed moments like this. Some ten feet away he saw a higher-ranking official whom he'd interviewed only a few days previous about a gambling raid. "Hiya, Lieutenant," he called, ignoring the patrolman. "They sure picked a beauty of a day for it, didn't they?"

A group of men stood just inside the open gates, and Paul headed straight for them. He could see flames leaping high into the air from somewhere inside the Yards, and he had to step carefully now, for a maze of canvas-covered hoses, twelve inches in diameter, seemed to cover the ice-glazed street and the frozen earth. Blue uniforms predominated, and Paul quickly recognized the Fire Commissioner and three police captains. This was really a serious fire, for the Commissioner certainly wouldn't leave his own house on a Saturday for anything less than a major catastrophe. Seven or eight men in mufti stood nearby, too, and one detached himself from the others as Paul approached.

Tony McCloskey was a veteran reporter who had become old at forty; his overcoat looked threadbare and he hunched his neck inside its upturned collar. But he knew his business, and he wasted no time as he briefed Paul on the situation. "Glad you're here, kid. This is a lulu. Mann is checking the various offices, Phil is getting local color and I'm standing by for any pronouncements the moguls care to make. No estimate on damages yet, but two firemen are reported killed so far."

"Where do you want me, Tony?" Paul hauled copy paper and pencils from his jacket and crammed them into the pocket of his overcoat. As he did he wished he had remembered to transfer them earlier: it would have been more professional.

"There's a rumor that the pens at Gilbert and Company have caught fire. Nose around down there and find out what you can. If there's anything to the story, let the office know right away, before you report back to me. I suggest you use the phones at the Saddle and Sirloin Club. Last time I tried 'em the wires were still open there."

"Okay. Where's this Gilbert outfit?" To Paul the vast acreage of the Yards, with its administration buildings and factories, slaughterhouses and processing plants, was a foreign world.

"Straight down there." McCloskey pointed with a thin finger. "You can't miss it. Good luck, kid."

Paul trotted off in the indicated direction, and for the first

[44]

time he felt the full impact of the catastrophe. To his left was the gutted skeleton of what had once been a four-story wooden building, and a half-battalion of firemen methodically played water from three heavy pipes on the smoking remains. Off to the right flames were licking at the walls of a long line of sheds, and rubber-coated, masked figures were disappearing into the blaze, armed with chemical extinguishers, only to emerge again in a few seconds, exhausted.

It was bitterly cold, too, Paul realized. His finger-tips felt frozen, and he flexed his hands as he increased his speed. This was definitely not going to be a pleasant day. Directly ahead now he saw a billboard sign bearing the legend "Gilbert and Company," and from behind a small concrete office building a thick cloud of dense, blackish-grey smoke was rising into the air. All that Paul knew about the Gilbert people was that they were one of the smaller packing companies, and that he had seen advertisements for their hams and their chops. If the smoke was any indication, he would need to learn considerably more in the immediate future.

Rounding the corner of the administration building he paused to take in the situation. In front of him now were the covered wooden pens where the animals the company had purchased were kept when they first arrived at the Yards, and the sight was appalling. The wooden structure, which was approximately two stories high, was a solid sheet of fire. A thick puff of soot-laden smoke swirled in Paul's direction and he gagged for an instant. But he was reminded that he had a job to do and he ran toward the cluster of three fire trucks which seemed to be the center of activity. Men with grime-smeared faces were working frantically, directing streams of water onto the fire, battling with chemicals and drenching the adjoining slaughterhouse which was still, miraculously, intact.

The smoke grew denser, the fumes more choking and Paul gasped for breath as he pressed nearer to the pens. Somewhere in this holocaust would be a man of authority who would know precisely what was happening here, how bad the damage was and what the future might hold in store; it was a reporter's duty to find that man. Fire fighters, intent on their work, dashed to and fro, and a mere observer had difficulty in keeping himself from their path, but at last Paul saw the person he was seeking, a Battalion Chief who stood off to the right some ten yards closer to the burning pens, directing operations through a megaphone.

Paul heard the frenzied screams of the animals trapped inside the building now, and as he neared the Battalion Chief he could feel the intense, searing heat of the fire. The noise was deafening at such close range, too: the flames roared as they consumed livestock and timber, the water from the hoses hissed and sang, and the men who were trying to bring the blaze under control all seemed to be calling to each other at once.

The Chief was unaware that someone stood at his elbow until Paul tapped him on the shoulder, then he glanced up with eyes that were smoke-reddened and a little glazed. "Yeah?"

"Express, Chief. How bad is it here?"

The fireman had dealt with reporters before, and he had no time to waste. "This building will go. Maybe five hundred pigs and sheep in it. No idea of the property damage. But if the wind holds it won't spread to the bigger pens and the slaughterhouse. That do it for you?"

Before Paul could answer, the Chief suddenly reached out and dealt him a staggering blow on the chest with the heel of his hand. And before Paul quite realized what was happening, he heard a tremendous crash and felt a sharp pain on the inside of his left foot, just above his shoe. Then only did he see that a section of the pen wall had toppled forward; a chunk of hard wood the size of a large cantaloupe had landed on his leg, and there was debris scattered on all sides. "Thanks, Chief," he said, "that was close."

"You better move back," the fireman replied. "This is no place for anybody except professionals. We got to take chances, you don't."

There was no opportunity to dispute the point, for he began to bawl a new series of orders through his megaphone, and Paul retreated. Within a few minutes he located an official of Gilbert and Company, who stood mournfully watching his firm's property disappear in smoke. It took but a few moments to learn an estimate of the damages and the extent of insurance coverage, and Paul limped off toward the telephones at the Saddle and Sirloin Club. The pain had spread, his whole ankle throbbed by now, and he was sure it was swollen, but he was too busy collating facts in his mind to pay much attention to his injury.

And he forgot it completely when he called the Express and was put through to one of the desk men who was handling the details of the fire. "I've got a little to add to what you already have, Charley," Paul drawled into the mouthpiece, hoping he sounded sufficiently cold-blooded and indifferent to meet the requirements of the newspaper profession. "The number three pen at Gilbert is gone. Five hundred and forty sheep and pigs, two million loss, about three-quarters of it covered by insurance."

As he hung up he thought again of the terrified screams of the dying animals.

*   *   *

It was almost nine o'clock that night when Paul dragged himself into his family's house, showered and shaved and changed his clothes. While he dressed, his mother came in and fussed over him; again and again she expressed the fear that he had caught cold, and although he was grateful for her concern, it nevertheless irritated him. There were times, he thought, when he was strongly tempted to take a bachelor apartment for himself. The family storm that would result would rage fiercely, but thereafter he'd have a little peace. His sense of annoyance continued to grow, and he was about to say something unpleasant when his father unexpectedly wandered into the room.

It was unusual for Gordon to come in here, and Paul always felt flattered on the rare occasions when his father did drop around for a chat. They grinned at each other and Molly, aware of an unusual spark of comradeship between them, hurriedly departed to attend to some little emergency that she invented on the spur of the moment. Gordon sat on the edge of Paul's bed and watched in silence for a few moments while his son jabbed links into the cuffs of his shirt. Then, before speaking he cleared his throat, as though it were an effort to say something.

"Pretty rough today, Paul?"

"A little." They were always so reticent with each other, Paul thought, and moved to his clothes closet for a necktie.

"Hurt your leg?"

"A hunk of Stockyards fell on it."

"Mother know about it?"

"No, Dad. I was careful not to move around the room while she was in here."

Gordon chuckled quietly. "Good. She'd stew around all night if she knew." Suddenly he sobered. "Suppose you'd better see a doctor about it?"

A show of sympathy from his father was always embarrassing. "We Dawsons are men of steel, Dad."

"You bet." Again Gordon cleared his throat, then stared for a moment at the pattern on the rug. "Paul," he asked suddenly, "did you enjoy yourself working out that fire today?"

There was a long, uncomfortable silence; it would be easier to lie, but Paul refused to stoop to that. "No. I didn't."

"I see."

The calm acceptance was too much. Dad had patently made up his mind in advance. "I don't think you see at all," Paul said sharply. "It's the screams of those dying animals. I can't get the sound out of my head."

"Some day," Gordon replied gently, "I'll tell you about a fire in the stables of a barn where I spent a few summers when I was a boy. There were horses in those stables. And cows in the adjoining barn." He stood and wandered to the window, rubbed away a patch of frosting and looked down at the snow-covered lawn.

"Sorry." Paul was abashed and felt very inadequate, very young.

"Sure." Gordon sounded as though he were speaking from a great distance. Suddenly he turned and jammed his hands into his trouser pockets. "Do you think you're too good for the grocery business? Is that it, Paul?"

"Certainly not!" The sudden switch to a hated subject was unexpected, though Paul should have anticipated it. "I don't think of myself as too good for it, or too highly educated, or too intellectual—or too much any of the things you've accused me of being at one time or another."

"I never thought I was too good to go into my father's business—a business that has provided a fine living to the men of our family for more than forty years!" Gordon had an infuriating habit of hearing only what he wanted to hear, of shutting out ideas that conflicted with his preconceived notions. "I'm proud to be a wholesale grocer. And none of my friends are ashamed to associate with me, either. What's more, what I do is important enough to have won me a place in Who's Who. I don't see anyone at your newspaper listed in it!"

This was likely to develop into a real argument, and Paul wanted no part of it. He was tired, he was late for his date with Joan and he had been over this same ground with Dad so many times that they both knew their speeches by heart. Slipping into his jacket he adjusted a handkerchief in his breast pocket with great care, picked up his wallet and keys and turned away from his dresser with what he thought was an air of calm and dispassionate forbearance.

"I've told you a hundred times—I have a great respect for you, Dad." To Paul's annoyance his voice was shaking slightly. "I'm just a guy trying to do the kind of work that I want to do. You wouldn't like it any more than I'd enjoy doing your kind of work. I can live and let live. I don't ask you to understand what I'm doing. I only ask you to show a little of the same kind of respect I give." Disturbed, he ran his fingers through his hair.

They started for the door at the same moment, and Paul stood aside to allow his father to precede him into the corridor. As they approached the stairwell Paul hesitated for a moment. "Good night, Dad," he said.

Gordon continued on to his own bedroom, neither replying nor looking around.

CHAPTER FOUR

Traffic seemed unusually heavy, and although Joan's home was only a few blocks from Paul's own house, he was forced to sit and fume through several changes of stoplights. At last the long line of cars began to move and the cause of the trouble was revealed: a bus had stalled on the boulevard. Ordinarily Paul would have been indifferent to a delay, but he knew that Joan would be annoyed because he was late, and he himself was anxious to begin the evening. Not that he was looking forward with any special pleasure to his date with Joan. He was forced to admit that his principal motive at the moment was to get the taste of his quarrel with Dad out of his mouth. These endless arguments only increased existing tensions.

It was painfully clear that he and Dad simply didn't speak the same language. Paul felt a strong urge to discuss the whole problem with someone, but there was nobody to whom he could turn. His mother, if he approached her, would weep and dutifully repeat all of his father's arguments. And Joan, whom he would see in a few minutes, would be bored. Not that she wouldn't try to understand, but she had been raised in an atmosphere in which women never interfered in business matters, and it would be hopeless to explain even the fundamentals to her.

Paul wished, suddenly, that he were seeing Helga Bjornson tonight. Now there was a girl to whom he could pour out his heart, a girl who would give him the sympathy he craved. Perhaps it was just as well, he thought as he parked the car, that he wasn't dating Helga. He didn't know her sufficiently well to unburden his most intimate problems on her.

It was ironic that he couldn't really talk freely to Joan, whom he had known longer and had dated more frequently than any other girl. Parental expectations had created barriers between them, but he was unable to break down the walls. Both families confidently expected that some day he and Joan would be married and, having reached this conclusion, looked on the relationship with benign calm.

Paul was disturbed by their attitude, but what actually bothered him even more was his suspicion that Joan herself believed that she would some day become his wife. He had never discussed the subject with her; on the contrary, he had taken pains to avoid it. But she revealed her inner convictions in the proprietary attitude she displayed toward him. And she had probably confided her expectations to several of her friends, for a number of them behaved toward Paul as though he wore a tag with Joan's name on it.

The thought had often occurred to him that he might have fallen in love with her if the senior Dawsons and Adamses had not made him feel that he was being crowded into a corner. There was no question in his mind about his own feelings: he was very definitely not in love with her. Yet, at the same time, he could not deny that he felt completely at home with her, that he understood her most of the time, and that many successful marriages had been built on far less than the similarity of background and spirit of mutual good will that he and Joan shared.

It was close to ten o'clock when he limped into the living room of the Adams house. The maid, who had opened the door for him, disappeared to tell Joan he was here, and he crossed the room to greet Mr. and Mrs. Adams, who were playing bridge with a couple who looked vaguely familiar. The men rose and shook hands with him, and the ladies beamed at him in fond indulgence, as though he and Joan were sixteen and were going out for the first time together.

"Hello, Uncle Matt," Paul said. "Aunt Martha, you look as though you've just made a grand slam."

Matthew Adams threw an arm around the younger man's shoulders. "Paul, you remember Mr. and Mrs. Hardy. They're old friends of your Mom and Dad."

"Of course." Paul forced himself to smile, though he couldn't place these people; nevertheless he dutifully made a mental note to mention them to his mother tomorrow.

"How's the newspaper business?" Adams, who was a grain broker on LaSalle Street, had a habit of rocking back and forth on his feet when he was being jovial.

"We're still publishing. And we'll sell a pile of papers tomorrow. I guess you've heard about the fire."

Mr. Hardy, who had been about to seat himself, tugged at his watch fob. "I've been listening to the radio all day. I have a good many customers out at the Yards. Do you know anything about the fire, Dawson?"

"Yes. I spent the day out there. It was rough." Paul wasn't being intentionally ungracious, but it was impossible for him to transform his experiences of the day, his memories of the tortured, dying animals into light social chat. All the same, there were certain amenities that had to be observed, and he thought that it wouldn't hurt him to add a few details. "Practically every company out there suffered. The last figure I heard before I was relieved was that more than fifty million worth went up in flames. The insurance people will have their preliminary survey finished tonight, so the full results ought to be ready in time for the final editions tomorrow morning."

[53]

Mrs. Hardy smiled brightly, anxious to enter into the conversation. "The fire is all out now, though, isn't it?"

There was only one response to such an inanity. "Yes'm," Paul said.

Joan's mother, who had been shuffling a deck of cards diligently, raised her head. "Where are you children going this evening?"

She knew perfectly well where they were going, Paul reflected. This was exactly the same sort of question his mother would ask, and he had no idea what prompted it. "There's the biweekly dance down at the Meridian, Aunt Martha," he said politely. "So I thought we might look in on it."

He could predict her response: an animated, "How nice!" followed by several banal comments on the pleasures and comforts to be found at the Meridian Club. But he was spared, for at this moment Joan came into the room, or rather, made her entrance.

It was something of a responsibility to be the most attractive girl in a large "crowd" that had grown up together, but Joan Adams carried her obligation with easy benevolence. And by any standards she looked like a lovely young lady. She was of medium height, with a lithe, trim figure, and was conscious of her erect posture. Her eyes and mouth were large, and she made the most of them; expressions that would have looked feigned in someone else appeared natural when she used them.

Her dress was a semi-formal evening gown which she had probably bought either at Marshall Field's or at one of the better New York shops. It was made of a soft, silky material, and its violet color matched her heavily fringed eyes. Severe but feminine, it had a little rolled collar in the front and dipped to a modest "V" in the back.

Her gauntlet-length white gloves were correct and demure, and so was her fur-trimmed evening wrap of soft white wool. Only in her choice of bracelets was Joan somewhat daring;

ladies supposedly wore jewelry that was not ostentatious, but on her left wrist was a heavy mass of gold charms, her trademark, and on her right wrist was a wide gold band of square medallions, each of which was engraved with a scroll pattern, and set with a pseudo-stone. Her defiance of the standards of her elders was definite but limited.

Joan stopped near a glass-stemmed lamp. She smiled at everyone but at no one. "Good evening," she said in her clear, sweet soprano.

She did not look at Paul, and he knew at once that she was angry with him. She would be still more upset when she learned he had hurt his ankle and couldn't dance. He waited until the others had greeted her, and then he addressed her softly. "Hi, cutie," he said, knowing she hated that form of address.

The violet eyes regarded him coolly for an instant, then Joan held out her wrap to him. "We're more than a little late. I think we'd better go, don't you?"

It was simple enough to ignore her reproof in the flurry of conversational goodbyes as they left, and as Paul followed her to the car, helped her into the seat and crossed to his own side he actually forgot for a few moments that she seemed to be annoyed with him. For a long time now he had felt an uncomfortable sensation whenever he had escorted Joan out of her house: he was sure that Uncle Matt and Aunt Martha were sitting back and speculating on how long it would be before they would be in a position to make an "important announcement." His mother and Aunt Martha had often discussed the possibilities, he knew, for Marcia had eavesdropped on more than one occasion and had gleefully reported back to her brother afterwards.

Paul shook off a faint feeling of depression and stepped on the starter. "You look terrific tonight, Joan," he said politely.

"I had enough time to get ready, so I should," she replied frigidly. "I'm still waiting for your apology."

"I was pretty late, wasn't I? I'm sorry." At moments like this he felt as though he *was* married to her, and he didn't like the sensation.

"Pretty late?" She drew back into her corner of the car, even though it took her farther from the heater. "You were due almost one hour ago, thank you. Everybody at our table will think we're not even going to be there."

"I had to work." He swung the car onto the Outer Drive and began to drive a little faster than was safe on icy roads.

"This is one night when I particularly wanted to be on time, too. Doris and Jack are announcing their engagement, and we may miss all the fun."

"They'll still be around so we can congratulate them." Doris and Jack were a couple Paul disliked mildly, and he could not share Joan's disappointment, although he sympathized with her. Of greater importance was his discovery that he was ravenously hungry, and he suddenly remembered he had eaten only a ham sandwich and had drunk a few cartons of sirupy coffee at the fire. This was one night he was going to enjoy the Meridian's supper-dance buffet. "There was a whale of a big fire out at the Stockyards, and I had to cover it. I was there all day."

"You could have phoned me." She sounded more hurt than angry now.

Paul always imagined that Joan looked down on his vocation as something slightly less than respectable. "It was just like in the movies," he said quietly. "There weren't many phones and there wasn't much time. What's more, a lot of other reporters had to use them, too. They wouldn't have liked it if I'd tied up a wire for social purposes."

Joan caught a hint of exasperation in his tone and promptly backed down. "I'm not being critical, Paul. Now that you've explained, I understand and I accept your apology." She smiled at him, leaned forward and snapped on the car radio. Something behind the smile, something intangible, suggested that she was

[56]

sure of him and that she was waiting with as much patience as she could muster for him to declare himself.

Paul glanced at her obliquely. He wondered how Helga Bjornson would have reacted under a similar set of circumstances. He felt positive it wouldn't have been necessary to say anything at all to Helga; she would have understood completely, without an explanation.

* * *

Two hundred or more couples milled around on the dance floor, shuffling and gliding and dipping and stomping to the rhythms of a six-piece orchestra, an aggregation of Northwestern University students who provided music for weekend gatherings at a reasonable fee. There was a sustained buzz of conversation beneath the wail of the clarinet and beat of the snare drum, and those who were not on the dance floor visited at each other's tables, wandered around and chatted with friends they had not seen in all of one or two days. In a few highly conspicuous instances, couples paired off in corners and indulged in romantic murmurs. The ballroom of the Meridian Club was not considered the place for intimate conversations, however, and those who broke the unwritten rules knew full well that they would be the topic of gossip and speculation for days to come, that they would be closely observed by their friends, who would view their every move as a preliminary to the announcement of an engagement or an elopement to the local Graetna Green, Crown Point, Indiana.

Almost everyone was acquainted with everyone else, and although there were various cliques and crowds, no one group was considered to be the superior of any other. The undergraduates who were still attending the local universities tended to band together, and those who had only recently been awarded their bachelors' degrees at Harvard or Chicago or Dartmouth or Michigan or Williams found that they still shared numerous mutual interests with their former classmates.

The young men who had been out of school a little longer, however, were now impelled to organize according to their vocational ties: there was a large table of young LaSalle Street brokers, another of budding steel magnates and several of potential meat-packing tycoons. The males in one party were exclusively composed of future mail order corporation executives, and at one ringside table was the loudest group of all, five nattily dressed young men who were employed in the rapidly-growing radio broadcasting industry. Their forced hilarity was somewhat self-conscious, for they had broken another of the Club's silent rules: they had gone outside their own social circle for their dates, and had escorted mildly flattered, budding actresses to the affair. No outsider could have distinguished between these heroines of the airwaves and the young ladies of family standing who were present, but the truth had circulated the ballroom very quickly, and most of the guests, the girls in particular, went out of their way to ostracize the future radio network vice-presidents who had dared to display such bad taste.

Strangely, there were remarkably few married couples at the Club. Here and there a pair of newlyweds could be seen with those who had once been a part of their "gang," but in general those who had taken the plunge into matrimony soon drifted away from these dances at the Meridian. Paul, sitting alone at the table he and Joan were sharing with four other couples, thought that in these times not even the sons of substantial families could afford to take part in the expensive frivolity on what they themselves earned. Almost all needed parental financial assistance. And when they had marital responsibilities, ten dollars was better spent on a week's food supply than on a meaningless evening.

Paul shifted in his chair discontentedly, stubbed out a cigarette and moodily lit another. He wondered why he had bothered to come here in the first place, and he looked contemptuously at the couples on the floor. Most of them, he told himself, had never indulged in a single deep or constructive thought in their lives. They were sheep who dutifully followed in the footsteps of their parents, hailed the signs of improving economic conditions as an indication that they would soon be restored to their full heritage, and never bothered to look outside the confines of their own little cliche and prejudice walled world.

It was not their fault, of course. Paul realized that much. Just as he himself could not really be blamed because his own family had remained unscarred by economic catastrophe and was therefore insensitive. It required real effort, he believed, to rise above the limitations of one's environment and background, and most people were trapped without even knowing it.

He interrupted his reverie when he saw Joan watching him over someone's shoulder from the dance floor. She smiled at him politely, mechanically, and he knew what was in her mind. As his swollen ankle prevented him from dancing, she was willing to do her duty and stop having fun; if he wished, she would return to the table and would sit with him. She seemed to be indicating that a lady was required to abide by the spirit of noblesse oblige if a gentleman demanded it, and she would not shrink from what was right.

In the past Paul had always thought of Joan as an amusing companion, someone who thought mostly in terms of her friends, their clothes and her own, their romantic problems and her own. Although her intellect was limited he liked her because her wit was never sharp, her manners were impeccable, and she was almost completely without malice. But at this moment Paul discovered he had no desire for her company, and a notion, ridiculous but at the same time seemingly reasonable, flashed through his mind: he and Joan really had nothing in common.

He forced a grin as he looked out toward the dance floor and shook his head negatively; Joan seemed relieved and winked cheerfully. Paul was startled when a hearty male voice spoke, close to his ear. "What's the matter with you, Dawson? Letting all those guys take your girl away from you?"

"Hello, Hank," Paul said without enthusiasm. Henry Gidelle was one of those bluff young men with a false, ingratiating smile, a locker room approach to contemporaries, an exaggerated gentlemanliness toward girls and a sickening sycophancy to any elder who might be wealthy or important. He was like his father, in whose brokerage firm he now worked; Dad always maintained that the elder Gidelle was a phoney. So was Henry.

"How about that, friend? How come you aren't out there fighting with sword and shield for little Joanie?" Henry flashed a toothy smile that implied numerous unnamed indecencies.

To almost anyone else Paul would have explained about his injured ankle, but this was a boor. "I'm like Marconi," he said flippantly, trying not to let his dislike show. "I handle 'em by remote control. Some day maybe I'll sell you the secret. I'll tell you this much now—I do it without wires."

Gidelle was uncertain whether the jibe was a direct thrust at him, and his bushy eyebrows furrowed. Then he caught sight of Joan again on the floor, and his brow cleared. "Don't say I didn't warn you, brother."

He walked quickly to the floor, cut in on Joan and leered triumphantly as he whirled her to the opposite side of the floor, where they were lost from view. A girl in a pale silk dress executed a complicated tango step directly in his line of vision, and he thought that the color of her gown was a precise match for Helga Bjornson's hair. He wondered how Helga would look in the dress, and that raised the question of whether women ever wore clothes the shade of their own hair. He had no idea of whether they did or didn't, but there was no opportunity to delve into the problem. Two couples of his group, breathless and slightly moist, approached the table and all four, feeling unnecessarily sorry for him, began to talk to him at the same time. He tried to sort out their babble, to reply first to one, then another; everything they were saying was inconsequential, but they were trying to be friendly and helpful, and the very least he owed them in return was a measure of appreciation and courtesy. Yet all he could think was that he wanted, at this instant, to be anywhere but at the Meridian.

Nothing here was real, nothing was significant, nothing was genuine.

*　　*　　*

Social evenings for everyone who was young, unmarried and lived on the South Side invariably ended at one place, a diner located on the fringe of the Hyde Park district, near Lake Michigan. The hard-working owner of this establishment had purchased an old streetcar, had hauled it to its present location and had converted it into a restaurant of sorts, with a counter occupying the center section in front of the stoves and hot plates, and with cramped booths at each end.

There was nothing unusual about the diner other than that it was enormously successful in spite of being ordinary and commonplace. The ventilation was at best adequate, the lighting was harsh, the decor non-existent. And the unchanging menu offered hamburgers, eggs with bacon or ham and three or four kinds of sandwiches. The most popular post-midnight beverage was milk, although the occasional truck driver or night worker who happened to find himself in the place drank coffee. Not many mature adults were habitues, however, for the average patrons were in their early twenties, and the din they created was incessant.

It was not at all strange for the occupants of a booth to start singing anything from a Big Ten marching song to a popular ballad, nor was it uncommon for total strangers to join in the chorus. The relaxed, convivial atmosphere of the diner certainly contributed as much to its success as did its low prices and convenient location. An adjoining gas station did a roaring business, too, and wisely permitted the clientele of the eating house to leave their cars on its property.

The available parking space was crowded by the time Paul brought the Plymouth to a halt; several other cars were moving in at the same time. Snapping off the ignition, he turned to Joan and to the couple in the back seat, friends who had no car and who had begged a lift. "Looks like the joint is crowded," he said. "We might have to wait for a table, so—"

"We could always go somewhere else, if you'd like," Joan interrupted.

"Not unless you want to."

She shook her head and there were muttering noises from the rear. "Okay, then," he directed. "The three of you go ahead or everybody else from the Meridian will be here ahead of us and we'll never grab a table."

"What about you, Paul?"

"It'll take me a minute to lock up the car, and I can't run too fast on this ankle. So scram, all of you."

They obeyed and hurried ahead; he took his time, and after climbing out of the car he paused for a moment and inhaled deeply. It was less cold tonight, and there was a sweet, fresh breeze sweeping inland from the lake. The sky was a clear, blue-black, and the wind had cleared away the smoke haze that usually settled over the city after rising from the chimneys of the steel furnaces and industrial factories of the suburbs to the south. Several stars showed here and there, and as Paul glanced up at them he experienced a lifting of the depression he had felt ever since he had left the Stockyards fire.

He limped slowly toward the diner entrance; through the damp frosting of the glass he could make out a mass of dark shapes and hoped there wouldn't be too long a wait for a table. He was hungry again, although he had eaten a plate of cold meats, spaghetti and salad at the Club, and he had a strong hankering for a hamburger with an onion. He hoped Joan wouldn't object too strongly to the onion. She never ate them herself, and it was their custom for him to kiss her goodnight.

A party of six in evening clothes sauntered out of the diner, and Paul was amused by the appearance of one of the girls. Her shoulders and neck were bare, yet she wore her fur jacket casually over one arm, leaving considerable quantities of skin exposed. She was undoubtedly chilly, but her vanity was such that she preferred discomfort. Grinning sourly, Paul watched her as she and her companions made their way toward a car at the far side of the gas station.

"Well, hello."

There was a voice he recognized instantly, and he saw Helga Bjornson not four feet away. She was smiling, plainly glad to see him, and he moved to her at once, removing his hat. "Hi. Fancy meeting you here." No sooner were the words out of his mouth than he was annoyed with himself; if he had tried he could not have thought of a more banal remark.

A young man, hatless and wearing a lightweight tan overcoat, stood slightly behind Helga, and near him were two other youths and a girl. The hatless one was manifestly Helga's date, and Paul sized him up swiftly. The fellow was quite young in appearance, bland and with a weak chin. All that really mattered was that he was plainly not seriously interested in Helga, for he moved off with the others to an old Chevvie and stood there patiently waiting. Paul concentrated his full attention on the girl.

"I see you've hurt your leg." There was genuine concern in her eyes, and her voice was gentle.

Paul felt enormously flattered; Joan hadn't noticed that anything was wrong with his ankle until he had called it to her attention. "It isn't anything serious. But there's quite a story that goes with it."

[63]

"I'd love to hear it." Helga's directness, her ability to shed all subterfuge was more than refreshing; its impact was so strong that it was almost physical.

"I'll call you tomorrow." Her companions, Paul noted, were becoming a trifle impatient.

"Will you?" She didn't bother to hide her pleasure. "After one-thirty. I'll be out in the morning."

"After one-thirty," he repeated. "Good night, Helga."

"Good night, Paul." She smiled, then went to join her friends.

Paul, glancing after her covertly as he continued on to the diner, realized that she was wearing the same black coat she had used the previous evening, and that beneath it was the same dress. Such things really didn't matter; clearly she could not afford an extensive wardrobe. All the same, he had never before known a girl who owned so few clothes that she was forced to wear the same dress two evenings in succession, and the realization was disquieting.

CHAPTER FIVE

Sunday dinner in the Dawson house was more than a meal, more than an event. In a sense it was a ritual, and as was the case in all ceremonials, certain solemnities were carefully observed. Chief among them was punctuality; the family sat down promptly at one o'clock, and all three children, at one time or another, had been punished for tardiness by being denied a place at the table. Delcie always wore her black silk uniform with a thin, white silk apron, a costume she otherwise donned only when there were guests. And the main course alternated between roast chicken, roast beef and roast turkey.

When Paul had been twelve years old he had been ordered never to appear in a colored shirt for Sunday dinner, and from that day forward he had invariably worn a white one, putting it on as automatically as he switched on his alarm clock every work night. His father even went so far as to wear a special type of white shirt on Sundays, with a pleated front and a stiff collar, and his suits were solid-colored. His mother appeared at the table in her prettiest daytime dresses, and there were strict rules to guide the younger generation: Paul was not permitted to wear a sports jacket, and sweaters and skirts were forbidden for the girls.

And no one was excused from the table prematurely; the entire family entered and left the dining room together. Right there, Paul thought as he glanced at his watch for the fifth time in as many minutes, was one of the most senseless of all the Sunday dinner rites. Molly was dallying over her ice cream and coffee, and there was no choice, thanks to the discipline of life-long habit, but to remain until she was finished.

It would be so simple to say, "I've got to make a phone call. It's almost two o'clock and I promised to make this call at one-thirty, so please pardon me." He would then leave the table. In theory it sounded fine, but he would sit and continue to fume until his father performed the final rites; Gordon would look at each person's plate in turn, nod gravely and say, "Shall we go into the living room?" Then everyone would rise and the ordeal would be ended—until next week.

Molly poured a few drops of cream into her coffee and glanced at her son. "You'll be here for supper tonight, Paul." It was a statement rather than a question, but there was an under-lying note of concern in her voice.

"I'm not sure, Mother." That was the truth. He was hoping that Helga would be free to go out with him, and in that case he planned to drive somewhere for an inexpensive meal. His cash was running low after a heavy weekend, but the important thing was to see Helga rather than to take her someplace where the cuisine was the principal attraction.

"You said you'd be here!" Molly sounded upset. "The Bar-hams are coming over for a pick-up Sunday supper tonight. I told you all about it several days ago, and you said you didn't have any dates for this evening."

Paul vaguely recalled a conversation on the subject, but he shrugged it off. "The Barhams are friends of yours and Dad's, not mine."

"They're bringing Dorothy with them!"

Now Paul remembered. Dorothy was the seventeen year old daughter of tonight's guests, and he was expected to entertain her. The mere idea of his being used in this way, of his being forced to spend a boring evening in the company of an adolescent was annoying, and his mother's calm assumption that he would willingly accept the role was infuriating. Granted that he had certain family obligations, and he had no desire to shirk them. But he did not think that they included spending several hours in the company of a girl not yet out of high school, a child who would expect him to dance with her to music provided either by the phonograph or radio and who was incapable of expressing a coherent thought on anything beyond the level of her juvenile problems.

This wasn't the first time he'd been pressed into playing host to the under-age offspring of his parents' friends, and the whole routine was drearily familiar. The girl was inevitably overawed by finding herself in the presence of someone whom she considered to be an "older man," and he therefore had to put twice as much effort into every word and action as he did on his own dates, or the young guest would remain miserably ill at ease.

"Can't Dorothy Barham talk to Marcia about volleyball and that terrible geometry teacher who talks through his nose? I'd think they'd have quite a bit in common."

Marcia emerged from a luscious day-dream long enough to make a wry face. "Dotty Barham is stuck up," she said. "She thinks she's something, but she isn't anything at all. If you ask her, she's the queen of the whole senior class, but if you ask anybody else about her—ouch. Excuse *me*." That disposed of Dorothy.

Molly stirred her coffee more vigorously than was necessary. "You haven't answered me, Paul. You surely haven't made an engagement for this evening?"

"Not yet, but I—"

"Then don't make one!" Gordon entered the conversation for the first time, and he spoke in his best executive voice, crisp, authoritative and final. "Mother and I don't ask so much of

[67]

you that you can't do us a favor now and again. We've done one or two for you over the better part of a quarter of a century, you know."

"Sure, Dad. It's just that I—"

"We'll expect you here at—what time are the Barhams coming, Molly?"

"Seven-fifteen."

"At seven-fifteen, Paul. And if you have any consideration for us, you'll give little Dorothy the benefit of all the charm and wit that you bestow on the sophisticated ladies who are your usual social companions."

Paul knew that if he said one word there would be an explosion. He was aching for a fight, and he could feel a vein in his left temple throbbing. But Marcia brought him back to earth. Gently, unobtrusively, she extended one leg under the table and pressed her foot against her brother's shoe. This unexpected demonstration of sympathy steadied and sobered him; he was not alone in recognizing the injustices that were being perpetrated, and the knowledge strengthened him. He could not trust himself to speak, however, and merely bobbed his head to signify agreement.

Molly was perturbed over the tensions she had so unwittingly created, and she knew only one way to alleviate them. "I've finished dinner," she announced, although her coffee was virtually untouched.

Gordon needed no urging. He looked perfunctorily around the table, then asked, "Shall we go into the living room?" and stood quickly without waiting for a reply.

Paul allowed his parents to precede him out of the dining room, then squeezed Marcia's shoulder and tried to grin at her. She winked and he responded by tugging at a lock of her hair. There were times when he forgot what a loyal, sensitive kid she really was, but this was one occasion he wouldn't forget.

"You going to be on the phone long?" she asked in a conspiratorial whisper. "I have a couple of calls to make, too."

"How did you know that I—"

"Oh, don't be silly," she replied with a shrug intended to indicate that she was wise far beyond her years.

Paul didn't wait to pursue the point. He pulled her hair again, and this time smiled at her openly. Then he hurried through the living room, not glancing in the direction of his parents, who were already seated in "their" chairs. He closed the door of the front hall closet behind him, and the overhead light came on automatically. An electrician from Gordon's company had installed the device for Molly three or four years ago, and everyone in the family except Paul still enjoyed the sensation of seeing the light switch on seemingly by itself.

Helga's telephone number had been in Paul's mind all morning, but in his agitation he forgot it, and was forced to look it up in the directory. He dialed the instrument, and thought the closet was incredibly stuffy. Here it was midwinter, but he was perspiring. He heard the phone ring very briefly at the other end, then the receiver was lifted.

"Hello."

"Hello, I'd like to speak to Helga, please."

"This is she. How are you, Paul?"

He was amazed and delighted; he had only spoken to her on the phone once before, yet she had recognized his voice instantly. It was true that she had probably been expecting his call, but she undoubtedly heard from other young men, too. "I'm fine," he said. "You recovered from last night?"

"Oh, we just went to a movie, so there wasn't much to recover from." There was a faint undercurrent of amusement in her voice which disappeared as she asked, "How is your leg?"

His ankle was much improved, and he had scarcely given it a thought all day. "Couldn't be better." The closet was stuffier and warmer than ever. "Look, Helga—are you free this afternoon? I thought we might get together for a little while."

"I'm not doing a thing, and I'd love it."

Her direct, unruffled approach, so unlike any he had ever known, was still rather startling. "I had nothing special in mind, you understand. I just thought we might drive somewhere—"

"With the streets so slippery? You wouldn't get much fun out of that. Why not come over here and we could talk?"

"Okay. Sounds swell." He knew that his eagerness and pleasure showed too plainly, but this was one girl with whom it seemed unnecessary to play cautious games of give and take. "How soon?"

"I'll be here all afternoon."

"Thirty minutes, then. Set your watch by it." They both laughed, and Paul waited until he heard a click at the other end of the wire before hanging up. Then, as he opened the closet door he realized that his shirt was soaked and that he would have to change it. That closet could be worse than the fabled Hole of Calcutta.

* * *

When Paul had dated Helga on Friday, he had picked her up at the house of one of her friends, a girl who lived on the near-North side; as Helga had worked late at the office that day, she had taken her party clothes with her and had first changed, then stayed overnight at the conveniently located apartment of her friend. Consequently Paul was seeing, for the first time, the building in which she lived. And in the watery afternoon sunshine he was acutely conscious of the surroundings. The neighborhood was poor but respectable; this was no slum district, but hundreds of thousands of Chicagoans lived on blocks identical with this one. Scattered here and there down the length of the street were a few tiny houses of red brick, each boasting an infinitesimal yard. The majority of buildings were weather-beaten grey houses of wood, unimaginative and utilitarian structures that were only slightly larger than their more modern counterparts. And there were three apartment buildings made of grey stone, all of them built prior to the World War, all of them without elevators, all without character. In the largest of these, a five-story structure that tried to achieve tone via an insignificant little courtyard, was the Bjornson apartment.

Paul rang the bell, and when the buzzer sounded he shoved open the downstairs inner door and began to trudge up three flights of steep stairs. He had, in the course of his newspaper duties, seen so many buildings like this, and he was painfully familiar with the dusty bannisters, the cheap flowered paper peeling from the walls or the cracked plaster of the ceilings. Similarly, he was very much aware of the conspicuous trash cans and empty milk bottles that decorated the entrance to each of the four apartments on every floor.

His sense of smell was none too good, but he was nevertheless conscious of the odors that seemed to choke the stairwell. There was a stale flatness to the air that indicated a lack of ventilation, and from one apartment on the second floor there emanated the sharp, penetrating smell of fried fish. Elsewhere in the building someone had been cooking onions and from above came the unappetizing stench of burned fat.

The excitement and happiness he had felt at the prospect of seeing Helga subsided somewhat, but flared up again when he saw her as he approached the third floor landing, where she stood in the open door of her family's apartment, smiling at him. Her overall appearance puzzled him somewhat, as he had always taken it for granted that girls dressed up for dates, just as he put on a clean shirt and a "good" tie. Helga, it was plain, had made no special effort for this afternoon, however. She was wearing a faded, somewhat wrinkled housedress, and over it was a cotton apron on which she was drying her hands. She

[71]

wore no jewelry, and she had not even bothered to put on lipstick.

She still managed to look radiant. "I've been watching you
come up the stairs, and your leg really is better," she said.
"What did happen to you?"

A flippant answer was on the tip of Paul's tongue, but he
changed his mind. "The Stockyard fire yesterday," he replied.
"A hunk of building landed on me out there." He reached her
side and took the hand she extended in greeting.

"It sounds dreadful, though you seem rather pleased. Come
in, won't you?" she added with a touch of prim formality.

The front hall was tiny, and a little table bearing a tired
potted plant filled up most of its inconsequential space. Beyond
was the living room, and Paul's first reaction was one of surprise, for it was smaller than his own bedroom. Two windows
at the far end were curtained in some cheap yellow material,
and the furniture consisted of a sofa covered in rough wool,
with maple arms and back, and three chairs to match. The only
item of interest was an unpainted cabinet that stood against one
wall and reached from floor to ceiling. Most of the shelves were
lined with books, two others held a scanty supply of china and
glassware, and a small, inexpensive radio had been set into a
cubicle at shoulder height. A varnished drop-leaf pine table
stood near an open door that led into the kitchen beyond, and
was probably used for dining. On one wall were a pair of prints
depicting lakes and mountains that suggested Sweden, and on
a little lamp table at one end of the sofa were a number of
family photographs, most of them stiff and faded. There were
no other decorations.

"Ma and Pa," Helga said, "this is Paul Dawson. Paul, these
are my parents."

Paul found himself confronting a tall, solidly built man with
rugged features and a shock of grey hair. He wore an old-
fashioned collarless shirt with a gold collar button holding it

together at the neck, a pair of rumpled trousers and carpet slippers. Helga's mother was half-hidden by her husband for a moment, but as she stepped forward Paul saw that she was as blonde as her daughter and carried herself with the same proud, regal air. She had once been a beautiful woman, and she still showed evidences of it, in spite of her wrinkled skin and the deep, permanent smudges under her eyes.

Mr. and Mrs. Bjornson measured Paul silently as he shook hands with both of them; he was unaccountably embarrassed and groped in vain for something to say. Helga promptly came to his rescue as she took his hat and coat. "Paul worked at the big fire yesterday. The one we read about in the newspaper this morning. Isn't that exciting?" She disappeared through a door into what was probably a bedroom.

"We are glad, always, to meet a friend of our Helga."

"Sit down, Mr. Dawson," Bjornson commanded.

He spoke with a marked, pleasant Swedish accent.

"You are a fireman, Mr. Dawson?" his wife asked as Paul obeyed and perched on the edge of a chair.

"No, I have a job with a newspaper. I reported the fire."

"In Stockholm," the older man declared, "I had once a cousin who also was in the newspaper profession. He worked— how do you call it?—in the printing presses. It was very interesting, he used to tell me."

"Do you also find your work interesting?" Mrs. Bjornson inquired politely.

"Yes, very." Paul ordinarily prided himself on his ability to get along with anyone, and was vastly irritated with himself. Never in his life had he been so tongue-tied, and he tried desperately to think of something to say.

Again Helga was his salvation, and she spoke from the doorway as she reentered the room. "Paul writes for his newspaper," she explained, crossed the room and picked up the news section of the Sunday Express. "You wrote part of this, didn't you?" She pointed to the columns devoted to the fire.

"Yes, I did." It would be too complicated to go into the differences between the functions of a reporter and a rewrite man. He was sure that neither of Helga's parents would know what he was talking about if he told them that he had telephoned his news to another man whose specific duty it was to put that story on paper.

"Oh, a writer." Bjornson was patently impressed and shook his big head. "We have here the work of many writers." He waved a big hand in the direction of the cabinet. "Helga is all the time reading. Do you know the play by our Swedish author, Strindberg, called *The Father*? This we saw many years ago, in Stockholm."

"I read it in school, but I can't say I remember it too clearly."

Mrs. Bjornson frowned. "It was a play about unhappy people, and there is already in this world enough unhappiness, is it not so?" Her accent was softer, slightly more Americanized than her husband's. She dropped the subject, and her eyes, so like Helga's, returned to Paul. "The name 'Dawson,' it is not Swedish?"

"No, my ancestors were English, way back somewhere, I guess." He would be overbearing and pompous, he thought, if he told a pair of immigrants that his mother's family had been in the country since the French and Indian War of 1756, and that the Dawsons had come over during the Presidency of Thomas Jefferson.

"English. That is good stock, also." Bjornson showed no self-consciousness, and Paul understood from whom Helga had inherited her direct approach. "Bertha." He turned abruptly to his wife. "We have still from our dinner some of your good meat balls?"

"Enough for tonight and tomorrow night, too, Olaf."

"Helga. You will offer to your guest some of your Ma's meat

balls?" The carpenter's hospitality was unfeigned, and he was completely relaxed.

"Would you care for some, Paul? I assure you they're delicious."

"I'm sure they are, but I couldn't eat a thing right now, thanks. I just finished dinner a little while ago myself." Paul thought of the huge kitchen at home, of Delcie's meticulous preparation of the five-course Sunday dinner.

"Some tea, then?" Helga was being a quietly efficient hostess now, having absorbed her father's implied rebuke that she was neglecting her duties. "We're great tea drinkers here."

"Not at the moment, thanks," Paul said. "But don't let me stop anybody else from having some."

"If we want, we get," Mrs. Bjornson commented cheerfully, then stood. "We go now, Olaf."

Her husband looked up at her blankly. "This afternoon we stay home."

She laughed, and Helga joined in. Even Paul could not resist a faint smile. "We go in the next room, so these young people can talk to each other. About Strindberg they do not care. Other things they talk about."

Comprehending, Bjornson pulled himself to his feet and offered his big, hard-palmed hand to Paul. "It is good to know you, Mr. Dawson. You will come to us again soon."

"Thank you, sir. I will."

Mrs. Bjornson shook his hand, too, and her clasp was firm. "We hope you will, Mr. Dawson. Goodbye."

She followed her husband out of the room and closed the door behind her. Through the thin wall Paul could hear a faint murmur of conversation, though he could not make out its substance. They were, of course, talking about him. Helga, who was looking at him, followed his train of thought. "They like you," she said.

"Really?" Paul was somewhat surprised.

"I'm not just saying it, I mean it. When Pa invites somebody to come back, well—it's quite a day. If I knew you better I'd tell you how I used to despair when he was rude to boys who called for me on dates."

"Good for your father. I hope he's rude to all of them—except me."

They laughed together, then Helga sobered. "You are truly all right, Paul? Your voice on the phone sounded—well, urgent."

"As a matter of fact, I felt that way." Without having intended to say any such thing he found himself telling Helga the full story of how he'd hoped to take her out to dinner somewhere and how his family's plans had interfered. There was something about his relationship with this girl that he couldn't understand: although she was very attractive, highly intelligent and warm, a man had no right to unburden himself like this on a second date.

And the surroundings were hardly conducive to an air of romance. The odors of fried fish from the apartment downstairs crept into the room insidiously, the cheap furniture and general atmosphere of refined poverty were completely alien and made Paul feel nervous and more than a little distressed. Yet here he was telling a girl he barely knew about his family's commitments for him. He felt a growing anger at himself; under any circumstances it was wrong to apologize to a girl for a nonexistent date.

Helga listened to him without comment until he finished, and then she seemed lost in thought, her eyes grave. "I hope you don't mind my saying this, Paul, but you're wrong. It doesn't do any harm to give your parents a helping hand. And it won't be any hardship on you, actually. There I go, opening my big mouth and interfering, but you told me, so I had to say what I think."

Paul felt rebuked. "What can I talk to a seventeen-year-old about?" he demanded.

She smiled at him impishly. "The same things you talk to a twenty-one-year-old about. And if the seventeen-year-old doesn't understand what you're saying, she'll never let on to you, not if she were shot for it."

Hurt, he wanted to sulk, but knew he'd look foolish if he did. "I'd still prefer to spend the evening with you," he insisted.

"I'd like it, too," she said candidly. "But I have a date, it so happens."

"Oh." He experienced a stab of jealousy. "We could always make it some other night, if you wish," he added lamely.

"I would." Helga's words were perfunctory, but her manner indicated that she really meant what she said.

Paul shifted his position on the uncomfortable chair and wished he could shut out the drone of the elder Bjornsons' voices through the wall. "What kind of evenings do you enjoy most? I mean, going to the theatre, or—"

"Oh, I love the theatre. Who doesn't? But most of the boys I know can't afford to buy tickets."

"Neither can I, but I go anyway." Paul laughed a little self-consciously, then felt impelled to tell her more. It seemed important in this household, where every expenditure was carefully measured, for Helga to know that he was not the spend-thrift son of a wealthy man. It was ridiculous, he knew, to feel apologetic and somewhat ashamed of the hard fact that he came from a family of some substance, that he therefore enjoyed luxuries and advantages denied to her. But it was therefore all the more urgent that she should be made to realize he stood on his own feet.

"I support myself," he said slowly. "I give my family a chunk of my salary every week for my room and board. They don't quite understand that I'm doing it as a matter of principle. Because, you see, they don't actually need the money." There, that had been extraordinarily difficult to say.

"Good for you, Paul." The blonde head nodded in emphatic agreement. "I've known one or two rich boys before, and they never had the urge to do anything worthwhile."

"The whole point is, I'm not rich!" He could not hide his irritation; she had totally missed what he was trying to convey to her. "My father is pretty well fixed, but I'm not. He makes about as much in two or three weeks as I earn in a year. Good for him is what I say. That doesn't mean I'm going to accept handouts from a private breadline."

"You're very proud."

He wasn't sure whether she was being critical or admiring. "Sure I am. Like last summer, the family—that is, my parents and my two sisters—went off to Banff and Lake Louise. They had quite a jaunt. They wanted me to come along, but I wouldn't. I just couldn't accept a fancy vacation that cost somebody else a small fortune." He said it defiantly, secretly hoping she would approve the stand he had taken.

Helga was thoughtfully silent for a time, and when she spoke she seemed to be thinking aloud. "It isn't easy for me to imagine that my father could be a man of wealth. But I'm trying to suppose that somehow he was. Then he would offer me something wonderful, let's say. Maybe it would be a vacation trip. Or a fur coat, real fur. I'd accept, because I'd know he offered it to me in love."

Paul's sense of mortification became sharper, more pronounced. "It's different with you," he said, an edge to his voice. "It isn't the same with a girl as it is with a man."

"Of course not. We look at things in different ways." If she was aware of his annoyance she gave no sign of it.

"I could have gone into my father's business. I preferred to make my way on my own. I have to do it myself."

"Every man must do that which makes him happiest. I don't

know much about the world or about people, and I've never been anywhere. But if I've learned anything from my reading, I know that every individual has to find his own contentment in his own way." She gazed searchingly at Paul for a moment, and he could not fathom what was in her mind. "Your father is the owner of his own business, isn't he?" she asked a trifle hesitantly.

"Yes. My grandfather was the founder of it, and the family had me neatly stashed away there—from the day I was born. I upset their calculations for them."

"You don't like being in the grocery business? It bores you, perhaps?"

"I want very much to own my own newspaper. I told you about that. Also—I don't like working for my father." There was the truth, and she could make of it what she would. He had opened the subject, so he could scarcely blame her for pursuing it, but in spite of the inconsistency he recognized in his own thinking, he resented this prying attitude she was displaying. No, that was too strong; what really bothered him was that she didn't automatically agree with him. On the other hand, if she simply echoed him and praised him, he would be incapable of feeling any respect for her.

"My grandfather owned a little farm which he left to his eldest son," Helga said quietly. "And my father is just a carpenter who sometimes finds work these days and sometimes doesn't. So I wouldn't know what it was like to have an inheritance and a heritage. What's more, I'm not a man, and I don't think as a man thinks, I don't feel as a man feels. So—will you forgive me if I say something that maybe I shouldn't?"

There was only one possible answer, although Paul braced himself for whatever was to come. He had asked for this, and he had to take it. "You say whatever you please," he assured her, not really meaning it.

"I don't know what I'd do if I were you." Her luminous eyes

[79]

were solemn, and she looked extraordinarily appealing. "I think that traditions are important. Family traditions, I mean. I believe that members of a family must love each other and respect each other. If they don't have that, they have nothing. But I also believe that everyone must do what he is convinced is right for himself. And so I don't know what happens when family loyalties and personal ambitions and happiness come in conflict with each other. It's very confusing."

Paul felt a sense of relief; she was not condemning him after all. "It isn't confusing to me," he said emphatically. "What I've done is right—for me, anyway."

"That's all that counts."

"No, it isn't. What counts is that here I've come calling on you on a Sunday afternoon—and all I do is burden you with my personal problems."

"It's no burden," Helga protested. "I enjoy talking to people I like about themselves. I honestly do."

In a girl less forthright, less honest, Paul would have been sure that the "slip" to the effect that she liked him had been deliberately flirtatious and provocative. But what attracted him most to Helga was that she spoke her mind without currying favor and without fear. Her candid approach to any subject, her sincere attitude that was so free from shams more than compensated for the shabbiness of these surroundings, for the discomfort he felt in being here. Their backgrounds were totally dissimilar, and he knew that his world was as alien to Helga as her way of life was to him. Yet they could meet on the common ground of truth, of frankness, and that was more than he had ever been able to say of any other girl he had ever known.

"Let's have dinner together some night this week," he suggested. "And maybe I can rustle up enough to get us seats for *Of Thee I Sing*. We could meet somewhere in the Loop right after work. What do you say?"

"I say it's far too expensive," she retorted, and laughed to take the sting out of her words.

Paul grinned at her and felt a sense of masculine domination. "You let me worry about that," he announced. "Now, what's the best night for you?"

"Thursday?"

"Thursday it is."

He was surprised when Helga stood, and he glanced surreptitiously at his watch. He had been here only a little more than an hour, but she was hinting that the visit was drawing to an end. He could have remained longer, but she apparently had other things to do, and there was no choice but to accede gracefully; a girl who worked had very little time left to herself and he was being selfish by taking up so much of it.

So he arose, too, and Helga went into the adjoining room for his hat and coat. As she opened the door the voices of her parents stopped abruptly, and did not resume again until she returned and again carefully closed the door behind her. Then the indistinct murmur began once more, and Paul thought that people who lived under such conditions must be subjected to a never-ending strain. Real privacy was unknown to them.

He struggled into his coat and Helga walked to the door with him. "Thanks for dropping over," she said. "I'll remember this as a specially nice Sunday."

"So will I. And I'll call you before Thursday night." He looked down at her and felt the impulse to kiss her. He knew that she was aware of his feeling, and that she would not protest, but he refrained. He didn't want her to get the wrong impression: this was only the second time he'd been alone with her, and he was afraid she might think it was too soon. Besides, he was too conscious of their "rich boy—poor girl" relationship.

Helga seemed to recognize the struggle he was going through, and apparently she understood the reasons for his restraint. She smiled at him softly, and there was a maturity in her eyes that exceeded her years. She held out her hand and Paul took it, then allowed his fingers to linger on hers for a moment longer than was necessary. "Tell your mother and father I was very pleased to meet them," he said, "and thanks for letting me barge in like this."

"It was fun." She disengaged her hand gently. "Goodbye, Paul."

She stood at the landing and watched as he started to descend the stairs, then he heard the door close. He felt a warm glow as he thought of Helga, but other elements, disturbing elements intruded themselves on his consciousness. The odors of fish and onions were stronger than before, the trash cans looked dingy and the ugliness of the cracked plaster and the dirty, torn wallpaper made him realize anew that he and Helga had very little in common. With all of his brave talk about his independence, his self-sufficiency, he would be miserable if he were ever forced to live in an atmosphere like this.

And Helga, he told himself, would be equally out of place in a spacious, well-appointed house where luxury was taken for granted. It was wrong to see too much of her, to allow their relationship to grow. Under the best of circumstances and conditions, a couple needed to exercise all of their good will and intelligence to achieve a happy marriage. There was so much in Helga's background that was foreign to him, so much in his own that would bewilder her.

As he opened the front door of the apartment house a thought struck him with an impact far greater than that of the cold air. After only two dates he was toying with the notion of marrying Helga! Hunching his shoulders and hurrying to his car, he told himself firmly that he must be mad.

CHAPTER SIX

"I think I like the Club best on Monday nights when it isn't so crowded," Molly announced, sipping her coffee.

Her husband and son nodded in agreement, and as Paul leaned back in a deep leather chair and looked at the logs blazing in the fireplace of the Meridian's main lounge, he thought that there were few places that gave him such a feeling of comfort and security. "It was sure bright of you to think of coming here for dinner tonight, Mother."

"Yes," Gordon added, "I always like these last-minute going-out-for-dinner arrangements."

Molly carefully refrained from saying that she had planned the evening carefully in advance, knowing that both of them were fond of such sudden shifts in dining plans. But she could not stop herself from smiling and commenting, "You look like a pair of little boys who've just gotten away with something."

"We did," her husband chuckled. "A mammoth dinner."

"The best broiled whitefish in town," Paul declared enthusiastically.

"You've always been pretty keen on it here. I can remember when I used to bring you here for lunch on a Saturday when you were no more than five or six, and you packed away enormous portions."

[83]

"Well, I'm consistent, Dad. I'm still doing it. Could either of you tolerate another cup of coffee?"

"Not for me, thank you," Molly said, then glanced at her husband. "And none for you either, dear. A second cup keeps you awake."

"I'm brow-beaten," Gordon replied contentedly, lighting a cigar.

"If you're going back to get some for yourself, Paul, you might see if you can find Marcia. I'm not sure where she's gone."

"I won't bother just for myself, Mother, and you needn't worry about Marcia. She ran into the Halliday brat and they've gone off into one of the empty card rooms. I saw them in there a few minutes ago, sitting in a corner and whispering to each other at a mile-a-minute rate. And giggling! Two giggles for each word spoken, I'd estimate. Dad, what do you suppose little girls find to whisper about?"

"The same thing that adult women talk about, but on a simplified level, would be my guess." Gordon smiled, waved amiably to an acquaintance across the lounge, then continued. "But you're coming to the wrong person. Ask Mother—she's the expert, not I."

"How about that, Mother?"

Molly immediately sensed that they were going to tease her, and decided to indulge them. "I'm sure that girls discuss the same things boys talk about. Just as women's conversations are more or less on the same subjects as men's."

"Now there's nonsense if ever I heard it," her husband declared solemnly. "Right, Paul?"

"Absolutely right, Dad. As Mother has never heard an all male conversation, she couldn't possibly know what men talk about. So I think we'll have to dig to the root of this problem by ourselves."

As much as his mother enjoyed the teasing, she wasn't going to give up without a struggle. "The subjects are the same.

[84]

There's only one difference. Men like to think they settle the questions that confound the world, but the women actually do settle them."

"When they won the right to vote, Paul," Gordon confided in a stage-whisper, "they lost their sense of perspective, and it hasn't been restored yet. I was against suffrage, and I'm still against it. Defies all the laws of nature."

"All the laws of man, you mean," Molly said promptly.

Paul chuckled and looked at his parents; they were having so much fun that he was happy for them, pleased that he was their son. "If you ask me, Dad, it's a conspiracy. They brood over dark secrets."

"Right! And they try to cover up their machinations by giggling madly."

"This isn't fair," Molly protested. "It's two against one. If Betsy were only here, I'd have some help."

A wistful expression crossed Gordon's face. "You sure would."

The spirit of sheer joy in just being together seemed about to evaporate and Paul wanted to keep it alive. Evenings like this were wonderful: he was proud of his heritage and he revelled in the warmth and closeness that each member of the family showed toward the others. "I've got the real inside dope, Dad. A private investigation has been made, and although I'm not at liberty to reveal my sources, I can pass on the lowdown to you."

"Now we're getting somewhere." Gordon looked buoyant again as he winked at his son.

"Naturally, you aren't to repeat this."

"Not to a living soul, I give you my word."

Paul, pretending that his mother wasn't present, leaned forward in his chair. "They gossip," he said pontifically.

"Ah! So that's it."

"That's it. Little girls, medium-sized girls, big girls. All ages. Gossip. No less—and, certainly, no more."

Gordon was laughing as he turned to his wife. "Well, madam. You've heard the findings of the court. Have you anything to say before sentence is pronounced?"

Molly kept a straight face. "There are times when I think I have four children, not three, and that you're the youngest of them."

"Recriminations won't get you anywhere." Gordon stood, crossed the few feet to Molly's chair, bent down and kissed her.

"Gordon! In the Meridian lounge!"

"I can't think of a better place," he replied imperturbably, and would have bent down again but she held up a hand and fended him off.

"What will people say?"

"I can answer that one for you, Mother," Paul said. "A rumor will sweep this place and shake it to its foundations. A story will spread like wildfire to the effect that my father and my mother love each other. Naturally the reporters will come to me for corroboration—it's very helpful when they find that a spokesman for a family happens to be a member of their own profession. Of course I'll have to be prepared for them. So what shall I tell the gentlemen of the press?"

Molly smiled softly. "You may tell them that I love my husband as much—no, more—than I did on the day that I married him. You may also tell them that I have three wonderful children whom I love and that I consider myself the most fortunate person on earth."

"I'll amend that statement." Gordon took her hand but addressed Paul. "I agree with all of it, except for one very important point. I'm the one who's lucky."

"A further amendment, if you don't mind." Paul was faintly surprised at the huskiness in his own voice. "As your one off-spring who is of voting age, I believe I'm qualified to speak for my sisters as well as for myself. We're the ones who are pretty darn well off."

His parents were deeply touched, and Molly's eyes looked suspiciously damp. Gordon puffed hard on his cigar to hide his emotions, and all three were silent. Paul, somewhat embarrassed by his own frankness, tried to think of a comment that would lead the conversation back to a level of bantering conviviality. But the few remarks that occurred to him were flippant, so he gave up the effort.

Gordon was struggling to find a new topic, too, when a young man, slightly Paul's senior, approached from the other side of the lounge. Tall, with carefully combed blond hair and a thin, trim mustache, he was impeccably dressed. Paul, who had never seen him before, took an instant dislike to him and was reminded of a department store dummy.

"Good evening, Mr. Dawson," the young man said in a smooth, controlled voice as he held out his hand.

"Hello, Victor." Gordon sounded genuinely pleased to see him. "I didn't know you were a member here."

"I'm not. I'm here as the guest of my aunt. You probably know her. Henrietta Fredericks."

"Of course." Gordon turned to his wife. "Molly, this is Henrietta's nephew. Mrs. Dawson, Mr. Victor Fredericks. And my son, Paul. You two boys ought to have quite a lot in common."

"Oh?" Paul thought as he shook hands that the fellow looked as though he was baring his teeth when he smiled.

"Glad to know you. I've seen your by-line on quite a few stories in the Express. They're good stuff."

"Thanks."

Molly, sensitive to Paul's antagonism, spoke quickly. "You sound as though you know something about newspapers, Mr. Fredericks."

"I was in the business, for a time, up in Detroit. Before I moved into advertising."

"You're not a Chicagoan, then?"

"No, ma'm. At the moment I'm a visitor, although I hope to make my home here." Fredericks glanced obliquely at Gordon, then away again. "I'm staying with my aunt."

"Be sure to give her my love."

"I certainly will, thank you. And I've enjoyed meeting you." The young man bowed to Molly, shook hands again with Paul and then turned to Gordon. "May I hope to hear from you soon, Mr. Dawson?"

"I'll telephone you in the next day or two. In fact, there's a letter in the mail to you right now saying you'll have our final word before the end of the week." Gordon sounded brisk but pleasant.

"Thanks very much, sir. I appreciate that." Fredericks bowed again and made his way back across the lounge to the far side, where he joined a small group of people.

Paul lit a cigarette and resumed his seat. "If that guy was ever a newspaperman, I'll eat my hat. It must take him half an hour just to tie his necktie and adjust his breast-pocket handkerchief every time he gets dressed."

"I'm afraid you're wrong, Paul," Gordon said. "He had a good record in Detroit, and his references are excellent."

"Are you thinking of hiring him, dear?" Molly, who knew little about her husband's business, was nevertheless curious.

"That all depends." Gordon studied the ash on his cigar.

"I must say he has good manners."

"Maybe I do the guy an injustice, but I didn't like him," Paul said. "He's a little too oily for my dough."

"I hope he won't be too oily for mine." There was an undercurrent of tension in Gordon's voice. "That is, if I give him the job." He eyed his son speculatively.

"What job is that, Dad?" Paul really didn't care, but felt he had to say something.

[88]

"Director of public relations, promotion and advertising. Carl Murphy is leaving us, you know."

"No, I didn't."

"He's had a rather serious operation and his doctors have advised him to move out to California for his health."

"I see." Paul ran his fingers through his hair nervously; he saw a great deal. Carl Murphy's job was one for which he had been groomed; he had worked during vacations as Murphy's assistant, and his father had told him repeatedly that his experience at the Express qualified him for the position.

"Of course, I hate to bring in an outsider if it isn't necessary."

"I quite understand, Dad."

"It takes a long time to bring in someone who is totally unfamiliar with our operation. You know what I mean as you've been exposed to Whitmarket and Company all your life."

"That's very true." It was, too. From the time Paul had been in high school he had studied company charts and pamphlets, and his father had spent countless evenings describing various departmental functions to him.

"Young Fredericks could do a good job for us, I feel sure. The year he spent in an advertising agency would be valuable for our purposes."

"Then you have no problem, Dad."

Molly could not hide her dismay as she looked first at her husband, then at her son. The spirit of family unity that had seemed so strong only a few minutes previous had evaporated, and the taut restlessness of the two men reminded her of the wild animals she had seen when her children had been younger and she had taken them to the Lincoln Park Zoo. She wanted to intervene, but could not; the issue that was causing the split between them was one they would have to settle themselves.

"No problem? I hate to pay out good money to an outsider when it could go to someone considerably closer to me, someone who will inherit Whitmarket and its responsibilities some day."

"I'm satisfied where I am, thanks."

"It's a bigger salary than you're making at the Express, Paul. Don't be too hasty about this."

"I'm flattered at the offer, but I have no kicks over what I'm making, Dad."

Gordon adjusted his glasses and fought for self-control. He succeeded, and when he spoke again the edge that had crept into his voice was gone. "Think about it for twenty-four hours before you give me an answer, Paul. You'd be a real help to the company if you took over Murphy's spot. Henry Thayer was talking to me about it this morning after our monthly directors' meeting. Like to hear what he said?"

"I—"

" 'That job is made to order for Paul, and he's made to order for it.' That's what he said to me. And it's an accurate picture of the situation, Paul. Nobody is flattering you, nobody is being kind to you, nobody is trying to drag you into the business through a trick of some kind. We could really use you and your talents."

"You make it pretty tough for me, Dad." Paul stubbed out his cigarette.

"I won't pretend that there isn't more to it than this immediate job." Gordon was at his executive best, cool and authoritative, seemingly impersonal. "Let's examine the picture analytically for a minute or two. The man who sits in the public relations and promotions hot-seat knows just about everything that goes on at the company. Although he ranks as a junior department head, he dips into almost every phase of the business."

"So I learned, those summers I worked for Carl Murphy. Carl was practically a walking encyclopaedia on the wholesale grocery business in general and Whitmarket in particular. I

[90]

think he had a copy of practically every report that was sent in to the front office."

"Exactly." Gordon drew a deep breath and his left hand tightened imperceptibly on the arm of his chair. "There's no better stepping-stone to the top than from his position."

"If somebody is interested in getting to the top in that particular line of work, of course." Paul was carefully trying to match his father's air of calm. "I'm sure it's a very attractive opening for somebody. On the other hand, a guy who wants to devote his life to a different kind of vocation wouldn't get excited over the prospects."

"Why wouldn't he?"

"I'm a professional man, Dad. A doctor serves the community. A lawyer serves the community. So does a newspaperman. I want to spend my life serving people rather than sell consumer merchandise."

Molly picked up her gloves and handbag. "Isn't it time we find Marcia and start for home?"

"Just a minute, dear. I'd like to finish this with Paul first. There's one angle he forgets. I won't live forever. Some day Whitmarket will belong to him and to his sisters. And somebody is going to have to know what makes the company tick. Somebody is going to need sufficient knowledge to protect the investment that I've built up and that my father built before me."

Paul shifted uncomfortably in his chair; this argument always made him feel guilty, but his father had used it so often before that repetition made it less potent. And he could not compromise his principles. He had meant what he had just said, and if Dad refused to take him seriously, that was too bad. "I can't answer that line of reasoning, and you know it, Dad," he said evenly. "I can only hope that either Betsy or Marcia will marry someone who'll fit your specifications for taking over the business."

Gordon rose abruptly. "Excuse me for a moment," he said to his wife. "I think I'll go over and tell young Fredericks that he has the job. It's an unorthodox way to handle such a matter, but he's so eager that it'll be a great relief to him. Meantime you might round up Marcia. I'll be ready to leave for home as soon as you are."

CHAPTER SEVEN

At around five o'clock each afternoon the clatter of typewriters in the city or "local" room of the Express reached a crescendo, punctuated by the incessant ringing of telephones and the shouts of rewrite men and reporters for copy boys. At the west end of the half-block long, cement-floored room was the sacred precinct of the city desk, which was separated from the outer world by a maze of partitions and doors, all made of glass. Actually there were four desks inside the cubicle, one for the City Editor himself, which he always occupied at this hour although he might have preferred to retire to his private office, two for his assistants and the fourth for the "slotman" who routed telephone calls and kept one eye on the clock, ever-conscious of the approach of the deadline for the first edition of tomorrow morning's newspaper.

Just outside the partitions and at right angles to it was the copy desk, a dignified oasis where six rather elderly gentlemen corrected the grammar in the stories written by the staff and prepared headlines. These veterans, who had spent their lives in newspaperdom, were calm, unflustered and seemingly never altered their work pace. They were the exceptions, however; the rest of the city room was bedlam.

Small typewriter desks were lined up in rows of three down

the length of the cavern, after the manner of a schoolroom. The nine seats closest to the city desk were occupied by the rewrite men, whose task it was to reduce to paper the news stories provided over the telephone by reporters. Perhaps half of the remaining desks were currently occupied by various of the reporters themselves; for one reason or another they had come into the office and were writing their own stories. In some cases this was a zealously-guarded privilege, and the chief political reporter, the humorist who found something light in the human side of the news and the two hard-bitten women who prepared stories for the special edification of feminine readers were in this category.

The remainder just happened to be allowed to do their own writing, and never knew from one day to the next when lightning would strike them. Paul was in this group, and at the moment he was feeling highly pleased with himself, for this was the third day in succession on which he was being permitted to write his own story. He sat at his desk near the rear of the room, pounding furiously on his typewriter and shouting, "Boy, copy!" as he worked against the pressure of the five-eighteen deadline. Page after page came out of his machine, and copy boys appeared on the run to take each new portion of his article to those who would process it.

Although the pace of the moment was frenzied, Paul was content. He had been the first reporter on the spot after a bus crash in which three people had been killed and eighteen others had been injured, he had talked at length to the survivors before they had been taken off to hospitals, and the net result was a story that would appear on page one. Later tonight, he knew, a reaction would set in and he would begin to feel desperately sorry for the victims of the accident; their suffering as people, as individuals, would bother him for days. Right now, however, he was taking quiet pride in the professional skill he was showing, in the feeling that he was doing his job competently.

His mind raced two paragraphs ahead of his actual writing, and a hasty glance at the clock showed him that he would just finish his story in time to beat the deadline. Then, unexpectedly, the rhythm of his work was jarred by the ringing of his telephone. He snatched off the earpiece, a quaint device equipped with a special wire loop that fitted it to a man's head. "Dawson," he snapped, and continued to write his story with his other hand.

"Hello, Paul." He heard his mother's voice at the other end of the wire.

"I'm awfully busy. I'll call you back, Mother."

Molly was not one to be put off so easily. "Are you coming home for dinner tonight, dear?"

"Yes. I'll call you back."

"Oh, I'm so glad. I wonder if you could do us a favor, dear, and—"

"I'll have to call you back." He slammed the earpiece back on its hook and returned to his story. For a second or two the words wouldn't come, but he used self-discipline to dismiss his mother from his mind and wrote all the more rapidly to make up for the precious time he had lost.

At last he brought the article to an end and leaned back in his chair to enjoy the luxury of a cigarette. He had beaten the deadline by precisely four minutes, and he felt satisfied. Feeling a need to stretch his legs, he stood and wandered to the water cooler, where a rewrite man and two other reporters were already gathered. Paul filled a paper cup, drank greedily and then exchanged a few words with the others; nobody was in a conversational mood at the moment, for the tensions of the work just completed still lingered. Strolling back to his own desk, Paul deliberately avoided looking through the glass at the men on the city desk. If one of them caught his eye now, there

[95]

was always the chance he'd be held over for an hour or two on some special assignment instead of being permitted to go home in another half-hour.

Settling back in his chair he picked up his carbon copy of the piece he had just written, and read the first three pages before he suddenly remembered that his mother had called him. Feeling faintly guilty he reached for his phone, dialed "9" for an outside line and then hastily put in his call. Molly was apparently sitting close to the telephone in her bedroom, for she answered at once. "Hello."

"Sorry I couldn't talk to you before, Mother. I was very busy." There was no point in explaining the urgencies of deadlines to her, for she wouldn't understand. He had made several futile attempts in the past, and knew better than to repeat his error now.

"You were really quite rude, Paul. Unnecessarily rude." Her voice was high, as it always was when she was angry or hurt.

"It was unintentional, I give you my word." He was sure she would dwell on the subject if he gave her the chance, so it was better not to linger. "I think you said there's something or other you want me to do?"

"If it's no trouble for you." She was still stiff and remote, in spite of his apology.

"I'm sure it won't be."

"Well, then. Could you drop by Dad's office and bring him home? Something happened to the boiler in the basement, and Evans is working on it, so it would be more convenient to let him finish instead of sending him for Dad. If you're sure you don't mind, that is."

"I'm quite sure, Mother." She was sure, too, though she wouldn't admit it, and Paul could not resist adding, "Does Dad know that I'll be over for him?"

"Yes, Paul," Molly replied, not realizing what she was admitting, "I phoned him before I called you."

"Okay, then. We'll be seeing you." Paul hung up and smiled to himself, half ruefully, half in amusement. There was no one, he thought, quite like his mother, no one who could arouse in him the simultaneous but contradictory feelings of tenderness and exasperation.

He finished reading the story he had written and was vaguely dissatisfied with it; for some unknown reason it didn't seem to hang together as he had at first so fondly believed. At least the city desk hadn't called him down, and that was something for which to be grateful. It was almost time to go home, and he killed a few minutes by chatting with a reporter who covered the criminal courts and had an ambition to be a drama critic. The conversation was desultory, as neither had any real interest in the other, and Paul at last saw that he could leave without having to face the accusation of being a clock watcher. It was now five minutes past his authorized departure time.

Donning his jacket, hat and coat with a deliberation that would make anyone looking at him think he was indifferent to the hour, he started to stroll toward the exit, but stopped short as he heard someone call his name through the open door of the partitioned city desk area.

"Dawson!" Mr. Austin, the City Editor, the only man in the room who wore a jacket while working, was beckoning.

It was a standing joke in newspaper circles around town that Harry Austin actually looked and acted far more like a certified public accountant than like the editors in movies. But his own employees, whom he ruled with the strong hand of a minor despot, could see little humor in the remark. From a distance he gave the appearance of being mild, even frail, for he was short and slender. But his pale blue eyes, cold and calculating, gave a better indication of his character, and his iron-grey hair, always combed, and a thin mustache, which he kept neatly trimmed, hinted at his fastidiousness.

He invariably tapped a hand or a foot, apparently finding

an outlet for his restlessness in incessant movement, but he rarely showed emotion in any other way. Paul hurried to him, and as always it was impossible to judge from the boss' expression whether he was about to bestow praise or blame. It was inconceivable, Paul thought, that anyone could ever become really friendly with the City Editor, but by the same token no one in the industry could fail to respect him. Local room humorists enjoyed saying that there was but one difference between a newspaperman and a journalist: the latter carried a cane. Yet everyone in Chicago who had ever come in contact with Harry Austin was willing to concede that he was a journalist in the best sense of the word.

"Yes, Mr. Austin?"

"See me in my office first thing in the morning. I've given instructions that you're not to be marked down for any outside assignments until I've seen you."

Austin returned to a study of a pile of papers which he removed one by one from a spike, and Paul was dismissed. The other men on the city desk either didn't know what the Editor had in mind or else they were taking pains to conceal whatever knowledge they possessed, for all three pretended to be busy and preoccupied. Paul headed for the elevators, reflecting that he might be out of a job by morning. There had been rumors during the past couple of weeks that a new economy wave was pending, and although similar stories were circulated regularly, it was possible that this time they might be true and that Paul's head would be the first to roll.

The idea was disquieting, but Paul was determined to continue on the path he had chosen for himself. If he should be discharged tomorrow, he would make the rounds of the other newspapers, and if no position opened up on any of them, he would try the radio stations, each of which now boasted its own news broadcasting department. One way or another he would land on his feet and would acquire the experience he needed if he was to some day own and publish his own small town daily newspaper. One way or another, regardless of setbacks, he would build toward the future that would mean so much to the region that his newspaper would serve.

His car was where he had left it early this afternoon, with a sign, proclaiming the owner to be a member of the press, prominently displayed inside the windshield. Possession of such a placard enabled a man to park anywhere and Paul knew he would feel a great sense of loss if he had to turn in his precious square of pasteboard. Every newspaperman felt that he was a member of a very exclusive club, and the trifling privileges which a reporter enjoyed became more important in his eyes when he feared they might soon be taken from him.

Traffic was unusually light as Paul drove north across the Chicago River via the Clark Street Bridge, and within ten minutes he arrived at the main offices of Whitmarket and Company. Leaving his car in the lot reserved for executives, he paused for a moment as he looked up at the six-story grey stone building. Then he walked in through the main entrance, wondering why he invariably felt depressed whenever he came here. In the main reception room were oil portraits of Grandpa and the two partners with whom he had formed the concern, but Paul did not glance in the direction of his distinguished ancestor. As a child he had too often been forced to stand and stare at the painting, to simulate an admiration for someone he had never actually known.

Most of the employees had already departed, and only one of the three elevators was still running. The operator was apparently new, for he did not recognize the young man whom he transported to the executive offices on the top floor, and Paul was grateful; above all else he hated being fawned upon by people who drew their paychecks from Gordon Dawson. The reception desk on the sixth floor was empty, and Paul walked down the long corridor lined with the offices of vice presidents and department heads to the suite which the employees privately referred to as "the big tin."

Lights were blazing in a large office that stood between the presidential suite and the rest of the company, and Paul felt a sense of pleasure and relief as he poked his head into the open door. This was the domain of Henry Thayer, Whitmarket's Senior Vice President, who had begun his career with the company's founder and was Gordon's closest associate. "Uncle Henry" had been closer to Paul than almost any blood relative, and there had always been a rather special sense of rapport between them. In fact, Paul had often thought that if he suffered any real regrets over having chosen another career for himself, it was because he would not be in business with this man whom he so liked and admired.

Henry Thayer was sitting behind his desk, immersed in work, and his position was typical of his whole approach to life. His feet rested on the top of his scarred telephone table, he was in his shirtsleeves with his necktie loosened, and as he finished reading sales reports he dropped them onto the floor. His patient secretary, who lived in a cubicle beyond his office, would spend a quarter of an hour picking up documents and restoring order after he left for the day.

There was nothing delicate about him, either physically or in his approach to living. He was six feet, four inches tall, with a ruddy face, an enormous appetite and an unlimited capacity for work and for fun. His deep bass voice intimidated underlings, dominated sales conferences and silenced colleagues at meetings of the board of directors, yet he was a curiously gentle man, sensitive to the feelings of others and as unsparing in his efforts to help a friend as he was tireless in safeguarding the interests of the company which he had joined as a clerk at the age of sixteen.

Paul grinned and pretended to clear his throat. "I hear you got skunked three sets in a row today," he said. It was a private joke; Thayer, who played tennis at noon every day to keep his waistline down, had taught Paul the game.

Papers fluttered to the floor, and the big man bounded to his feet. "You little rascal, I'll give you a three game handicap in every set and still beat you every time!"

They met in the center of the room and Paul was enveloped in a bear hug. "Uncle Henry, you look wonderful."

"That's because I feel wonderful." Thayer took a step backward and his dark eyes studied Paul. "Which is more than I can say for you. You're pale, boy. Get away from that sweatshop you work in and meet me some noon. I'll put a little tone into your muscles."

"I wish I could, Uncle Henry. But I'll take you on any Saturday you like."

"Saturdays? They're for my grandchildren." Thayer smiled, then sobered. "We don't see much of you any more, Paul. Aunt Helen was asking about you only a couple of nights ago."

"I've neglected both of you terribly. I'm sorry." Paul was genuinely regretful. Some of the brightest memories of his childhood and adolescence were centered around Uncle Henry and Aunt Helen, and it was wrong to repay their kindness now with indifference.

"What are you talking about, youngster? You've got your own life to live. Live it!"

If only his father felt that way, Paul thought. "I'm doing my darndest."

"See that you do. Get yourself a nice little girl, settle down with her—and have fun. Remember my motto, Paul. Get your kicks out of life every step of the way. If you don't, you're better off dead." Thayer glanced at an old clock on a table. "I've got to get out of here. We've got seats for the fight tonight." His hand crashed down between Paul's shoulder blades. "Do less worrying and get yourself some fun. You stick to your old Uncle Henry's recipe, and you can't lose."

[101]

"I'll try." Paul started for the door. "Give my love to Aunt Helen. And I'll be seeing both of you, soon."

"Only if you want to. Otherwise, to heck with us, to heck with everybody!" Thayer's deep voice echoed into the corridor.

The outer door of the presidential suite was open, and Paul steeled himself. The contrast between the atmosphere here and that of Uncle Henry's office was so sharp that he could almost feel it physically. A grey-haired woman, deceptively soft-faced and mild-mannered, wearing one of her unobtrusive tailored suits, was arranging file folders at a desk. She glanced up quickly, her spinster's eyes hostile. Suddenly she softened and smiled.

"Well, Paul. We haven't seen you in a long time. Too long a time."

"Hi, Miss Keebling." Matilda Keebling had been his father's secretary since a year or two before Paul's birth. She unquestionably knew everything there was to know about the wholesale grocery business, she was fiercely loyal to her employer and she was, as Gordon so often said, worth her weight in gold. Paul always had the feeling that she thought of him as a ten-year-old, except when she remembered that he was disloyal to the organization to which she was devoting her entire life. At such times, Paul was convinced, she disapproved of him heartily.

"We're very pleased with your wonderful progress, Paul." She never referred to herself in the first person; it was one of her idiosyncrasies. "We were so pleased to see the article in the paper yesterday with your name on it. 'By Paul Dawson.' My. It's hard to realize, it really is."

"There'll be another piece with my byline on it tomorrow morning—I think." Paul hadn't meant to boast and took no pleasure in the quick smile that lighted up Miss Keebling's tired, lined face.

"We'll certainly be looking for it." She leaned forward slightly across her desk, and lowered her voice confidentially.

"You must keep a scrap-book of all the things you write, don't you?"

"No, as a matter of fact, I don't." The notion had never occurred to Paul.

"Then I'm sure your Mama does." That disposed of the matter in Miss Keebling's mind.

"I see you have some new plants." Paul could never distinguish among the little potted green gems that lined the window, but it was a safe bet that there was at least one recent acquisition.

"There are two new ones, and they're both doing beautifully!" Miss Keebling declared enthusiastically. "We've had so much unusual sunshine this winter that they're all thriving. And it was very clever of you to notice." Suddenly she stiffened and inclined her head slightly in the direction of the heavy oak door behind her. "But we mustn't keep you out here jabbering. You're to go right in, Paul. Your Papa is expecting you."

"Nice to have seen you, Miss Keebling," he murmured, walked quickly to the door of his father's office and tapped lightly, then entered.

This was the room that some day would have been Paul's had he chosen a different path for himself, but he felt no sense of identification with it, no regret that he would never spend his working life here. It was a somber room, heavy and oppressive, or so it had always appeared in Paul's eyes. Panels of dark, unobtrusive oak lined the walls, and the swivel chair of worn, green leather in which the President of the company sat was located midway between a long mahogany desk and a large table; Gordon could swing from one to the other without rising from his seat.

A miniature telephone switchboard stood at the left side of the desk, and on the right was a large photograph of Molly. There were pictures of Paul and his sisters on the work table; significantly, those of the girls had been taken in the past year or two, but that of Paul was the one that had appeared in his high school annual the year he had been graduated. Apparently his father still thought of him as being sixteen or seventeen.

A dark green sofa stood on the far side of the room, and it always looked slightly dusty, although it was not. Paul had never seen anyone sit on it except his sister Betsy. There were five or six comfortable visitors' chairs, and near the three large windows on the left was a table on which were pyramided samples of the canned goods and other products which Whitmarket sold. The walls had always been bare of ornamentation, and Paul was surprised to see a large chart hanging from one of them now. No lamp had been lighted on that side of the office, and the big square of beaverboard was too far distant for him to make out the writing on it, but the graph itself was very clear: whatever it indicated showed a long, slow decline.

Gordon, unrumpled despite a long day, was talking on the telephone, and waved a hand at Paul, who wandered to the window and looked out at the brilliantly-lit Wrigley Building and the Gothic bulk of Tribune Tower behind it. It was possible, he told himself, that he might find himself on a job-hunting expedition at the Trib tomorrow.

He had no interest in the phone conversation, but it was impossible to shut out the sound of his father's voice. "We can't pay those prices and they know it!" Gordon was saying heatedly. "We have fixed costs like everybody else, and we're entitled to a profit—like everybody else. This Administration in Washington is putting the Indian sign on us—and on a thousand others like us. If they'd just leave us alone, we'd be all right. If they keep sticking their noses in and telling what we can and can't do, we might as well tack up the bankruptcy sale notices right now!"

There was silence as he listened to the voice at the other end of the wire, and Paul hoped devoutly that this wasn't going to be a springboard for a lecture that would last all the way home.

He already knew in detail what his father thought of President Roosevelt, and he had learned, too, that no matter what he himself might say in reply, it would be wrong.

"Tell them we've made our final offer," Gordon said, his voice hard and cold and unyielding. "They can take it or leave it, and if they haven't confirmed by noon tomorrow, the whole deal is off." He slammed the phone down into its cradle, then lifted his head and observed mildly to his son, "Sorry, Paul. I was on long distance."

"Take your time, Dad. I'm in no rush." Mother, of course, was planning to serve dinner precisely at six-thirty, but that was her problem.

"I'll be with you in a minute. You might read this, meantime. From your sister. It came today." Gordon reached into the inner pocket of his jacket and pulled out a letter, which he tossed across the desk.

"Thanks." Paul wondered if the lighting in the office was deceptive. Gordon's complexion was pasty, the wrinkles around his eyes and at the corners of his mouth were sharply etched and his shoulders seemed to have narrowed and sagged. For year after year, Paul suddenly thought, we see our parents through the eyes of our childhood. We never really look at them. Then, without warning, we see them as they are and we realize that they're growing old.

He felt a wave of affection for his father so deep that it almost overcame him, but he could not let his emotions show. Any demonstration of his love and regard would be excruciatingly awkward for both of them, so he averted his gaze and carefully unfolded the letter from Betsy. "This," he said a shade too loudly, "must be something. As Marcia would say, if she's written you here instead of at home, she must want money again."

Gordon did not reply but studied his son covertly, while pretending to busy himself with a large ledger that was opened on the desk in front of him. He and Paul were alike in so many

[105]

ways, yet so different. He could look across the desk and see himself some thirty-odd years ago, but this was not simply a copy of what he himself had been. There was a coldness, a spirit of rejection in Paul that he himself had never felt toward his own father, and it was this alien attitude, this lack of sympathy and understanding that was building the walls of estrangement higher and higher.

The pity of it was that Gordon could feel for the boy. In his own youth he had wanted to be a composer, and to this day he loved good music passionately. Yet when his father had come to him and had said, "I need you in the business," he had put his romantic, adolescent dreams behind him and had buckled down to his duty. He wondered how Paul would react right now if he were to say, "Son, look at this ledger. Here's what's happening to Whitmarket and Company. I need you here with me. I need someone on whom I can rely completely, someone I can trust."

He was afraid to make the experiment. If Paul showed callousness and indifference—and his past attitude made it highly likely that he'd shrug off such an appeal now—there would be a definite break between them, a cleavage that could never be bridged. And so, feeling uncertain, Gordon decided to leave well enough alone. There was at least a truce, and as long as it continued there was a possibility, regardless of how remote, that Paul might some day be persuaded that his place was here.

Totally unaware of his father's thoughts, Paul was reading Betsy's hastily scrawled note for the second time: *Dearest Daddy, I'm writing this to you at the office because I'd like to sound you out on something—privately, before I spring it on Mama. I'd dearly love to bring my room-mate, Mary Jane Stone, home with me over the Easter vacation. She's a darling, and I know you'll all be as crazy about her as I am. There's just one thing that worries me a tiny bit—I'm sure she can't afford the trip all the way out to Chicago, and as a good hostess I really should offer to pay her fare. Do you suppose the old exchequer could stand the strain? I'll be writing a real letter in the next couple of days, but am dashing this off between classes and really must fly. All my love to you and Mama, a hug for Marcia and ditto to the Boy Wonder. Ever your Bets.*

"Hah!" Paul said, and shook his head.

"I see no reason she can't bring her room-mate out here with her," Gordon declared, his tone a shade defensive.

"Of course you don't. That's why she wrote to you in the first place." Paul spoke without rancor and a broad grin softened his words. It was a family joke that Betsy could always twist Dad around her little finger, that he had never been known to deny her anything. "You've already dictated an answer to her, I suppose."

Gordon cleared his throat. "I happened to be cleaning up a considerable amount of correspondence today, so I—"

Paul laughed outright. "I salute Bets on the achievement of another brilliant *fait accompli*. Mother will have a minor fit and say you're spoiling her, so you'd better have your arguments ready."

Gordon joined in the laugh, a trifle self-consciously, and this was as close as he would ever come to an admission that he privately favored Betsy over his other children. It was wonderful to see that Paul showed no jealousy and had not, in fact, for many years. "I guess we'd better be on our way. You're parked downstairs?"

"Yes, Dad."

Again they smiled at each other companionably, and the barriers that separated them seemed for a moment to have vanished. They were co-conspirators, and Gordon chuckled as he took Betsy's letter and stuffed it back into his pocket. They walked together into the outer office, and as the President of Whitmarket and Company took his hat and coat from the clothes-closet, his secretary, who was locking her file cabinets, felt a surge of hope. She hadn't seen Mr. Dawson and Paul so at ease with each other in—well, she just couldn't remember how long. Maybe there was still a chance that Paul would join the staff here.

"Good night, Miss Keebling," her employer said amiably, and started down the corridor with his hand on his son's shoulder.

The silent offices on either side of the carpeted hall looked a little less grim to Paul now, though he didn't quite know why. He tensed slightly as they passed the door to the room that was about to be occupied by Victor Fredericks, the newly-hired public relations, promotion and advertising man. But Gordon said nothing, so Paul relaxed again.

They rode down to the ground floor in silence, it being a fixed habit of the company's head never to talk in elevators. It was one of his maxims that everything he said was overheard, then repeated in a distorted way, and members of his family were as familiar with his rule as were his associates. Gordon continued to smile until he caught sight of his father's oil portrait in the principal reception room. He looked at it briefly, then glanced at his son. And the amity, the well-being in which both had been enveloped vanished as abruptly as it had sprung into existence.

CHAPTER EIGHT

Paul arrived at the office early on Thursday, forgetting in his anxiety over his appointment with the City Editor that Mr. Austin rarely came into the office before late morning. The assistant in charge of the city desk and the slotman who helped him tried to keep the young reporter busy handling odd assignments inside the office, but not much was stirring at this time of day, and Paul spent the better part of the morning sitting glum and unoccupied at his desk. He read the early editions of the afternoon papers that the copy boys brought him, but little local news interested him. The only item that caught his attention was a foreign story: Hitler, the head of the German government, had made another of his violent speeches last night, and the domestic bigots were applauding it this morning.

Otherwise there was nothing out of the ordinary, and Paul's own problems were uppermost in his mind. If he should be fired, he thought, he might break his date for this evening. He wouldn't be fit company for Helga, and he felt sure she'd understand and agree to a postponement if he told her the truth. Maybe it was just as well that he'd been unable to buy tickets for *Of Thee I Sing* for tonight; a man without a job wouldn't be in a mood to enjoy a musical comedy.

"Paul!" Eddie, the day slotman, beckoned and nodded his

head toward the private offices that were located behind the city desk.

The gesture was sufficient for Paul to know that the boss had arrived. Stubbing out a cigarette, he wiped the palms of his hands on a handkerchief and headed straight for the inner sanctum. A secretary, one of those rare creatures in the newspaper world, with whom reporters had almost no contact, sat on guard outside the City's Editor's small office. A luscious blonde who would have been more suitable in a theatrical agency, she was pasting some clippings from the morning's final edition on sheets of copy paper, and she didn't look up.

"Yes?" she asked brusquely.

"Mr. Austin wants to see me. Paul Dawson."

The girl didn't bother to reply. She rose sinuously to her feet and disappeared into the inner office. She came out again a moment later and said curtly, "Go on in." Then she resumed her seat and started to work again, still not having glanced once in Paul's direction.

The City Editor was marking the final edition of the Express with a thick copy pencil, and he continued with his task as he heard his visitor enter. "Sit down, Dawson."

"Yes, sir." Paul had never before been invited to sit in this bare, cramped room, and he was sure now that something extremely unpleasant was in the wind.

"Dawson, you're not a very good reporter." The pencil encircled a small article, and Mr. Austin scribbled something on the page beside it. "You aren't hard-boiled enough. You're too sensitive, too much aware of the feelings of people. That hurts your ability to see a story clearly, to milk it for every angle. Mind you, I'm not saying you're bad. You have energy and initiative, and you're conscientious. But you just aren't good."

"I see." This is it, Paul thought miserably. In three minutes or less he'd be on his way to the cashier for his final salary check plus one week's severance pay.

The thin, parched face cracked in a semblance of a smile. "Relax, boy," Mr. Austin said. "I told you the worst as an appetizer, so you wouldn't get a swelled head. You may not be a reporter, Dawson, but you can write. You have the potential of becoming as good as any man on the staff. I've been trying you out these past few days. I've been putting the heat on you, and there's a real place in the newspaper world, take my word for it, for a man who can bang out clean, lively copy when there's pressure on him. You're all right."

"Thanks very much." Paul was thoroughly confused now; praise from the boss was rare, and coming on top of harsh criticism it made no sense at all.

"So, as of now, you're no longer a reporter. I'm adding you to the rewrite battery. You'll get fifteen dollars a week more, effective with next week's paycheck. And if you make good as a rewrite man, we'll have another talk in a couple of months and maybe I can squeeze a few extra pennies out of the budget to boost you up to the same level as the other boys."

This was so different from what Paul had expected that he was stunned. Then, very slowly he grinned and inhaled deeply. For an instant he was at a loss for words, but knew he had to say something and groped desperately for the right phrases. "I—I appreciate this, Mr. Austin. I—"

"Tell Eddie I said to give you the end desk in the third row." The copy pencil was busy again, and the interview came to an end.

"Yes, sir." Paul walked out quickly, and barely restrained himself from thumbing his nose at the secretary, who was now drinking coffee from a paper carton as she stared blankly into space.

In less than a quarter of an hour Paul had changed his few belongings to his new desk, had accepted the congratulations of his colleagues and was hard at work, writing small news items that would be used to fill the spaces between bigger stories. It

[111]

was difficult to concentrate, even on anything as simple as this routine work, and he felt a giddy pride, a sense of triumph. Suddenly, on an impulse, he reached for his telephone and a few seconds later he heard Helga's voice.

"Hi," he said. "All set for tonight?"

"Why, yes." She sounded a little remote, and he thought that someone was probably in her office with her. "We're to meet at the entrance to the Cape Cod Room at seven o'clock, as I understand it. Unless something has come up that's caused you to change your plans?"

So that was it. She was apprehensive, thinking he was intending to cancel the date, and Paul laughed buoyantly. "Nothing could make me change tonight's plans! We're going to have a real celebration!"

"Oh?" He could feel her relief at the other end of the wire. "I didn't know there was something to celebrate."

"There wasn't—until a few minutes ago. But there sure is now. I've had a promotion. And a raise. And—well, I'll tell you about it later." He brought the conversation to an abrupt end, selfishly wanting to savor Helga's pleasure and congratulations in person rather than through the comparatively impersonal medium of the telephone.

A copy boy brought him several more small stories for rewrite; one was an account of a knifing in a West Side slum area, and had come from the news agency that handled all such trivia for the metropolitan newspapers. He would be required to spend a little time and effort on that one, but the others were mere single paragraph fillers, and he could knock them out at his leisure. He ran fresh copy paper into his typewriter and started to work in earnest. The tempo increased, reporters began to phone in stories from the outside, and within an hour Paul was too busy to sit back and enjoy the heady taste of his triumph.

That may have been the reason why it was mid-afternoon

[112]

before he remembered to call his mother and tell her his good news.

* * *

Paul arrived at the Drake ten minutes early, sauntered through the hotel toward the entrance to the Cape Cod Room and leaned against the wall outside the door; he had never before been this meticulously prompt. And although this would be the third time in less than a week that he had seen Helga, he didn't mind in the least discarding his bachelor's caution and fear of involvement. The danger signals were flying, but he preferred to ignore them; after all, he had just had a salary raise, he was about to spend the evening with an extraordinarily attractive girl, and he decided to have fun for its own sake and let the future take care of itself.

Suddenly he saw Helga approaching, and he glanced at his watch. It was only three minutes to seven, and it occurred to him that it was typical of her to be on time. Some girls, like Joan, made it a point to keep a fellow waiting for at least a quarter of an hour. Helga had not yet seen him, and walked slowly, looking in the windows of the exclusive shops located in the hotel's arcade, so Paul approached her quietly.

"Boo!"

"Hi, Paul."

Her pleasure at seeing him was so warm and frank that he barely controlled an impulse to kiss her. He was afraid she would read his mind and spoke hurriedly. "I hope I didn't startle you or anything, but I couldn't resist sneaking up on you. You were so engrossed in looking at all the junk in these windows."

"Junk? Why, I've never seen such lovely things, and I couldn't take my eyes off them. I don't get into the Drake very often," she added bluntly, "and I hardly do my shopping in stores like these." Smiling, she pointed at a hand-tooled jewel case. "Do you call that junk?"

[113]

"I take it all back." Paul grinned and looked at the little leather box. It was similar to one his mother owned, and he could not refrain from asking, "Would you really like to have that?"

"Actually have it for myself?" Helga laughed merrily. "I could never afford to own anything as beautiful and expensive. I just like to look at it. In the same way I admire that bracelet." She indicated a thin band of diamonds and rubies in the adjoining window.

"I don't care about owning it, though." She moved closer to the glass and gazed in fascination at the bracelet. "Aren't those stones clear and cool? But when you move just a little, and the light hits them from another angle, fire seems to come out of them. There's a Swedish poem my father often quotes that describes the way they look. If I can translate it for you, *'The sunrise belongs to everyone. Even a pauper may enjoy beauty.'*"

Paul stared at her and thought that she was the only girl he had ever met who could look at unattainable objects and appreciate them for their own sake, without covetousness. She was content to revel in the beauty of the diamonds, which were symbols of a world she had never known and would not know, yet there was no envy in her. She was unique, he told himself, and any man who failed to evaluate the true worth of such a girl deserved contempt.

Helga, suddenly aware that he was watching her, became embarrassed. "Well." She lifted her head and looked a trifle uncertainly in the direction of the entrance to the Cape Cod Room.

"We aren't going to eat here at all," Paul said, taking her arm and piloting her rapidly along the tile-floored arcade to the Walton Place entrance where he had parked his car. "We're going to Julio's instead. Ever been there?"

"No, I—"

"Swell. You'll love it. Ever hear of the joint?"

"No, I don't believe I—"

"Can't blame you. It's a newspaper hangout. We use it as our Mecca in times of success and times of tragedy. If I'd been fired today, we'd have gone there and spent all my money. Instead we'll go there and spend all my money. In fact, we'll tear the roof off the place!"

Helga slowed her pace and her smile faded. "Is it a terribly expensive restaurant, Paul? Because we don't have to—"

"Sure it's expensive. And we do have to go there. That's the whole idea. They have wonderful atmosphere, wonderful steaks, it's a wonderful evening—and here we are! What more can anybody ask or want—and get?"

They were out the door now, and he gave her no chance to reply as he helped her into the car. In his present mood it was impossible for him to remain quiet, and as they drove to the nearby restaurant he gave her a detailed account of his interview with Mr. Austin. He was just finishing as they arrived at Julio's, and Helga paused inside the entrance, looked up at him and put her gloved hand on his arm.

"I think it's the nicest thing I've ever heard. And thank you for sharing it with me, Paul."

Her sincerity implied far more than she actually said, and it was an effort for Paul to appear outwardly calm as Julio, the short, balding owner of the establishment, led the way to a corner booth and saw his guests comfortably seated at a candle-lit table complete with red and white checkered tablecloth and napkins to match.

Helga removed her black cloth coat, and as she painstakingly repeated the gesture of folding it that had so bothered Paul at the Balloon Room, he saw her costume for the first time. Now he realized the significance of something she had told him on the phone about changing at the apartment of a girl who worked in her office. She had bought new clothes for tonight,

[115]

and she had obviously spent more than she could afford. She was wearing a simple, tailored suit with a soft white wool sweater. A necklace and earrings of jade-green beads matched the suit perfectly.

No girl whom Paul knew had ever dressed in better taste, and he felt a sense of great relief. Here was proof positive that Helga was willing and able to learn, that she could be as smart as the young ladies who had been drilled in such matters since earliest childhood. Paul knew only too well that he was carrying his innate snobbishness to absurd limits, but it was better to be honest than to fool himself.

"You look beautiful," he said.

Helga blushed, and it was the first time he had seen her completely flustered. "Do you like this suit?" she asked timidly.

"I think it's lovely—and you're lovely in it."

"I spent all of last week's salary on it. I really splurged. Wasn't that dreadful?" Even in her sudden shyness she could not avoid candor.

"It was not dreadful," Paul said forcibly. "Is this the first time you've worn it?"

She nodded.

"I'm glad. I just hope you didn't go and spend a lot of money on account of—us." He knew he should stop there, but could not. "Of course, you understand that as far as I'm concerned, you'd look like—like nobody else has ever looked—even in an old burlap sack."

Their eyes met and something electric passed between them. Helga was the first to look away and gazed down at the table-cloth. "I'll have to try an old burlap sack some day."

Neither of them thought the attempt at humor succeeded, and there was an uncomfortable pause which Paul wanted to break by reaching across the table and taking Helga's hand. But he did not quite dare: this was not a girl with whom a man could play silly, flirtatious games, and he knew that any gesture of affection he might make would land him in deep water, deeper than he had ever been in before.

Again it was Helga who led the way to safer ground. "You must feel very proud of your promotion."

"Sure, it feels swell. The really important thing about it is that it brings the day when I can own my own paper that much closer. I've been thinking about it all afternoon, and I've raised my sights a little. Maybe I'll aim for a town of about twenty-five or thirty thousand. Some place that's big enough to support a daily newspaper. Some place where an editor who has something to say can roll up his sleeves and really slug—without fear or favor."

"I don't think you'd be afraid of anybody or anything."

"I couldn't let myself be afraid. Maintaining real freedom of the press is an editor's obligation."

"What made you decide in the first place that you want to own your own newspaper?"

"People," Paul replied emphatically. "I want to help them. In times like these, when everybody is confused and worried, a newspaper that defines issues and takes a stand on the things it believes to be important has an enormous contribution to make."

He was about to add more, but at that moment Julio returned to take the dinner order, and a few moments later the first course was brought to the table. For the next hour and a half two healthy young people devoured a meal of fresh shrimp cocktails, minestrone, T-bone steaks with baked potatoes and broccoli, mixed green salad, spumoni, cheese and coffee. Julio's prices were as high as Paul had hinted; a complete dinner cost two dollars and twenty-five cents, and not even the best hotels charged more.

But the food was indeed superb, and as Paul had said, the atmosphere alone was worth the price of admission. He and Helga lingered over a second cup of coffee, then a third, and

[117]

Paul was later unable to recall just what they had discussed. He remembered talking about his sisters, and he knew that Helga had described in detail a summer vacation she had spent with some distant cousins in northern Wisconsin. The rest was a vague but extraordinarily pleasant blur.

Only when they were once again in the car did Paul consider the immediate present. "It's too late for a movie, I'm afraid," he said, glancing at his watch.

"Good. I don't feel like going to one anyway."

"Neither do I. What'll we do?"

"You decide, Paul." She leaned back in the seat, completely relaxed, then leaned forward again to turn on the heater.

"Wait till the engine warms up," he cautioned as he started toward North Michigan Boulevard. "Let's see. We could go somewhere and dance—"

"No." Helga's voice was firm. "You've spent enough money on one evening already. Just because you've had a salary raise doesn't mean you've got to get rid of it before you even earn it."

"Okay. I'm just trying to think, a tough process at best. This isn't exactly the weather for a stroll along the lakefront."

"Oh, you go ahead if you want to, Paul. I'll stay in the car and wait for you."

"No, I think I'll be on your side. Suppose we just drive around for awhile. The streets are dry enough."

"Fine," she agreed. "With or without music?"

"Up to you."

"With, then."

Helga snapped on the radio, but reception was poor until Paul reached the Randolph Street bridge and moved past the skyscraper office buildings onto the Outer Drive. Then the static cleared and Helga tried first one station, then another, finally settling for a dance orchestra on WGN. She hummed softly to herself for some minutes and neither she nor Paul made any effort to talk. They were happy to be together, and their easy, companionable silence was the strongest of all possible signs that they were really content.

Paul drove aimlessly south through the park, then doubled back again onto the Drive. Very gradually, almost imperceptibly, the atmosphere changed to one of tension. Helga stopped humming and stared out her side window; Paul felt his nerves growing taut, and the music began to grate and jar. Suddenly he reached out and turned off the radio, but Helga did not seem to notice. And, for no valid reason, he began to drive more rapidly.

It was Helga who finally broke the silence. "We've been driving for a long time, Paul. It's after eleven."

"Yes."

"And tomorrow is a work day."

"Sure is."

"I guess—you'd better take me home, then."

Something in her tone arrested him, and he glanced at her, but her face was hidden in the shadows. Had there been a note of regret in her voice? Was it possible that she was yearning for a sign of affection, that she felt as he did?

The idea intrigued him and he forgot to turn west at Seventy-first Street, realized his error just too late and muttered under his breath. Helga laughed, but didn't sound like herself: the sound was high-pitched, almost shrill. At last he drew up in front of her apartment house and turned off the ignition, then dropped the car key into his overcoat pocket.

"Thank you for a lovely evening," Helga said carefully. "I've had a marvelous time."

Paul looked at her, and before he stopped to consider what he was doing he tossed his hat into the back seat, took Helga into his arms and kissed her. She returned his fervor measure for measure, and they clung to each other dizzily, breathlessly, for what seemed like a very long time.

CHAPTER NINE

It was unusual for Paul to make a date with a girl for the daylight hours on a Saturday, but as Helga had previous engagements for the weekend nights, he had to settle for what he could get. And so, anxious to see her again, he took her to lunch on Saturday. They drove to a restaurant in Chinatown, ate large quantities of unfamiliar but delicious dishes, chatted unceasingly through the meal and thoroughly enjoyed each other's company.

Afterwards, as they were heading back toward the Outer Drive from Twenty-second Street and the buildings of the World's Fair loomed up directly ahead, Paul had a sudden thought. "How'd you like to go into the Fair grounds?"

"There's only one thing wrong with the idea," Helga said promptly. "The Fair is closed for the winter."

"Answer the man's question. Yes or no?"

"Yes, of course I would."

"Okay, then." He swung the car onto one of the specially constructed roads leading to a main Fair gate. "There's an ill-founded rumor that one of my ancestors was a sorcerer, but I'm now going to prove to you that the pen is mightier than the sorcerer. My press pass will get us in."

Helga laughed, then watched with interest as the watchman

on duty at the gate waved them into the grounds after taking only a cursory glance at the pasteboard card issued by the Commissioner of Police. "I *am* impressed."

"Don't be." Paul shifted into second gear, was silent for a moment and then felt a compulsion to explain. "That guy wasn't letting me in because I'm me. He was just being polite to somebody who happens to have a job with the Express."

A truck was parked beside the delivery entrance to one of the exhibition halls, another made its way slowly along a narrow, ice-packed side road and a passenger car stood in front of the Globe Theatre, the reproduction of an Elizabethan entertainment hall where Shakespearean plays were given when the Fair was open. Otherwise the grounds seemed deserted and the contrast between the summer crowds and the silent atmosphere of the place now was so marked that neither Paul nor Helga spoke for several minutes. Then his face lighted up and he grinned.

"I'll take you to a spot you've never been before, I'll bet."

"I think I've walked over every inch of the Fair grounds, Paul."

"Wait and see." He drove more rapidly, then braked at the entrance to a plain, solid building that was devoid of signs or ornamentation. "Ever been here before?"

Helga frowned, trying to recall. "What is it?"

"The press building."

"Oh. Then I haven't been here. You're right."

"It's reserved for the use of working newspaper folk. Come on. There's something really worth seeing."

"Can we get in?" she asked.

"Oh, sure. This and the administration building stay open all winter. They even have steam heat." He climbed out, hurried around to the other side of the car and took Helga's elbow as he guided her across the ice.

The door was unlocked and a faint trickle of heat took the

chill off the main lounge, which was empty. From an office in the rear came the sound of a typewriter, and Helga looked up in surprise.

"Who on earth is working here now?"

"Somebody on the publicity staff of the Fair, would be my guess. We go this way." Paul led her to a flight of stairs at the far end of the lounge and they started to climb. "I hope your wind is good. We've got a long way to go."

"You haven't told me where it is we're going."

"To coin a phrase, curiosity killed a cat. But I'll give you a hint. I'm very proud of myself for being so smart. The weather is what started my mind working."

"All I can answer is that it's a lovely day." She sounded mystified.

Paul chuckled but said nothing more until they arrived at the top of the stairs, then he murmured, "Here we are," and opened a door.

They walked out onto an open balcony, at least forty feet long and twelve feet deep, and both paused for a moment, blinking. Chicago was enjoying one of its rare days of winter sunshine and the glare on the snow that covered the Fair grounds was momentarily dazzling. They moved together toward the snow-covered railing, and Helga, still unsure of the treat that was in store, said, "There isn't a breath of wind this afternoon."

"That's right," Paul exulted. "The elements are conspiring with me today. Not a cloud in the sky, not a soul in sight except us, and for our exclusive entertainment, one of the grandest sights ever made by man. Look!"

He waved his arm and together they gazed down from the press observation platform onto the panorama of the World's Fair; from here as from nowhere else they could gain an overall impression of the majesty of the buildings, the bold grandeur of the architectural plan that had resulted in the construction of an international exposition along the lake front. Some of the bigger halls seemed close enough to touch, a few of the smaller ones appeared to have shrunk, but all fitted together in a pattern that could not be seen from the ground.

"Thank you for bringing me," Helga said.

"I've been up here a hundred times, but it always gets me. The first thing that always hits me is the courage of the people who planned and built all this—right smack in the middle of the worst Depression we've ever had. It makes me proud to be a Chicagoan."

"I never thought of it that way before, but—me too, Paul."

"And what strikes me most of all is the realization of how much accumulated learning and toil and sacrifice is represented in these exhibits. They like to call this Fair a symbol of Chicago's century of progress, but what they've got out there are thousands of years of man's development—all gathered into a few acres. It kind of takes my breath away when I think about it. It wasn't so long ago that our ancestors discovered fire and invented the wheel. But in the Hall of Science they've got marvels that are beyond belief, even when you see them. Think of the effort and the concentration that's gone into all the thousands of inventions and discoveries that make life what it is today."

Helga was so impressed by the depth and sincerity of his tone that she forgot about the World's Fair buildings and looked up at Paul instead. He wasn't seeing the structures of wood and plaster and stone, either; instead he was staring out into space and his eyes were dreamy, wistful. There was depth in this man, Helga thought, the real substance of one who has ideals and is willing to fight for them, the solid strength of the gentle person who never raises his voice because he knows that a shout conveys only bluster.

"All the arts are here, everything that we call civilization," Paul continued. "And I'm naive enough to get a huge kick out of just realizing how much man has done for his fellow man. It staggers me when I think of all the suffering and self-lessness that have gone into the long climb up from cave dwelling. I suppose you think I'm being romantic and foolish."

"Romantic, but not foolish. I think it's a wonderful attitude," Helga said softly.

There was something more he wanted to say, and her sympathetic tone encouraged him. "It's all symbolized to me in those young saplings they've planted out there, beyond the Fair grounds." He nodded toward the south. "In another twenty years or so, there'll be fine, strong trees lining the Drive. And for generations to come people will enjoy a park where there was once nothing. I'm looking forward to watching those trees grow, year by year." Afraid he had revealed too much of himself, he became embarrassed. "Sometimes I'm inclined to shoot off my face," he muttered, "so don't encourage me."

"I'll never forget what you said about the trees, Paul. Every time I see them, I'll remember."

They looked at each other and the same current they had felt on Thursday night flowed between them. This time it was stronger, more insistent, and they were in each other's arms. They kissed passionately, and when Helga would have drawn away Paul tightened his hold on her and buried his face in her neck. The World's Fair was forgotten as they stood, conscious of something so strong, so insistent that everything but their own feeling was blotted out.

Again they kissed, then pulled apart breathlessly. "I think," Helga said, her voice shaking, "that we'd better go."

"Yes." Paul kept an arm around her shoulder as they moved to the door, then allowed her to precede him down the stairs.

They were quiet as they got into the car, and neither spoke as they rode out of the Fair grounds onto the Drive. Paul realized that Helga's eyes were on him, but when he turned to her she looked away quickly. She seemed about to speak, but

[124]

changed her mind, and he said nothing, either. Rarely had he been so at peace with another person.

Then, unexpectedly, circumstances intervened and there was an abrupt change in the atmosphere. Near a road leading out to the Drive a knot of people were gathered, and a police car stood at the edge of the Drive itself. Paul immediately remembered that he was a newspaperman. "Something going on here," he said. "Let's find out what it is."

Parking directly behind the police car, he caught a glimpse of a body on the ground and instructed Helga, "Wait here."

He got out of the car and showed his press card to the uniformed police sergeant who was in charge. The sergeant told him what had happened: a thirteen-year-old boy had been knocked down by a hit-and-run driver while trying to cross the road. The child had suffered a broken leg, an ambulance had been summoned and was expected momentarily.

Paul scribbled the few facts on the back of an envelope, then hurried back to the Plymouth, white-faced. As he climbed into the car he quickly told Helga what had occurred, then asked, "Do you mind driving downtown with me? I want to get the story in to the Express."

"Of course, Paul."

"It's a day off for me, but to heck with that. There's something here that needs to be written, and I'm going to write it." He pressed his foot hard against the accelerator.

Helga wanted to ask what he meant, but knew better. He would tell her whatever he wanted to say, and she would have to wait; it would be wrong, she knew, to annoy him with questions. Meantime she was astonished at the change that had come over him. His eyes, no longer wistful, were stormy, and his mouth had tightened in a grim, hard line.

"It's an outrage!" he said at last, his voice quivering. "That's the eighth accident in the past year at that intersection—to my knowledge. Maybe there have been even more. In a way I can't blame the driver of the car, although it was criminal of him to race off without stopping. Even so, the real criminal is you. And me. All of us."

Not understanding, Helga could hold back no longer. "I'm sorry, but I don't—"

"There ought to be a 'Stop' sign at that intersection," Paul interrupted angrily. "Every time something has happened there, the City promises to do something about it. Every time there's an accident, the Park Board makes promises, the Police Department makes promises, a couple of aldermen make speeches. But what happens? Absolutely nothing!"

"But that's awful!"

"It won't go on any longer if I have anything to say about it. I tell you, Helga, I'm so grateful to be a newspaperman that I can't see straight. Just you watch the tempest my article will stir up. And it darn well should! When I think of that kid lying there with a broken leg that'll take weeks and weeks to heal— thanks to the carelessness of men who are in positions of responsibility—I want to yell. And I will yell, too. In print."

She put her hand on his arm. "Good for you, Paul," she said quietly.

Paul was so deep in thought that he paid no attention to her words or her gesture, and he did not know that her admiration for him increased accordingly. "I think I'll start the article by saying, 'There's a killer loose in the streets of Chicago. That killer is every citizen.'" He repeated the sentences, then nodded. "That'll do it. I hope they've got some asbestos paper, because I'll sure burn up any ordinary stuff."

Traffic was light, as was usual on Saturday afternoons, and in a few minutes they arrived at the Express office. Paul parked the car, and with Helga shyly accompanying him, hurried to the local room. There he gave her a chair and copies of the afternoon newspapers to read while he was busy, and after explaining his reason for coming in to the slotman on the city desk, he walked quickly to his own typewriter.

He lost all awareness of time as he wrote, and was somewhat surprised, after turning out three solid pages of copy, to discover that only twenty minutes had passed. The piece needed virtually no editing, he was pleased to discover, and after shouting, "Boy, copy!" he took a carbon of the article to Helga, who had been drinking in every detail of the scene, from the green eyeshades of the editors on the copy desk to the remarkable performance of a lugubrious rewrite man who pounded out his work with the forefinger of his right hand.

"Here," Paul said proudly. "See what you think of it."

Helga read intently, and looked up as she reached the middle of the second page. "It's wonderful," she said, her eyes shining. "It's—"

"Dawson!" The slotman was beckoning.

"Excuse me," Paul said, and walked quickly to the city desk. Mr. Austin was sitting in his big swivel chair, his face bland and expressionless, and the slotman inclined his head in the boss' direction. Paul moved to him and saw that the City Editor's right hand was resting on the article.

"Yes, Mr. Austin?"

"What the devil do you mean by writing this kind of tripe, Dawson?" Harry Austin's voice was coldly impersonal.

Stunned, Paul could only stare at him. "I—I don't quite get you, sir."

"This is an editorial. For your information, editorials are written upstairs, by editorial writers who take their orders direct from the publisher."

"But—"

"In this department we write news, we do not conduct crusades."

"It all actually happened, Mr. Austin. I was there myself not five minutes after the accident—"

[127]

"What of it? Look here, boy—are you deliberately trying to ruin this newspaper's connections?"

"Ruin—?"

"Don't you understand—can't you get it through that foggy young head of yours that the Express is on good terms with City Hall? We get along fine with everybody—the Mayor, the Police Department, everybody. But if I were to run this fervent insanity of yours in tomorrow morning's paper, it would be a declaration of war on the administration. Please try to remember after this that we helped to elect that crowd in City Hall, and we support them. We do not rip into them. And we'll have no future difficulties if you'll let the men who are paid to write editorials write them!"

Very deliberately he fingered Paul's article, tore it in half and dropped the remains into a large waste-basket. Then he picked up his telephone and dialed an outside number.

Paul turned and walked away slowly. The hard-boiled world of practical newspaperdom certainly did not fit his idealistic concept of it, and he was deeply disturbed. Nevertheless, he told himself fiercely, he could still do more to help people by being a newspaperman than he could in any other business or profession. And certainly one disappointment, one setback was not significant. Assuredly, too, there were vast differences between the Express, a huge metropolitan journal, and the little newspaper somewhere that he would own and operate.

All the same, when he saw Helga waiting for him, her eyes still glowing, he could not bring himself to tell her that his story would never appear in print.

CHAPTER TEN

The magnet of Helga Bjornson was irresistible, and Paul saw her with increasing frequency. Knowing that his family approved only of girls who were daughters of their friends or members of the same social set, he said nothing at home about these dates, and he enjoyed Helga's company too much to worry over the fact that his emotional involvement with her was growing deeper than any he had ever had with a girl before.

All that mattered was that he wanted to see more and more of Helga, and see her he did. They often ate dinner together, they held hands through an occasional movie, they went dancing several times and they covered hundreds of miles driving to nowhere and back in the Plymouth. They attended a concert given by the Chicago Symphony Orchestra, and one night they saw *Of Thee I Sing*. They had fun, and the fun cost money, but Paul didn't care; he spent the better part of his salary on Helga, in spite of her constantly reiterated protests.

Over a period of a month they came to know a great deal about each other, they developed great sensitivity to each other's moods and at times they seemed to forget the existence of anyone and everyone but themselves. Neither mentioned the subject of love, however, and Paul was content to continue this way indefinitely, taking each day as it came, savoring it for its own sake. Never had he been so buoyant.

No two people could be thrown together so constantly, though, and maintain an approach that was simultaneously warm but cautious, intimate but uncommitted. Today might be pleasant, but tomorrow and a long string of tomorrows loomed ahead, and it was inevitable that something should happen to change the nature of this relationship that seemed to be suspended in time.

The shift came when it was least expected, on an evening that seemed like so many others. Paul ate dinner at home with his parents, then picked up Helga and took her to the Tivoli Theatre, where they saw a movie, a light, romantic comedy that provided entertainment for an hour and a half but was forgotten as soon as they walked out onto the street again. They drove to a hamburger joint on the lakefront, and it bothered neither of them that there were numerous closer eating places to which they could have gone; it was no chore to drive several miles out of the way, as that was part of the joy of just being together.

At around eleven-thirty, Paul started to drive Helga home, and both were seemingly relaxed; certainly Paul had no worries and he assumed that Helga felt as he did. He whistled softly under his breath as he drove, and she sat close to him, though not quite touching him. The proximity satisfied him, and presumably she was at peace, too. Neither felt the urge to talk, and it crossed his mind that it was very comfortable not to be forced to make conversation for its own sake. Here was the first girl with whom he could be completely himself, who didn't demand unceasing attention and flattery as the price of a date.

Paul broke off in the middle of a tune. "Tomorrow is pay day," he said. "So what do you say if we go to the Balloon Room tomorrow night? We'll make it a sort of an anniversary, seeing that we started there."

Helga stiffened slightly, and there was a long silence. When she replied an undercurrent of concern was evident in her voice. "I'm—not so sure, Paul."

"Now, now," he replied indulgently. "We've been through all this before."

"No, we haven't. I—"

"Let me say it for you. 'Paul, I won't let you spend all your money on me.' See? I know the line by heart. And you know my answer to it. If you've forgotten it, I'll repeat it for you. It goes something like this. 'Helga, I don't know anything that I'd rather spend—'"

"Please, Paul."

"All right, I'll stop being cute. But I honestly mean every word of the way I feel, and you know it. So the Balloon Room it is."

"I wasn't thinking about—the money."

"Oh? Then—"

"It's more important than that."

He stole a glance at her, and saw that she was staring straight ahead. Something was bothering her, that much he could tell. Instinctively he knew what it was and felt a strong urge to side-step the issue. "Nothing is more important than being extravagant," he said in a bantering tone. "You've told me that often."

"Paul, I'm being serious."

"Must we be serious?"

"I—I don't see any alternative."

"There are lots of alternatives. Unless you insist—"

"I have to insist."

"Okay. Shoot."

"I can't talk until you stop. Look, there's a parking place over there, right in front of my house."

"Okay." He maneuvered the car deftly. "Now, what did—"

"I don't think we ought to see each other tomorrow night."

He stared at her in dismay. "Why not? Have I—"

"You haven't done anything." Helga stared down at her hands miserably.

"Then I don't get it." Paul snapped off the ignition, removed

[131]

the key as though it offended him and dropped it absently into his overcoat pocket.

"It's just that—well, I don't see any of my other friends any more. I haven't seen anyone but you in weeks."

"To heck with any other guy!"

"It isn't fair to you, either. You haven't seen any other girls, Paul."

"I don't want to see any." He tried to put his arm around her, but she drew away from him.

"Ma and Pa think I should date other boys, too."

"Well, I don't! I—will you look at me, please? I can't talk to you when you're staring down at the floorboards."

"All right."

"I love you, Helga," Paul said, and his voice was harsh and distant in his own ears. The words had popped out suddenly, unexpectedly, without premeditation.

"I'm glad," she murmured. "Because I love you, too, Paul."

Suddenly she reached out, opened the door and fled into the apartment house. Paul was startled, and she moved so quickly that she vanished inside the building before he could follow her. He was too numb to think clearly. All he realized at the moment was that he had seemingly committed himself and his future. He had been sincere when he had blurted out his feelings for Helga, but he wasn't at all sure that the emotion was permanent, that he really wanted to go as far as he had.

As of this instant he thought more highly of her than of any other girl he had ever taken out, but an open declaration of love implied numerous complications. Helga might well assume that he had proposed marriage to her, particularly in the light of his constant attention and devotion these past weeks, and her own avowal of love would not be given lightly. She was not the sort of person who would say what she did not mean, nor would she be carried away by the romantic mood of a moment.

Paul felt trapped, but he could not tell Helga the truth without hurting her and he shrank from the idea. Perhaps, he thought as he started the car, it would not be necessary to make any sharp or immediate decision on the subject of marriage. Sometimes these things had a way of taking care of themselves, and if he didn't press too hard or too quickly for a solution, the question might conceivably be resolved without his having to take any drastic steps.

A sense of relief stole over him as he drove through the quiet streets, and he finally came to the conclusion that his panic had been unwarranted. Simply because he had told Helga he loved her didn't mean they'd have to apply for a marriage license to-morrow. Then, as he reached the boulevard and approached his family's house, his mood shifted again; ill-defined mental pic-tures of his parents flickered through his mind, and a cold, nameless fear settled in the pit of his stomach.

No lights were lit when he arrived home, and he went straight to his room. He was completely awake and alert as he undressed and he decided to smoke a cigarette before going to bed. His room felt unaccountably chilly, and he put on a heavy bathrobe, then settled into his easy chair. His thoughts were muddled, and he decided to read a magazine in order to ease his jitters. He reached for a copy of *Judge* on his desk, but neither the words nor the cartoons made sense to him. At that moment a gentle tap sounded at his door and he looked up, startled.

"Yes?"

The door opened slowly and Molly, wearing a flannel dress-ing gown, stood hesitantly in the frame. "I saw your light on, Paul, so I knew that you were still awake. May I come in?"

"Sure, Mother." He stood, gave her his chair and perched on the edge of his bed. "What are you doing up?" His attempt at jocularity sounded hollow in his own ears.

"I can never go to sleep until I hear you come in. You know that."

[133]

"Yes. I know." It was futile to repeat endlessly to his mother that he wasn't a high school boy any more.

"You're all right, dear?" Molly peered at him anxiously.

"You bet. Fine." He ran his fingers through his hair.

"I hope you don't mind my dropping in for a few minutes like this. We see so little of you these days that you're almost a stranger to us, so I've got to make opportunities for little visits with you." She sounded wistful.

"I don't mind at all. I'm not in the least tired. I just don't want to keep you up." He tried to smile, to sound gracious, although there was nothing he wanted less at this moment than to indulge in a meaningless chat with his mother.

"Oh, I'm wide awake," Molly said brightly, settling into the chair. "Where was it you said you were going this evening, dear? I don't quite remember."

Paul had to laugh. "The reason you don't remember is because I didn't say. As a matter of fact, it was one of my usual riotous nights. I took in a movie at the Tivoli and then had a hamburger afterwards."

"You didn't go alone?"

"Oh, no."

"With Joan, then?" she persisted.

"No, Mother. Someone else."

"I see. Is she someone I know, Paul?"

"You've never met her."

Molly waited for him to continue, but he did not and she tried to conceal her nervousness. "I wrote a letter to Betsy this evening," she said, changing the subject with an effort. "I left it open in case you want to add a few lines."

"Go ahead and mail it. I dropped her a note last week. Or maybe it was the week before."

A silence followed, and Molly's discomfort grew. It was obvious to her that something was disturbing Paul, and it was equally apparent that he had no intention of disclosing what was on his mind. And so she tried to soothe him in the only way she knew. "It's really late, dear. You ought to be going to bed."

"I'm not at all tired, Mother. But I'm sure you must be," Paul said, rising.

Molly was not going to be dismissed so easily. "You need your sleep."

"Oh, I can get along on practically none." His tone was gentle and teasing, and he tried to hide his resentment. Some day his mother would realize that he was an adult, but from present indications that time was far distant. "I'm not a growing boy any more."

"You aren't so far removed from your adolescence as all that." A look of determination appeared on Molly's face as she stood. "I'll go down to the kitchen and heat some milk for you."

"Thanks all the same, but please don't bother."

"It's always made you sleepy, and I'm sure it will tonight. You just climb into bed, dear, and I'll have a glass for you almost before you know it."

"I really don't want any milk, Mother. Honestly." Paul put an arm around her shoulder and led her to the door. The whole atmosphere in this house was so stifling that he could scarcely breathe, he thought, and his feeling of frustration soared anew. Out of a need to break away from his mother's possessiveness, and out of an impulse to do something about Helga that might relieve his sense of guilt toward her, he formed a sudden plan. "Are you and Dad going to be home tomorrow evening after dinner?" he asked in a quiet, tight voice.

"I think so, though I'm not really sure." Molly turned in the frame and looked up at her son questioningly.

"I'll appreciate it if you'll let me know in the morning. You see, I want to bring a girl over to meet you."

His tone of voice and the tension in his face were as significant to Molly as his words, and she could only nod.

"Good night, Mother." He closed the door gently but firmly behind her.

* * *

Breakfast was the one almost silent meal in the Dawson house; the men read their morning newspapers, Marcia crammed food into her mouth in a frantic race against the clock and her school's "tardy-bell," and only Molly, who usually appeared in a silk dressing gown, seemed untouched by the pressures of work-day existence. She sat now, surveying her brood and interrupting their attempts to concentrate with such comments as, "Would you care for more toast, Gordon?" or "Are your eggs done the way you want them, Paul?" And through her cheerful conversation ran the refrain, *"Please* don't gulp your porridge, Marcia dear. Sit up straight, eat like a lady and do show a little consideration for your tummy."

Gordon, who was reading the financial pages of the Tribune, grunted something unintelligible, and Paul, who had been absorbed in an article he had written on the first page of the Express, glanced up in some irritation. He had been analyzing his work, pulling the story to pieces and then putting it together again in sharper, more succinct wording, and the interruption was annoying. "Speak to me, Dad?" he muttered.

"Yes." Gordon continued to look down at the folded newspaper on the table before him. "All this nonsense I've heard ever since a little education gave you the wisdom of the world. 'All that matters is people, Dad.' What you can't ever get through your head is that the people suffer when the nation's economy isn't sound. And do you know what happened yesterday? The market went down again. Ninth consecutive day. That precious crowd of yours in Washington doesn't seem to be stabilizing conditions, in spite of all their promises and speeches and loose talk."

It was useless to protest that the present Administration wasn't "his," Paul thought. Whenever the stock market dropped, Dad always sounded as though his only son was personally responsible for the election of President Roosevelt and a Democratic Congress. There was only one way to avoid an argument, and Paul knew it. He remained silent, spread butter on a slice of toast and pretended to be devoting his full interest to his own newspaper. However, far more was on his mind than the avoidance of a political discussion, and he turned at last to his mother.

"Do you know yet about tonight?"

Molly exchanged a significant glance with her husband, and Marcia, aware that something out of the ordinary was taking place, lost interest in her oatmeal. Gordon cleared his throat, ran a forefinger along the crease of his newspaper and looked at Paul. It was plain that the unusual request of last night had received considerable attention, and the head of the family was taking charge of the situation.

"I'm usually pretty tired on weekday nights, so I never go out if I can help it. Saturday is my night to howl. So we'll be here this evening. Mother says there's some girl you want to bring to the house?"

"Yes, Dad. I have a dinner date, and I thought we could drop in on you and Mother afterwards. If that's convenient." He paused, but no one said anything. "I thought you'd like to meet her, and I'm sure she'd like to meet you."

"We'll be very happy to see her," Gordon said quietly.

Molly, who had slept poorly, was too tired and nervous to be subtle. "Who *is* the girl, dear?"

"Her name is Helga Bjornson." The tension continued to mount, and Paul drained his coffee.

Marcia became aware of cross-currents beyond her depth and took refuge in her breakfast. Her glass of milk suddenly became fascinating to her, and she held it up to the light for several seconds before tasting it. Gordon neatly cut the remainder of his fried ham, trimmed off a bit of fat and ate stolidly. As a man accustomed to the give-and-take of business on an executive level, he was adroit in concealing his thoughts. But Molly could not hide her reactions.

"I don't believe I've ever heard you mention her before, Paul."

"To the best of my knowledge, I haven't." Paul couldn't stop himself from adopting a defensive tone.

"It would be nice to know something about her before greeting her as a guest." Molly was sweet but nonetheless insistent.

"Well, let's see. She works as a secretary. I met her in the office where she works. It's an insurance company and I was doing some checking for the paper. I've had a number of dates with her. I like her. Very much. So I thought it'd be okay to bring her around tonight. Unless you object, of course—in which case I won't."

Gordon tapped on the rim of his saucer, but his voice was calm as he said, "We're always happy to meet your friends, Paul. Mother and I will be here all evening, so please do bring the young lady over. We look forward to meeting her."

His wife raised troubled eyes to his. "You remember the Bromley girl, Gordon? Arthur's and Cora's daughter? When poor Arthur's business collapsed two years ago, their girl went to secretarial school, and I understand she's found a fine position for herself since. The Bromleys have been very gallant. I bumped into Cora in the restaurant at Field's last week, and you'd never in a million years guess from her attitude that they've had such tough sledding. I'm always a little amazed," she added in a self-conscious rush, "at how many of our friends' daughters are working. It seems to be the thing to do these days."

Paul took a deep breath, then exhaled slowly; he badly wanted a cigarette, but his parents disapproved of smoking at the table. "Helga isn't being gallant by working," he said coldly. "I doubt if it ever occurred to her that she'd do anything

[138]

except work—after she finished getting educated at a public high school." His antagonism, his method of presenting facts were only increasing the already considerable difficulties that loomed ahead, but his mother's smug, narrow view made him reckless. "You see, she's never been in a position to enjoy many of the advantages. Her father is a carpenter."

Marcia giggled nervously and entered the conversation for the first time. "You're kidding," she said.

Paul flushed angrily, but his father intervened before he could speak. "I'll be late for work and have to fire myself if I don't hurry," Gordon said diplomatically, glanced at his wristwatch and rose abruptly. "We'll expect to see you and Miss— uh—your young lady around nine, Paul."

CHAPTER ELEVEN

From the moment that Paul met Helga at the spaghetti place for a quick dinner he knew that something was off key, that no good would come of the evening. Something about her appearance puzzled and disturbed him, and by the time they finished their minestrone he figured out what was wrong. Her most blatant mistake had been her heavy-handed application of make-up. No lady wore mascara, but Helga's eyes were now heavily fringed and the blackened lashes were incongruously dark against the background of her fair skin and blonde hair. She had painted her lips too heavily and had used rouge on her cheeks.

The net effect of her appearance was to make her look cheap and common, if not vulgar, and Paul wanted to tell her as much. But he could not; he had enough sense to realize that she had done this in order to impress his parents. And if he criticized her now for her ignorance, she would be miserably self-conscious.

Although he knew very little about women's clothes, he suspected that the way Helga was dressed had something to do with his discomfort, too. He should have warned her, he supposed, to wear something conservative and quiet for her first meeting with his mother and father, though he had assumed that she would. Now it was too late.

She had chosen a glossy, gold satin blouse for the occasion, and it was so shiny, so eye-catching that Paul knew it was in bad taste. And even he was able to tell that her tailored skirt was part of a suit, the jacket of which was absent. Her accessories were off-beat, too: a wide leather belt with a heavy gilt buckle; an over-sized leather purse; flimsy patent leather sandals with spike heels. It was all wrong, he knew instinctively.

Unfortunately Helga seemed unaware that her costume was a jumble of badly-matched items, and Paul, keeping one eye on his watch, managed to get through dinner without comment on the subject. He found it difficult to find topics of impersonal, mutual interest to discuss, and Helga was not much help. She seemed preoccupied and slightly depressed; several times she was on the verge of speaking out on something that was obviously preying on her mind, but each time she seemed to bite back the words, and, shaking her blonde head slightly, remained silent.

As the hour for the visit drew nearer, the tensions increased markedly, and neither had said a word for at least ten minutes when they at last climbed into the car for the drive to the Dawson house. Paul, to whom nothing was more nerve-racking than a prolonged silence, reached for the knob that would turn on the radio, but Helga covered his hand with hers and as she looked at him her eyes seemed to beg for continued quiet. Paul leaned toward her, kissed her gently and started the car without touching the radio again.

As they headed south on the Outer Drive he could hear Helga's even, steady breathing, and at last he felt impelled to say something. "They're not ogres, you know. My parents, I mean."

"Of course they aren't!" Helga laughed, and the sound seemed genuine.

"You act as though they are," Paul declared accusingly, unsatisfied.

"Oh, I'm so sorry. I don't mean to give that impression." Her regret was real, but something continued to trouble her. "It's—you, Paul."

"What about me? There's nothing wrong with me!" Stepping on the accelerator, he shot past a chauffeur-driven Pierce Arrow.

"Of course not, darling." Helga's voice was soothing, very soft and tranquil. "I simply noticed that you've been a little upset, that's all. It's natural enough, but I haven't known what to do about it, and I wish I could."

Paul simulated a loud laugh of denial. "Now why in blazes would I be upset? You're my girl and I'm taking you to meet my parents. You bet it's natural. Thousands of fellows have done it, and everybody involved has survived."

Helga was too wise to reply. Plainly he would quarrel with her if he could, in order to relieve his sense of strain, so she said nothing. Instead she moved closer to him, linked her arm through his and leaned lightly against his shoulder. For a moment he remained rigid, then gradually, almost imperceptibly he began to relax, and finally he smiled. Unthinkingly he reached forward and snapped on the radio, and this time Helga made no objection. His need for distraction was manifestly greater than her own desire for quiet.

The ride seemed endless, but at last it drew to a close, and as Paul approached the Dawson driveway he waved vaguely. "This is it," he said.

"Oh, is this your house? Imagine that! I've passed it so many times, and I've always admired it!" Surprise and enthusiasm were both evident in Helga's tone.

"It's where I live, but the house isn't mine." Paul jabbed the foot brake too hard and the Plymouth's tires squealed in protest. "The difference may seem academic, but it isn't."

He jumped out, hurried around to her side and opened the door. As she emerged from the car he felt a sudden wave of tender protectiveness and would have taken her in his arms, but

Helga demurred. "Not now," she said, "but thank you for wanting to."

Paul opened the front door, and saw at once that most of the lamps in the living room were lit, as was customary when guests were expected. "Let's go," he muttered, more to himself than to the girl at his side, then called, "We're here."

Molly and Gordon had been sitting in the living room, reading or pretending to read, and both rose to their feet, forced smiles on their faces. Paul noted that his mother was dressed in the sort of clothes she wore when she went calling on elderly relatives. Her silk suit was a solid, dark grey, fitted her perfectly and was inconspicuously expensive. Her one concession to jewelry was the diamond fleur-de-lys brooch she wore on her jacket.

Paul resented that diamond pin: it represented more money than a carpenter could earn in a year these days. "Mother, Dad," he said, suddenly cold and devoid of all feeling, "let me present Miss Bjornson."

Everyone else took over, and there was a quick babble of polite, meaningless conversation. Gordon was never in better form than when he played host, Helga seemed to be in absolute control of herself, and Molly was making her most charming, fluting social noises. For a moment Paul was forgotten, then his father turned to him as though he were a small boy. "Intending to stand there all night? Why don't you make yourself useful and take Miss Bjornson's coat?"

"You're right. Why don't I?" Paul grinned aimlessly, helped Helga out of her coat and then turned away quickly as he saw his mother take in every detail of that inappropriate costume and heavy make-up. The opportunity to escape for a moment from this scene which he had been dreading relieved him, but at the same time he could not stand being out of the room for a single minute.

He hung up Helga's coat and his own, and by the time he returned to the living room the others were seated. Helga had taken a place on a long sofa covered in heavy, tufted gold silk, and her choice had been an unfortunate one, Paul thought, for her blouse clashed with it and became all the more prominent. He sat beside her, but no one seemed to notice that he had come into the room.

"Oh, yes," Helga was saying, "I'm a native Chicagoan. I've lived all my life on the South Side."

"Well, that gives all of us something in common, then," Molly replied, and turned to her son. "Paul, dear—wouldn't you and Miss Bjornson like some refreshments?"

Helga shook her head before Paul had a chance to speak. "Not just now, thanks," she said. "We just finished an enormous spaghetti dinner a little while ago."

"Really?" Mother looked incredulous. "Paul will never touch spaghetti at home." She laughed synthetically.

Paul had no desire to launch into a discussion of his food likes and dislikes, but Dad stepped into the breach before he had a chance to defend himself. "It just shows you," Gordon declared heartily, "how little parents really know about their children these days. I dare say your mother and father would be amazed at half the things you eat, Miss Bjornson."

"No, I think not." Helga smiled easily, and Paul thought she was by far the most self-contained person in the room. "I was brought up to eat anything and everything. We've always had a struggle, and if I didn't want what was put in front of me, I could go hungry." She glanced at her hostess, then her host. "There were a few times, when Pa couldn't get work, that we truly did go hungry."

Frankness was a virtue, but it could be carried too far, Paul thought, wishing she would drop the subject. He wanted to say something, to interrupt, but he could not. It was as though he was watching a nightmare develop but was powerless to halt it.

"I remember once," Helga continued, "we had nothing but

baked beans and canned corn in the house for about ten days. It was very filling, I'll say that."

Gordon was the first to recover from the embarrassed silence that followed Helga's painful revelation of her family's struggles. "Really?" he murmured. "Our company handles beans and corn. A couple of brands of each."

"I know." Helga seemed blithely unaware of her errors. "Paul has shown them to me. To be honest with you, Mr. Dawson, I'd never heard of them before."

"You don't say." Gordon withdrew a trifle into a shell.

"Ma always bought the cheapest kinds. And yours are expensive. Two or three cents more than what we got."

"You look well nourished, Miss Bjornson," Molly chimed in sweetly, "so let's hope your troubles are behind you."

If they didn't drop the subject of food, Paul thought, he would do something violent. He could not think coherently for the moment, and felt only a burning anger against Helga for betraying such a gauche, ingenuous attitude. And when he saw her about to speak again, he could barely restrain himself from clamping a hand over her mouth.

"I'll always have a good appetite, I'm sure, Mrs. Dawson."

"Do you hear that, Paul?" Molly's bright eyes focused on her son for an instant, then she turned to her husband. "Gracious, when I think of the cooks we lost when Paul was little. There was that wonderful German woman—you remember the potato dumplings she made, don't you, Gordon? And after her we had that treasure of a Scandinavian, but she wouldn't stay, either." Leaning toward Helga she said confidentially, "You just can't imagine a more finicky eater. He still is, you know."

Paul froze, and although Helga said something in reply, he did not hear her. Surely his mother hadn't made an accidental slip, and his resentment shifted suddenly and was directed at her. The reference to a Scandinavian cook had been both deliberate and malicious, and he could not believe otherwise.

[145]

Gordon seemed to feel that the conversation was getting out of hand, too, and he broke in before Helga finished whatever she was saying.

"Your voice startles me, Miss Bjornson. You sound remarkably like my elder daughter. Don't you think so, Mother?"

Molly thoughtfully considered his question for a moment, then smiled. "No, I don't. You see," she explained to Helga, "he misses Betsy so much that he spends half his time thinking he sees her double on the streets."

"Now that's an exaggeration," Gordon declared stoutly, chuckling. "She's off at college now. Wellesley. I gather that you didn't care to go to college, Miss Bjornson?"

"I wish you'd call me Helga. 'Miss Bjornson' is so formal. And I did want to go to college—very much. It was my lifelong ambition, really. But my parents couldn't afford it, and I missed winning a scholarship, so that was that."

The room was not overly warm, but Paul discovered that he was perspiring freely. He tried, desperately, to think of some way to stem the tide of talk, to direct it into less personal channels, but his father, launched now on a favorite theme, gave him no chance. Gordon leaned back in his big leather chair and folded his hands over his stomach.

"Every girl should go away to school for awhile," he said, apparently deaf to Helga's explanation that a lack of funds had prevented her from doing just that. "It's the sort of opportunity women often don't get again in later life. Gives them a taste of real freedom."

"Yes, it must." Helga spoke so softly that Paul, as close as he was to her, could barely hear her.

Gordon, however, wasn't listening. "And it gives a girl a higher education, too. That's important. The day when women were thought to be the inferior of men is over. Provided a woman has the chance and the desire to exercise her mind, that is. The urge to improve herself, to learn, that's what

[146]

counts. And that's what our Betsy has, I'm glad to say. She isn't the type who'll ever sit back and just expect some man to support her for the rest of her life."

It was impossible to tell whether Gordon was thinking only in terms of his own daughter or whether he was hinting in a none too subtle way that Helga was interested in Paul because he was the son of a wealthy father. One covert glance at the girl beside Paul was enough to indicate her reaction, however. The color had drained from her face, and she looked as though she had been slapped.

"I'm very much in favor of women working, Mr. Dawson," she said very clearly, emphasizing each word. "I believe in the principle so strongly that I intend to continue with my job, regardless of whether I'm married or single."

Molly was aware of the younger woman's tension, but her husband was either a superb actor or else he was unconscious of the atmosphere he was creating. "Of course Betsy doesn't spend all her time working. Glamour and excitement are necessities for young ladies, or so I've always been told, and Betsy is getting her fair share of both." He chuckled and shook his head. "The little minx wheedled enough extra out of me to make a trip down to New York this weekend with a couple of her friends. They have dates tomorrow night with some cadets from West Point. Oh, it's great to be young and carefree, all right."

Paul was completely outraged, so angry that he began to tremble. It was unforgivable of his father to go on like this, to babble about the benefits his daughter enjoyed when his audience was a girl who had never tasted luxury in all of her life. Thinking of the mean little apartment in which Helga and her family lived, of the careful saving that had gone into every stitch of clothing she wore, Paul wanted to reach out and strike his father.

And his own indecision melted in the face of his fury. Let both of his parents sit here in judgment, his father demonstrating a lack of sensitivity, his mother hiding behind her tight little superior smile. So they thought Helga wasn't good enough, did they? He'd show them! He would marry her at the first possible moment. And he felt ashamed of the sense of reluctance that had been confusing him. There were no real issues holding him apart from Helga except those he had created in his own mind. They loved each other, and that settled the matter.

Molly was saying something now in her dulcet voice, but Paul did not listen. Very deliberately he reached out and put his hand over Helga's. His move apparently startled her, and she plainly thought he was being indiscreet, for she made a gentle effort to disengage herself. But Paul would not release his hold, and rather than make a scene she allowed him to continue to cover her hand with his.

Suddenly he became aware of the new turn the conversation had taken, and told himself savagely that he had to pay closer attention to every word that was being said. So far the evening had closely resembled a bad dream; now the elements of a real nightmare were creeping in.

"You have every right to be very proud of Paul," Helga was saying. "Not many people have the courage of their convictions, but he has."

"Of course he has," Molly replied with a vague smile.

"Did he ever tell you about the article he wrote after a hit and run driver knocked down a little boy at an intersection where there should have been a 'Stop' sign?"

Paul tried to catch Helga's eye to silence her, but she was not looking at him and he became panicky. He had told her the truth about Harry Austin's hard-boiled reaction to his impassioned article when she had searched for it in vain in the columns of the Express. But she failed to realize that if she repeated the story now she would be handing ammunition to his father. To Gordon it would prove again that there was no ethical difference between the newspaper profession and the grocery business and that a man who turned his back on the world of commerce was an adolescent idealist who was deluding himself.

"He wrote one of the most wonderful articles I've ever read," Helga continued enthusiastically. "Really, it was inspired."

Something had to be done, and quickly. Paul was about to interrupt rudely, to change the subject by sheer force, but Marcia saved him the trouble by choosing this moment to enter the room. From the way she carried herself, from the expression on her face it was obvious to Paul that she was miffed. He could not know, however, that she had overheard Gordon and Molly discussing this evening in terms uncomplimentary to the girl who was to visit them, and that her conduct was a calculated effort to demonstrate her loyalty to her parents in the face of what she considered to be Paul's abandonment of the family's standards. She had even dressed with meticulous care, and everything about her attire was correct from her dark wool dress of Navy blue to the matching ribbon in her hair and her low-heeled kid pumps of the same color. Paul seized on her appearance as a welcome interruption, and beckoned to her as she hesitated in the archway.

Marcia ignored him and addressed her mother. "May I speak to you for a minute, please, Mother?" she asked in her most dignified tone.

"Of course. Come in, dear."

What happened next was as shocking to Paul as it was momentarily incomprehensible. Marcia walked straight to Molly and did not seem to be aware of the presence of a stranger in the room. She was showing her feelings in the most graphic terms she was capable of conceiving, and Paul's rage reached a new high. Helga would be sure to think that his parents, by not rebuking Marcia for her insolence, were actually condoning her bad manners.

"Miss Bjornson," he said in a cold, clipped voice that sounded very much like Gordon's, "permit me to present my younger sister, Marcia, whom we all hope will some day be dry behind the ears. Marcia," he added in scathing condescension, addressing her as one would a five-year-old, "say how-do-you-do to Miss Bjornson."

Helga tried to pass off the incident and reacted as though Paul had made a feeble joke. "Hello, Marcia," she said warmly. "Pay no attention to him. You'd be surprised how he brags about you when you're out of earshot."

"Hi," Marcia replied in a chilly, disinterested voice, not deigning to look around. "Mother, I just talked to Mary Louise on the phone, and she wants to know if I can spend overnight at her house tomorrow."

Molly considered the request briefly, ignoring her daughter's obvious, intentional rudeness. She would speak to Marcia about the matter later, but she would not administer a rebuke in the presence of a guest. Nevertheless Paul wished that just this once his mother were less restrained; if he had his way, he would paddle Marcia until she wept.

"I see no reason why you can't go, dear."

"Thank you, Mother." Marcia started to leave, her back rigid, when Gordon stopped her.

"Marcia," he directed, "go out to the kitchen, if you please, and bring in a bowl of fruit." He, at least, was trying to compensate for an unwarranted display of very bad manners.

There was silence for a second or two, then Marcia shrugged her pudgy young shoulders. "Can't you get Delcie to bring it in?" she asked indifferently. "I have to call Mary Louise back."

If there was one thing Gordon could not tolerate it was a gesture of defiance from one of his children. In this instance he knew full well that Marcia was not striking out at him, that on the contrary she was trying to demonstrate family solidarity in the presence of an intruder, but her insolence was too much all the same. "You'll do as you're told when you're told to do it," he said in the authoritative tone that every member of the household invariably recognized as the final word.

Helga, however, had no intention of allowing herself to become the center of a controversy, and she seemed to be in awe of no one, not even of Gordon. "Please don't bother on my account," she said in a sweet, unruffled voice, and Paul wondered how much effort that air of calm was costing her. "I've enjoyed our visit very much, but I really must be going."

She stood, and somehow she managed to smile. Molly and Gordon rose, too, and Marcia retreated to the front hall, from which dark vantage point she could study this creature from another world. Molly murmured her routine regrets which she always expressed at the pending departure of a casual guest, and Gordon, the incident with Marcia forgotten, beamed in seeming good will. Paul, faintly dazed, was the only person still seated, and Helga turned to him.

"Please," she asked, "will you take me home?"

CHAPTER TWELVE

Paul said nothing until he had driven out onto the street, and even then he spoke only when Helga placed a hand gently on his arm. It was she who had been hurt, yet she was consoling him, and the realization increased Paul's anger against his family. "I'm sorry," he said, his face dark and his voice ugly. "They're a pack of impossible, insufferable boors and I'm very sorry."

"No, Paul. They feel very deeply about you, and that's why they act as they do." Even though Helga had been humiliated, she retained her sense of proportion and her ability to think clearly and dispassionately. "They just try to protect you against someone they fear will take you away from them. You see, they think of you as being part of themselves still. Many parents make that mistake. They aren't the first and they won't be the last. So you truly mustn't blame them for feeling as they do. Really, you ought to be proud that they care so much about you."

"And Marcia?" he demanded, grinding the gears as he shifted them savagely. "I suppose I ought to be proud of her, too."

"Some day, if you have a daughter," Helga prophesied quietly, "you'll be flattered if she's so loyal to you, just as your father was pleased, in spite of his annoyance."

"Any daughter of mine," Paul declared in a thin, tight voice, "will have better sense. That is, if she's your daughter, too."

Helga remained silent and sat very still. And Paul, realizing the significance of his words, hastily pulled into a long parking place, then turned to the girl beside him. She stared straight ahead and seemed to have withdrawn from him.

"I'm not very good at this sort of thing," he said, "because I've had no practice at it. This is the first time I—Helga, I know I'm being clumsy, but I—well, anyway, here's what I'm trying to say. I want—to marry you, Helga."

She drew in her breath sharply. "Really, Paul? Are you sure?"

"I'm sure," he replied stridently.

He pulled her to him and kissed her, but was too numb to feel the touch of her lips against his. A passing car honked loudly, and someone in it shouted derisively. Paul and Helga moved apart, realized that they were parked almost directly beneath a street light, and on a major thoroughfare at that; they grinned at each other uncertainly and self-consciously. Then Paul abruptly started the car, and although he was ordinarily a good driver, he let out the clutch too fast and the Plymouth shot ahead jerkily.

Neither said anything for several minutes. Finally he felt impelled to speak. "I love you, Helga," he said, and he sounded very firm, very positive.

"I love you, too. It's just—." She broke off and stared out of the frosted window.

"Just what?"

"There are so many reasons we shouldn't be married. Ma and Pa have talked to me by the hour about us. And, now, meeting your parents and all, I—well, I can't help wondering, that's all."

"I know what I want. Naturally, a lady is privileged to change her mind."

"Oh, Paul." Helga's composure deserted her, and she choked for an instant. "I've never really loved anybody else before. I know I'll never feel like this about another man, not as long as I live."

By way of answer he put his right arm around her and drew her to him, and when they stopped at a boulevard because of traffic, he bent down and kissed her again, tenderly this time. "What are we worrying about?" he asked, and if there was an abandon in his gaiety he did not know it.

"There's a campaign on against one-arm drivers," she murmured, settling comfortably into the crook of his elbow. "You've probably written half of the articles on the subject yourself. And I'm worried for fear you'll bump into another car. The streets are still slippery."

Paul laughed exuberantly. "Ma'm," he said, "you've never been as safe as you are at this very minute. Your security rests in the driving skill, and the unerring wisdom of Paul Dawson, Esquire. And I assure you that Mr. Paul Dawson will never let Mrs. Paul Dawson down."

They laughed together, nervously but bravely, banishing their fears and their doubts, and there was little more to say on the remainder of the ride. When they stopped at last in front of Helga's shabby home they kissed, then embraced for several long minutes, and all of the evening's frustrations dissolved. They mounted the stairs together slowly, hand in hand, and when they arrived in front of the apartment Helga unlocked the door and left it open a crack. As she turned for Paul's goodnight kiss, a voice sounded from the partly-darkened living room.

"Is that you, Helga?"

"Yes, Pa." She and Paul instinctively moved apart.

"Your young man is there with you?" Olaf Bjornson moved to the door and opened it wide.

"Yes, Pa. Paul's here. How did you know that he's my young man? He really wasn't—until tonight." She forced a laugh, then added, "We—have something to tell you."

"Come in, please, both."

Paul shook hands, then followed Helga and her father into the cramped living room, and thought incongruously that the odors of fish and of cabbage seemed to be ever-present here. Helga, who always seemed so fearless, showed distinct signs of being upset at what was patently a departure from her father's usual custom when she came home after a date, and she rolled her gloves into a ball in her hands as she asked, "Is everything all right, Pa? You're feeling all right, and Ma, too?"

"I wish to have a talk with your young man. Go in to your Ma until I call you," Bjornson replied heavily.

She obeyed at once, and as Paul removed his coat and dropped it on a chair, he noticed that Helga's father had dressed as if he had expected the occasion. He had put on a stiff collar, but his unaccustomed necktie was loosely knotted and revealed the gold of his collar button. He wore a jacket and vest, too, and an old-fashioned watch fob from which hung a yellowed chunk of ivory. "Sit down," he commanded, and waved toward the couch.

"Thank you," Paul replied, but did not obey at once. Instead he waited until Helga closed the bedroom door behind her.

"I call you Paul now."

"Yes, I wish you would." It was difficult to guess what was going on behind those intense, pale eyes.

"In the old country, always a man came first to a girl's pa and asked for her hand to be married. Always I thought this would happen here, too, but I forgot I live in America. I have been here so many years, but sometimes I still forget." The huge, strong hands moved restlessly for a moment, then became still again.

"I'm sorry, Mr. Bjornson," Paul said, and meant it. "I should have come to you first." He tried to smile, but the effort was too great. "Let me make up for my mistake now. I love Helga. And I want to marry her." He discovered that his heart was thumping so hard he felt a little dizzy. "Do I—do we have your permission?"

"This is not a good marriage." The carpenter stood abruptly and clenched his fists. "You are the son of a rich man. Helga is the daughter of a poor man."

Paul was thoroughly fed up with that theme and all of its implications. "I don't give a hoot," he said brusquely, "and neither does Helga. Nothing matters except the way we feel about each other, nothing."

"Now nothing else matters, this is true." Bjornson shook his massive head sadly. "But in six months, in a year, after the rose becomes not so fresh, then it will matter. It was a great Swedish scientist and writer, Linnaeus, who said, 'If a tree dies, plant another in its place.' But this cannot so easy be done after a marriage. Then the mistake is made. Then the work to tear out what is wrong is hard. Now, before the mistake is made, this is the time to think over what you wish to do."

"I've given it a great deal of thought," Paul said, trying to match the other's dignity and wishing he didn't feel like a schoolboy being punished for an error in judgment. "And I see no reason why Helga and I can't make a real go of it. Of course, if you think it's such a big mistake—"

"Is a mistake." The deep voice was stubbornly certain.

"I'm afraid I can't agree with you, sir," Paul said sharply.

"Sure not." A rumble of totally unexpected laughter welled up in Bjornson. "If a young man agrees so easy, then he is not fit for my Helga, and I beat him down the street with my own hands. Sure not. You love my girl. So you think all will be fine, like in the story books."

Paul was bewildered by the sudden change in approach. "I don't understand you," he said flatly.

Helga's father reached out and clamped a hand on Paul's knee, squeezing so hard that the younger man had to control himself to keep from wincing. "Fairy tales do not come true,"

[156]

Bjornson said slowly. "The poor know this. The rich, sometimes they do not know it, but money does not make for them the happy end of the fairy tale, either."

"Right now I'm earning a salary of fifty-five dollars a week, and while I have hopes of getting another raise in a couple of months, I'm hardly what you'd call rich. I have nearly eight thousand dollars in bonds and in a savings account, all of it inherited. And that's all I have." Paul wanted to add that his family would probably disown him the day he married Helga, but he refrained from saying it.

"Helga!" the old carpenter called, and said nothing more until his daughter reentered the room.

She looked first at Paul, then at her father. "Is—is everything all right? I heard your voices, and I thought you might be quarreling."

"We do not quarrel," her father said. "We do not agree, but we do not quarrel."

"Your father is opposed to our getting married," Paul explained.

"I know. He's told me, too." Helga touched Paul's sleeve tentatively, then sat on the arm of the couch and rested her hand on his shoulder.

Bjornson cleared his throat noisily. "I do not forbid this marriage. If I forbid, you will marry the next day. The young in every land are like this. My Helga and her man are not different from others."

"You mean it, Pa?" Helga clutched Paul's shoulder and he put his arm around her to steady her. "You'll withdraw your objections? You and Ma will—"

"I object, but I do not forbid. All your life, Helga, I teach you to think. Now is the time when you must think. I do not do it for you, I cannot do it for you. And you think, Paul." He walked to the bedroom door, and paused with his hand on the knob. Turning, he looked very old, and there actually were tears in his eyes now. "For my Helga I want only happiness. All these years, this is all I want. So think, both." Suddenly he opened the door and disappeared into the next room.

Paul and Helga looked at each other; there was so much to say that neither could speak a word, and they took refuge in each other's arms. They were both trembling and there was no joy in their kiss, only pain.

*   *   *

The front of the house was dark when Paul arrived home, but as he approached his own room he saw that a light was on there, which surprised him, and when he entered he found his father seated in the maroon-covered easy chair, reading a novel.

"Hello," Gordon said, marking his place and closing the book. "You're back earlier than I thought."

"Yes." Paul was bone tired, and the last thing he wanted was a discussion with his father. If he tried to avoid it, however, he would merely postpone the inevitable, so it would be better to get it over and out of the way here and now. He reminded himself sternly, insistently, that he was not to indulge in any recriminations. No matter what was said, he was not to utter any criticism of the family for the insults that had been tendered to Helga. His father would leap to the defense, and there'd be an explosion that would only increase the bitterness and solve nothing.

Gordon promptly demonstrated that he was more sensitive and perspicacious than his son realized. "I hope you don't mind my waiting up for you like this. It's the first time I've done it in years. But I wanted to apologize to you."

"Apologize?" Paul felt suddenly deflated, and had a feeling that he was being "handled."

"We gave Miss Bjornson a pretty uncomfortable evening, Marcia in particular. I've stopped her allowance for two weeks as a punishment. I hope you'll tell Miss Bjornson how sorry we

[158]

are. Matter of fact, I'll tell her myself next time I see her." He took a cigar from a case in his breast pocket, regarded it thoughtfully and gave Paul a chance to digest what he had said. Then, after carefully applying a match to the cigar, he leaned back and smiled. "She's a pretty girl, Paul. A very pretty girl."

"Thanks. I think so myself." Uncomfortable at this unexpectedly soft approach, Paul took an ash tray from his desk and placed it on the edge of the chair for his father's convenience.

"I don't suppose you can see the resemblance, but she reminds me a little of Mother many years ago."

"No, I'm afraid I don't see any similarities, Dad." Paul lighted a cigarette and stood directly in front of his father. His legs ached but he didn't want to sit; he felt more in command of himself and the situation by standing and looking down at his father.

"Of course there's a difference in hair color, and Miss Bjornson is much taller than Mother. As I remember my gay blade days, I never took out tall girls. Don't really know why." Gordon examined the growing ash on his cigar. It was unusual for him to smoke at this time of night, so he apparently wasn't as self-possessed as he appeared.

"Helga is just right for me," Paul declared, trying not to sound belligerent.

"So I gather, son."

"And I wish you'd start calling her 'Helga,' not 'Miss Bjornson.' You'll have to begin sooner or later."

"Right. 'Helga' it is." Gordon grinned amiably, without guile.

"Sure is."

"Have you known her very long, Paul? I hope you don't mind my asking." A new note crept into Gordon's voice, something stronger and more purposeful.

"No, Dad." It was pointless to lie, even though the truth would result in certain inevitable reactions. "Ask anything you like. And I haven't known her long. But long enough," he added, raising his voice, "to know that she's right for me."

"I went out to Kansas City when I was about your age," Gordon said calmly. "My father sent me out there on a business trip, and I had to spend two or three months there. There was a girl who worked as a cashier in the hotel, I remember her well. In those days you didn't find many women working, you understand. Well, I lost my head over her. On the third evening I had dinner with her, I proposed to her. And she accepted me." He took a long, slow puff on his cigar, then chuckled. "All this is between you and me, of course. It's a subject I don't discuss with Mother. But I tell you, it was Romeo and Juliet all over again. I even composed some poetry for that girl, if you can imagine me writing poetry."

In spite of himself, Paul smiled. "Was it pretty bad?"

"It was terrible. I came back home, and all my plans were made. I was going back to Kansas City in a month and marry that girl." He paused and flicked a half-inch of ash into the tray.

"What happened?" Paul's bitterness was very evident now. "Grandpa convinced you that a hotel cashier wasn't good enough for somebody with the name of Dawson, I suppose."

"Not at all." There was a wistful expression in Gordon's eyes, and he sighed gently. "I was a big boy, Paul—big enough to make up my own mind. When I got away, I saw a few things more clearly. I saw that my background and the girl's background were different. I saw that her way of life and my way of life weren't the same at all. We had different standards, different goals, different ideals."

"Didn't she have enough class for you?" Paul stubbed out his cigarette viciously.

"It wasn't a matter of class," Gordon continued gently. "I'm not as much of a snob as all that. I deal with farmers and produce men in my business and have, every day of my life. They're as good as I am, and I know it. But I have enough good sense to know they'd be as uncomfortable in my shoes as I'd be if I wore theirs. It has less to do with money and country clubs and opening nights at the opera than you'd imagine, son."

Paul couldn't stand any longer and sank to the foot of the bed, where he leaned back and clasped his hands around one knee. Never had his father spoken to him like this before, and as a consequence he was thoroughly confused. If only there were something against which he could strike out, the air would be cleared. But this reasonable approach, this cool delivery that was so free of his father's usual pompous bombast took the wind out of his sails. He wanted to fight back, to shout that he loved Helga and had every intention of marrying her, that this talk was a waste of time.

"What's your point, then?" Paul asked, a huskiness in his voice betraying his fatigue. "If it isn't money, what then?"

Gordon considered the question for a long minute, and there was no sound in the room but the ticking of Paul's alarm clock. Here was the crux of the whole argument, and one wrong word could spoil it all. "The important factor, the determining factor is how people fit into their environment. You've been brought up in a certain way. I don't say it's any better or any worse than the way someone else has been raised, but you're still the product of your background. If you were suddenly to find yourself in a New England village, living among fishermen—or in a coal mining town in Pennsylvania, let's say—you'd be out of your element. You wouldn't be comfortable."

"It seems to me that you're getting away from the issue, Dad."

"Far from it. I—"

"Are you so certain that you wouldn't have had a good marriage and a happy life with the girl from Kansas City?"

"I'm positive of it, Paul. From everything I've ever observed —and mind you, I know men and women in all walks of life—

I have no doubt whatsoever that I'd have been walking into sure disaster if I'd married that girl."

"Times have changed," Paul insisted. "The values that mattered when you were young aren't so significant today."

"People are the same today as they were a hundred years ago and as they will be a hundred years from now. You're asking me to be broad-minded, so I'm asking you to open your mind to what I'm saying, too. Fair enough?"

"Fair enough, Dad." Paul leaned forward, rested his elbows on his knees and cupped his chin.

Gordon glanced at him and was shaken; when Paul had been a small boy, before he had learned to read, he had sat nightly in this position when listening to a bedtime story. And at this moment he looked as young, as innocent, as defenseless as he had seventeen years ago. It was almost impossible to realize that this was a headstrong young man contemplating marriage, and that he had a mind of his own.

"I'm simply urging you to be sensible, Paul."

"I *am* being sensible." Paul began to lose his self-control.

"You're also being stubborn, you know." Gordon's voice became louder. "I'm trying to think of you and your welfare. The least you can do is to be courteous."

"All right, Dad. I'm listening." Their increasing hostility showed in the glares they exchanged.

"The best way I know of putting it to you is to beg you to consider this thing in relation to your mother and your sisters."

"Mother has her life. She's married to you."

"All right. We'll leave her out of it. What about Betsy?"

"Well, what about her, Dad?"

Gordon was annoyed and frowned. "Can you imagine Betsy and this—this Helga as sisters-in-law?"

"I hadn't thought of it."

"Well, do so. And you'll see what I mean."

"I can't see that it's important one way or another."

"Surely it's important to you whether or not your wife fits in with Betsy—with your family!"

"It's more important whether the girl I marry fits with me. If you must know, I don't give a hang what the family thinks."

"Now there's a fine attitude for you! Not caring about your family. It's plain to me that you're just being stubborn, that you won't listen to reason and that you're blindly set on making a mistake. I'm trying to help you to prevent it, rather than watch you struggle to rectify it later on. But if you won't listen, then you won't!"

Gordon stood, shook his head in exasperation and stamped out of the room, muttering unintelligibly as he left.

Paul was so tired that he stumbled several times as he undressed and dragged himself to bed. But the raw Chicago dawn was beginning to streak the sky before he finally fell asleep.

CHAPTER THIRTEEN

Day-to-day living was unreal, and over the course of a week Paul came to feel that only his work had any substance. Everything else in his existence was vague, almost dreamlike, and there were times when he seemed to be submerged in a deep nightmare from which there was no escape. His conscience and his sense of obligation, which was sharpened by what his mother kept referring to, between tears, as "traditions of the family," were balanced on one side of the scales, and on the other was Helga. The problem was ever-present and he found surcease only when he was busiest at the office, when the pressure of deadlines forced him to concentrate exclusively on his job.

He spent as little time as possible at home, but when he was there the family never ceased to remind him that he was the cause of unnecessary tragedy in their lives. His mother appeared red-eyed at the breakfast table every morning and sat glumly throughout the meal. She addressed Paul only when asking him if he would be home for dinner, and when he said he would not she invariably looked as though she would weep again. His discomfort in her presence was made all the greater when he repeatedly discovered that she was gazing at him sorrowfully, and although he tried to tell himself that she was merely acting for his benefit, he actually knew better. His mother's grief was genuine.

Relations with his father were more complicated. Gordon had presumably expected that eventually his son would react to the advice he had given. But Paul continued to see Helga every evening, and his father was therefore hurt and angry, apparently feeling that his very considerable efforts had been wasted on a headstrong, stubborn young man. Each day Gordon withdrew more and more, and by the end of the week he was exchanging no words with Paul other than a muttered, "Good morning."

It was simpler to deal with Marcia than with her elders, of course, and Paul put her in her place by ignoring her. She returned the compliment by pretending he did not exist, but finally broke down one morning and, drawing him aside, asked him in a fierce whisper, "How dare you break Mother's heart like this?" The question had been so silly that he hadn't lowered his dignity to answer it.

Even Betsy had been called upon to support the family position. She had telephoned from Wellesley on Sunday morning, and after an extensive conversation with her parents had asked to speak to Paul. When he had come to the phone they'd had little to say to each other. "I hear they've put the heat on you," Betsy had said, and when Paul had agreed, curtly and morosely, she had laughed. Strangely, he'd since thought he had detected a sympathetic note in that laugh.

Sunday dinner had been a grim affair, and even now, two days later, he shuddered when he thought of it. He had hurried to Helga's as soon as he could, only to discover a similar atmosphere of gloom at her house. Together he and Helga had fled to his car and had driven aimlessly for hours. It was extraordinarily difficult, Paul thought as he sat idly at his desk in the Express city room, to obtain a clear perspective on what was happening, but of one thing he was sure: his romance with Helga was depressing everyone whom it touched.

Worst of all was the effect on Helga herself. She had lost her buoyancy, there were dark smudges under her eyes and her silences seemed to grow longer every evening. Certainly she was getting no more enjoyment out of the relationship than was Paul. Each night they had dinner together at some inexpensive restaurant, and thereafter they were confronted with the choice of either driving around for the sake of driving or else taking in a movie they did not really want to see. Under the circumstances they felt they would be welcome neither at her family's apartment nor at the Dawson house, and their sense of frustration and of loneliness was magnified accordingly.

Now, in the quiet office, Paul's sense of insecurity and conflict made him restless, and he thought that if he could see Helga he'd feel better. He shoved back his chair and walked up to the slotman on the city desk, determined to take advantage of the day's lull. Every once in awhile the world seemed to stop manufacturing news, and the lack of activity was intolerable; it gave a man too much time for brooding.

"Eddie," Paul said, "do you see any good reason why I shouldn't go out for lunch today?"

"Help yourself, kid." The slotman passed a grubby hand over his bald head. "It's dead around here today. Just be sure you come back this afternoon, huh?"

"I'll be back. And thanks, Eddie."

"Is she a good-looker, kid?"

Paul did not reply but returned to his desk and called Helga's office. She was in the file room, another girl told him, but could he wait for a minute, please? He waited impatiently, and at last Helga came to the phone and said, "Hello" breathlessly, as though she had been running.

"Hi." Paul wasted no words. "How about meeting me for lunch today?"

She was surprised. "I thought you could never get away at noon. You haven't been fired?"

"No, I've simply made arrangements to get out for lunch,

that's all. How about Henrici's at twelve-thirty? That's half-way between your place and mine."

"I—all right, Paul. Twelve-thirty." Her momentary hesitation indicated that she wanted to inquire if anything was wrong, but had refrained. "And thanks for asking me," she added politely, then hung up quickly.

Although it was the warmest day in months, Paul shivered as he walked across the Loop to the restaurant and hunched his shoulders under the weight of his overcoat. A damp wind was blowing inland from Lake Michigan and seemed to penetrate his bones; the sky overhead was dull and grey, and seemed to fit his mood. The Randolph Street theatres looked shabby in the daylight, and streaks of dirt showed on their unlit marquees. Businessmen, stenographers and shoppers were bustling in every direction, giving substance to the theory that Chicagoans walked faster than the people of any other city. In spite of their speed, however, most of them looked tired and drawn, and Paul thought, not for the first time, that few members of the human race were ever cheerful for any sustained period of time.

Helga was waiting for him just inside the entrance, and they looked at each other for an instant; they were still too new to each other to kiss in a public place. "You're early," Paul said, almost accusingly.

"Well, this is an occasion, isn't it?" She smiled up at him as they walked side by side behind the head waiter to a marble-topped table at the rear of the establishment. "After all, it's the first time we've ever met for lunch."

Paul nodded, pleased that they were being given a quiet table against a wall. He helped Helga into her chair, and as he seated himself he saw a friend of his father's nearby, so he waved politely and called a greeting.

"Who's that?" Helga craned around to see.

"Nobody." Paul was irritated at her lack of manners, and

thought she should know better. Then, as so often happened, he was ashamed of his hyper-critical attitude; he took a grip on himself, then smiled. "How much time do you have?"

"An hour. But nobody will object if I take a little longer." Helga picked up her menu. "How about you?"

He shrugged and caught the attention of a waiter. "There's so little news today we're coming out with a blank paper tomorrow. I'm going to have the tongue and eggs, pancake style. They're wonderful here."

"That sounds good to me, too."

Paul gave the order, instructed the waiter to be sure to bring them some salt-stick rolls, then leaned back in his chair and lit a cigarette. Helga, he thought, looked as though she had spent a sleepless night, and the circles under her eyes were more prominent than ever.

Helga, who had been momentarily occupied with her own thoughts, leaned across the table impulsively and touched Paul's wrist. "You're smoking too much," she said.

He knew she was right but hated to admit it. "And you're getting along on no sleep."

"Hardly. Though I haven't been getting much lately," she conceded. "But that's still no excuse for you."

"We're a fine pair." He took a long, deliberate drag from his cigarette, then decided that he was being childishly defiant and stubbed it out.

"I think we're a very fine pair." Helga spoke quietly but with deep conviction. At this moment the waiter arrived with lunch, and she said nothing more until he served the food and left. Then she asked, "Was there some special reason you wanted me to meet you this noon?"

"No, not really. I just wanted to meet you, that's all."

"Thank you."

"For a minute you sounded worried."

"I was worried, frankly." She toyed with her lunch. "We've

[168]

never met at noon like this before, so I jumped to conclusions, I guess. I shouldn't have, but I did."

"What kind of conclusions?" All girls loved to indulge in day-dreams, bad and good, Paul thought. He grinned at her and wanted to take her hand.

"Well, I've been scared. About us."

"What is there to be scared about, for Pete's sake? There are enough problems in the world without making up new ones!"

"We have no real plans, Paul. And that worries me." She put her fork on her plate and looked directly at him. "Are you sure that you want to marry me?"

"Of course I'm sure!"

"But you've changed the subject when I've tried to talk about setting a date—"

"Because I think such a discussion is premature, that's why. We've got to wait." Paul began to grow uncomfortable.

"Why must we wait?"

"It's no secret to you that my parents aren't exactly jumping up and down with joy at the prospect of our getting married, Helga!"

"If they're opposed to a marriage between us now," she said quietly, "they'll be just as opposed in two months or six months or a year."

"That's where you're all wrong. I know my mother and father better than you do—"

"Well, of course."

"And I say that if we give them enough time and don't do anything to get their backs up, they'll get used to the idea. Eventually."

"But you'd like to be married right away? Just as I would?"

"Tomorrow, if it were up to me!"

"It *is* up to you, darling. And to me."

"I tell you, my parents would be up in arms!"

"Paul, dear, I have a very great respect for my parents.

Nobody could love a mother and father more than I love mine. But I live my own life."

"Just as I live mine!"

Helga saw that he was becoming upset, but she had taken the plunge and it was too late to back out now. "A child shows love for his mother and father by obeying them. And they respect him for his obedience. But when he grows up, he learns to be independent of them. The only way they'll respect him then is if he does what he believes to be right and good. Then there's respect both ways, from the parents to their grown-up child and from the grown-up child to the parents."

"If we rush things, there'll be a permanent break with my folks. It's that simple!"

"You'd better eat before everything gets cold," Helga said, and poured a little cream into her coffee.

Paul ignored the suggestion. "The way I see it, you're urging me to disregard my parents!"

"No, I'm not. I—"

"Well, that's precisely what we'd be doing if we decided to get married right away. And all your talk about showing adult independence is gibberish. People can be independent without being rude or defiant!"

She was treading on delicate ground, but their whole future together was at stake, and this was no time to be subtle. "We aren't getting married in order to defy your mother and father, at least I hope we aren't. We're getting married because we love each other."

"At last we agree on something!"

"All right, then. You want to be married right away. So do I. It's our lives we're dealing with, not those of your parents or of my parents. I don't pretend to know how your mother and father would react. I hope they'd respect you. Maybe it would take time for them to adjust their thinking, but surely they'd come to respect you, Paul. I can't believe they wouldn't."

Paul was too angry to think clearly and lit a fresh cigarette to give himself a moment in which to steady himself. "It seems to me," he said slowly, "that you're trying to push me into a corner."

"Darling, I'm not. I'm just—"

"And I don't like the feeling. I'm a guy who needs enough room to move around in. What's all the great rush for? We have the rest of our lives ahead of us, so what difference does a few weeks or a few months one way or the other make?"

"Now you're upset, Paul."

"Upset? Hardly. You're the one who's upset."

Helga looked far more composed than she felt, but the effort of maintaining a surface calm was almost too great. "I'm trying to think of you and me. And of our future."

Her choice of words was unfortunate, but she could not know that Gordon had used an almost identical expression and that she had consequently struck Paul on a spot that was already sore. "I'm capable of looking out for my own future, you know," he said brusquely. "I must say your opinion is interesting. And revealing. Even if I don't agree with it. I believe I have a lot of foresight! And the stand I'm taking right now proves it!" It was bad enough to be forced to defend himself to his father, but this was intolerable.

It would be easy to let the matter drop, Helga thought. She could agree and achieve momentary peace, but the basic problem, that of somehow opening Paul's eyes to the need to stand on his own feet, would be no closer to a solution. "Paul, I'm not very expert in expressing myself. You know how to handle words better than I can. So try to bear with me. I'm just trying to show you that there's a difference between respecting one's parents—and just blindly trying always to please them." Having gone this far, she decided to take the final step, too. "An adult must stand on his own feet."

The waiter approached, saw that both plates were virtually

[171]

untouched and would have gone away again, but Paul gestured to him curtly. "We're through," he said.

There was a long, dead silence while the table was being cleared; Paul's rage was so great he could barely control himself, and he spoke the instant that the waiter moved away. "Would you mind repeating what you just said? I can't believe I've heard you right!"

"All I've tried to do is to show you—"

"You've shown me plenty. You've shown that you want me to break with my parents!"

"No! Not break with them. Just stand up to them by having the courage of your convictions. Respect for parents doesn't mean you've got to give in to their wishes—"

"I've heard enough!"

"Oh, Paul—"

"If you'd had the kind of background and family life I've had, you couldn't set out deliberately to break the hearts of people who devoted their lives to you. But you aren't that way. You're callous and hard-boiled, and it's a good thing I found it out now instead of later!" He shoved back his chair savagely and rose to his feet.

"Darling, you're twisting it all around. Please be sensible. Sit down again, and—"

"It's better for both of us if we end this whole thing right here and now. You couldn't have been clearer or plainer. All right. If that's the way it has to be, then that's the way it's going to be. Blood is still thicker than water. So goodbye, Helga." Removing his hat and coat from a wall hook, he walked quickly to the cashier's desk, paid his check and left the restaurant without once looking back.

The wind was sharper now, but Paul was unaware of the elements as he hurried back to the Express office, and not until he arrived at the city room did he realize he had carried his coat the entire distance. A few routine items were on his desk, and he rewrote the stories automatically, almost unthinkingly. People spoke to him and he replied; a reporter stopped at his desk to tell him a joke, and he found himself laughing at it, though he hadn't heard a word. He felt numb and guessed that he was drained of all feeling. Later, he told himself, a reaction would set in. He thought of sending Helga some flowers with a note apologizing for walking out on her at the restaurant, but it was probably better to leave well enough alone.

Gradually the tempo of work increased, and when a boy brought a sheaf of copy to Paul, he ran fresh paper into his typewriter and started to study the first story, an account of a rather sensational divorce case that had been heard in court that morning. But he could not concentrate for a moment and looked up. He was free, he told himself fiercely. He had narrowly escaped making the greatest mistake of his life, and he tried to convince himself that he was very wise, very strong, that Helga herself would be grateful to him.

Suddenly he picked up his telephone ear piece and dialed a number, and while the phone rang at the other end he tapped rapidly on the edge of his desk with the blunt end of a pencil. "Hello." A metallic voice cut into his thoughts.

"Hello, Mother," he said. "I just wanted to let you know that my plans for tonight are changed." The pencil drummed faster, then stopped. "I'll be home for dinner after all."

CHAPTER FOURTEEN

For two weeks Paul could not bring himself to tell his family that his romance with Helga was ended. He would not discuss his reasons for breaking off with her, and he dreaded seeing the pleasure on his father's face and the relief on his mother's when they learned his news. There was another cause for his reticence, too, one he could not quite define. He told himself repeatedly that he had done the right thing, that a marriage between them could not have been successful, yet he felt a sense of shame at having abruptly terminated the most important relationship he had ever enjoyed with any girl.

Helga, he told himself again and again, was a wonderful person, but she was wrong for him, just as he wasn't right for her. And he should have allowed the subject to drop out of his mind right there. But he could not, and instead behaved erratically, moodily. He had no desire for the company of his parents, and made several last-minute dinner dates with colleagues at the office. Twice he ate alone, which he hated, and over the weekend he had made his sole appearance at the family table on Sunday; naturally, no personal crisis was so great that he could avoid the Sunday noon obligation.

On Saturday night, at a loss for anything better to do, he had driven over to the University and had dropped in at his old fraternity house. Somewhat to his surprise he had discovered a dance in progress, but he had no interest in it. The girls all looked and acted like adolescents, and finally he and three other bored alumni locked themselves in the upstairs library and played several rubbers of bridge. Paul had never cared much for the game, but it passed the time and he wasn't left alone with his thoughts.

Repeatedly as the days passed he felt the urge to call Helga, but each time he knew the gesture was meaningless unless he intended to see her again. What bothered him most was that his feeling of restlessness and dissatisfaction remained with him. Instead of lessening it seemed to grow more intense, and he became increasingly aware of the need to do something about it. No man had a right to feel sorry for himself for more than ten days, and Paul's good sense at last reasserted itself. His sulking and moping were doing no one any good, and he was succeeding only in hurting himself; he began to lose respect for himself and decided it was time to stop.

And so, on the fifteenth day after his break-up with Helga, he took active steps to resume his social life. He came home for dinner, and was forced to admit to himself that his parents had behaved toward him with unexpected discretion. Certainly it was obvious to them that he and Helga were no longer seeing each other, yet there had been no comments, no questions, no leading remarks. This unusual display of reticence, this conscious effort not to interfere in his life heartened and buoyed him, and he dominated the dinner table conversation, telling stories and quipping at such a furious clip that even his father, who had been silent and somewhat withdrawn, began to mellow and finally sat back in his chair and laughed heartily.

Marcia was the only member of the family toward whom Paul still felt resentful, but it was impossible to continue a feud with a child who knew no better, and he patronizingly addressed several remarks to her. The eagerness with which she responded demonstrated how starved she had been for his regard, and his sense of well being expanded even more. By the time the meal ended, everyone was in good spirits, and Gordon bestowed the highest accolade at his command.

"I wish Betsy had been here tonight," he said. "Then it would have been just perfect."

Paul hurried to his room, changed into a freshly-pressed suit and returned downstairs to take his hat and coat from the hall closet. Then, assuming an air of casual disregard, he strolled into the living room. Gordon was reading one of the evening papers, Molly was thumbing through a magazine and waiting until someone stopped concentrating on other things long enough for her to open a conversation. Marcia, who should have been in her room doing her homework, sprawled on the floor before the radio cabinet. The machine, a new fifteen-tube super-heterodyne set capable of pulling in KDKA in Pittsburgh or WGY in Schenectady as clearly as local stations, was playing softly, and the youngest of the Dawsons was lying on her stomach, surreptitiously reaching out for chocolates in a box on a coffee-table, just within arm's length. An open magazine was on the floor under her nose, and she was avidly examining a picture of Greta Garbo.

No one looked up until Paul cleared his throat. "I'll say good night," he announced, then added unnecessarily, "I'm going out."

"Oh?" Molly's quiet matched her son's, but her eyes were watchful and alert.

"I'll be home fairly early," Paul said carelessly. "I'm just dropping in on Joan, that's all."

The announcement had the effect of a bomb falling through the roof. Gordon lowered his newspaper, Molly stared openly and even Marcia stopped chewing a chocolate-coated caramel. Gordon was the first to recover. "That so?" he murmured, then conveniently buried himself once more in his paper.

Molly, who had been containing herself for days, was unable to let the matter rest. "I hope she knows you're coming over, dear," she said, smiling brightly. "After all, Joan is a very popular girl, so she may have another date and—"

"She's expecting me," Paul interrupted.

"Well, that's fine, then," Molly beamed, and the implications of the situation made her forget her caution. "I'm so glad, Paul! You just can't imagine how we've been feeling for this past month and we—"

Gordon cut his wife off with an imperative cough, but in his own way he showed his own feelings just as clearly. "If you have no special plans for the evening, son," he declared loudly, making it impossible for Molly to continue, "I have some charge accounts around town that are just gathering dust. So if you feel like going to the Empire Room or the College Inn, just say the word and—"

"Thanks all the same, Dad. But the gay, giddy whirl would be too much on a work night." Paul knew it was wrong to feel the old, familiar annoyance; Dad was merely trying to be helpful and to encourage a romance he believed to be eminently proper, but it was a nuisance all the same to feel the pressure of a strong, guiding hand.

Molly was uncertain how to interpret Paul's refusal and Marcia lost interest in the situation; the shape of Garbo's eyebrows was more intriguing. Gordon, however, was equal to the occasion. "Any time you want to squire Joan around town, just say the word and I'll turn my hotel credit cards over to you." Having made his point with what he firmly believed was subtlety and finesse, he started to read an account of the Federal Reserve Board's new regulations on bank loans.

Paul felt a vague sense of disappointment; the reactions had been roughly what he had expected, yet he felt cheated, as though something had been withheld from him. Realizing that he was being inconsistent as well as a trifle foolish, he smiled absently and left, only half-hearing his mother's admonition to put on his coat and hat before going out into the night air.

As Paul drove to the Adams house he tried to put himself in his parents' position and wondered how he would have reacted to the brief scene that had just been concluded. If he were a father, he guessed, he would feel relieved at learning that his son wasn't going to marry a girl whom he and his wife considered unsuitable. On the other hand, what would his own standard be under such circumstances—how would he measure his son's intended bride? He guessed it would depend on the woman to whom he'd be married, and his sense of confusion increased. A person like Helga would have a broad and tolerant view; Joan, however, would be more inclined to share the orthodox approach of his family.

Such speculation, he told himself firmly, served no useful purpose. Slamming on his brakes with greater vehemence than was necessary as he arrived in front of the Adams home, he thought that he was slipping into the bad habit of analyzing everything he said and did, that he was spending more time worrying than he was in living. There was no reason to indulge in such purposeless, vain practices, and he reminded himself that he was young, healthy and unattached, that he had a good job and a future that only his muddled reasoning could limit. He pressed the doorbell far longer than was necessary.

Joan herself answered the summons. "Hi, stranger," she said lightly.

"Hello, kid." Paul removed his hat, kissed her impersonally and stepped into the house. Several lamps were lit in the living room, but Joan's parents were conspicuously absent. "Where are the master and his lady?"

She lifted an eyebrow as she took his hat and coat. "Oh, they developed a date somewhere the very minute I told them you were coming over."

Paul glanced at her out of the corner of his eye; her tone

[178]

was unusual and so was something about her appearance. Joan had always been glad to see him in the past, and she had invariably made it a point to dress up for him. But tonight she wore a skirt and sweater and her hair was tied back with a ribbon in a careless, childish fashion. It occurred to him that she might have heard of his romance with Helga, that she had consequently felt jealous and would now try to punish him with indifference. If that was the case he'd have her straightened out in no time at all. They had known each other too long to take umbrage over what, in the long run and from the proper perspective, would be seen as a minor incident.

"If I know your family," he said airily, "they probably dashed over to see my folks."

"I doubt it."

She spoke so flatly that Paul was taken aback for a moment. "Is there someplace special you'd like to go tonight?"

"No, not really."

"A movie, maybe?"

"If you'd like, Paul." The indifference was apparently genuine!

Somewhat nettled, he jammed his hands into his pockets. "Maybe you'd rather go dancing. The Empire Room, perhaps."

"I was rather looking forward to having a little talk, so we could stay right here. I have one or two things on my mind, and it's possible you might want to talk about some things yourself. After all, it's been ages since we've seen each other. And a lot has happened in that time. So unless you really want to go out and hit the high spots, I'm perfectly content to stay right here—and get reacquainted."

Her inferences were not lost on Paul, and he achieved a blank expression as he followed Joan into the living room and sat down beside her on the low sofa of orange-flecked tweed. "I've been busy lately," he murmured.

[179]

It was wrong of Joan to laugh, but she could not conceal her merriment. "You sound exactly like a man!"

"That's good," Paul grinned, lighting cigarettes for her and for himself.

"I suppose you think you live in a vacuum."

"No, not precisely. The newspaper world is a strange and mysterious—"

"Pooh. I'm not talking about your job, and you know it." There was nothing malicious in Joan's attitude. She simply knew he was embarrassed, and she could not resist teasing him. "You've been seen all over town with a beautiful blonde. Same girl, evening after evening. Shall I tell you who saw you—and where? I'll have you know that I've had daily reports from some of the dearest, most kindly, well-meaning friends—" She broke off abruptly as she saw a look of pain in Paul's eyes.

"Don't bother to tell me who saw me where," he said at almost the same instant, his voice thick and heavy. "It's all over and finished now."

"I'm sorry, Paul." Joan was genuinely contrite, and, reaching out instinctively, touched his hand.

He reacted without thinking, and before he quite knew what he was doing his arms were around her and he was kissing her, hard. He realized that they should feel something sharp and clear and definite, yet the moment was flat, curiously empty. Even as Paul held her, his lips pressed against Joan's, the thought crossed his mind that he might as well be kissing a lifeless statue instead of a pretty girl. Disgusted with himself, he released her as unexpectedly as he had reached for her, and they stared at each other for an instant, sober and unemotional.

"Impetuous, that's what you are," Joan said. "And you've ruined my lipstick."

"Not to mention my handkerchief." Paul scrubbed his mouth.

"Well," she said, "that was a noble experiment. It just happens to have been made too late."

[180]

Paul wanted to avoid a discussion, but that was impossible. He had started something, and as a gentleman it was his duty to face the issue he had created. However, it would be better not to be more serious than was necessary. "If it weren't that I've known you for so long, I'd apologize," he said. "Under the circumstances I'll just say I'm terribly sorry. Am I forgiven?"

Joan's mood was unlike any he had ever known. "I hate cliches," she replied, "but there's really nothing to forgive." She sat down near him on the sofa again, and her violet eyes searched his.

"We're both suffering from a malady known as taking-for-granted. We've been afflicted since birth, both of us. There are some who claim the disease is hereditary, but Dr. Paul Dawson has proved conclusively that the environmental atmosphere is chiefly responsible for—"

"We should have been able to get together, Paul. Don't be funny, please. Because it really isn't very funny, you know."

"Okay." All the things that should have been left unsaid would come out into the open now. "There's no spark between us, that's all. You don't go for me and I don't go for you. I suppose there are a thousand reasons why, but none of them are terribly important—except academically. Or clinically."

Joan regarded him steadily. "Have you felt this way for very long?"

Paul hesitated for an instant before replying. "I don't want to sound ungracious, but I've never felt any other way." The room seemed to be suffocatingly hot and he wanted to open a window.

She laughed suddenly, and he thought he detected a note of tenderness in her mirth. "May I tell you something—and no hard feelings?"

"Sure." He ran his fingers nervously through his hair.

"I used to imagine—to tell myself that you were secretly in love with me, but that you were too shy to tell me so."

[181]

"I'm sorry."

"There's no need to be sorry any more. For a long time I *thought* I loved you. I guess I really *did,* though it's hard to believe now."

He tried to smile. "Why is it so hard?"

"Because I don't any more. All these weeks we haven't seen each other were good for me, Paul. Time was—one of the things that made me see you in a different light."

"I'm glad." He wasn't actually glad at all; now that Joan was unexpectedly beyond his grasp he wondered if he had perhaps made the greatest mistake of his life in not having proposed to her at a time when she would have accepted him.

"Then all's well that ends well."

"You bet."

Joan leaned forward and hugged him impulsively. "It's a shame, you know, it really is."

"They'll be broken-hearted." He sounded more jovial than he felt. "My mother will take it the worst of any of them."

"No, mine will." Joan giggled and fluffed her hair, then suddenly sobered.

There was something in her attitude that was new, Paul thought; he was only vaguely aware of it, he could not put his finger on it, yet he was conscious of its presence. She seemed more certain of herself than ever before, as though she had grown from a girl into a woman. He tried to dismiss the notion and told himself that he had, in all probability, never really seen her clearly until now.

She became aware of his silence and sat erect. "I'm so sorry, I'm being the world's worst hostess. There's some scrumptious pineapple upside-down cake left from dinner, and you always love it, so—"

"Not for me, thanks."

She regarded him severely. "You've lost weight, Paul."

"A little, maybe. I guess I've been off my feed lately. Nothing serious."

Either Joan was strongly intuitive or she had known him too long to be fooled. "You must be terribly in love with her." She made the statement calmly, unemotionally.

Paul blinked at her. "Who said anything about being—"

"All right. It's none of my business, so we'll let the whole thing ride. But I'll tell you something. I didn't just sit home and pine after you disappeared. I've got me a fellow."

"That's swell! Anybody I—"

"Yes, you know him." From Joan's tone it was evident she was going no further in her identification. "We're not saying anything until he lands a new job he's been trying to get. And then—well, stick around and watch the fireworks. They'll be able to hear Daddy as far west as Des Moines, if the wind is right."

Paul was bewildered; if he knew the man whom Joan wanted to marry, it was obviously someone who belonged to the "right" crowd, so he couldn't imagine why she would face parental objections. Comparing her situation to his own when he had planned to marry Helga, he could only shake his head. Joan simply didn't know when she was well off. "Don't dream up obstacles," he said.

"Oh, I'm not. It's just that he doesn't have a nickel to his name. His family went broke in '30. So did most people, but Daddy won't think of that. He'll rant, scream and rave—which will be too bad for him."

"How come?"

She stood and her small, delicate hands were clenched. "I know what I want and what's right," she said emphatically, with a display of strength Paul had never before known in her. "Daddy—and Mother, too—will have to face reality, that's all. I'm a big girl, and I have every right to marry the man I love. That's precisely what I intend to do."

As Paul watched her, his own sense of inner turmoil increased. Joan was right, of course, and he truly admired her for the first time in all the years he had known her. She had the courage to carry out her convictions, and that was more than he could say for himself. Now that it was too late he felt sorry he had never loved her; she would be a wonderful wife, and he almost envied the man she was going to marry.

CHAPTER FIFTEEN

In books and plays, Paul thought, something dramatic happened and thus caused a major turning point in a man's life. In his own case, however, the void in which he existed grew and deepened, and he could find no escape from his basic dilemma, either through association with others or within himself. Even if he were to reverse himself and try to resume with Helga, he was convinced that she would have nothing to do with him. He couldn't blame her, of course, after his treatment of her. And the knowledge that Joan Adams had the vision and the integrity to make a decision and to hold fast to it increased his sense of self-dissatisfaction.

His most acute feeling was one of utter loneliness. The men he knew at the Express were business associates with whom he had virtually nothing in common except work. And his old friends, some of them college classmates and others childhood and summer vacation companions, were all engrossed in their own lives. It was difficult to find and hold a good job, and almost everyone Paul knew was concentrating on his own security. Some of his friends were already married, and to them the struggle was even more intense; the majority of the others had matrimony in mind and were trying to build toward it vocationally with all possible speed.

No one was particularly interested in the problems of a lucky devil who came from a comfortably well-to-do family, who himself possessed a good and even glamorous position and who, for whatever the reasons, happened to find himself on the loose. The hard fact that nobody was really concerned over anybody else was borne in on Paul rather forcibly on Sunday morning. He had stayed home on Saturday night, had remained in his own room and had read until his eyes ached. So, when he received a phone call from Phil Gray, a classmate who was captain of an amateur baseball team and who told him a game was being organized, he was glad to get together with a group of young men he had long known. For ten years, more or less, the gang had congregated in Jackson Park on Sunday mornings in Spring and Summer to play a game of softball. Paul was delighted at the chance to work off some energy and see some fellows he had liked.

But the atmosphere, he discovered when he reached the hard-packed diamond, was different this year. Maybe he himself had changed, but he was sure that the atmosphere was the more responsible for his feeling. Two recent bridegrooms brought their wives to watch them play baseball, and the girls sat together in a car parked on the road near home plate, gossiping and chatting, and occasionally unrolling a window to shout a word of praise or encouragement to their mates.

It wasn't just the presence of the women that disturbed Paul, however. He could not help but notice that most of the players looked tired, with deep smudges under their eyes and the beginnings of lines in their foreheads; worst of all, their gayety, their spirit of camaraderie was forced. It was as though each man was trying to turn back the clock to the days when he had been carefree and without responsibilities. Such magic was impossible, and by the time Paul returned home for Sunday dinner he was saddened rather than refreshed.

The most disturbing factor, one which contributed heavily

to Paul's loneliness, was the disintegration of his relations with the family. Ever since his date with Joan, his parents had adopted the attitude that the prodigal had returned to the fold, and their attitude was a constant irritation to him. His father's narrow political views and his mother's limited, decorous social horizons filled him with contempt, but he had to keep his opinions to himself. After all, he was still living under their roof.

The idea occurred to him repeatedly that he might take a bachelor apartment, that the day was rapidly approaching when he would have to take such a step, for neither he nor his parents was benefitting from their present relationship. Although it was not easy to admit to himself, the most significant events in his personal day-to-day living now were the moments when he exchanged a few pleasantries with Delcie and the less frequent occasions when his boredom and his inability—or unwillingness—to speak Gordon's and Molly's language caused him to tease Marcia rather unmercifully.

Over the period of almost a month he dated a number of girls, but found even the vivacious ones dull. Those whom he had known for years and whose parents belonged to the right clubs were interested solely in the doings of their own confined set; a female reporter at the Express with whom he had dinner one evening was too hard-boiled for his taste; and two girls with whom he had gone to the University and who were surprised but pleased to hear from him, proved to be vapid.

And so he floundered and drifted in an intricate maze of his own making, finding and taking satisfaction only in his work, which, as he soon discovered, became little more than drudgery when there was no one with whom he could share his triumphs and his disappointments. He might have remained indefinitely in a state of suspended emotional animation if, after all, there had not been an incident that shook him out of his lethargy.

It happened at the dinner table, and it began insignificantly and quietly. Both Gordon and Paul had been eating silently, and the burden of conversation fell on Molly and Marcia, who chatted over inconsequentials. The head of the family, who had just been carving a second helping of roast lamb for everyone, looked up from his labor and remarked, half to himself, "That was certainly a stupid editorial."

There was silence for a moment, then Molly filled the gap. "What editorial, dear?"

"In one of tonight's papers, I don't recall off-hand which one. They were offering advice to businessmen."

Paul knew better than to say anything when he heard that familiar edge of sarcasm in his father's voice, but he could not hold back. "What kind of advice, Dad?"

"Some great, ink-stained brain had the temerity to say that the business executives of America must change their outlook and lift their eyes to new horizons. New horizons!"

"What's wrong with that?"

"I'll tell you what's wrong with it. I'm a businessman. I operate a large company. I've run it, successfully, for a lot of years, and I resent having some pseudo-intellectual who has spent his whole life in the world of books telling me what I'm to do or not to do. I've had practical experience in the school of hard knocks, and I know what I'm doing."

The discussion should have ended right there, but Paul felt that his basic concept of living was being challenged. "Maybe the guy who wrote that editorial knew what he was doing, too, Dad."

"Rubbish."

"Not at all. Maybe you're too close to the forest to see the trees. Maybe—"

"Are you implying that I don't know how to conduct my business, Paul?"

"Certainly not. But I am saying that the man who wrote that editorial was fulfilling his right and proper obligation to society. Maybe he sees the business scene more dispassionately and objectively than you do."

"Paul, I will not tolerate your—"

"And whether he's right or wrong, he's doing the right thing by bringing his views into the open. That's the function of a newspaper's editorial page. He's stirring up controversy. He's making people think."

"Think, eh? Do you suppose my company simply runs itself? Do you imagine that I spend my time just staring out of a window, waiting to look important when a visitor comes in to see me?"

"I didn't say that, Dad. I'm only trying to explain to you that it's a newspaperman's duty to speak the truth as he sees the truth!"

"Even if what he's saying is gibberish?"

"I'm damned if it's gibberish!" Paul knew he was shouting, but his father had raised his voice first. "Any newspaper that doesn't take a stand on vital issues is failing in its duty to its readers. Why do you think the Constitution of the United States guarantees freedom of the press? Why do you—"

"There's a difference between freedom and license," Gordon roared.

"Now you're deliberately trying to confuse things. But I can promise you this much, Dad. When I own my own newspaper, I'm going to come right out with the things that I believe in. I'm going to lay my views on the line, without fear of anyone. I'm going to—"

"You and your newspaper. A boy playing at being a man!"

"You can't talk to me like that!"

"Oh?"

"You're my father, and I try to show you that I respect you. But that doesn't give you the right to insult me—or to belittle my principles!"

"Principles? To blazes with false principles! I know my busi-

[189]

ness. I've spent my whole life in it. Anybody who tries to tell me that I'm running it in the wrong way is out of his mind. And that's all I have to say!"

Gordon threw his napkin to the floor and stamped off to the living room, his lips compressed, his eyes wildly stormy and a thin white line showing around his mouth. Molly, whose every instinct told her to follow him, first urged Paul to apologize. To her amazement he glared at her, stood without a word and stalked out of the house. Unconscious of where he was going and not really caring, he walked to the lake and sat down on one of the high rocks of the breakwater. There was a matter of principle at stake, he told himself repeatedly. His father was dead wrong, but lacked the courage and integrity to admit that he was in error. It was typical of him that he believed he knew more than anyone else, that all he needed to do was to express an opinion, which thereupon automatically made whatever he said true and right and just.

Such an attitude was nonsensical, and to a son who still lived in the home he provided it was intolerable. Once again the idea flashed into his mind that maybe he should have married Joan when he'd had the chance. At least he'd have escaped his parents' domination that way, and without objection from them. Then he dismissed the notion abruptly. Marriage without love was no marriage.

Paul smoked cigarettes furiously, until his mouth and throat were raw, and stared with unseeing eyes at the placid waters of Lake Michigan. In his anger he had forgotten to put on a topcoat, and several times he shivered, but was only dimly aware of his discomfort. Not until he passed his right hand across his face and felt the cold of his fingers did he quite realize where he was and that Chicago's early spring, in spite of its promise of better days to come, was certainly not balmy.

He pulled himself to his feet, discovered that his joints ached and dragged himself home. Although he didn't know why, he was trembling as violently as though he were suffering from a high fever, and his mind would not function clearly. Only one thought filled his consciousness: he had lost all respect for his father.

When he arrived at the house he went straight to his room, undressed and tumbled into bed. He was exhausted and slept soundly, but when his alarm awakened him in the morning he was vaguely conscious of having been disturbed by a series of ugly, distorted dreams. And he felt even more depressed than before. But he was determined to show nothing, and when he arrived at the breakfast table he greeted his parents civilly and quietly. Molly raised her troubled face for a good morning kiss, which was unusual, but Gordon behaved as though nothing at all had happened.

"Morning, Paul," he said. "The stock market held steady yesterday."

A civilized blanket of good manners covered the ragged edges of feeling and somehow the meal ended as it had begun, on a note of dignity and quiet. Paul was still in something of a daze as he drove to work, and not until he neared the Express Building and parked his car did a resolve form within him. Through the morning it hardened into a core and took form, and finally, shortly before noon, he requested and received permission to leave for the day an hour earlier than usual. From that moment forward he was able to devote only a portion of his mind to his job; he knew what he intended to do, but even the realization that he was deliberately planning the most drastic action of his life did not excite him. If anything, his new calm and self-containment convinced him that the steps he contemplated were right.

Shortly after five in the afternoon he cleaned up his desk, slipped on his topcoat and left the Express office. He was so deep in thought that he momentarily forgot that his automobile was nearby; he walked across the Loop to Michigan Avenue,

[191]

headed north to Wacker Drive and arrived at the London Guaranty Building at precisely five-fifteen. As he well knew, Helga Bjornson worked until five-thirty, so, unless she was released unexpectedly early today, he had a quarter of an hour to kill.

He bought a pack of cigarettes at the lobby tobacco counter, then wandered out to the street again. A freighter was moving slowly from the Chicago River into the lake, and he watched the Michigan Avenue Bridge being raised and lowered again, keeping a careful eye on the entrance to the building all the while. By the time the vessel had reached a point just opposite the Tribune's loading wharves on the river-front, it was almost five-thirty, and he hurried back into the lobby. The elevators were discharging load after load of workers now, and he wanted to take no chance of missing Helga.

When she did not appear it crossed his mind for the first time that perhaps she was ill. There was also the possibility that she had left her job and had taken another one elsewhere, and he thought that he should have telephoned her company first to find out if she was still employed there. It was too late to duck into a phone booth now, however, for he might miss her, and he cursed himself for his shortsightedness. Gradually the crowds thinned, he began to give up hope, and grinding a cigarette butt under his heel he decided to wait just five minutes longer.

Then, suddenly, he saw her. Helga came out of the elevator with two other girls, one of whom was talking animatedly, and she seemed to be completely absorbed by what her companion was saying. Paul studied her intently, and thought she looked thin. But she was still lovely, more attractive than any girl he had ever known.

After listening to her friends for what seemed like an interminable time, Helga finally turned to leave the lobby and Paul stepped away from the wall. His calm suddenly deserted him

[192]

and he felt his heart pounding, then he forgot everything but his nearness to Helga. He'd planned a score of speeches, but as he touched her arm lightly he found himself saying only, "Hi."

She was startled at the sight of him, but composed herself quickly and scarcely slackened her pace. "Why, hello," she said politely, in the tone one would use to a distant acquaintance.

Paul fell in beside her. "I've been waiting for you," he declared, feeling woefully inadequate. Helga did not reply, and he was forced to add, "I'd like to talk to you, if I may."

She remained silent until she reached the bus-stop on Wacker Drive, then she looked up at him, her blue eyes displaying no emotion. "Really?" she asked.

"Really," he repeated firmly. "Is there someplace we could go for a few minutes and—"

"I'm afraid I might miss my bus." Helga seemed to be staring through him now.

"I know I've behaved like the worst kind of a heel," Paul said. "I walked out on you that day in the restaurant after making an unwarranted scene. I've neglected you ever since, and you did nothing at all to deserve that kind of treatment. So if you don't want to waste your time on me, I can't blame you." He realized that two men and a woman who were waiting for the bus were listening avidly, and he lowered his voice. "I'm not very good at street corner orations," he muttered.

Helga relented unexpectedly, and a smile touched the corners of her lips although her eyes remained grave. "I suppose I can spare a little while," she conceded.

Together they headed west on Wacker Drive, then turned south when they came to State Street. Paul knew that his planning had been haphazard, and he became even more upset. He should have thought of some specific place to take Helga; instead here they were, wandering almost aimlessly in the rush-hour crowds. Neither spoke until they were passing the Chicago and State Lake movie theatres, and then Paul, still trying

[193]

desperately to remember some quiet and secluded place that would be suitable, found his voice.

"How have you been?" he asked inanely.

"Fine, thank you."

Helga did not return the compliment, he noticed, and made no inquiries after his health. His feeling of panic mounted, and then, as they reached the corner of Randolph Street, he caught a glimpse farther down State Street of the entrance to one of the favorite eating establishments of his childhood, Kranz' old-fashioned ice cream parlor. Relieved beyond a degree justified by the circumstances, he guided Helga to the place, barely touching her elbow now and again with the tips of his fingers.

As they entered, they immediately became aware of the strong, rich odors of chocolate, and an elderly lady in a crisp black uniform with a white collar smiled at them benignly and led them to a marble-topped table. The restaurant was almost deserted, and only two waitresses were on duty; this was not an hour when most people wanted sundaes or banana splits. Paul would have helped Helga out of her jacket, but she merely opened it, then concentrated, or at least pretended to concentrate, on the glassine-covered menu that stood in a little metal holder on the table. Paul studied her covertly and thought that never had she looked so appealing.

"I'll just have a cup of coffee, please." Not until Helga spoke did Paul become aware of the presence of a waitress.

"Two coffees," he amended, and as the woman departed he reached into his pocket for his cigarettes, then changed his mind. He had no desire to smoke.

"You wanted to see me?" Helga glanced at her plain, rather old-fashioned wrist-watch.

"You're very decent to have come here with me. I appreciate it, though I don't deserve it." Paul hadn't intended to say any such thing, but plunged on. "Helga, I was an idiot, and I've

[194]

never been as miserable or as lonely in my life as I've been in these past five and a half weeks. If it's any consolation to you, if it'll give you any satisfaction, I've been paying through the nose for my mistake."

"I get no satisfaction out of knowing that someone else has suffered." Helga was glancing down at her handbag, and she flipped its handle to and fro.

"The reason I acted so disgracefully was because I was torn two ways." Paul smiled faintly in self-scorn. "I wanted to marry you. My parents were opposed. So I took it all out on you. On you, of all people on earth."

Raising her head sharply, Helga looked straight at him. "Do you think me so insensitive that I didn't know why you were in torment? That's what I tried to tell you, Paul. I tried to make you understand that we couldn't make a happy and successful marriage if you carried a burden of guilt and resentment around on your shoulders." She paused as the waitress arrived with the coffee, then continued. "Anyway, I'm glad you know now. But I'm sorry you had to go through so much to find it out. You've become very thin—you don't look well."

The edge of concern in her voice lifted his spirits immeasurably, but he couldn't let her see his reaction, so he stirred his coffee vigorously. "Thank you for being generous," was all he could say.

"There's no reason to thank me." Helga lifted her cup, then set it down again. The coffee was too hot to drink. "But you still haven't told me why you sought me out today."

Paul met her gaze for the first time. "Because," he said clearly, "I think I've learned how to value and measure and weigh. I know what's important to me now and what isn't. And there you have it. If you want to turn the tables on me—and walk out right this minute, you can have the last laugh, a long, loud one."

"I could never laugh at you. I never have." A slight, barely audible catch in her voice hinted that her calm was only surface deep.

"Please, will you forgive me?" Paul had difficulty in speaking and wanted to kick himself. At this moment, of all times in his life, he should have been master of himself and of the situation. "Helga, I want to marry you. I want you as my wife more than I've ever wanted anything."

She lowered her head again, and he could only see the top of her blonde head. For an instant he thought she was crying, but when she spoke her voice was clear. "Are you sure, Paul? Truly sure? You see, I'm not a very modern girl. Oh, I'm emancipated, but I don't believe that freedom has given women the license to become promiscuous. I intend to be married just once, and to stay married all of my days. I can only be married to a man I love, and to love him I must honor him and his principles."

Grey flecks in the marble of the table-top seemed to dance and dart around. Paul leaned forward, and his face was only a few inches from Helga's. "I let you down," he said huskily, "so I'm afraid you can't have a very high opinion of me. But I've found my principles now. And the best way I know to put them into words is to tell you—that I love you."

"I love you, Paul."

"You do?" The little table rocked, and the coffee cups and saucers were in peril of crashing to the floor.

"I never stopped." Helga's control evaporated and there were tears in her eyes. "To me love isn't something that can be turned on and off like a faucet. Everyone has weaknesses, everyone makes mistakes and—well, even if I'd never seen you again, I couldn't have stopped loving you."

The few customers in Kranz' ice cream parlor, the waitresses and the cashier were treated to a unique spectacle as Paul stood, lifted Helga to her feet and kissed her. Never in the long history of the establishment had sedate tradition been so upset.

CHAPTER SIXTEEN

Helga's parents were the first to be told the news, and they took it quietly. Her mother wept a little and her father threw one arm around her and gripped Paul hard with the other. The time for opposition and argument, the old carpenter knew, was past and he accepted the situation solemnly but gracefully. If he felt any misgivings, he kept them to himself.

Paul and Helga both wanted to be married by a minister, but the question then came up: would they go to her church or his? Either way there would be one set of parents who would be hurt, and so they decided it would be best to have a judge perform the ceremony. This was a time when they needed to be sensible, and they were intent on erasing obstacles, not on creating new ones.

Helga began an intensive apartment hunt almost at once, and on the first Saturday after she and Paul had come together again, when they both enjoyed a day off from work, they spent all morning and the better part of the afternoon searching for a place to live. Almost without discussion they settled on the near North Side as the part of the city on which they concentrated. Neither had ever lived in this district, which was within easy walking distance of the Loop, and by unspoken consent they seemed to feel that their future would be less complicated if they began their married life in a section where neither had known close social ties.

Both of them realized that their union would be a rather unusual one, and although they said almost nothing to each other about the special problems that would inevitably arise, they were nonetheless conscious that they were going to face a series of intricate difficulties that most newlyweds did not encounter. First on the list, of course, were Paul's parents and what to do about them, but he avoided the subject on the few occasions that Helga ventured a tentative remark, and she finally dropped the matter. It was enough, in the flush of romantic excitement and activity, to feel confident that everything could and would be worked out.

Paul deliberately told his family nothing, preferring to wait until all plans were set, and he threw himself into the arranging of details with furious energy. His first act was to withdraw two hundred and fifty dollars from his savings account, and from a wholesale jeweler who was related to a fellow rewrite man at the Express he bought Helga a one-karat square-cut diamond as an engagement ring. The solitaire was mounted in a plain setting of platinum, and the evening he gave it to Helga was an occasion neither would ever forget. He had intended to present the ring to her over a candle-lit dinner table, but the little box burned a hole in his pocket, and when they were setting out in his car, he took the box from his pocket and handed it abruptly to her. Without a word, she opened it and gasped with delight. He kissed her and then they both laughed at the unromantic setting in a car under a streetlight. The romantic dinner-table atmosphere subsequently proved to be decidedly anticlimactic.

One afternoon Helga telephoned Paul in considerable excitement to say she had learned of an apartment on Elm Street that sounded perfect, and he met her there immediately after work. The place was even better than they had hoped to find:

the building itself was quiet and dignified, boasted a self-service elevator, a part-time doorman whose very presence would discourage burglars, and was equipped with such modern features as individual incinerators for garbage disposal, basement laundry facilities, and a private parking area in an adjacent vacant lot.

No couple could have asked for more than the apartment itself offered. The exposures were east and north, there were plenty of windows to insure air and light, and the management agreed to decorate with two coats of paint in any colors Helga chose. There was an unusually large living room, a spacious bedroom and a compact, utilitarian kitchen. Paul was quickly satisfied, and when Helga found that closet space was more than adequate, she put her stamp of approval on the place, too. There was only one fly in the ointment, and that was the rental of sixty-five dollars per month. Paul was afraid his salary wouldn't stretch, but he signed a two-year lease all the same. They had seen a dozen or more apartments and the place on Elm Street was the first to which they both felt drawn, so he decided to allow the financial future to take care of itself. This problem, too, was resolved with unexpected speed, but the solution became the grounds for the only real disruption of pre-marital harmony.

The storm blew up as the result of a brief talk Paul had with the City Editor. He asked Mr. Austin to allow him to take his two-week vacation in the immediate future instead of waiting until summer and explained, in confidence, that he was going to be married. To his intense gratification and surprise, his superior promptly raised his salary by twenty dollars to the more than respectable sum of seventy-five dollars per week.

There was no longer any reason why Helga needed to keep on working, and Paul told her so. She demurred and said she wanted to continue with her job, at least for a time, but he refused to listen to her reasons and informed her flatly that his wife was not going to work. The discussion ended on a distinct note of strain, but Helga was eventually forced to give in, for Paul was adamant.

A judge of the Municipal Court, Andrew McCloskey, about whom Paul had written a number of flattering articles, readily agreed to perform the wedding ceremony in his chambers, and Jim Haskell, an old friend with whom Paul lunched one day and who was told of the forthcoming marriage after being sworn to secrecy, immediately offered his lakeside lodge in northern Wisconsin as a honeymoon cottage. Then, one memorable noon, Paul met Helga and they went together to the Marriage License Bureau at the County Building and filled out the necessary forms. Both of them felt strangely shy after they had procured the necessary document, and they were silent for some minutes as they walked hand-in-hand up Clark Street afterwards.

Helga's mood changed subtly, and Paul could feel her growing tension in the grip of her fingers. He glanced down at her inquiringly, and saw she was frowning. "You can't wait any longer, darling," she said abruptly. "You've got to tell your family now."

"Yes, I suppose I do," he agreed uncomfortably.

"Tonight?"

"Okay, tonight."

"Do you want me to be there with you when you do it, Paul?"

"No, I prefer to tell them alone. I'm not sure how they'll—anyway, I think it's better if I just handle it myself."

Helga squeezed his hand and they said no more, but both were tense that evening throughout dinner, and as soon as they finished eating Helga murmured something about having to join her mother to do some sewing on her trousseau. Paul drove her home, and neither made any reference to what loomed directly ahead until, as they were parting, Helga asked Paul to telephone her later in the evening and he promised that he would.

When he arrived at his family's house, both Gordon and Molly were in the living room, but Marcia, fortunately, was not there. His parents greeted him with quick smiles, and both were obviously so pleased to see him and to assume that he had chosen to spend at least a part of his evening with them that he felt a twinge of guilt. He sauntered into the room, but remained standing as Gordon tossed aside his copy of the current issue of The Literary Digest. Molly was darning socks, a chore she always performed herself and refused to delegate to servants, and Paul's discomfort grew more intense when he saw that at the moment she was mending one of his.

Gordon, who seemed for some unaccountable reason to look more tired and drawn each day, made an effort to sound sociable and hearty. "Look who's here, Mother," he said. "Where have you been keeping yourself lately, Paul?" His searching eyes contradicted his jocularity.

"I'll tell you about it." Paul's mouth felt dry and he rocked back and forth on his heels, suddenly unable to stand still.

Something in his tone made Molly look up, and she dropped the sock and darning-egg into her sewing basket. "You're all right, dear?"

"I've never been better in my life," Paul replied with far more vigor than the question warranted. He smiled with an effort. "I hope you're going to be free, both of you, next Friday. A week from tomorrow at twelve noon."

They stiffened, though neither of them knew it. "What will happen then?" Gordon inquired cautiously.

"There's going to be a wedding in the private chambers of Judge McCloskey. Miss Helga Bjornson is going to marry Mr. Paul Dawson. R.S.V.P." One look at their stricken, incredulous faces was enough, and his attempt at humor seemed in the worst possible taste. "There'll be nobody there except you—

and Helga's folks," he added hastily. "We don't want anyone else."

Molly said nothing, but jumped to her feet and raced from the room, weeping silently. For several seconds Gordon did not appear to have heard; he eyed Paul with what seemed to be a curious detachment, and when he spoke his voice was quietly, unemotionally conversational. "Do you think you're doing the right thing?"

"It's right, Dad. I know it's right."

Again there was a silence. Then Gordon picked up his magazine, folded it with meticulous care and tucked it under his arm. Without a word he started toward the stairs, then paused and turned as he reached the archway at the far end of the living room. "I don't agree," he said in the same dead, flat voice. "I think you're wrong. I think you're making the greatest mistake of your life."

He disappeared and Paul was alone in the room. It was hard to realize that he had broken the news at last, that whatever might happen now would be an aftermath and that the peak of the storm itself had passed. Very slowly he walked to the telephone in the front hall closet, and in a voice remarkably like his father's he gave Helga a verbatim report of what had just happened. Then he climbed the stairs to his own room and sat down in his easy chair.

This furniture that had so long been his actually belonged to his parents, of course, and he had no claim on any of it, he thought. He would miss the chair, his desk, everything in the room. Sometime in the next day or two he'd have to start packing his personal belongings and arrange to have them shipped up to the apartment, but that could wait a bit longer. Certainly he felt in no mood for any such activity tonight.

For a short time he heard the sound of voices from the other end of the corridor, principally the sustained, angry mutter of his father. Then all became silent again, and Paul continued to sit, unaware of the passage of time. Apparently Marcia had been told the news, for she appeared unexpectedly in the doorway, a red-checked wool bathrobe over her flannel pajamas. There were no greys in her uncomplicated life; the blacks were as sharp as the whites; at this instant she hated her brother with every ounce of her being.

"You're a fine one," she declared, her voice harsh and grating and surprisingly mature. Then she flounced off down the corridor and slammed her own door to emphasize her feelings.

It was time, Paul thought, to turn in. He felt no bitterness toward Marcia, nor, at the moment, did he resent his parents' attitude. He was proud, not ashamed of what he was doing, and it was they and not he who would have to make the adjustments. He stood, and as he started to remove his jacket he heard the soft patter of slippered feet on the hall carpet. He hesitated, and Molly stood in the frame clutching her silk dressing gown about her, her eyes red.

"May I come in for a minute, dear?"

"You bet." On sudden impulse Paul crossed the room to her, hugged her tightly and kissed her forehead. His mother didn't seem to notice.

"There are a great many things I'm not going to say," she announced as she settled herself in Paul's armchair, bobbing her head up and down vigorously as though to remind herself that she intended to remain calm and sensible and practical. "It's really going to be—in a week, Paul?"

"One week from tomorrow, at noon." He loosened his necktie and leaned against his dresser. Watchful and wary, he was uncertain what attitude she was going to take.

"Under the circumstances and considering everything," Molly said thoughtfully, "it's wise, I suppose, to hold a private civil ceremony, although I'm sure Dr. Gates will be hurt that he hasn't been asked to officiate." She paused for a moment, but her son made no comment. "What sort of plans are her parents making for a reception afterwards? Helga's parents." She seemed to have difficulty in speaking the name of her future daughter-in-law.

"There won't be any reception, Mother. Jim Haskell is lending us his lodge up in Wisconsin, and we'll drive straight up there after the wedding. We'll be gone for a couple of weeks. And when we come back, we're taking a place on Elm Street. If you'd like to see it, we'd enjoy taking you up there over the weekend."

Molly could think of only one aspect at a time, and her mind was not on apartments. "Your aunts will be dreadfully insulted if they aren't there to see you married."

"They'll get over it," Paul replied with unnecessarily brutal candor. "And I don't think they'll mind as much as all that."

"But your sisters will. Surely you want Marcia there. And you could postpone the wedding, couldn't you, until Betsy comes home for her spring vacation next month?"

"We could not postpone it, Marcia isn't invited because we've decided we want only our parents, and if either of my sisters objects, she can get even with me by not inviting me to her wedding when the time comes." This sniping, Paul thought, only created antagonism, so he softened at once. "Try to look at it our way, Mother. Helga and I have had a pretty tough row to hoe. Her folks aren't—well, you don't know them. So we want as little fuss and embarrassment as possible. After all, the basic idea is to get married, not to hold a pagan festival."

Part of what he said seemed to make sense, and Molly's gloom dissipated somewhat. "There will still have to be a reception," she said briskly.

By exerting tremendous will power Paul succeeded in hiding his elation. In effect his mother was admitting defeat; she was no longer opposing the marriage itself, apparently realizing that such a stand would be unsuccessful. So if it made her happy to quibble over unimportant details, Paul was ready to humor her. "There's only one thing that stands in the way of a reception," he said gently. "Helga's father doesn't have the kind of money it would cost to toss a big shindig."

"It needn't be anything fancy, you know. Just a simple, quiet—"

"Mother, he's a carpenter. And he's had some lean times. Your cook and your chauffeur have averaged higher wages than he's been paid in the past four or five years."

Molly would absorb these facts later; right now she had a specific goal in mind, and she wasn't to be put off. "I wouldn't dream of asking Mr. and Mrs. Bjornson to bear the expense," she said firmly. "That never crossed my mind. I can reserve one of the private rooms at the Club with no trouble at all, and we can have the chef there attend to the catering and—"

"No, Mother." Their eyes met and Paul saw how wrong he had been to assume that she was accepting his marriage to Helga without any further struggle. All she had been saying was a thin facade, but when it was ripped away her hostility was still there, stubborn and unyielding and self-righteous.

"I was hoping," she said, speaking rapidly, "that we could salvage at least the—the outward appearances of respectability. I was hoping we could at least present a certain picture to our friends of a conventional and good marriage. But if you insist on shocking the world—"

"I'm not interested in shocking anyone. All I care about is marrying Helga. And if it's of any interest to you, Mother, I don't give a hang about all the 'right' gestures to appease all the 'right' people. I know it's going to be a good marriage, and that's enough for me."

Molly had the last word. Standing, she moved with great dignity to the door, seemed on the verge of breaking into tears but conquered the urge. "Your father," she said emphatically, quoting the final authority, "does not think it will be a good marriage."

* * *

The day of the wedding seemed in many respects like any other. Marcia went off to school at the usual time, Gordon drove to his office after breakfast, having arranged with Molly to meet her at Judge McCloskey's chambers, and Molly took the newspapers to her own room, where she could read them at her leisure over a second cup of coffee. Paul, telling himself repeatedly that he was not at all excited, deliberately waited until everyone else had cleared out of the dining room before going down for breakfast, then discovered he had no appetite whatsoever and was forced to reject the hot cereal, sausages and eggs that Delcie offered to him.

He finished packing the last of his belongings in the suitcase he was taking up to Wisconsin; all of his other clothes had gone off to the apartment two days previous. He had no idea what had happened to them there, for all that was Helga's department. She had quit her job, and had spent most of her time haunting second-hand stores for furniture, and when she hadn't been out shopping she had been at the apartment, arranging and unpacking and supervising the activities of the truckers who arrived daily with a new load of purchases.

Paul felt a little removed from the house-decorating sphere; all he knew was that he had cashed in seven hundred and fifty dollars worth of bonds, which Helga protested was too much, and he was leaving the details to her. As a matter of fact he hadn't even seen most of the items she had bought, but he was sure he would be satisfied. Helga was content, and that was what counted most.

He shaved with the utmost care, but managed to nick his face three times, and as he dressed he tried to control his growing nervousness. He remembered all the old jokes about bridegrooms wanting to run away, to disappear somewhere during the final hours before their weddings, and he grinned feebly at himself in the mirror over his dresser. Suddenly, inexplicably, he felt very lonely. The whole atmosphere was wrong, he told himself angrily, and it was the family's fault.

Marcia, who had been surly and uncommunicative, had merely poked her head in the door to call, "Good luck, congratulations," before she had hurried off to school, and his mother and father had been positively phlegmatic. In fact their politeness during the entire past week had been nerve-racking. Helga had recognized Paul's hurt, of course, and two evenings ago she had said that his parents' hostility was temporary and would surely dissolve. He clung to that thought, even though he didn't actually believe it and suspected that Helga didn't, either.

Now, glancing at his watch, he thought he would phone Helga, just to make sure she was all right, but at that moment Delcie tapped on his door and, opening it, handed him a telegram. Ripping open the blue-and-white Postal Telegraph envelope, Paul saw it was a message from Betsy, the first word he'd had from her since he had written her a brief note telling her his plans.

"NEVER THOUGHT I'D LIVE TO SEE THE DAY," he read. "YOUNG HERO VOTED MOST LIKELY TO SUCCEED LEAVES ANCESTRAL HEARTH. WOULD FIND DETAILS OF DRAMA MUCH MORE FASCINATING THAN CURRENT STUDY OF 'BEOWULF.' JUST MY LUCK TO MISS YEAR'S BIGGEST CIRCUS. SAVE SOME POPCORN AND SPUN SUGAR CANDY FOR ME. BETSY."

Even after reading the wire three times, Paul could not be sure whether the elder of his sisters was being facetious at his expense or whether she was showing guarded sympathy for him. He hoped she approved, as he'd always been much closer to Betsy than to Marcia, but he was afraid that like the rest she would consider him a traitor to the family, to their traditions. Stuffing the paper into his inner jacket pocket, he made a mental note to be sure to show it to Helga. It was her right to know that the enemy on the other side of the barricades had, it seemed, gained a new recruit.

Hurrying downstairs to the phone, he put in his call, and much to his surprise Helga herself answered the ring. "Good morning," Paul said. "By a process of elimination and identification it may be possible for you to guess that this is Mr. Dawson."

She laughed and tried to sound stern. "You shouldn't have called me. We aren't supposed to talk to each other this morning."

"Who says?"

"Superstition, that's who. It's supposed to mean bad luck."

"Would you like to know what Paul the Dauntless has to say to that? And in a single word of one syllable? I quote. Pooh." He waited until her laugh subsided, then asked tenderly, "You all right, honey?"

"Fine. I guess. I'm not thinking very coherently this morning."

"How very strange. Unusual symptoms. How's your pulse, ma'm?"

"Beating like mad. Just exactly like yours. And if I stand here spouting nonsense when I still have a million things to do, I'll be late for my own wedding."

"And that would never do," Paul agreed with mock solemnity. "Helga," he said abruptly, "I love you."

"I love you." She seemed to be standing very close to the telephone, and he could hear the sound of her breathing plainly.

There was a sudden silence; both were swept away by the emotions of the moment. Paul was the first to recover, and he tried to sound crisp and authoritative. "My future wife," he said, "doesn't permit me to hold long telephone conversations, so I'll have to say goodbye to you now."

"An hour and a half from now, darling."

"You may consider it a date. That's final, and I give you my word on it." Paul hung up and stepped out of the closet, smiling softly to himself.

Molly, still in her dressing gown, was just inside the entrance to the living room, rearranging ash trays and statuettes on a table. Obviously she had been waiting for him, and Paul's glow of intimacy with Helga diminished. "Why, you're all dressed and I haven't even started yet, Paul."

"A stitch in time saves nine, but haste makes waste," Paul replied, wishing she'd come to the point of whatever she intended to say to him.

"I was just wondering, Paul—." Molly started to speak, then broke off and pursed her lips.

"Yes, Mother?"

"Wouldn't it be more convenient for you to ride downtown with me in the big car?" Apparently she couldn't quite bring herself to mention Judge McCloskey's chambers by name.

He thought it was probably very natural for a mother to want to spend the last minutes of her son's bachelorhood with him, and he made a real effort to be gentle. "That wouldn't work. Right after the ceremony Helga and I are driving north, so I've got to have my car handy."

"Yes, of course. How stupid of me. I wasn't thinking." Molly started to turn away, but Paul put his arms around her shoulders. "Why don't you drive with me instead, and let your car pick you up later on?"

"That wouldn't be practical, dear. I called your father a little while ago, and instead of meeting me at—City Hall, I'm to stop at his office for him first."

"Sure, Mother. That's the way you'll have to handle it, then." He could feel her trembling, and he was afraid she would start to cry any second. "Just so we all get there, huh?" Never had he tried so hard to sound gay and light, and never had he failed so miserably.

All of Molly's fears and hurts were reflected in her eyes as she gazed up at her son. But she, too, knew that this was the most inopportune of all moments to reveal her doubts, her grievances and her worries about the future relationships between those she loved most. "Paul," she said. "Oh, Paul." Reaching up, she took his face in her hands and kissed him.

For no good reason he wanted to break down and weep. Instead he took refuge in gruff, masculine pragmatism. "Helga says you stopped by our apartment for a few minutes yesterday, while she was there fixing it up." He appreciated the gesture and guessed it had been made at considerable cost to her pride.

"I just happened to be in the neighborhood. It's a darling little place, Paul."

"Glad you like it." He interpreted her remark as condescending, and immediately stiffened. Sheer curiosity, not love, had prompted her visit to the apartment, he thought. And that reminded him of something that had been bothering him for several days: as yet there was no sign of a wedding present from his parents. He had no interest in receiving a valuable gift, but he saw the complete lack of a gesture as an indication of displeasure. He wanted to ask his mother if she had seen the chest that Mr. Bjornson had made with his own hands and had presented to his daughter and her husband-to-be as a token of his love. But pride interfered, and he clamped his jaws shut.

Molly had no idea of what was going through his mind, but at this moment he looked so much like his father, and yet so different, too, that she could no longer hold back her tears. "I pray for you, Paul. I pray for your happiness," she said.

CHAPTER SEVENTEEN

At one corner of the long, highly polished oak desk was a bronze plaque which read, "Andrew T. McCloskey, Judge, Municipal Court." An American flag dominated the space behind the desk, two walls were lined with law books that showed a faint coat of grime, and on the south exposure the spring sunshine streamed in through a pair of windows in need of washing. A green twill carpet covered the floor, and on a slightly dusty oak conference table surrounded by straight-backed chairs were a large thermos jug and several water glasses. Two trays heaped high with papers stood on the desk, and prominently displayed on the telephone table were autographed pictures of the President of the United States, the Governor of Illinois and the Mayor of Chicago. In all, the setting was dignified, utilitarian, and bleak.

The Judge was still on the bench, and Paul stood alone in the office, conscious of the clatter of typewriters in the outer office of the bailiff. He looked at his watch five times in as many minutes, restrained himself from smoking a cigarette and began to pace up and down. It served him right for arriving too early, of course, and he wished he had stalled a little longer at home. The thought of "home" was wryly amusing; from this time forward his parents' house was not his. He would need to acclimate himself to the fact he lived on Elm Street.

He wandered to the windows and looked across Clark Street, only half-seeing the huge electric sign on the Grand Opera House. Neither then nor later could he have told anyone what was playing at the theatre. He turned as he heard the door open behind him, and the Judge's secretary, a rather vapid mouse-blonde, ushered in his parents.

Gordon said, "Well, Paul," and then betrayed his emotions by removing his glasses and wiping them meticulously. Molly did not trust herself to words, and instead simply tried to smile. It crossed Paul's mind that it was tragic, in this moment, that he and his parents had nothing to say to each other. It was some comfort to him, however, to realize that the occasion was of sufficient importance to his mother so that she bought a new outfit. As a matter of fact, she looked particularly smart in a dress and jacket of thin blue wool with her furs draped casually over her shoulders.

The silence became increasingly long and uncomfortable, then the door opened again and Helga's parents were ushered in. Paul, already unbearably nervous, thought that his mother-in-law to-be looked like Delcie on her day off in a print dress, old-fashioned short coat with velvet collar and a black straw hat which perched on the top of her head. Olaf Bjornson, although he appeared out of place in a shiny blue suit and stiff, high collar with a thin, string necktie, was more at his ease than anyone. He smiled quietly and held out his hand to Gordon, and Paul, who had felt himself incapable of speech or action, pulled himself together.

"Mr. and Mrs. Bjornson—my mother and father, Mr. and Mrs. Dawson." Even as he said the words, their strange stiffness increased his discomfort, and as he watched his elders solemnly shaking hands with each other, he had to control a wild and stupid impulse to laugh.

"In Sweden we have a saying," Bjornson remarked with seeming casualness. "When the sun shines on a wedding, that marriage will succeed."

Gordon had never looked firmer. "I hope you're right," he said bluntly.

There was an instant's pause, and Molly moved in smoothly. "Has Helga come with you?" she asked, smiling.

"She has gone with one of the young ladies of the office to paint on her face more lipstick," Mrs. Bjornson replied. "Always today the young must paint their faces."

Molly, who never wore more than a trace of light lipstick, nodded. "I know. My daughters are the same way. The little one, who's really still a child, actually gets insulted when I won't allow her out of the house with that stuff smeared all over her face."

"My Helga never puts on her face too much," Mr. Bjornson intervened. "My Helga is a fine girl."

"There's no better boy than Paul anywhere," Gordon responded quickly, an undisguised note of belligerence in his tone.

"Both are good," the old carpenter agreed, his eyes solemn. "And if each truly loves the other, that will be the most good."

Paul could only wish that Helga would hurry and appear; he felt awkward, powerless, and he was suffused by a fear, senseless yet potent, that a violent argument would break out at any second. His heart leaped when the door opened again, but the newcomer was Judge McCloskey, who beamed impersonally as he removed his black robe.

"Well! Are we all set?"

"Not quite, Your Honor," Paul said with a shaky laugh. "The bride will be here in a minute." He proceeded with introductions, carefully presenting Helga's parents first.

The telephone rang, and the Judge picked up the instrument, frowning faintly as though to indicate that calls were inappropriate when he was about to perform a wedding ceremony.

Then he became involved in an animated conversation and, speaking in low tones, turned his face toward a wall in order to insure greater privacy. As he spoke he ran the fingers of his free hand through his unruly white hair, and occasionally he rubbed the side of his broad nose reflectively. Suddenly he spun around and his eyes, as blue as those of the Bjornsons, were twinkling. "That's a great story, Dave. Save the rest of it for lunch, huh? I've got a wedding on my hands. Yeah, young fellow from the Express."

At this moment Helga entered the room, and Paul caught his breath. Never had he seen anyone so radiant, so alive, and he forgot everyone and everything else. He knew she had been working hard making her wedding dress, a gown of cream-colored silk, and the results were worth the effort. On her left shoulder she wore a spray of three white orchids, the largest Paul had been able to find, and she looked like what she was, an ecstatically happy girl.

He hurried to her and kissed her gently, but neither spoke; at this moment neither was capable of speech. Paul's parents approached, and as Molly gingerly kissed Helga's cheek, Judge McCloskey hung up the phone. "If we can get started here," he said jovially, "I can kiss the bride in a few minutes myself." He laughed as Paul started to introduce him to Helga. "I know who she is, my boy. I've been ringmaster at enough of these circuses to know the bride when I see her."

Gordon tried to echo Judge McCloskey's laughter, but there was a forced, hollow ring to the sound. No one else as much as smiled, and Mr. Bjornson shifted his weight from one foot to the other and back again, while his wife looked faintly concerned and Molly studied the grain of her alligator handbag. Paul and Helga glanced at each other, and again there was an awkward moment of silence, which the Judge broke.

"Gather around the desk," he said briskly. "Move in, all of you. I'll have you two youngsters right here, if you please."

[214]

There was a shuffling, and Paul, standing very erect, took his place beside Helga at one edge of the desk. Her face was very pale, and Paul wondered if she might be trembling as hard as he was, yet somehow not showing it. Then, as the Judge opened a small, thin book, he forgot everything but the ceremony itself.

His Honor read for several minutes in a dry, rapid monotone, and at times it was difficult to hear his words. Then he paused and said, loudly and clearly, "will you, Paul, take this woman to be your wife, will you love her and protect her and cherish her, in sickness and in health, so long as you two shall live?"

His reply, "I will," came out loud and clear.

Now it was Helga's turn to be questioned and to respond; Paul relaxed slightly and let his left hand stray to the pocket of his jacket. There he groped for a moment, then found the plain band of white gold that Helga had selected three days ago. An incongruous thought flashed through his mind: it would have been nice if he had asked his father to carry the ring for him. Then he forgot the intrusion of his conscience, for the Judge asked him to place the ring on Helga's finger. He was mildly amused to discover that his own hand was visibly shaking.

"Under the powers vested in me by the Corporation of the City of Chicago," Judge McCloskey said, "I pronounce you man and wife." No one moved, and he grinned. "If you don't kiss her first, I will."

Helga and Paul turned to each other, but their kiss was shy and quiet, almost no more than a token touching of lips. This was a sacred moment, the most significant in their lives, and their feeling of awe was intense.

They parted, and Paul whispered, "I love you," in Helga's ear. She looked at him, and her eyes said more than she could have expressed in mere words. As they turned, a sudden babble of conversation welled up, and Paul was astonished to see that not only were both mothers crying, as he had more or less expected, but that Gordon's cheeks were wet, too. Only Olaf

Bjornson, fingering the top button of his old-fashioned jacket, was dry-eyed.

Molly, first hugging Paul fiercely and then Helga more cautiously, wept openly now, but Bertha Bjornson managed to control her tears. Everyone seemed to talk at once, but no one listened to anyone else. Finally the voice of Judge McCloskey cut through the din. "You folks stay as long as you like," he declared. "But don't mind if I run along. I have a lunch date with a Congressman, and you know how those fellows are. Touchy." He shook hands all around, then dashed out.

Gordon, at his social best, tried gallantly to create a festive atmosphere. "Why don't we all go out for lunch together some place or other?" he suggested.

Helga brightened and looked as though she might agree, but Paul answered before she had a chance to speak. "Thanks all the same, Dad, but we've got to hit the road. We have a four hundred mile drive ahead of us."

"That's reasonable enough," his father replied, showing no outward regret. "We'll do it when you youngsters come back into town. Is that a date?"

The Bjornsons, very much ill at ease, could only nod, but Helga was equal to the occasion. "It's a date," she said firmly, and smiled up at her new father-in-law.

He grinned back at her, and for an instant there seemed to be an understanding, a rapport between them, and Gordon's expression indicated that he accepted her for her own sake. Then he apparently remembered that this was the girl who had irrevocably widened the breach between him and the son in whom he had placed so much hope, and he stiffened. "I guess we'd better be on our way then, Molly." He turned in polite inquiry to Helga's parents. "We have our car downstairs. Can we give you folks a lift anywhere?"

"You are kind. But thank you, no," Olaf Bjornson replied softly, offering no fuller explanation for his rejection.

Molly touched her husband lightly on the arm. "You're forgetting something, dear," she said meaningfully.

"So I am." Gordon struck himself lightly across the forehead, then reached into his inner pocket and pulled out his wallet. Fumbling in it for an instant, he drew out an oblong piece of paper and handed it to Helga. "This will help to take care of the furniture. It's for both of you," he added abruptly, his voice suddenly husky and his manner awkward.

"It's with our love, children," Molly amended gently.

There were tears in Helga's eyes as she hugged her parents-in-law, and not until she finished was Paul able to glance over her shoulder and see the size of the check. It was made out in the amount of one thousand dollars, and the generosity of his mother and father overwhelmed him.

It would be ridiculous to behave like a small child and cry, he told himself as he kissed his mother fiercely, then, for the first time in years, threw his arms around his father. It was a considerable effort to say anything, and "Thank you," was the best he could muster, in spite of his realization that the expression was inadequate.

"Look, Pa!" Helga exclaimed breathlessly. "Isn't this wonderful, Ma?"

The money as such made no impression on the old carpenter, but he bowed with quaint formality to Molly, then patted Gordon on the shoulder, a familiarity that even close golfing companions would have been hesitant to attempt. " 'He who is truly generous is truly wise.' This is a proverb which all in Sweden know. And I know now that this marriage will succeed. One who is the son of such loving parents must himself be loving."

Bertha Bjornson wanted to say something, too, but she had to struggle for a few seconds before she could find the words she wanted. "For our daughter," she said at last, "we thank you."

There was no adequate answer, and while Molly searched for something gracious and not condescending, Paul concluded that it was time to leave. "Mrs. Dawson," he said, taking Helga's hand, "would you like to come with me to the north woods?"

"I think I could be persuaded," Helga said in the same tone, her grip tightening in his.

There was a final flurry of goodbye kisses, and Molly once more began to weep. Paul and Helga started out of the door, then paused in the frame and looked back. Their parents stood clustered together, watching them, and the memory of these couples who had so little in common was strong in both their minds as they rode down in an elevator crowded with city and Cook County employees and walked through the cavernous lobby of the building. Then, suddenly, as they reached the street, the realization struck them that they were alone.

They halted, and Paul would have taken Helga into his arms but she evaded him, blushing. "Not right out here in public, darling!" she protested.

"A man is privileged to kiss his wife any place, any time. Which reminds me. Did Judge McCloskey give me the certificate?"

"Yes, Paul. You put it in your pocket. That one."

"Oh, good. Now, as I was saying—"

"Wait until we get to the car, at least. Where is it?"

"Mrs. Dawson, you're going to get kissed right here and now." To the delight of a trio of stenographers who had just come out of City Hall, he accompanied his words with vigorous action.

Then, laughing a little breathlessly, he tucked Helga's arm into his and started south on Clark Street. "The car is right down near the corner. I used my press card so we wouldn't get a ticket. By the way, I ought to change the insurance on the car if you're going to drive. And that reminds me—do you drive? I've never thought to ask you."

"Where in the world would I have had a car to drive?"

"Okay, then, I'll teach you. Though it's only fair to warn you

[218]

that more than one promising marriage has been busted up that way."

"I'll take a chance, darling." Helga stopped and waited while Paul unlocked the door, then smiled at him as he helped her in.

He walked around and had to tap on the window so she would raise the lock button on his side; she seemed to be daydreaming. He climbed in, throwing his topcoat into the back seat, and as he started the engine he noticed that Helga was carefully unpinning her corsage. "Hey! What do you think you're doing, Mrs. Dawson?"

"This is too beautiful, Mr. Dawson. I can't wear it on the road."

"You put it back on you this instant, ma'm. Flowers are meant to be worn."

Unexpectedly, Helga turned scarlet. "But every car we pass, any place we stop to eat—they'll all know I'm a bride."

"And so you are, honey. The loveliest bride there's ever been in all this world."

The start of their journey was delayed by another kiss, this one infinitely sweeter and more tender.

CHAPTER EIGHTEEN

The blue-green little lake sparkled beneath a dazzling sun, and the budding trees of the woods that fringed the shoreline were mirrored in the still water. Somewhere high in a tangle of spruce and oak and pine a bird chirped merrily and talkatively, then fell silent again. There was a rustle in the underbrush as a small animal, a rabbit or a chipmunk, perhaps, scurried toward some hidden destination. The air was fresh and clean, with just enough nip left in it, despite the warmth of the sun, to serve as a reminder that winter was not far past.

After the noise of the city, the quiet seemed to be all the more intense, and the sound of water dripping from Paul's paddle as he lazily propelled a canoe across the lake was loud and distinct. Helga was curled up in the stern of the little craft, her heavy wool skirt tucked around her legs, and she let the fingers of her left hand trail in the water. Neither of the honeymooners had spoken for some minutes; both were supremely content.

Their eyes met and held, and their whole world was made up of each other. "Don't freeze your hand in that water, honey," Paul said.

"I won't. It feels nice."

"Just be sure, that's all. This isn't swimming weather. And that hand belongs to me."

"Yes, darling. It belongs to you."

Again they looked at each other; Paul stopped paddling and allowed the canoe to drift. "I never knew there could be anyone as sweet and as wonderful as you, Helga. If I'd known marriage would be like this, I'd have married you years and years ago."

She laughed, and all the depth and intensity of her feelings showed in her face. "Just think of all the decades we've wasted."

"We'll make up for all of them." An idea crossed his mind, and he glanced at his watch. "Congratulations, Mrs. Dawson."

"For what, darling?"

"It's now our anniversary."

"Is it?"

"Yes, honey. We've now been married for twenty-four whole hours."

"It seems as though we've been married—forever."

Paul bent toward her after first securing the paddle beneath his seat. "Lean forward, honey," he said.

Helga complied, though not understanding for a moment, and Paul kissed her, gently at first, then with mounting fervor. His hands gripped her slender waist, and she curled her arms around his neck. At last Helga disengaged herself.

"We'll tip the canoe over," she said breathlessly. "And then we'll have a swim, whether this is the season for it or not."

Paul wanted to hold her again, but he took up the paddle. "You're right. There's a time and place for everything. This is the time—but not the place."

He steered for the shore. They didn't speak, but the current between them was strong. After what seemed much more than the actual ten minutes, Paul swung toward a little dock that had been built mid-way between the honeymoon cabin and a sturdy boathouse. Still sitting, he made the canoe secure, then climbed onto the dock and helped Helga ashore.

The moment her feet touched the timbers he drew her toward him, and she moved into his arms eagerly. They kissed again, fiercely, and their bodies pressed together. Their ardor was natural and frank, sweet and unrestrained. At last they turned, then moved toward the cabin with their arms around each other.

* * *

A huge single room made up the whole of the attractive log cabin. Off one corner was the bathroom, which, architecturally, was virtually an annex; the rest of the space, almost as wide as it was long, was used for sleeping, eating, cooking and sitting. One of its principal charms came from its many windows, which were hung with red and white checked gingham curtains, and which on one side framed a magnificent view of the lake, whose shore was no more than fifteen yards from the steps leading up to the building's only door. On the other sides Paul and Helga could look out on the deep forests of pine and birch and maple and spruce, and here and there little paths lost themselves in the deep shadows.

The furniture was simple but pleasant and comfortable. In the center of the room were two wicker arm chairs, each holding a thick red and white checked cushion, and between them stood a table on which stood a tall reading lamp with a wrought iron base; electricity had been installed in the cabin within the past year. In one corner was the large bed, with a window above it, and on the opposite wall, near the sink, was an old-fashioned black pot-bellied stove, which was more picturesque in appearance than it was convenient for cooking. However, Helga, whose capabilities with a skillet were apparently limitless, made no complaints.

In front of the stove were a gleaming scrubbed pine table and four chairs, above which, from a low beam, hung a quaint lantern which gave off a gentle glow. The walls of natural, unpainted wood were dotted with an assortment of fishing rods, tackle and racks of colorful feathered fishing flies, and at irregularly spaced intervals there were thick wooden pegs for hanging clothing. And completing the arrangement, the better part of the pine floor was covered by a green and yellow rug of woven hemp.

The overall atmosphere was masculine rather than feminine, but Helga's presence made the difference, an emphatic difference. Paul, who had wandered down to the crude boathouse and narrow jetty, while Helga had started breakfast preparations, opened the door and stood in the frame, sniffing appreciatively. "You didn't tell me that we're having sausages this morning," he said severely. "And you've been married for almost two weeks now, so by this time you ought to know better."

Helga, in a yellow sweater and heavy, brown tweed skirt, busied herself with a long fork and poured a measure of fat out of the frying pan. "No girl should tell a man everything she knows, not even if he's her husband," she replied demurely. "How is it out in the great big world today?"

"Swell. A little warmer than yesterday, I think." He unbuttoned the collar of his flannel shirt and, leaning against a wall as he watched her, jammed his hands into the pockets of his slacks. "Want to take another canoe ride this morning, honey?"

"I'd love to, but I know you're anxious to go into town again." Helga frowned as she expertly broke eggs into a bowl. "You said you'd like to snoop around that newspaper office some more."

"So I would. I don't actually think it's a paper I'd ever want to buy, but I'm learning plenty by asking questions. What bothers me is that you don't get any fun out of just sitting and watching a linotype machine clattering away."

"Of course I'll enjoy it, silly. If we're going to have our own newspaper in a couple of years, the more you can find out in the meantime, the better it will be for us."

Paul's mood changed and he frowned slightly. "There's plenty I want to find out, I'll say that. You remember I told

[223]

you the editor poured out his troubles to me the other day? Well, I'm not sure just what to make of it all. For instance, he said the town playground is in need of repairs and he wants to write an editorial about it. But he claims he doesn't dare, because the head of the park system, the organization that runs the playground, is also the president of the lumber yard. And it seems the lumber yard is the newspaper's biggest advertiser."

"So the editor is afraid of offending an advertiser?"

"That's it. He's told me three or four stories like that, and I'd like to dig a bit deeper. He sounds to me like the sort of a guy who's scared of his own shadow and toadies up to anybody who'll keep him safe and secure. Anyway, I want to get a better line on him."

Helga, who had learned a great deal about the world of newspapers in recent months, was beginning to develop her own ideas, but hesitated to express them. There was a moment's silence, then she decided to go ahead. "Maybe there isn't so much difference between big city and small town newspapers as you thought. I don't mean to imply," she added hastily, "that newspapers can be bought or influenced. I'm sure they can't. All I'm trying to say is that maybe the editor up here has practical problems that are as serious to him as the ones that the publisher of a big city newspaper has to face."

"Of course they're as serious." It was difficult for Paul to admit, even to himself, that his idealism had been damaged or tarnished in any way. "I simply want to satisfy myself that this guy is a coward, that's all. Then I'll have a better perspective."

It was obvious that he was disturbed, and Helga took a deliberate step to brighten the atmosphere. "I can only say that I'm delighted we're going into town. Do you want to know why?"

Paul responded instantly to her teasing though loving tone. "All right. Why?"

"Because," she said with a laugh, "I can drive the car."

He clapped his hand to his head in a mock gesture of despair. "That's what happens to an upright citizen when he gets married."

"Come again?"

"Okay. From the beginning. He sees a pretty face—"

"Thank you, darling."

"He gets dizzy, he falls for it—and wham! He can't call his soul his own any more. Even worse, he can't call his car his own."

"Your orange juice is on the table, darling."

"That's right, bribe me."

"And would you hand me a couple of plates from the cupboard, please? The big ones."

"Not without adequate payment, I won't. Payment in advance, Mrs. Dawson."

They kissed and Paul's arms tightened around her. Finally Helga broke away, laughing. "If you don't stop, breakfast will be spoiled. Of course if you like burned eggs—"

"I love 'em." He reached for her again.

"No, Paul, really. Breakfast is ready right this minute. If you want to do something constructive, why don't you start the toast?"

"There's an old saying—something about the devil finding work for idle hands—that I'm strongly inclined not to remember." Nevertheless, he obediently put two slices of toast into the machine.

Helga slid the eggs onto the plates, added the sausages which had been draining on paper and approached the table. "When do you want to leave, right after breakfast?"

"Sure, if that's okay with you. But what'll you do while I dig around at the Daily Eagle, honey?"

"Oh, I'll wander around town for a while and then join you. I'd do some marketing, but there's nothing that we need except coffee at this point. And we'll take the better part of the can

[225]

back home with us tomorrow, whatever we don't use here. But I don't want to buy anything perishable that will be left over when we'll only have three meals left here after this one."

Paul was impressed; he had never known much about the details of housekeeping, but he was sure his mother had never planned so carefully. "We'll buy you another present when we reach town," he said.

"We'll do no such thing. We've bought something for me almost every single day. Earrings and perfume—and goodness knows what not. We have a lot of expenses ahead of us, darling, and we've got to start facing the realities of existence."

"Imagine that. A female who doesn't want to be spoiled. The honeymoon is over." Paul laughed, then sobered. "You know, honey, it's hard to realize that it really will be over tomorrow. And in forty-eight hours from now, I'll be back at work."

"Me, too. When I think of all the things I've got to do to get the apartment into shape, I become positively dizzy. But the honeymoon won't be over, Paul. It'll never be over for us."

"Of course not. You know what I meant." He buttered a slice of toast and stared down at his plate, frowning.

"To be truthful with you, no. I don't."

"We've been living in the present, Helga. We haven't been exactly thinking in terms of what will face us when we get back to Chicago."

She looked across the table at him, and her concern was mirrored in her eyes. "You sound as though something worries you, darling."

"I wouldn't say I'm worried, exactly."

"Then what?"

"Oh, the complexities of family relationships."

"You make it sound as though we have ogres for parents," Helga said gently.

"Hardly that. And your folks are fine. They love you, and I'm reasonably sure they won't make any problems about

[226]

accepting me." He broke off abruptly, realizing that he was showing his fears.

She recognized his implications but was quick to refute them. "No one is going to make any problems, darling. Just you wait and see."

He had his doubts, but she was so earnest that he kept them to himself.

* * *

Rush-hour traffic was even heavier than usual; Madison Street was crowded with cars and the spring air was heavy with the fumes of gasoline. Paul, who had just thrown away a cigarette, lit another and hoped that Helga hadn't become involved in a crack-up. Maybe he shouldn't have let her take the car alone on their first day in the city; on the other hand she had navigated without difficulty when she had gone out to see her parents this noon and she had been full of confidence over her abilities when she had spoken to him on the phone just half an hour ago, so it was silly to worry. She was lucky that Illinois, unlike some other states, didn't require a driver's license. In any case, like husbands everywhere, he told himself, he was just plain stuck, waiting for his wife.

His wife. The very words gave him a pleasant glow, and he realized that he had used the phrase again and again at the office all day. "My wife says," and, "As I told my wife this morning," or, "My wife and I believe" had crept into practically every conversation he had held with his colleagues. And the knowledge that he and Helga would be going right now to his family's house gave him a feeling of proud possessiveness.

A reporter came out of the Express Building and called goodnight to Paul, who returned his wave. At that moment a horn honked lightly, and the Plymouth pulled up at the curb. "Taxi, mister?"

"Hi, honey." He hurried to the car. "Want me to drive?"

[227]

"Not unless you insist. I manage very well. I had an excellent teacher."

"Okay." He grinned as he climbed in beside her, they kissed and Helga put the car into gear and started smoothly. "Hey, you look pretty."

"Thank you, darling."

"Snappy dress."

"This is what I wore when we were married."

"I know. That's why I think it's snappy." Paul leaned back, thinking she was handling the car remarkably well. "How'd everything go today?"

"Oh, the apartment is still a shambles, darling. It'll be ages before I have everything the way I want it."

"I don't believe that for a minute. When we walked in last night it looked as though we've lived there for months."

"Gracious, Paul! I still have the kitchen shelves to line, and all the glassware and china to wash and put away, and there are books all over the place and—"

"I'll help you with the books over the weekend. Or tomorrow night. That's when we'll do it. How were your folks?"

"Just fine. They both said to give you their love, and I invited them to come up for supper on Thursday—"

"Swell."

"Ma is just the same as ever. She never changes, just never." Helga swung the car onto the Outer Drive and smiled as she started south. "Pa starts to work next week on a new job. They told him there'll be six months' work, at least."

"That's wonderful, honey."

"Oh, Pa always gets along," she said in quiet pride. "What's this party tonight all about, darling? You sounded so rushed when I spoke to you on the phone the first time that—"

"I didn't mean to. Mr. Austin wanted to see me, so I had to talk fast. But I told you all I know. The party is for Betsy. I have no idea if it's going to be family stuff, or some of her friends, or what. I don't even know if her room-mate has come out from school with her. I've been a little out of touch lately."

"Well, no matter who's there, we'll have a nice time," Helga said firmly, then launched into an account of the difficulties she had encountered in finding the type of bolt Paul hd wanted her to buy so they could double-lock the front door of their apartment.

There was so much to talk about that they reached South Shore Drive almost before they realized it, and when they pulled into the driveway of the Dawson house they saw that two other cars were already parked beside the garage. "You'd better go in there next to the Lincoln," Paul directed, "otherwise we'll block the drive. I'm not sure who owns the LaSalle over there, but the Lincoln belongs to Uncle Henry, so this is a family party, all right."

"I didn't even know you had an Uncle Henry."

"I don't." Paul reached over, turned off the ignition and pocketed the key. "I just call him Uncle Henry. Actually, neither he nor Aunt Helen is related to us. Henry Thayer is first vice president of Dad's company. They've been in business together all their lives, so they automatically show up at each other's family parties. Like ham goes with eggs." He jumped out, hurried to the other side and opened Helga's door. "What's wrong, honey?"

"Nothing." She moved a foot or two away from him on the gravel roadway.

"You mean that slightly stricken expression is natural?"

"I'm just a little nervous, meeting your sister and friends of your parents and some of your other relatives—or whoever. That's all."

"I've never heard such nonsense." Paul kissed her at the base of her throat, then took her hand and held it tightly as he led her toward the house. If he said anything more, he thought, he'd only increase her tension.

[229]

They mounted the steps and Paul reached for the brass knob, knowing the door would be unlocked as there was a party in progress. Then he stopped abruptly; this was no longer his house. He rang the doorbell, feeling a trifle awkward, and was about to mention his reactions to Helga when the door opened and Betsy was revealed in the light of the front hall.

People often said that if Betsy Dawson were four years older she could be Paul's twin. She was tall and slender, and her dark brown hair was the same shade as that of her brother, although curlier. She wore vivid lipstick which was striking against her pale skin and her dress, a bright green silk, with a full, pleated skirt, was both becoming and stylish.

Helga immediately saw one major difference between Betsy and her brother, and that was in their eyes. Paul's were wistful, and their dreaminess reflected his idealism. Betsy's, however, were alert and direct. She had somehow met the challenges that life had presented to her, and had consequently come to terms with herself; she seemed, in this first impression, to be forthright and honest.

Paul hugged her, then freed one arm and put it around Helga. "Mrs. Dawson, Miss Dawson," he said, cautioning himself that he would need to exercise self-control if Betsy treated Helga with the same reserve the rest of his family had shown.

The two girls eyed each other for a moment, and Paul wondered if they were going to bother to shake hands. His sense of apprehension increased, then a mysterious feminine current which he recognized but could not understand passed between them, and to his infinite relief they smiled and kissed each other.

"You're exactly as I imagined you'd be," Betsy said.

"I'd certainly have known you anywhere," Helga replied, her nervousness miraculously gone.

"Come on up to 'the sorority house' and powder your nose before you greet the hordes. And that'll give us a chance to get

[230]

acquainted." Betsy linked her arm companionably through that of her new sister-in-law.

"Not so fast, Cutie," Paul said. "Don't you have even one word of greeting for your distinguished older brother?"

"Of course. Hi, Ugly." Betsy turned and pinched his cheek affectionately. "How'd you ever get a girl who looks like Helga to marry you?"

"When you get to know her," Paul grinned, "you'll realize that beauty is only skin deep. The reason she married me is because she's soft in the head."

Helga immediately entered into the spirit of the moment. "I humor my husband. It prevents him from becoming violent."

"Good." Betsy nodded sagely.

All three were laughing as they moved into the house, and as Betsy led the way to the stairs Helga turned for an instant and directed a look of infinite tenderness and love at Paul. Then, as the two girls mounted the steps, chatting, he drifted toward the living room, inwardly glowing and outwardly expansive. A dozen or more people were in the room, standing about in small groups, and for the moment no one noticed Paul. He started forward, then stopped abruptly. The closest person to him was Henry Thayer, and never had he seen so startling a change in any human being.

In three months Whitmarket and Company's Senior Vice President had become an old man. His once robust frame was painfully thin, his broad shoulders drooped and his skin, which had always been ruddy, was sallow and drawn. Now, as he felt Paul's eyes on him, he glanced up, smiled wanly and walked toward the younger man with a shuffling gait.

"So you're back, are you? Where's your bride? And don't try to hide her from me, because I'll find her!" There was no vitality in the deep voice, only a husky weariness.

"Hi, Uncle Henry." Paul wanted to ask if Thayer had been ill, but decided it would be more politic to make his inquiries of others. "You bet she's here. She'll be down in a minute. How are tricks?"

"No complaints, Paul, no complaints." The older man's attempt to strike a note of hearty joviality seemed false. "You know me!"

"I'll say I do." Paul caught a glimpse of Mrs. Thayer across the room, and although "Aunt Helen" was smartly dressed in a black dinner dress, she looked weary, too, as though she had just seen her husband through a siege of illness, and Paul felt uncomfortable. The realization that a robust man who savored every moment of life could age so quickly made him insecure; in his mind Henry Thayer, like Chicago's skyline, had been solid and unchangeable.

There was no chance to dwell any longer on the matter, however, for Elsa and Mark Harper, sedate cousins of his mother's, called out greetings to him, and Marcia, who had been talking to the eleven-year-old son of the Harper household, waved casually to him. He hurried across the big living room to her, pleased to see her and forgetting his previous rancor toward her. She looked very pretty in a pink and white dress with a black velvet sash, and he intended to compliment her on her appearance. But her coolness, her deliberate remoteness, brought him up short.

"Hello, Paul. Did you have a nice trip?"

"Very nice." He wanted to lash out at her, to topple her from her pedestal of adolescent superiority, but held himself in check. "Where are Mother and Dad? I haven't seen them yet."

"Daddy's right over there." Marcia nodded in the direction of the bay windows, then turned away.

Paul paid no further attention to her and caught his father's eye; Gordon promptly broke away from a knot of male relatives and took his son's outstretched hand. "It's good to have you here, Paul."

"It's good to be here, Dad."

[232]

"How's everything?"

"Oh, fine. We're both fine." The least his father could have done, Paul thought resentfully, was to ask after Helga. "We got into town last night. It was too late to call and say hello until today."

"Yes, I got your message from Miss Keebling. Sorry I couldn't talk to you when you phoned this morning, but I was tied up."

"So I gathered. You look tired, Dad."

Gordon shrugged indifferently; he had never been one to dwell on the state of his own health. "Your mother is in the dining room, supervising things there. She's anxious to see you, I know."

"I'd better wait until Helga comes downstairs. There's this whole crowd to introduce her to."

"Your mother will be disappointed if you don't go in to say hello."

"Okay, Dad. If Helga shows up while I'm out of the room, you tell her where I am, will you?"

Paul started off to the dining room, pausing to accept the congratulations of his mother's sister, Cora Haines, an older and heavier version of Molly. Just before he reached the closed double doors he was stopped again, this time by his cousin, Richard Haines, a stolid man some ten years his senior, with whom Paul had never felt anything in common, and with whom he exchanged a few hearty but vague pleasantries.

Once more he edged toward the dining room doors, then paused and glanced briefly at the assembled guests. These were all people with whom he should share some feeling of kinship, he knew, but there was no real bond at all. They were smug and self-satisfied, content to live within the comfortable, narrow confines of their prejudices. Aside from his sister Betsy, Uncle Henry Thayer and his parents, he didn't really give a hang about any of them. The path he had chosen for himself was a different one, and he felt superior to them all, as only one who had broken out of the rigid mold could feel.

It was strange, then, that he should be anxious to show Helga off to them and to win their approval of her. If their opinions were of no consequence, what did it matter whether they liked her or not? The answer was beyond his grasp.

CHAPTER NINETEEN

Paul stood just inside the dining room doors, which he closed softly behind him, and looked first at his mother, then at the plates and platters of food she was arranging. And, as he glanced at the delicacies and unusual dishes, he shook his head; his mother, who had not seen or heard him, was smiling to herself in quiet satisfaction.

It had become a custom in the past year for Chicago's hostesses to compete with each other in the preparation of new and different meals, and it was evident from Molly's air that she knew her reputation as a leader was deserved and that tonight's buffet would not dim its luster. She examined her heavy silver tableware, her rich Spode and the fragile lace cloth which was a perfect foil for the yellow and red roses, and she seemed very pleased. Her impressive coffee service rested on a little table of its own, and the flickering tapers in the twin candelabra on the sideboard made the room festive.

Her son could not subdue a bitter thought: why was it that she, who could be do daring in the planning and execution of a menu, should cling so stubbornly to hidebound traditions in every other way? Then it occurred to him that she was not exceeding the limits of her self-imposed proprieties. On the contrary, her very efforts in creating this meal were conservative; she was actually just copying the practices of her friends and relatives.

Molly, unaware that she was under Paul's critical eye, surveyed her table carefully and felt elated. Tonight's supper, she told herself proudly, was going to be one of her best, and she was certain that every woman present would talk about it for days to come. She had to admit that she had achieved a completely successful blend of the expected and the startling.

There was a platter of cold shrimp in a pink mayonnaise sauce, and beside it stood a hot chafing dish of tiny meat balls in a rich gravy of mushrooms, dates, peppers and pickled walnuts. On a large plate were thin slices of lean smoked ham rolled and skewered around cold asparagus tips, and lending a piquant touch was celery stuffed with caviar and cream cheese.

Another hot plate held light pastry shells filled with creamed chicken and chives. The most plebeian dish was one of miniature slit frankfurters stuffed with sliced olives and skewered with toothpicks. There were halved tomatoes stuffed with minced lobster, and at one end of the table stood a platter on a bed of ice with Molly's most renowned recipe, her special salad. Individual molds of sliced cucumbers, hard-boiled eggs and artichoke hearts in clear aspic, each served on a firm lettuce leaf, were a never-failing delight at Dawson parties. And, as a final touch, there were light, hot biscuits made of dough mixed with blue cheese and caraway seeds.

Molly told herself that in her husband's mind this was a party in honor of Betsy, but she knew better. To her this was a reception for Paul and, of course, for his bride. A mother who had been cheated out of the wedding luncheon that should have been held two weeks ago had her own way of achieving the results she desired. And, she thought with satisfaction, everyone was here tonight who should have been in attendance when her son was married.

Suddenly she heard someone speak directly behind her. "Hi, Toots."

"Paul!" She hugged hm, unaware until this moment just how much she had missed him.

"You look wonderful, Mother." That, Paul knew, was a lie. Granted that his mother's navy blue silk dress looked trim and attractive, she herself showed signs of fatigue. There were smudges under her eyes, as there were under his father's, and he wondered whether these indications of sleeplessness were something new or whether he had simply failed for a long time to notice either of his parents closely.

"Do I, dear? Thank you. I think you've lost more weight, Paul."

"I don't see how that's possible. I've been eating like the proverbial pig. Helga's a sensational cook."

"I must tell her about some of your favorite dishes, the first chance I get." Molly blinked as she looked up at her son. "This is quite a night for me, and for your father, too. It's the first time in a great many months that we've had all three of our children under our roof together."

"You make it sound as though we're scattered all over the face of the earth."

"Hardly that. But it will take time to acclimate myself to the thought that you're living way off on the North Side."

"Thirty minutes by car, no more. As you'll see later this week. We want to have you up for dinner while Betsy is in town."

"Oh, we wouldn't dream of imposing, Paul. It will be so much easier on Helga and on you, too, for you to come out here."

"Helga will settle the details with you as to when she'd like you to come up," he replied firmly. There was little more to say, and he was ready to return to the living room when his mother touched his arm.

"Are you going upstairs—to see your room?"

"I hadn't thought of it, no. Is there something special that you want me to see, Mother?"

"No. It's just that we—always think of you as being in it. You don't know how lonely it's been here without you, Paul."

"Hey, none of that." If he knew his mother she would start to cry soon, and the best way to prevent tears was to surround her with people as quickly as possible. "You'd better come out and see if everybody is here. From the looks of things your spread is ready, and you don't want the hot things to get cold or the cold things to get hot, do you?"

Very gently, with an arm around her shoulders, he guided her to the double doors and led her into the living room. Helga and Betsy had come downstairs and were surrounded by half a dozen guests; judging from appearances, Paul guessed that his bride had already been introduced to everyone present. When she saw her mother-in-law, she broke away and kissed Molly warmly, and Paul saw a new, different excitement in her face.

"Having a good time, honey?" he asked as his mother drifted away to count noses and make sure that all her guests were assembled.

"It's more than fun, darling. I love meeting all these people who are related to you—and having them tell me how fond of you they are. You've said so little about them that I'd never have guessed they're so—nice."

"You sure got along with Betsy like a house on fire."

"She's very sweet. And she's so much like you, darling. You can't imagine what it's like, Paul, for someone who has never had any sisters or brothers, to know she's going to have a sister like Betsy. And Marcia, too."

"Now you're letting your enthusiasm carry you overboard."

"No, I can understand how she's felt, and I have sympathy for her position. Remember, she's very young."

"For my dough she's a little brute."

"She's no such thing and we both know it. We're old enough

to have more sense, so it's our place to make the gestures to her. We can't spend the rest of our lives feeding on hurts and feuds, and there's no time like right now to begin doing what's right."

Helga looked quickly around the living room, located the younger of her sisters-in-law and walked to her, deliberately and purposefully. Marcia, who was apparently somewhat bored with the gathering, was standing alone, pretending to examine the titles of books on a shelf to the left of the fireplace. "How soon does your school have spring vacation, Marcia? Paul says you don't have the same schedule as most other schools."

"Week after next," was the suspicious, faintly sullen reply.

"Oh, good. We want to have you up one day—just by yourself."

"If I have time."

"I hope you will have. I thought we could make it some weekday, while Paul is off at work. Then you and I can do whatever we decide we'd like to do. And you could stay overnight, if you'd enjoy that. I know we would. Our living room sofa makes up into a very comfortable bed, or so the man said who sold it to me. You could be the guinea pig and try it out."

"I guess Mother and Daddy would let me stay over." Marcia began to thaw, reluctantly but visibly.

"I'm positive they will. Just be sure not to mention that in our house there's *no* bedtime curfew."

"Okay." For the first time Marcia smiled.

"It's a date, then. There's really no fun like staying overnight with people."

"How did you know that?"

"It hasn't been so very long," Helga said quietly, "since I was in school myself."

At that moment Molly announced that supper was ready, and there was a concerted move to the buffet in the dining room. Paul caught a glimpse of Helga helping herself at the table, then he lost sight of her for a few minutes and didn't see her again

[239]

until he had heaped food onto his own plate. He had waited until the majority of guests had served themselves. Then he discovered Helga with Betsy on the cushioned window seats in the living room; they made room for him between them, but conversation was desultory at best while all three ate heartily.

The dessert, one of Molly's specialties, created a minor sensation of its own when the guests returned to the dining room for it, and it was worth the attention paid to it. A confection of several thin layers of light sponge cake, it was filled with rich chocolate cream and chopped almonds and topped with a thick icing arranged in elaborate snowy peaks and garnished with glazed cherries and marzipan leaves. It tasted as good as it looked.

Afterwards, over coffee, conversation was subdued, and the loud hum that had filled the first floor of the house gave way to a low murmur. Paul had noticed that Henry Thayer, who had always been an enthusiastic trencherman, had eaten virtually nothing, and he asked Betsy, "Has Uncle Henry been sick? He looks pretty terrible."

"Something has been the matter," was her reply. "I had to go up to Daddy's office this morning—you know how he insists that I come in and make the rounds of the place. And I saw Uncle Henry then. I asked Daddy about him, but I didn't find out much. All Daddy would say was, 'He has problems.'"

The very thought was depressing, and Paul fell silent. Helga, almost instantly aware of his mood, began to tell Betsy about the little newspaper they had investigated on their honeymoon. Paul brightened at once, Betsy proved to be a deeply interested listener, and Helga warmed to her subject. She became so engrossed in her description that she failed to notice that her father-in-law, coffee cup in hand, had wandered over and stood at the end of the window-seat, half behind her, listening.

"The paper was really too small for what we want," she said. "It had a circulation of only three thousand copies a day, and

Paul said that isn't enough. And even more important, the town wasn't big enough to assure the publisher of any sustained local advertising. See how much I've learned, darling? But it really was a cute little plant, Betsy. They had a very nice press, and the linotype machine was practically new. I learned how to operate it—well, not really, but almost. The owner of the paper gave me a couple of lessons. It isn't too hard at all, when you know typing."

Gordon took a step forward and interrupted. "Paul," he said, forcing a smile, "I wonder if you could tear yourself away from these beauties for a few minutes. I'd like a word with you."

"Sure, Dad." Paul gripped Helga's shoulder lovingly, stood and moved off with his father.

"Let's go upstairs, shall we? Too much jabber down here."

"Anything you say."

They climbed the stairs together, then Gordon turned to the right. "I suggest your old room. It'll be quieter back there."

"Okay." Patently something of importance was on his father's mind, and Paul searched his face for a clue, but could find none.

"Well. How does it feel to be an old married man?" Gordon headed straight for the easy chair and settled himself in it comfortably.

"Swell, Dad. Wonderful. Any time the Association of Benedicts wants a testimonial, they've got mine."

"That's fine. Cigar, son?"

"No, thanks."

Gordon lit a match and applied it carefully to the end of his cigar. "How do you think Betsy looks?"

"The same as ever."

"The same? What's happened to your eyes?" Gordon chuckled indulgently. "She gets prettier all the time."

"It's fine that you're so proud of her, Dad." It was strange to be back in the room that had been his for so long.

"I'm proud of all three of my children. Just as I hope they're proud of me."

"We are. All four of us."

"Four? Yes, of course. It takes a little time to get accustomed to the idea that the family has grown." Gordon fell silent, then lifted his head and looked straight at his son. "Do you remember that chap Fredericks we met at the Meridian Club one night?"

"Of course. You hired him."

"That's correct. To do our promotion and public relations job. Well, he isn't working out quite as I'd hoped he would."

"I'm sorry to hear it." Paul was indeed sorry, for he felt sure he knew what was coming.

"Henry Thayer thinks he's too slick. Henry says he manages to stay just on this side of ethical business practices. Personally, I wouldn't go quite that far in my criticism."

Paul wasn't sure what to reply, and so said nothing. But he braced himself; the trend of his father's conversation was unmistakable.

"Here's the way I see it. There are certain business trends these days, and certain circumstances in which the company finds itself that would make it highly advantageous to us if we could take our promotion and public relations man into our confidence. When I say 'we,' I refer to Henry and myself, of course."

"I'm not sure I follow you, Dad. What do you mean by 'trends' and 'circumstances'?" Paul asked, trying to divert his father's mind from the inevitable.

"Let's not put the cart before the horse. I asked you to come up here because I wanted to sound you out, as you've undoubtedly gathered."

"I have," Paul replied dryly, running his fingers through his hair.

"We need your talents—and your loyalty—more than ever, Paul."

"I wish I could go along with you, Dad. For your sake, I wish I could see things your way. But I can't. I'm a newspaperman."

"You're an adult now. And it's time you face facts. This won't be easy for me, but I'd better tell you the position that Whitmarket and Company is in."

Paul heard only the first portion of his father's remark. "I do face facts. And one of them is that I have the courage of my convictions. I live according to what I believe is right."

"There's a difference between daydreams and reality." Gordon raised his voice without realizing it. "There's a difference between a man throwing away his life and making something of himself. He's got to have a reason for living and working."

"I have plenty of reason." Paul was speaking more loudly, too. "My principles—"

"Spare me the idealism. The future of an honorable company has to be protected!"

"Everybody is entitled to his own concept of what has to be done. What I'm doing satisfies Helga and me, and that's all that—"

"She's encouraging this unreasonable streak in you. I knew it when I heard her talking downstairs. You were bad enough before you married her, and now you're impossible." Gordon stood and glared at his son.

Paul felt his temper beginning to soar. "You leave my wife out of this. Just because she happens to believe the same way I do is our concern, nobody else's."

"You're my concern. Just as your mother and your sisters are my concern! And that is why the company is my concern, too. I'm trying to make the future as secure and solid as I can. For my family. And in spite of all my efforts, an outsider comes along and upsets—"

"Are you referring to Helga as an outsider?" Paul knew he was shouting now, but he didn't care.

"I certainly am. And I'll tell you something else. Her influence on you is the worst thing that ever could have happened to you!" Gordon was working himself into a rage, and his eyes grew shiny. "I've spent years trying to straighten you out, trying to make you see that you'll destroy yourself unless you get all those fool notions out of that juvenile head of yours. Then you spout your rubbish to a pretty girl, you see yourself reflected in her eyes—and you wreck yourself."

"You're the one who's spouting rubbish, Dad! You don't know what you're talking about!"

Paul was suddenly aware that Helga and Betsy were in the doorway. But Gordon, whose back was to the door, did not see them. Even if he had, Paul suspected he was too aroused to stem the bitter recrimination that was welling up within him.

"I've spent fifty years in a vacuum, is that it? I've gotten where I have in business and in the community through some kind of a fluke. My experience counts for nothing, my knowledge counts for nothing, my success counts for nothing. I'll revise my standards and accept those of a self-opinionated boy who won't listen to his father. You prefer to drink in the advice of a penniless, baby-faced blonde who married you because she thought she was snagging a good catch!"

"That's enough!"

"You're an insolent, ungrateful pup who's lost whatever sense you ever possessed! You—"

"If you weren't my father, I'd punch you in the face! But there's nothing to make me stay here and listen to your insults. It was tough enough when you made cracks about me. But nobody can talk about my wife as you have—not you or anybody else!"

Paul turned, put an arm around Helga's shoulder and started blindly toward the stairs.

[244]

CHAPTER TWENTY

Paul's sense of outrage deepened and became more intense during the twenty-four hours following his argument with his father, and when he arrived at the little apartment on Elm Street the following evening he felt a bone-weariness greater than any he had ever before experienced. He let himself in with his new latchkey, called, "Hi, I'm home," and then headed for the kitchen, where he heard noises.

Helga, in an old grey flannel skirt, a shirt and low-heeled shoes, was mashing potatoes in a bowl. She showed the effects of the unexpected crisis, too, and although she tried to smile the effort was too great. "Hi, darling. You're late."

"Yeah. I had to do a round-up story on a train wreck, and every time I thought I was finished there was another batch of information that made me revise everything all over again." He tossed the evening newspapers onto the large, enamel-topped table, then put his arms around Helga and kissed her. They clung to each other, and when he at last released her she stepped back and studied him.

"You look tired, Paul."

"The same to you, Mrs. Dawson." He rubbed a hand across his face, then hesitated before speaking again. "Any phone calls since I called you this noon?"

"A laundry over on Rush Street earnestly requests our patronage."

"You know what I mean, honey."

"No. No calls."

"Nuts to 'em. I figured he'd be too proud and stubborn to apologize. That's just like him. He's never in all his life admitted he was wrong, not ever. But I certainly thought Mother would call to say she was sorry about the whole mess."

"I was sure she wouldn't. After all, she's his wife."

"She's also my mother and your mother-in-law."

"Paul, dear, we talked almost all night last night. And it won't do us any good to go over the same ground again and again. To me there's nothing more important than a close family relationship—I see no point in anything unless people have that. But there's nothing we can do at the moment."

"At the moment? There's nothing you and I are going to do, ever! We're the ones who were abused without cause!"

"Yes, darling. I know. And I can only repeat what I said last night. Eventually everything will work out as it should, if we'll let it."

"There's only one way for all this to work out. We're going to have nothing more to do with them."

"That puts me in a position I don't like. I stand between you and your parents. I have all along. And that's wrong." Helga started to move across the kitchen to the oven, but Paul stopped her.

"Let's hold up dinner for awhile, huh? I'm not very hungry just yet. And as to your coming between my parents and me, you seem to forget that you were on the receiving end of just as many insults as I got!"

"No, I'm not forgetting. I simply know that it'll do no good for us to quarrel about it."

"Who's quarreling, for Pete's sake?" Paul demanded impatiently, irritated because she didn't seem to share his sense of

[246]

urgency. She had been hurt by his father's words, he knew, but her lack of anger over the incident puzzled him, and because he didn't understand her approach he was annoyed.

They were both so tired that a real argument might have developed had the doorbell not rung. "It's the janitor," Helga said. "He promised to come up and make the pilot light on the stove bigger."

"Okay, I'll let him in." Paul walked slowly to the front door and opened it.

Betsy stood in the frame, her hands plunged deep into the pockets of her polo coat. "Hi."

"Hi." Totally unprepared for her visit, Paul looked at her uncertainly.

"Am I welcome?"

"Of course, come in."

Helga, who had heard their voices, appeared behind him, then Betsy crowded past him and the two girls embraced. "I hope I haven't interrupted you at dinner, Helga."

"No, we haven't eaten yet. Paul just came home from the office a couple of minutes ago. Why don't you join us? Unless you have other plans—"

"No other plans." Betsy paused, then continued decisively. "All right, I will stay, if you're sure it's no trouble. I could pretend that I just happened to be in the neighborhood, but that would be absurd."

She exchanged a glance with her sister-in-law as all three stood in the tiny entrance hall, and Helga immediately took charge. "Paul, you show Betsy around the house, and I'll have everything ready in a few minutes."

"Wait. Can't I help?" Betsy asked.

"No, it's all done, thanks. And by the time Paul finishes his conducted tour, we'll be all set."

Helga disappeared into the kitchen, which led off the little corridor, and brother and sister stared at each other for a moment. "This is what is known as a hallway," he said. "That thing against the wall is a mahogany table, and that round, shiny oval above it is a mirror. And this is a clothes closet, which may or may not still be wet with paint, but if you're willing to risk it, I'll hang your coat in it."

"Thanks. Seeing you're so good to me, I'll take the chance." Betsy slipped out of her coat, handed it to him and then straightened the collar of the navy blue blouse she wore over a pleated navy blue skirt.

Paul snapped on a light and tried to simulate a bantering tone. "Directly in front of you is the living room, also the dining room. They happen to be one and the same thing. That hunk of furniture over there—"

"It is not a hunk of furniture. It's a drop-leaf gateleg walnut table, and you use it for purposes of eating, as I can judge from the chairs around it." Betsy was having trouble making light conversation, too.

"Smart girl. Why don't *you* take *me* on a conducted tour? To me a chair is just something you sit on."

Betsy forced a smile and moved into the living room and immediately thought that the atmosphere was cheerful and comfortable, even though little taste had been shown in the selection of the various pieces. Dominating the room were a sofa, an easy chair and a wing chair upholstered in matching shades of brown, and in front of the couch was a coffee table with a machine-tooled leather top. Somehow that table set the tone for the entire room: it was attractive enough, and it was elegant when contrasted with the furniture Helga had previously known, but it actually pretended to be something it was not, hence it was faintly shoddy according to the standards of someone who was familiar with genuine Chippendale or Louis XV.

"This is a very attractive room, Paul." Betsy fingered the heavy linen drapes.

"Glad you like it." He knew something was wrong, although he wasn't sure in his own mind why the whole apartment fell a little short of his expectations. He realized only that it lacked the quality that set his parents' house apart from that of ordinary people, and although he had tried to hide his reaction from Helga, he was afraid she was aware of it. Betsy, he thought, undoubtedly felt just as he did.

If that was the case, she was expert beyond her years in dissembling, and she ran a finger lightly across a row of books on the top shelf of an L-shaped corner case. "I left a lot of books at home when I went off to school," she said. "I suppose you swiped most of them."

"These, my dear child, are adult reading." He tried gallantly to adopt the note of raillery that had so long characterized their relationship. "Most of them are filled with words of at least two syllables. So, by definition, they couldn't have belonged to you."

"Ho-hum. Also hum-ho." The strain was as great on Betsy as it was on her brother. "Is this the end of the grand tour, or is there a place where you sleep, too?"

"There is. Line up in single file, please. No crowding, no pushing, no shoving. Just follow the guide, and don't try to duck under the velvet ropes, which have been put up for the benefit of the tourists as well as the protection of the museum."

Paul walked down a short corridor past the bathroom, which he indicated by a flick of his hand. It was ridiculous, he knew, to regard its peach-colored walls as offensive, but he would be less than honest with himself if he failed to admit that they bothered him. When he reached the bedroom he turned on the lamps that stood on Helga's kidney-shaped dressing table, then moved aside and watched his sister in silence.

Betsy inspected the suite, which consisted of twin beds, a man's dresser and a woman's dresser, all of pine stained to resemble blond mahogany, then she instantly transferred her attention to the one item of genuine interest. It was a wardrobe, six feet high, of real blond mahogany; it was double-sectioned, with mirrored doors, and was put together with carved pegs rather than nails. She inspected it, then reached tentatively for a handle.

"May I see the inside?"

"Sure."

"Oh, this is lovely, Paul. It's cedar-lined. Is it an antique?"

"No, but it will be some day. Helga's father made it for us."

"He must love her very much."

"He does."

There was a long, embarrassed pause, and Betsy turned her face away as she closed the wardrobe. "You think I'm pretty tactless, I suppose, but I'm not very good at opening subjects, and it seems to me the best way is to—"

"You still haven't seen the kitchen."

"—just take a deep breath. Paul, I wish you could try to understand that—"

"Do you want to see the kitchen or don't you?"

"Of course."

"Come on, then." He stalked out of the bedroom, leaving Betsy to follow him, and preceded her into the kitchen, where Helga was removing a pan of hamburgers from the broiler. "Last stop," he declared roughly. "Stove, sink, icebox. All the modern conveniences. Are there any questions? If not, there will be a brief period for fraternization with the natives before the cruise ship leaves. And please remember not to tip the guides. All expenses are included."

"I love your apartment, Helga. I think it's darling." Betsy edged past her brother. "Are you sure there isn't something I can do?"

"You might pour the water, if you really want to go to work."

"If you'll excuse me," Paul said, "I'll get cleaned up before we eat."

He left without waiting for an answer, and by the time he

returned, dinner was on the table at one end of the living room. The girls were both sitting, waiting for him, and he took his chair in silence. Helga served the hamburgers, mashed potatoes and wax beans, and Betsy murmured something polite to the effect that everything looked delicious. Helga smiled at her.

"I should have made a salad, I know. Paul loves them, I've discovered, so you must, too."

"Oh, I couldn't possibly eat a salad, not with all this."

"Next time you come up we'll have one. I'm just beginning to be salad conscious. In Ma's and Pa's house we almost never ate salad. I don't know why it is," Helga added candidly, "but poor people never seem to think in salad terms."

"We have sociology lectures with our meals around here," Paul declared, sensitive to his wife's bluntness.

He expected a response in kind from Betsy, but she did not smile. "I'll have to cram a lot of salads into the next few months at school, from the looks of things," she said. "I'll be going back next week, because my tuition's paid for through the rest of the term, but that looks like the end of it."

"What do you mean?" Paul raised his head sharply.

"I mean that last night was unfortunate." Betsy put her fork carefully on her plate and looked squarely at her brother. "Daddy was wrong. He blew off a lot of steam, and he said a lot of things that he shouldn't have said. But—"

"If he's sent you here to do some apologizing for him, he's chosen the wrong method!"

Helga leaned across the table and put her hand on his arm. "Darling, please. This isn't very easy for Betsy, and you're being rude to her."

"I meant what I said, all the same. If Dad isn't man enough to—"

"He doesn't even know I'm here," Betsy stated flatly, her eyes glazing slightly, as did her father's and her brother's in moments of great emotion. "And he'd shoot me if he knew

[251]

what I intend to say to you. This morning he had a talk with me at breakfast, after Marcia left for school. Mother had a dreadful headache after last night's fireworks, so Daddy and I were alone."

"How cozy." Paul salted his potatoes, unnecessarily and vigorously.

Helga was about to appeal to him again, but changed her mind and turned to her sister-in-law instead. "Don't mind him, Betsy. When he's all worked up this way, he'll say anything."

"Oh, I know. He's exactly like Daddy. They're identical peas out of the same pod."

"Whoever it was said that comparisons are odious sure knew what he was talking about." Paul ate stolidly, but tasted nothing.

"Daddy told me this morning that the business is in great difficulty."

"Well. What a pity." His heart sank, but his face showed no change.

"Really, Paul. They're on the verge of bankruptcy. Daddy didn't go into detail with me, but he said he wanted me to know. And I thought you ought to know, too."

"Okay, now I know. Thanks for telling me." Paul's anger was directed principally at himself. He had the feeling that he ought to do what he could to help Whitmarket and Company, but he reminded himself in almost the same breath that old loyalties and sentimental ties, all of which had to be discarded, were interfering with his judgment.

"Now you know why Uncle Henry looks like a ghost. And Daddy is almost the same way. That company means everything to them, Paul."

"Well, it doesn't to me."

Helga, who had been listening carefully, addressed herself to the other girl. "I have no hatred for your father, Betsy. What he said to Paul about me last night was untrue, so it was unjust.

But I can understand that if he has bad business worries, he had to find a target for his feelings."

"Exactly!" Betsy looked as though she would burst into tears, but managed to control herself. "And you were that target, partly because he and Paul haven't seen anything the same way for so long, and partly because he doesn't understand you."

"I know. It was some famous author who said that we are intolerant of that which is alien to us. I can't remember offhand who it was said it, but I'm not thinking very clearly."

Paul could no longer make a pretense of eating. "Unless I'm going mad, you're both standing on your heads trying to excuse and justify Dad's insults!"

"No, darling."

"That's the way I see it."

"Let me try, Helga." Betsy turned earnestly to her brother. "Dad was wrong. I know it and Helga knows it and you know it. And he's too intelligent and sensitive a man not to know it himself. You—"

"All you're doing is convincing yourself, Bets, not me. I can't and won't believe that any man who behaved as he did is either sensitive or intelligent, so help me."

"Paul, he was overwrought. You know how much that company has always meant to him. He hasn't been sleeping, and he hasn't been eating. Show him a little sympathy."

"Why should I?"

Helga sat erect in her chair. "Because he is your father," she said clearly. "All of his life he's felt secure. But now he has a crisis, and his security is threatened. A cousin of my mother's lost his mind when the little shoe repair shop he owned in Göteborg failed, and he was sent to a hospital for many months. That shop had meant security to him, just as it had to his father and his grandfather and, for all I know, his great-grandfather before him. It didn't matter that he could go to Stockholm and earn as much working in someone else's shoe repair shop in a

[253]

week as he'd made in Göteborg for himself in a month. In his own mind his security was gone, and for a little while he was like someone wild."

"I can see one parallel," Paul replied frostily. "Dad was a wild man last night, all right, and no mistake about that."

"Then it's up to us to show him compassion, darling."

"How many other cheeks do you want to hold out to him, Helga? Me, when I've been hit unfairly, I know better than to stick my jaw out again. If Dad is having financial problems, that's too bad. It's his worry, though, not mine. And where I stand is very plain. He took some cracks at me—which I'm used to taking, but which I won't take again. More important, he insulted my wife. That's something nobody can do, regardless of the provocation. So I'm through with him, once and for all, permanently!"

CHAPTER TWENTY-ONE

A fresh spring breeze was blowing off Lake Michigan as Helga applied the brakes to the Plymouth and halted in the driveway of the imposing home of her parents-in-law. She got out of the car, inhaled deeply, and for a brief moment was almost overcome by a sense of panic. This trip to see Paul's mother was no impulse of the moment; on the contrary, she had spent most of the night wondering what to do, and this visit seemed to be the most constructive step she could take. Paul's attitude last night, first while Betsy had been at the apartment, then later, after she had left, had been stubborn, unreasonable and intransigent, and if he would take no active steps to heal a breach that was wrong, then it was up to the woman who loved him to do what was necessary.

All the same, Helga felt insecure as she looked at the solid brick house. It was one thing to hear that Paul's father was in financial difficulties, but it was something entirely different to imagine that the foundations of this impressive pile of masonry might be weak. It was easy enough, in the black silence of three o'clock in the morning, to imagine herself coming here because of principles which she believed to be right. Now that she actually stood in front of the door, however, her self-doubts seemed stronger by far than her convictions.

She had arrived far too early in the morning, for one thing. She knew nothing of Molly Dawson's personal habits, but she felt sure that ten-fifteen was not an appropriate hour for a call, not even from a daughter-in-law. And certainly her tan, two-piece dress, which she had made for herself over a year ago and had often worn to work, was all wrong. If she had been thinking, she would have dressed in something more chic for her clothes-conscious mother-in-law, who always looked as though she had just stepped out of a bandbox.

Worst of all, Helga realized, she was risking a rebuff. She could not for an instant lose sight of the fact that Molly was Gordon's wife, and would therefore take her husband's side in a quarrel. But it was wrong for Paul and his father to be at odds, and Helga knew she had to do whatever she could do to reconcile them. Instead of ringing the bell she lifted the heavy brass knocker and let it fall again, resoundingly.

After what seemed like an interminable wait, a maid in uniform, a woman Helga had never before seen, opened the door a few inches and peered out suspiciously. "Yes?"

"I'm here to see Mrs. Dawson."

"I don't know for sure she's in. If she is, who should I tell her is calling?"

"Mrs. Paul Dawson."

"Oh." Badly flustered, the maid flung open the door. "Please to come in, Mrs. Dawson. I'm sorry, I didn't recognize you. I only had a little peep of you the other night through the glass window in the butler's pantry. I'm sorry. I'll tell Mrs. Dawson you're here."

Before Helga could assure her that no harm had been done, the woman hurried up the stairs. It was very quiet in the living room, the wood was polished, the leather was oiled and every piece of furniture, clean and neat, stood in its place. Slowly, almost hesitantly, Helga walked into the room, and new securities engulfed her. There was a difference between the gracious living that this house represented and her own apartment, yet she could not understand why. She had been proud of the furniture and accessories she had selected for her own first home, but she was sure Paul was disappointed. He had said nothing overt, of course; that wasn't his way. She had been able to tell, all the same, from the guarded expression in his eyes and the careful wording of his enthusiastic praise when he had complimented her on her choices.

Helga was jerked back to the present moment as she heard footsteps on the stairs and turned to see her mother-in-law descending. Molly, in a silk flowered dressing gown, looked haggard but had not lost her social poise. There were deep, dark rings under her eyes and her face, devoid of cosmetics of any kind, showed every line and wrinkle; nevertheless a fixed, polite smile was on her lips, and there was no discernible hostility in her eyes.

"How sweet of you to drop in, Helga." Molly embraced her daughter-in-law gingerly.

"I must apologize for coming so early in the morning, before you are dressed."

"Oh, not at all. I often stay this way until eleven or even twelve. It's a dreadful habit, I'm sure, but I've done it all my life and I suppose I'm too old to change now." Molly laughed a trifle self-consciously, then moved toward the bay windows. "Please sit down, won't you?"

"Yes, thank you." Helga perched on the edge of the cushion of Gordon's green leather chair and folded her hands in her lap.

"You're very kind to stop by. You're on your way to see your own parents, I suppose?"

"No, I drove out just to see you."

"Well." Molly ran the tasseled cord of her robe through her fingers.

"I think there is much that you and I can say to each other. If we are frank, we can help each other." Helga didn't realize that in her tension she was speaking a precise English reminiscent of the attempts of her parents to master the language. Her accent was that of a girl born and educated in the United States, but the cadence of her words was that of Sweden.

"I'm—I'm not too sure I know what you mean."

Molly was seeking a graceful escape, but none was available. According to her lifelong standards a ladylike face had to be maintained at all costs, but this unorthodox young woman seemed insistent on ripping through the fabric of polite convention. It was hard to decide what to say or do next, and Molly smiled in open relief as Betsy, carrying a cup of coffee, strolled in from the dining room. She wore a pink hand-knitted dress, and her mother thought with satisfaction that no young girl had ever looked smarter.

"I thought I heard voices in here," Betsy said. "Good morning to you, sister mine."

"Hi, Betsy."

"You make me feel like a real sluggard, coming all the way out to the South Side before I've finished my breakfast. I suppose you have all your housework done for the day, too."

"Not really. Just a little straightening up after Paul left for the office."

"I'm in the tight grip of a disease called spring vacation. Or maybe it was visiting my stupid brother and his adorable wife last night—and getting all worn out. Anyway, I couldn't wake myself up this morning." Betsy was about to sit on the sofa, then looked at her mother and sister-in-law. Placing her coffee cup momentarily on a table, she crossed the room, leaned down and kissed Helga. "I'm the one around here who says what she thinks, even when nobody wants my opinion. And I say that Helga Bjornson is the best thing, the very best thing that has ever happened to the Dawson family."

Neither expecting a reply or waiting for one, she walked firmly but without haste to the staircase and disappeared. There was a long silence, which Molly, her face still creased by an artificial smile, finally broke. "I congratulate you, I really do. Betsy takes to very few people."

[258]

"I like her," Helga replied. "I don't yet know her well, but I like her. She is a fine girl. Just as her brother is a fine man. And I love him."

The unexpected bluntness of her statement startled Molly, who wanted to weep but restrained her emotions. "Yes. Paul is a good boy. I was always proud of him."

"I am proud of him now, and that pride really belongs to you, for it is you who fashioned him. You—and his father." Helga was breathing rapidly, although her face still seemed calm.

The obvious kindness was too much for Molly, and her control vanished. Tears appeared in her eyes, and she wiped them away with a tiny handkerchief which she drew from a pocket of her dressing gown. "I've never known an experience like the one night before last. It was a nightmare."

"The other night doesn't matter," Helga said quietly. "All that counts to me is Paul's happiness. All that counts to you is the happiness of his father, and that of Paul, too. So we have the same aim. We want them to feel the love that a father and a son should feel, without bitterness. And without misunderstanding, for it is this which causes all the other ills."

"You really believe that. You aren't just saying it."

"Of course. Otherwise I could not have come to you this morning."

"You're a mystery to me, Helga, you confuse me. If I were in your shoes, I'd be so indignant—"

"I do not pretend. When I am struck, I bruise. But bruises heal. And more is at stake here than a few black and blue marks on my skin."

It was extraordinarily difficult for Molly, who had lived all of her life on a level in which social propriety was paramount, to face basic questions with someone whom she knew only slightly. Nevertheless she made the effort. "Why did you come here this morning, Helga?"

"Because we have learned, Paul and I, that your husband is having troubles."

"Betsy had no right to tell you."

"No, she was right. There are families so that each may help the other when there are problems. You have been afraid I came here this morning to argue, to upbraid you for what took place two nights ago. But that was the fault of no one, neither of Paul nor of his father. Much has happened over many years that has made unhappiness. And when there is a crisis, all that is bad comes out. But the harshness that exists between people only destroys, it builds nothing. And I am here because I want to build."

"I really believe you mean that."

"I mean it."

Molly began to weep; then ashamed of giving in to open emotion, she turned her face away, and Helga, who had been about to go to her and offer her comfort, deliberately refrained. There were times when a physical demonstration of kindness could do more harm than good, and at such a moment as this it was better to let Molly fight her way toward self-control alone.

For several minutes Paul's mother held her crumpled, soaked handkerchief to her face, then said in a choked voice, "I don't know what we're going to do."

"You'll do as everyone does. You'll go on as best you can." Helga knew her words were inadequate, but she could give no other reply.

"Apparently Betsy didn't tell you the whole story. Perhaps she doesn't realize herself just how terrible it can all be. If the company fails, everything will crash with it."

"Everything?" Helga was genuinely puzzled.

"This house will be lost. All of our investments. Everything we've built up in a lifetime of struggle. If Paul's father can't pull the company through its crisis, we'll be ruined."

"All of my life I have known poverty," Helga said slowly, "so

I am not frightened by being poor. It's easy for me to talk, I guess, and not easy for you to understand. You have always had servants, a lovely home, luxuries—"

"I've had security. And I'm frightened." Molly stopped crying and looked at her daughter-in-law.

"The poor know that there is only one kind of security. It doesn't come from how much money you have in the bank. Sometimes Ma and Pa didn't know how they would pay the rent, but always they paid it. Always, somehow, they managed. And they have had a good life together."

"They're used to scrimping and saving, counting pennies and doing without. I'm not." Without realizing quite what she was doing, Molly was seeking support and advice now from her daughter-in-law. "And my girls. If Whitmarket is forced to close, Betsy will have to leave college. And Marcia will never get there. They—"

"I went to no college," Helga interposed gently. "Yet I am healthy and happy. Betsy is a wonderful girl. She's worried about you and about her father, not herself. You needn't fear for her. And Marcia will be all right, too, even if the worst happens. You will help her, and so will Betsy." She paused and touched her lips, which were unaccountably dry, with the tip of her tongue. "If you'd let me, I'd try to help, too."

Molly could only stare at her for what seemed like a very long time. "You'd do that—for us?"

Helga raised her head, and her eyes showed quiet determination and something more, something that went beyond mere feeling. "You forget," she said, "that my name is Dawson, too."

Color suffused Molly's face and she stood quickly, as though someone had commanded her to rise. It had always been difficult for her to revise her judgments of people once they had been formed, and there had been so few occasions in her life when she had ever been forced to admit she had made an error that it was virtually impossible for her to apologize in so many words. And so the moment was a painful one for her, particularly as her reactions were complicated by so many factors.

She knew now that she and Helga were bound together by ties she had never before been willing to recognize. At the same time she could not lose sight of the fact that this was the wife of a son who had caused Gordon to suffer, and her husband, today as always, was more important to her by far than her children. Helga's gesture had to be answered in kind, of course, and Molly responded in the best traditions of one who had been taught early that dignity must be preserved at all costs.

"I forgot. Thank you," she said.

They faced each other somewhat uncertainly, neither sure of what to do next. They would have embraced, but Helga was too shy to make the first move and Molly was too reserved. Slightly ashamed of the emotion she had displayed before the younger woman, she struggled to gain domination of the situation. "I hope you and Paul will come up for dinner some night later this week," she said carefully. "Any night that's convenient for you will be fine."

Helga hesitated, then decided to speak her mind. "Would it be fine with Paul's father, too?"

"Oh, he'll be so pleased as soon as he sees that Paul is really sorry. All his father wants is a sign, a gesture of contrition from him, and—"

"Paul won't do that, I know he won't." Helga's voice was soft, barely above the level of a whisper.

"Surely he's willing to show the respect that's due his father!" Molly, shocked, reverted to the view of family relationships she had held for so many years. It was inconceivable to her that anyone could be guilty of such gross disloyalty to Gordon as to fail to look up to him or defer to him.

Helga saw the blind spot in the older woman's attitude, but there was nothing she could do to change or cure the condition. When she herself was groping for a secure base with the man whom she had just married, she was not in a position to criticize her mother-in-law, who had, in her own way, made a successful marital adjustment. Molly believed implicitly in her husband, accepted every pronouncement he made as final and loyally followed wherever he chose to lead her.

It would be impertinent to disagree, Helga thought, but Molly still had to be made to understand that everyone else's world, unlike her own, did not revolve around Gordon. The problem was to present hard facts to her in terms that she would understand. "You've known Paul many years longer than I have. So I'm sure it will be nothing new to you when I say that he's stubborn."

"Oh, I can't tell you how I've grieved when I've seen him close his mind and refuse to listen to reason!"

"Then you know what we face, you and I. Paul isn't as wise as his father. So if his father would be the first to hold out a hand, perhaps I could persuade Paul to meet him part of the way. I can promise you no results, but I give you my word that I'd try my very best."

"I'm sure you would." Molly brightened for a moment, comforted by the support of this totally unexpected ally, then her face darkened again. "I don't know that I can ask Paul's father to make any extra efforts these days, when he's devoting all of his time and thought and energy to his business. That's why I wish so that Paul would come to him, and relieve his mind."

Helga realized that anything else she might say would make no impression. She had established her own peace with Paul's mother, and that was something; at the very least, the ice was broken. "We'll both do what we can," she said, "and we'll hope for the best."

"It's all we can do," Molly sighed, unable to hear the optimism in her daughter-in-law's words. "It's all any woman can do, when her husband is in trouble."

CHAPTER TWENTY-TWO

Lamb chops, at twenty-one cents a pound, were exorbitantly expensive, and Helga was deeply disturbed at the sight of Paul toying with the meat on his plate. This was not the time to mention such matters, however; he was already violently aroused. It was difficult at best to maintain her own sense of balance when she saw him thrashing around, and she wanted to help him, yet felt inadequate because she could not. "Darling," she said earnestly, "if you'd only try to be a little more objective—"

"Objective? How could any guy be objective after what's happened?" Paul speared a chunk of carrot, looked at it without seeing it and then let his fork drop to his plate. "When I think of you going out to see my mother the other day, it makes my blood boil. Every time I'm reminded of it, I get so sore that I—"

"It was hardly a crime," Helga interrupted wearily, losing all interest in her own food. Every night was the same now, every conversation an endless, repetitive argument.

"I say it was wrong for you to go there. And if I'd known you were intending to do it, I'd have forbidden you to go."

"Forbidden? That's rather strong language in the twentieth century, Paul. I am an adult, you know. So I don't have to ask your permission before I—"

"You know what I'm getting at, so don't twist my meaning and don't put words in my mouth!" The thought crossed Paul's mind that he had barely touched his dinner, but he shoved his plate away and lit a cigarette.

"I know that your mother loves you, just as you certainly love her, so I—"

"Naturally I love her! She's my mother!"

"—so I was simply trying to do what little I could to end these terrible family misunderstandings."

"As my family is the one concerned, suppose you leave all that to me."

"Paul, won't you ever listen? I feel responsible. I'm the cause of all the ill feeling between you and your father. I have been all along. That's why we broke up once. And all the bad is still there, rotting away under the surface. A marriage ceremony didn't change it, just as you aren't going to improve anything by eating your heart out, striking at your father."

"He's a bigoted, unprincipled, narrow-minded man. And because he's an opportunist himself, he can't stand seeing anyone else living strictly according to principle, for the very sake of principle."

"What he objects to most of all is your marriage to me. And the reason it bothers him is because he doesn't understand it, that's all. If you'll just get outside yourself for a few minutes, you'll realize it." Helga doggedly finished her own chop, unwilling to see a delicacy wasted. "Your father doesn't resent me —as me. He doesn't know me well enough to have formed any opinion of me as a person."

"Just what I'm saying!" Paul replied triumphantly, leaning back in his chair with such force that the wood creaked. "This whole thing is no more and no less than a matter of principle."

Exasperated beyond her endurance, Helga stood. "Anyone listening to you would think you married me because of principle, not because you love me."

"You accuse me of being dramatic. But listen to who's being dramatic now!"

She made no reply but cleared off the table and carried the dishes to the kitchen. She felt numb, as though she were moving in a dream, and she could not even allow herself to glance at Paul. She had the distressing feeling as she stacked the plates in the sink, that he was more concerned with his running feud with his father than he was with fundamentals. A young man who recognized reality would see that his father was more absorbed in trying to save a tottering business than in beating out at a son who had behaved in an unorthodox manner. A young man who truly grasped the fact that his parents loved him in spite of their inability to understand him would demonstrate his own affection in return through consistent and forgiving action. He would not spend all of his efforts in trying to justify himself, in stubbornly demanding that others accept him on the basis of standards which, Helga was beginning to suspect, he had erected out of defiance rather than conviction.

For the first time in her life, she was badly frightened, immobilized by her sense of impotence. Loving Paul, she didn't know what to do.

She scrubbed the plates with a brush, not seeing them, and she was startled when she heard Paul's voice behind her. She hadn't heard him come into the kitchen. "Want some help?" he asked politely.

"No, thank you."

He disappeared again, and when Helga finished with the dishes she started back toward the living room, hesitated, then forced herself to continue. It was ridiculous to feel as she did, and the sooner she rid herself of disturbing notions, the sooner everything would return to normal. Paul was reading a magazine, or at least was pretending to read it, and did not look up as she entered.

"Would you like some coffee?"

"Oh, don't bother, Helga." Paul sounded supremely indifferent, as remote as though he were addressing someone he had never before met.

"It's no bother." She kept her voice under control with an effort. "In fact, I have it all made."

"Then I will have a cup, if you please."

She left, returning a few moments later with a tray containing a coffee pot, milk and sugar, and two cups and saucers. "Would you like some dessert? There's that blueberry pie that I made yesterday. We didn't even cut into it last night, so it's still fresh, and—"

"None for me, thanks. And I'll just take my coffee plain, if you don't mind."

"But you always like milk in it at night, Paul. You've told me so many times that you don't sleep well if—"

"There's nothing wrong with the way I sleep. And if I feel like drinking my coffee black—"

"Then that's the way you shall have it," Helga declared firmly. It was excruciatingly plain that he would make an issue out of any subject, that he would find an argument even where there were no grounds for one.

Paul took the cup she held out to him, grunted his thanks and buried himself behind his magazine. He knew he was behaving ungraciously, but he kept remembering that Helga had gone out to see his mother, in full and deliberate consciousness that he would be displeased, so he could not stem his feeling of impatience with her. Apparently she was too callous, too insensitive to be capable of understanding that she as well as he had been on the receiving end of his father's insults. And she was blatantly unable to see that he was demonstrating the greatest of all possible strength by refusing to have any contact with his parents until such time as they made an appropriate apology. He was tired of trying to make Helga recognize the light, and from now on she would have to gain an insight into his principles by herself.

If she was too young or too foolish—or whatever she was—to digest what he told her, that was her tough luck. He had more than enough on his mind. And she would have to become an adult on her own; he was her husband, not her teacher. He continued to sit, absorbed in thought, and gradually he realized that Helga was speaking to him.

"Paul," she said tentatively, for the third time.

"Mmm?"

"You seemed a million miles away."

"Not necessarily."

"I don't want to disturb you if you're thinking of something important—"

"Please, Helga. If there's something you want to say, then go ahead and say it!"

"All right. Another wedding present came today. From Mr. and Mrs. Henkle. He was my boss while I was still working. Guess what it is."

"I couldn't possibly guess."

"A salad bowl, of course." They had previously received four, and had indulged in considerable private joking on the subject, so Helga smiled broadly.

Paul, however, was in no mood to be amused. "I see," he said, wooden-faced.

"I'll get it and show it to you. It's a very pretty one, really, the nicest of all of them. I think it's made of cherry, and it has a silver-handled spoon and fork with it—"

"Don't bother. I'll look at it some other time." He began to leaf through his magazine.

"All right." A wall separated them, Helga thought, and although it was invisible it was still very real: she could feel its presence, high and thick and impenetrable. A wave of exhaustion crept over her. "I think I'm going in to bed, Paul."

"Okay. Good night."

Helga was already on her feet, and had he given her any sign of encouragement or softness, she would have come over to him. But his unyielding abruptness startled her, and she moved slowly toward the bedroom. This was the first time they hadn't kissed each other good night, but Paul seemed so indifferent, so removed that Helga left the room without speaking another word.

She was still awake when he came to bed some two hours later, and she had no way of knowing that he hadn't actually read a word in all that time.

* * *

By the time Paul came into the living room in the morning, putting on his jacket, Helga was dressed and the breakfast table was set. She was bustling around in the kitchen when he appeared in the doorway, and after saying, "Good morning," they exchanged a token kiss. Each had thought of many things to say, but neither wanted to be the first to speak. A single gesture from either would have sufficed to restore at least the aura of mutual good will, but a strange paralysis, a combination of pride, stubbornness and self-justification immobilized them.

And so they sat down in a silence that grew increasingly uncomfortable. Paul checked through the morning newspapers, marking them with a heavy copy pencil of soft lead, a task he ordinarily would have performed later at the office, and Helga, at a loss for anything better to do, busied herself making out a marketing list. Whenever one glanced surreptitiously across the table, the other seemed to be occupied, and the cleavage consequently became deeper.

Paul, who was prepared to forgive Helga if she admitted to him that she had been wrong, hardened himself at the signs of what he interpreted as her intransigence, and she, seeing his stony face, despaired. She could not refrain from speaking, however, when she saw that he was again leaving his meal virtually untouched.

"Aren't your eggs done the way you want them, Paul?"

"Sure, they're fine. I'm just not very hungry, I guess. Don't worry about it."

"But I do worry. You ate so little last night."

"I'm all right, I tell you."

"You can't put in a full day's work on an empty tummy. It just isn't right."

"Helga, will you please stop sounding like my mother? If I get hungry later in the morning, I'll have a sweet roll and some coffee sent in to me at the office. In the meantime what I'm eating right now suits me perfectly." He was sorry he had made the remark about his mother, but he'd only make matters worse if he called further attention to it.

"You'll do as you please, naturally." Having been rebuffed, she took refuge in her dignity. "I was merely concerned about you, that's all."

"Thank you for your concern. I appreciate it." That wasn't what he had intended to say at all. He wanted to tell her that he felt bewildered and lonely, that he didn't know how to go forward since his feeling that they were operating as a team, as a unit, had been destroyed. Then, remembering that it was she who had sided with his parents, he was engulfed by a new wave of bitterness.

Helga saw the sudden downward curve of his lips, but she had no intention of reopening a subject that had already been plumbed exhaustively and fruitlessly. "Will you be home at the usual time tonight?"

"Sure, unless some big story breaks. Why, do you have something planned?"

"Not a thing."

He drank the last half of his coffee in a single gulp and

glanced at his watch. "I'd better get out of here. I'm still not sure of the bus schedules."

"Take the car today, why don't you?"

"No need for that." Actually, he thought, he would have preferred to drive to work. But his conscience was uneasy, for he felt a faint but definite suspicion that he was being overly harsh on Helga, and his attitude would be somewhat mitigated if he punished himself through a form of self-denial.

She wanted to say that she was spending the day at home, but she recognized that his offer of the use of the car was a peace gesture, the greatest of which he was capable of making at the moment. "Thank you," she said.

Paul shoved back his chair. "I'd better get rolling. There are lots of words waiting to get written today."

Helga would have accompanied him to the front door, but he was gone before she could rise from her seat. His failure to kiss her goodbye hurt, but the pain wasn't as sharp as it would have been a day or two ago. Curiously, the longer the bad feeling between them persisted, the more numb she became.

*　　*　　*

No member of the Bjornson family ever acted on sudden impulse, and Helga had devoted great care and thought to tonight. She had spent the better part of the day finishing her new dress, and as she inspected herself critically in it now in the full-length mirror on the face of the cabinet her father had made, she felt sure it would please Paul. It certainly wasn't the sort of thing she ever would have chosen for herself, but when she had seen it on an advertising poster in front of a movie theatre two days ago, she had hurried down to the basement of the Boston Store, where a fabric sale had been in progress, and had bought the materials.

Her own taste was such that she didn't look like herself, but she told herself as she studied her reflection that it was the kind of costume a man was certain to admire. The dress was a sheath of shiny black satin, with a tricky neckline which dipped to a "V" in the front. It had short, frilly cape sleeves of bright, multi-colored striped taffeta, and there was a wide sash of the same material which knotted on one side. All in all, the effect was one of sophistication, and Helga, thinking she looked a trifle too pale, touched up her mouth with the darkest shade of lipstick she possessed.

Paul would surely recognize what she had done as an attempt at reconciliation, and if she was any judge at all, he would certainly drop the chip from his shoulder. Then, after real amity was restored, they would be able to discuss the problems of their relationships with his parents calmly, dispassionately.

It seemed as though he was much later than usual tonight, but when Helga heard his key in the front lock she glanced at the bedroom clock and saw to her surprise that if anything he was a few minutes early. "I'm home," he called, and Helga hurried into the living room.

"Hello, darling." She stood, self-consciously, in the center of the room.

"Hi." Paul started toward her, stopped and stared at her. "Who do you think you are, Jean Harlow or somebody? That's the most gosh-awful outfit I've ever seen!"

Helga, who seldom cried, ran into the bathroom, shut the door behind her and wept, hard.

CHAPTER TWENTY-THREE

Helga had seen enough of the houses of the well-to-do to realize that the apartment building in which her parents lived was little better than a tenement, but the familiar odors, the cracked plaster and the peeling wallpaper comforted her as she slowly climbed the stairs. This had been home for a long time, and she savored each moment, relaxing in the warmth of the security that she had always known here and had always taken for granted. Opening her purse, she took out the key she kept in a little inner pocketbook, unlocked the front door and walked into her parents' apartment.

Her father was sitting in front of the window, dressed in battered trousers and an old shirt with the sleeves rolled up. He was reading a thick book and Helga saw that it was printed in Swedish, that it was new and that, like almost everything her father ever read, it looked ponderous and beyond her grasp. He was so absorbed that he failed to hear her enter, and she stood very still for a moment, drinking in the scene.

The cheap, worn furniture was just as it had always been, and her father, solid and reliable, looked precisely as he had in her imagination during these past few days. She wanted to cry, but controlled herself; apparently she made some slight, involuntary movement, however, and Olaf Bjornson looked up.

There was no surprise in his face as he smiled, marked his place in the book with deliberation, closed it and stood.

"So, Helga. So."

"Pa!" It was ridiculous to feel as she did, but she buried her face in his shoulder as she hugged him fiercely.

"We did not know you would come to see us today," he said gently.

"I didn't know it myself—until I just came out. I should have telephoned first, I guess. There might have been nobody here, and the trip would have been wasted. Where's Ma?"

"To the butcher shop. Soon she comes back."

"You aren't working today, Pa?"

"Three days of work only we have this week. Next week is promised six days."

"Oh, that's wonderful." Helga began to wander around the room, touching familiar objects, almost caressing them with her fingertips.

"I do not complain."

"I know. You never have. Pa, I'm sorry about dinner the other night. Having to call it all off, I mean. But we want to have you and Ma up very soon. In the next few days."

Bjornson, who had been watching her carefully, managed to assume a bland expression. "Always the young they are busy. Too busy for the old."

"Oh, Pa!"

"I do not object. This all fathers and mothers must understand, that when their children grow up, they move out of the nest. And this the children must understand, too, so they do not feel guilty when they are too busy with the new nest to visit the old."

"Some parents understand it, and some children. But not all, I can assure you," Helga said bitterly. She was about to add more, but the words would not come and she turned to a little plant on the window sill, which she had herself bought several

[274]

years previously, and methodically wiped dust from its leaves with her fingers.

Her father studied her in silence, making no attempt to persuade her to reveal her troubles. In due time and in her own way she would unburden herself and disclose the reason for this unexpected visit. "You have on a new dress, Helga?"

"Yes, Pa. This is only the second time I've worn it." The dress, a part of her trousseau, was of tomato-red, printed with splashes of white, and Helga, who had copied it from a magazine pattern, considered it one of the most stylish things in her wardrobe.

"You have bought this at Marshall Field, maybe?"

"Hardly." She laughed at the suggestion. "I made it myself, just before I was married. Ma helped me." She turned and faced her father. "I'm sure we showed it to you. Don't you recognize it?"

The old man shrugged; one woman's dress was exactly like another to him, but he had helped Helga to forget her worries for a moment, and that had been his only aim. "The goods cost much money," he declared, fingering the material of the skirt.

"How you could have lived with Ma and me all these years and still know so little about things like this is beyond me! It's silk shantung that Ma bought at a remnant sale a whole year ago."

"There is much I do not know." Bjornson grinned harmlessly.

"But there's so much you do know, Pa. About the things that really matter." There was a catch in her voice, and before she quite realized what was happening, her father was on his feet again and was holding her in his arms.

"If Paul treats my girl bad, with my own hands will I kill him."

"He—doesn't mean to hurt me, Pa. It isn't his fault, really.

[275]

He can't help being the way he is, any more than I can help being the way I am."

"You want to cry, Helga? So first cry, then we talk."

She smiled instead, which was the reaction he had hoped for. "Why do you hate to see people cry, Pa? Is it because tears are a sign of weakness, and you're so strong?"

"Often the strong weep harder than the weak. I do not like, because to cry is to waste. When something is wrong, it must be made better. To cry, this does not help."

"In the kind of spot that Paul and I are in, I'm not sure anything will help, Pa. It's just what you told me, weeks and weeks ago, but I wouldn't believe you then. We don't seem to speak the same language."

Her father glanced idly at the dust jacket of his book. "In Babel people did not understand each other. For thousands of years, man tries to make his neighbor know what he says and to hear right what his neighbor says to him. So when two young people start together in marriage, it is no surprise that they need time before they make sense to each other." Although his words were calm and soothing, he was peering at Helga sharply from beneath his shaggy white brows.

"But it's so complicated. Paul's father is having business problems. Something is happening to his company that upsets him dreadfully, and he—"

"If I have in my pocket one hundred dollars, I think I am rich. If Mr. Dawson has in his pocket one thousand dollars, he thinks he is poor. The son feels as the father. Here it is you who must have the sympathy, Helga. When a man is afraid, it is wrong to laugh or to turn away from him, even if you know his fears are false. Your man shares the fears of his father, so these must now be your fears for him, too."

"Wait, Pa. You haven't let me finish. I understand they're afraid they'll lose their money, and I really do sympathize with the whole family. If it were only a question of money, do you think I'd be so concerned? I'm your daughter, remember, so the money is the very least part."

"Please to go on." Bjornson settled back into his chair, satisfied now that he had achieved his goal. Helga had spent at least some portion of her indignation on him, and hence was calmer than she had been when she had first come in. Now it would be possible to deal with her logically.

"Paul's father said some very unpleasant things to Paul about —both of us the other night. And Pa, I'm not complaining. I know he's in an awful state because of his business, so I didn't mind."

"This was sure to happen. The father holds too close to the son. The son wishes to be free, but when the hands of the father are no longer there, he fears he will fall."

"I've come between them, Pa. I've disrupted their whole family."

"No, they tear themselves apart." The old carpenter illustrated graphically with his strong hands.

"I still haven't told you all of it. I went out to see Paul's mother the other morning. I felt sorry for her, Pa. And she's good and decent and sweet. But Paul was furious. He's been angry with me ever since. He accuses me of taking sides with his family against him, as though—well, as though we were all in some big conspiracy together, just trying to hurt him. I've tried and tried to explain to him, but he won't listen to me. He keeps acting as though I've done him harm and he wants to hit me back."

"All this I have expected, but not so soon."

"He behaves as though he's engaged in some kind of a private war with his parents, Pa. And from the way he talks, either I've got to be on his side or I'm on the other side. I thought he had such a wonderful family life, but he doesn't even know what the word 'family' means. If he has any feeling for his father's problems, he keeps them to himself very successfully. I certainly can't see him showing anything, even though he must be suffering, I know he must."

"He suffers, Helga."

"But what am I to do, Pa? How can we ever build a successful marriage, and have a family of our own some day—if Paul is only interested in justifying himself? If he's just going to carry on a senseless feud—"

"Senseless? Not senseless." Rising slowly, Bjornson walked to the shelves at the far side of the room, looked for several seconds at the well-worn books in it and finally withdrew one. Calmly, deliberately, he thumbed through the pages until he found what he was seeking, then he returned to his daughter and handed the volume to her. "Here," he said, pointing. "Read."

Helga could not find the pertinent reference for a moment. Then she saw it and repeated it aloud. " 'He who flies from his own family has far to travel.' "

"Those words were written more than two thousand years ago in Rome. But Paul has not learned their meaning."

"Will he ever learn them?"

"Who can say?" The old man shrugged his shoulders expressively. "You remember, Helga, my cousin Gustav, who came with me to America from Sweden? Many years ago he died, but you remember him, I think."

"Not too clearly. He was a big man, always laughing. And he wore a silk shirt one time, I believe. It was the first silk shirt I ever saw."

"This was Gustav. In America all money is easy, this is what Gustav said. So if in his pocket he had twenty dollars, the next day in his pocket was nothing. Always he had to borrow, and when in Cleveland, Ohio, he died at the age of forty-seven, even the funeral was paid for by your cousin Carl and me." He paused, then drove home his point. "Forty-seven years old Gustav was, but inside he was a little child still."

"I don't see—"

"You are a woman, Helga."

"Of course." Her pale eyebrows furrowed, and she looked at her father in bewilderment. He was never one to talk for the sake of conversation, and at this critical time in her life he was not merely trying to soothe her. "I'm married now, so I'm a woman."

"Before marriage even, you were a woman. Now you see why I was afraid for you to marry Paul?"

"No, Pa."

"Paul, he is not a man."

"But—"

"Like my cousin Gustav, who did not learn how much is a dollar, Paul is a boy still. Gustav was a child about money. Paul is in other ways a child."

There was a long silence while Helga digested his words. "You mean," she said at last, "that he still clings to his parents like a little boy?"

"To his Ma and Pa, no, not now. Now he holds to you instead."

"But he's the man of our family, Pa. He supports me, and he makes all the major decisions and he—"

"Paul has not learned that to honor himself he must honor his Ma and Pa. And he does not know that if he is to have a marriage, he must love his wife."

Helga was deeply shocked. "Oh, you're wrong there, Pa. Of course he loves me! If he didn't, he wouldn't have married me. He wouldn't have faced the opposition of his parents and—"

"They did not want this marriage. That is why Paul wanted it. That is why he fought for it. That is why he married you."

"What are you trying to tell me?" she demanded, all of her own doubts and insecurities being forced to the surface by her father's quiet statements.

"Your Pa brought to America the ideas of the old country, this is what you thought, Helga. I said this marriage was maybe not good. And you said, 'My Pa is old-fashioned. In this country a poor girl and a rich boy together can be happy.' This is true, too."

"Now you're contradicting yourself, Pa. First you say one thing, then you tell me the exact opposite, until I don't know what you're trying to say." Helga's composure vanished completely, and she looked at her father frantically.

"In my own way I tell you. Sometimes it is said that a husband who is much older than his wife cannot make a fine marriage. This is not so. Sometimes it said that if the girl comes from one country and the man comes from another country, they cannot make a good marriage. This also is not so. To find that which is right and that which will last, a man and a woman need love. But *this* they *must* have."

"You keep hinting that Paul doesn't love me! Is that what you're trying to say, Pa? Is it?"

"Paul does not yet love you," was the unruffled reply, and Bjornson's calm seemed to underscore the gravity of his words.

"Then why did he marry me? Answer me that!"

"To Paul you were the sign of his wish to break away from his Ma and Pa. My Helga was not the daughter of a rich man. She did not go to schools that cost more money each year than a carpenter earns in that year. She did not wear fine and fancy clothes, and her friends were daughters of men who were poor, like her Pa."

"I was all the things Paul's parents thought were wrong for their son. And he was just defying them by marrying me. That's it, isn't it? That's what you're trying to tell me now."

"No, no." He stroked her tense hand and forearm. "To make you see clear, I explain too simply. You are something to Paul. He has met many girls, but you are the girl he wishes to marry, you are the girl he marries. He has feeling for you, but it is not the same as the feeling you have for him. This I have long seen. You love Paul very deep."

[280]

"Yes, Pa. I do."

"His love for you is not so deep. It is—I am old. In my mind now I do not remember how in America they call this kind of love he has for you."

"Puppy love?" She needed all of her reserves of courage to speak the words.

"Puppy love. So now you understand."

Helga tried desperately to regain her sense of equilibrium. "Won't he ever feel more than that, Pa? Will it always be this way?"

"Maybe. Maybe not."

"What can I do?"

"Nothing, my Helga. It is Paul who must do. You can give to him only from the outside. That which he needs must come from the inside." Bjornson stood and patted his daughter on the shoulder. "First he must know himself. When he does this, he will no longer fight his Pa, for he will know there is no need to fight. When this happens, he will become really a man. He will see everything in the world with the eyes of a man then."

"And how will he see me, Pa?"

"Who can answer such a question? Maybe to himself he will say, 'This is my wife. My wife I love.' Or maybe he will say, 'Marriage to the daughter of a carpenter is wrong.' If your love for him is so big and so strong that you can wait, then you will learn in time how he will feel about you."

"I love Paul." Helga stood, and with decision a sense of peace returned to her. "So I'll stick with him. I'll be right there when he makes up his mind whether he really loves me or not."

CHAPTER TWENTY-FOUR

Newspaper work, which always sounded so exciting to outsiders, could be dull and routine almost beyond belief, and Paul felt bored with his job, himself and the world. Not so long ago he had been proud of his position and had eagerly accepted the challenge that had awaited him each morning when he first sat down at his desk; he had gladly accepted the responsibility of preparing the day's news for public consumption and had considered himself a member of a highly trained professional team.

Now, however, he seemed to see everything through different eyes. All that distinguished today's news from yesterday's was a mass of unimportant detail, and his cynicism extended even to his opinion of his writing. The people who read his stories in their homes and on busses or suburban trains actually did no more than glance at his words, for they were too absorbed in their own problems. He realized, of course, that his own troubles weighed on his mind to the exclusion of almost everything else, but he told himself that he wasn't feeling sorry for himself, that he had a right to feel as he did.

He and Helga were living almost as strangers under the same roof these days, and it was absurd for a couple so recently married to behave with such mutual cold indifference, but ridiculous or not, that was the situation and he had to face it. At least she hadn't gone out to his parents again, and that was something for which to be grateful. Or if she had, she certainly hadn't said anything to him. And by this time it was plain enough what his father thought of both him and Helga, for there had been no word of any kind from Gordon.

Paul knew he could be roused to new anger just thinking about his father, so he deliberately concentrated on the material awaiting rewrite on his desk. There were some notes on an unpleasant and rather sensational divorce case, the details of which a reporter had phoned in to him from the Superior Court, there were a couple of minor crime stories and the inevitable advance copy of some politician's long-winded speech to be delivered at a dinner that evening. The most appealing of his morning assignments was to prepare a little feature story on the weather of the past twenty-four hours, which had been freakish, and he thought he would try his hand at it first. However, after three starts, none of which satisfied him, he discovered that he was in no mood to be amusing, and that everything he tried to put on paper about the ups and downs of the temperature was trite and stale. No matter what he might say about the city roasting one hour and shivering the next, someone else had said it before and had undoubtedly said it better.

He lit a cigarette, but the smoke felt harsh against the membranes of his throat and after taking a couple of puffs he stubbed it out. Several other rewrite men were sending a copy boy out for coffee and Paul thought of ordering some for himself, then changed his mind. Nothing he ate or drank seemed to sit right these days, and there was no point in deliberately making himself feel worse. A weariness that grew deeper and more enervating every day had taken hold of him, and as he glanced around the local room he thought that his colleagues all looked tired, too. Most of them were pale men with drawn skins and worried eyes and Paul wondered if they, too, had once thought of the newspaper world as glamorous and exciting. Worst of all, not even the prospect of some day owning his own newspaper, which had always roused him, could stir him from his lethargy; he had never felt like a crusader in his life.

Forcing himself to work, he wrote one of the crime stories, an account of a robbery, then started to work on the other. Although he was now concentrating on the material in his typewriter, he was nevertheless aware of the presence of Harry Austin when the City Editor appeared and conferred briefly with his assistant, only to vanish again in the direction of his private office. The assistant, a heavy-set, short man who wore thick spectacles, surveyed the local room, said something to the slotman and then returned to his perusal of the early editions of the afternoon papers. Paul gave the matter no further notice until he heard someone call his name and looked up to see the slotman beckoning to him.

"Okay, Eddie." Shoving back his chair, he thought that it would be in keeping with his present run of bad luck if he were given some particularly difficult writing assignment today, when the words weren't flowing as they should.

"You're a good guy, aren't you, Paul?" The slotman loosened his necktie.

"Sure. I'm a great guy."

"Always willing to help out some pals."

"Most of the time," Paul replied cautiously.

"Well, it just happens I've got a special job for you, kid."

"I knew it," Paul groaned.

"Oh, you'll like this one. It'll give you a chance to get out in the nice, fresh air for awhile instead of being cooped up in a dark, dirty newspaper office."

"Do me a favor and cut the gags. I'm not in a mood for fun and games this morning."

"All right, all right. A story has just broken, and we're shorthanded this morning. The North Side legman is home with the flu, and three other reporters are out sick, too. Everybody available is running around some place. And I'm stuck. Mr. Austin tossed this thing to Mr. Mack here, and Mr. Mack gave it to me. And now I've got to get rid of it."

"In words of one syllable, please, Eddie. I'm just a rewrite man, so I'm a little dim."

"I'm just asking you to do me a favor and not climb up on your high horse, Paul. Will you be a reporter again for a little while this morning? You're the junior on the rewrite battery, and seeing I've got to assign one of you fellows—"

"Okay, sure. Relax, Eddie. Where do you want me to go, and what's the story?"

"Something popped up on the near North Side. We just got the flash on it through the police radio, so I guess you'll have to pick up the details yourself. Here's where you're to go." The slot-man handed Paul a sheet of yellow copy paper on which an address was scribbled in pencil. "It's plenty early in the day, so you'll have lots of time to come back in and write your own story. And thanks for helping me out, kid. I appreciate this."

"Think nothing of it."

Paul walked without undue haste back to his desk, donned his jacket and automatically picked up a wad of copy paper, which he stuck into his pocket along with a couple of pencils. He glanced idly at the address on the sheet Eddie had given him, and was glad he didn't have too far to go.

Buttoning his collar and straightening his necktie, he jammed the paper bearing the address into a pocket of his jacket and deliberately sauntered out of the door. It was standard procedure that no newspaperman ever showed a sign of haste while still inside his own office. He might sprint after he had left the local room, but the professional always assumed a casual air until he reached the street. It was a way of demonstrating, Paul had long ago concluded, that the news-gatherer was blasé and that no story was worth getting really worked up about. Whatever the basic motive, he had fallen into the pattern himself, and his behavior this morning was automatic and unthinking.

[285]

Mid-morning traffic on Madison Street seemed normal, so Paul was annoyed to discover that there were no taxicabs parked in front of the Express office. On most days at least two or three enterprising cab drivers waited here to take members of the staff to various parts of the city on their assignments, and Paul told himself gloomily that his luck was running true to form. He moved to the curb in the hopes of hailing a cab and wished that he had taken the Plymouth today. Although it was true enough that his job usually kept him desk-bound, occasions like this did arise from time to time, and it would be convenient for him to have the car. Most days when he left it with Helga, she didn't use it at all, and he was willing to bet that at this moment it was sitting, useless, in the parking area next to their apartment house.

Two taxis appeared, one behind the other, but both were carrying passengers and Paul stepped down into the street, waving an arm. He waited, fuming, through three changes of traffic lights at the corner, then at last an empty Yellow Cab approached. "Where to, Mister?" the driver asked as Paul got in.

Paul was already fumbling with the paper bearing the address. "One-fourteen Moulton Place." He leaned back in the cab, lit a cigarette and looked idly out of the window. There were advantages to riding around town at his ease, on an expense account, and he realized he was being petty to begrudge Helga the use of the car.

Traffic on the Wabash Avenue bridge crossing the Chicago River was unusually heavy and the driver became talkative. "You see the White Sox ball game yesterday?"

"No, I didn't."

"What a catcher that Ray Schalk is! There's nobody in the majors in his class, even if the Sox don't win a pennant. Where at is Moulton Place, exactly? You know?"

"Right off Lake Shore Drive. It's a little street, about two blocks long. Go up to the Drive and I'll show you." Paul always was amused when his knowledge of the city's geography proved to be more extensive than that of a taxicab driver, and he chuckled softly to himself for he happened to know Moulton Place well. Uncle Henry and Aunt Helen Thayer lived there, and he had visited their house scores of times.

"You're the boss, Mister. You say it and I'll take you there. One-fourteen it was, huh?"

"Wait a second till I check. Yes, that's right." Paul crumpled the sheet of paper and tossed it out through the open window.

He settled back in his seat once more, and it occurred to him that he did not remember the actual street number of the Thayers' address. He tried to visualize the stone numerals on the front of their house, but could not. It was strange, he thought, that hardly anyone could ever remember the number of a close friend's address.

It was impossible, of course, that he was being sent to the Thayer home; no family in Chicago was more respectable or dignified, and certainly nothing would take place there that would be sent out over the police radio network. The mere idea of the Thayers becoming involved in melodrama made him smile faintly to himself, and he decided that if he finished his assignment with dispatch, he might drop in and say hello to Aunt Helen.

"Take the Cubs now," the driver said. "The way Gabby is hitting and Hack Wilson is hitting, they're like as not to wind up on top. It don't matter to me, though. I'd rather watch Bib Falk hit one little single for the Sox than watch the whole Cubs' team knock them out of Wrigley Field all afternoon."

Paul grunted, not encouraging conversation. They had just reached Oak Street, where there was a traffic jam, and if the driver was distracted they'd never get to Moulton Place.

Hurt by his passenger's indifference, the man fell silent, and Paul gazed out of the window as the taxi moved up Lake Shore Drive. He was glad he had been given this opportunity to get out of the office for a time this morning; the change in routine and the activity might help to curb his restlessness. He kept trying to squelch the recurring notion that his marriage was failing, but it wasn't easy. In the past couple of days he'd found himself thinking about Joan Adams, which made him feel guilty and disloyal to Helga, and that simply confused him all the more. Nevertheless he could not help but speculate on how different life would be if he had married Joan instead of Helga. He had recognized the strength and depth of Joan's character too late, and he wondered whether he might have fallen in love with her had he seen her more clearly years ago.

Angrily, impatiently, he put the subject out of his mind. He had to deal with a situation that existed: he loved Helga, he was married to Helga but he wasn't getting along with Helga. And suppositions over what once might have been wouldn't solve current problems that were very real and very pressing.

The car swung into Moulton Place, and Paul saw a police patrolman in uniform standing outside a solid and respectable grey stone house. Paul's shock was so great that he could neither think nor move for several seconds. The house was that of Uncle Henry and Aunt Helen Thayer.

"All right to let you off here, Mister? There's a couple of police cars parked right out in front of the joint."

"Sure." Paul handed the man a one dollar bill, and didn't wait for change.

There were indeed two police cars at the curb, and Paul's apprehension was so great that he felt physically ill. A heavy-set uniformed patrolman blocked his path. "Move along now, move along."

Paul wanted to shout that nobody could keep him out of Uncle Henry's house. Instead he took his wallet from his pocket and produced his press card. "I'm from the Express."

"Why didn't you say so in the first place? Second floor, turn to your left."

Paul had already pushed open the door and was sprinting up the stairs. He knew this house almost as intimately as he did that of his parents, and the policeman had directed him to the master bedroom. Although the flight of steps was short, he was out of breath by the time he reached the landing and stood for an instant, gasping. Off to the right, through an open door there was a low murmur of conversation and Paul made out the voice of Aunt Helen, then that of one of her sons. He thought that, as an intimate of the family, he should go directly to them to find out what had happened, but he was reluctant to barge in. He felt guilty at being here as a reporter. He turned to his left and in the dim light of the hallway he made out the form of another uniformed officer.

Wordlessly Paul extended his card, the policeman nodded and stepped aside, and Paul opened the bodroom door. His attention was first arrested by a detective in mufti, who seemed to be marking down a list of contents of a bureau in a small, worn black book. The man glanced up from his labors and shoved his hat farther back on his broad, high brow. "Who are you?"

"Dawson. Express."

"Okay. Over there." The detective jerked a thumb past his shoulder.

Paul had to force himself to turn, to look across the room. There, on one of the beds, was the fully clothed body of Henry Thayer. In his right hand was a small pistol, and it was evident that he had shot himself through the temple. His eyes, which had always been such a perfect mirror of his joyous vitality, were wide open, and on his face was an expression of bewilderment, almost as though he was bemused at the realization that life was over.

It was so quiet in the room that the scratching of the detective's pencil against the paper of the notebook sounded sharply, then suddenly it stopped. "You want to see the note? It's over there on the dresser, the high dresser. Just be careful you don't stick your own fingerprints all over it. The lieutenant is fussy about details like that."

Paul did not know he was even in motion until he found himself in front of the dresser, and he was only vaguely conscious that the blurred reflection he saw in a mirror above the cabinet was his own. Lying face up on the surface of the dresser was a letter written in Uncle Henry's characteristically bold, vigorous hand, but the words swam crazily before Paul's eyes. He steeled himself to read it. It was short and simple. Uncle Henry had written that he could not bear to live in a world in which the company that he had devoted his life to must fail.

The letter was penned on the engraved executive stationery of Whitmarket and Company.

"These old guys are all alike," the detective said as he continued with his inventory. "They've got everything in the world—money, fancy houses, the whole works. So their private gold mine gets shaky—and wham. They can't take it. I wish I had ten bucks for every case like this I've had to go out on the past few years. Boy, could I have me a night on the town!"

"Yeah." Paul dredged the word up from somewhere, but his voice did not sound like his own.

The impact of Uncle Henry's death was so stunning that Paul had to grip the edge of the dresser to maintain some contact with the world of reality. And the longer he stood here, the deeper the blow penetrated, the wider the area of his pain. He thought of a rock being thrown into a still pond, sinking to the bottom and sending its ever-broadening ripples across the surface of the water. Again and again, in his mind's eye, he saw the splash of the rock, and he thought he was going mad.

His grief for Uncle Henry was overwhelming: it was inconceivable that so happy a man, someone who had loved every facet of life so intensely, was gone. That he, of all people, had chosen suicide as a means of escape, was horrifying. In a remote corner of Paul's being there stirred the first feelings of sympathy for Aunt Helen and the other members of the Thayer family, but his own sorrow was so great that there was almost no room for any other emotion.

Then, gradually, he began to realize the broader implications of what had happened. Whitmarket and Company was of necessity in desperate shape for a man like Henry Thayer to act as he had. Yet his participation in the shares of the corporation had been small; granted that he had been the most highly valued and highly paid of employees, he had still been an employee.

The owner of Whitmarket was its President, Gordon Dawson. And, Paul thought, if Uncle Henry had been so wretched that he had killed himself, his own father must be totally without hope.

All the violent ill feeling between his father and himself that had come into the open in recent days was more clearly etched now than ever before, and Paul felt a sense of degradation almost as penetrating as his sorrow. How much his feud with his father had distracted Gordon's mind from the critical problems he'd had to face at his company Paul did not know, would never know.

The detective was peering across the room suspiciously. "Hey, did you know this old guy?"

"Yes," Paul said, "I knew him."

Turning quickly, he walked into the corridor, down the stairs and out of the house. Later, tomorrow perhaps, he would call and pay his respects to Aunt Helen. But right now he needed to think. He was alive, Helga was alive, his father and mother were alive, and the time had come when he needed to see all of them without distortion. He wanted to weep for Uncle Henry, but that would have to wait; there were the living to be considered at this moment, and he was grateful to God that those who were dearest to him were alive.

CHAPTER TWENTY-FIVE

Helga, completely unaware of the dramatic events taking place only a few blocks away, was spending her morning cleaning the apartment. She found some measure of relief from her frustrations in scrubbing the kitchen floor, in polishing every piece of furniture and in wiping away all vestiges of the soot that was the enemy of Chicago's housewives. In spite of her thoroughness she completed the task before noon, took a shower and changed her clothes. Now the problem was how to fill in the rest of the day.

She had no desire to read and could not, in fact, concentrate on words. And she felt no wish to see any of her friends or even her parents. It was easier, even if it was wrong, to give in to the unaccustomed lassitude that so often took hold of her these days, particularly after she had indulged in violent physical exertion. It had been one thing, she was discovering, to have told her father she would patiently and bravely see Paul through his inner crisis, but the execution was more difficult by far than the expression of her intention.

There were moments, and this was one of them, when Helga experienced a sensation of let-down, when the task before her seemed greater than her ability to handle it. For a long minute she stood in the center of the living room, shaken by doubt and confusion; then her good sense and her integrity reasserted themselves and she resolutely forced herself to abandon her mood of despair. There was much still to be done today, she told herself: she would go marketing, then prepare herself a bite of lunch. And a little later in the day she would telephone Betsy and arrange a private date. Her sister-in-law was about to return to school in a few days, so there wasn't too much time left for the get-together that Helga believed was essential. Perhaps there wasn't much that two girls could do to heal a family breach that seemed more irrevocable with each passing day, but at least they could try, and through discussing the problem they might arrive at some conclusion.

It was all well and good, Helga told herself fiercely, for her father to hold the view that there was nothing she herself could do to help Paul. Such an approach, by its very definition, was defeatist, and she wasn't going to accept the idea that she might have to wait for years before Paul became truly adult. If courageous action on her part could speed the process, she was eager to do anything and everything she could, even though she knew there was a considerable risk involved. It was certainly possible that when Paul saw himself clearly, he would reject her.

Nevertheless Helga was willing to take the chance. Her present experience, she was learning, was giving her a deeper insight into the nature of real love, and she realized that the essence of a deep and abiding affection for someone else was unselfishness. If Paul benefited, she would be content, even if it meant that she herself would suffer. Smiling wryly, she told herself that the cost of her achievement of maturity might be extraordinarily high.

The door buzzer sounded, but Helga was so engrossed in her thoughts that she did not hear it, and it rang a second time, more insistently, before it penetrated her consciousness. Still lost in the depths of her mind, she crossed the room and opened the front door; it was a second or two before she was fully aware

[293]

that the person waiting on the threshold was her mother-in-law.

"I do hope I'm not interrupting you when you're doing something important," Molly said hesitantly. "I really should have called you before coming up."

By way of answer Helga threw her arms around the older woman and kissed her. Molly was embarrassed by the unexpected demonstration, but she was relieved, too, and a little of the tension in her face evaporated as she stepped inside the apartment. Having been uncertain of her welcome, she became overly voluble.

"I was downtown shopping this morning," she said, "and after wandering around in Fields and Carsons for a couple of hours I decided I was being silly, because I wasn't really trying to buy anything that I actually wanted. So I just acted on impulse. I got on the bus and came up to see you. It was the first time in ten years that I've been on a bus, but I got the right one, I really must say that much for myself. Betsy and Marcia will never believe it when I tell them. They're convinced I'm helpless when I'm out alone. Helga, are you sure that I haven't come at an inconvenient time? If there's something you're doing or planning to do, please just say so."

"There's nobody I'd rather see at this very minute," Helga replied, and meant it.

"You haven't had lunch yet?"

"No, I—"

"Then you must come somewhere with me."

"We'll do no such thing! Are you going to deprive me of the opportunity of entertaining you the first time you've given me the chance? We'll have lunch right here."

Molly was about to argue the point, then thought better of it. "All right, if you'll let me help."

"That sounds just perfect. Shall we get things started right away, or would you rather wait for awhile?"

There was a silence for a moment, as Molly tried to bring

herself to open the subject that had brought her here. She could not, however, and so she took refuge in the amenities. "I'm dying to snoop around in your kitchen, I really am."

"Then you shall certainly snoop," Helga said quietly, leading the way into the kitchen.

Molly glanced at her quickly and saw there was no hidden meaning in her tone. "I was just joking," she said feebly.

Helga opened the refrigerator and peered inside. "There's some roast veal, and if you'd like that we could heat it up. And we had chicken last night—"

"From the looks of it, neither of you ate very much." Molly, who was at her side, was suddenly too worried to remember to be polite. "There's almost a whole chicken on that dish."

"I guess we weren't very hungry."

"I'm sorry, Helga. I'm so sorry."

"Please, it isn't your fault, you know."

"It's all our faults. You poor children. And you cooked the chicken the way Paul likes it best, too, fried in a bread-crumb batter. Helga, you've lost weight."

"I look better when I'm thin."

The door of the refrigerator swung gently to and fro, unnoticed. "My husband is ashamed of the things he said about you. I know he intends to apologize to you. I have no idea what he's going to do or how he's going to do it, because he didn't tell me and I didn't press him. But I thought you'd like to know. It may not help much, but I hope it will help a little."

"It helps a great deal. He's a fine man. I've always thought so, and I still think so, more than ever."

"Thank you." Molly looked as though she might burst into tears.

"I suggest that we have the cold chicken and a little salad, if that's all right with you," Helga declared briskly. "It won't take me any time at all to fix the salad."

[295]

She busily washed a head of lettuce, shook it dry and sliced a cucumber. Then, by the time she had mixed a dressing, her mother-in-law had regained at least an outward air of composure. Together they carried platters, dishes and silverware into the living room, and when Helga would have the table with a cloth, Molly demurred, insisting that they use the woven fiber mats which were already in place. There was little conversation as they started to eat, and Helga was content to say nothing, to let talk develop as it would. Molly, to whom silence was unnatural, was too occupied in sorting out her emotions to indulge in the light social chit-chat that would have come so easily to her under ordinary circumstances.

"Helga," she said suddenly. "I want your help. This is no accidental visit, and I really didn't just show up here because of an impulse of the moment."

"I don't know how I can help, but I'll gladly do anything in my power."

"It's Paul. This estrangement is so wrong. But I don't know what to do. I don't know how to reach him."

"Yes, it's very wrong."

"I've been a proud woman all of my life. I've struggled with myself, and I've swallowed my pride in coming to you. But I appeal to you now. I recognize—I've been forced to recognize that I don't know my son and never have. But you know him, Helga, as no one else ever has."

"What makes you think that I—"

"He married you. There's something in you to which he's responded as he never has to anyone before, ever. That's why I beg you now to tell me what to do. I don't know what to do."

Distressed at the spectacle of Molly humbling herself, Helga reached a hand across the table. "Don't blame yourself. You must not blame yourself."

"But I can't go on knowing there's bitterness between Paul and us." Molly reached into the pocket of her brown and white

[296]

striped shirtwaist dress and drew out a handkerchief. "There must be some way to establish the right relations with him again."

"So there is. If you do nothing and wait patiently, Paul will return in time to you. Eventually his bitterness will die and he will make the first move, the right move to you. But if any pressure is put on him, he'll react badly. He'll stay away that much longer, even though it's the last thing in the world he himself wants."

"I've thought so often of calling him, even of seeing him and begging him to make amends with his father. You truly think that if I do nothing at all, he'll change his attitude?"

"I'm sure of it." Helga tried to put all of the conviction she felt into her voice. "His anger is directed against his father, not against you, of course. But he would think that his father sent you to him, and that would keep the fires of his resentment alive. If no wind blows on the coals and fans them, they will die. Where there is real love there cannot be permanent anger, and Paul has a very real love for you and for his father. So that what he foolishly believes is his hatred will vanish."

Molly looked across the table, her eyes damp but bright. "I'm a very lucky woman to have you for a daughter-in-law. And Paul is the luckiest of all. I don't know that he deserves such a wife."

"Maybe he wouldn't agree with that." Helga, to her horror, found that she could not hold back the tears that were forming in her own eyes.

The role of adviser was far more familiar to Molly than that of suppliant, and everything in her that was maternal responded to the challenge of this sudden shift. "Tell me."

"I don't know what there is to tell. Everything I do is wrong. I try and try, but Paul is always disappointed. He criticizes the way I dress, the way I look, the apartment, everything. They're all little things, but they aren't really so little. It's me he's striking at—through all the little things. But if I could only know what really pleases him . . ."

Here was ground on which Molly was sure-footed, and she spoke decisively though gently. "Just you forget about those little things. We'll go shopping together one day soon, very soon, and I'll do all I can to help you. Don't worry about it, dear. It's—"

The ring of the telephone interrupted her, and Helga started at once toward the bedroom. "Excuse me," she said apologetically. "I would be very grateful for your help," she added with a grave smile.

She hurried to the telephone and lifted it from its hook. "Hello."

"Hi. Helga? This is Betsy. Is my mother there?"

The abruptness of the other girl's tone was startling, but Helga accepted it in her stride. "Yes, we've just been having lunch together, and—"

"Oh, thank goodness. I've been hunting all over town for her. Could I speak to her right away, please?"

"Of course." Helga put down the instrument and returned to the living room. "It's Betsy," she said. "She wants to speak to you."

"I wonder how in the world she ever located me," Molly murmured, rising. "Pardon me for a minute, Helga."

The minute stretched out into a very long time, and Helga, at a loss for something better to do, cleaned off the table and washed the dishes. She was almost finished when her mother-in-law appeared in the door, white-faced and trembling, and Helga immediately turned off the water and dried her hands.

"Henry Thayer is dead," Molly said in a low voice. "He shot himself. This morning."

There was no reply to such news, and Helga stood very still, saying nothing.

[298]

"I called Gordon just now, after Betsy told me. But I couldn't reach him."

"He's—all right?"

"I hope so. His secretary said his office was full of people, so he couldn't talk. He said to tell me he'd see me at home this evening. As usual."

Molly swayed slightly; Helga hurried to her and put an arm around her. "Let's go back inside and sit down."

"I've got to go home."

"In a little while. I'll drive you. I have the car here today. But first we'd better sit."

Molly's eyes were dazed as she sank into a chair. "It's the business. Gordon hasn't said much these past few days, but it's been getting worse and worse. I could tell. He hasn't slept. Or eaten. Oh, I wish I'd been able to get through to him when I called him!"

"Of course you do."

"Poor Henry. Poor, dear Henry. And Helen. How terrible for her. Betsy said she called there. She spoke to Dickie Thayer. They're all broken up. Helga, you don't suppose that Gordon will—will—" Her voice trailed away and she was unable to give voice to her fears.

"No, he won't."

"How can you be so sure?" Molly jumped to her feet in a sudden panic. "I'd better go to his office. I—"

"No, that would be no help to him. He must have much to do, and your presence would only distract him and upset him all the more. He knows you will be waiting for him when he comes home tonight, and that is what is most important to him. So don't be afraid. He will be there, just as he promised."

Molly, although still badly frightened, was somewhat comforted. "How do you know that he'll be—all right?" she persisted. "How do you know that he isn't so discouraged and downhearted that he'll—"

"Because he is Paul's father, and I know Paul." Helga spoke crisply, authoritatively now. "Just as you know his father. That is not how men of the Dawson family face their problems."

"How do they face them, then?"

Again Helga slid an arm around her. "They fight. They have too much pride to give in."

"Betsy said she called Paul to tell him, but he was out of his office. I thought he might know what to do. I feel so helpless. Gordon must be so—crushed."

"When the very worst happens, a man must wage his own battle. I have learned that from my own father."

"If Gordon has anything left to fight with. But in the meantime, what am I to do?"

Helga leaned down and kissed Molly on the cheek. "I wish I could answer you, but I can't. I can only tell you what I try to tell myself. We must wait. And pray for guidance."

CHAPTER TWENTY-SIX

"Keep your story down to two hundred words, three hundred at the most," the slotman said. "So many of these old money-bags have gotten panicky when their business has gone on the rocks and have knocked themselves out that they aren't news any more. Mr. Austin wants a straight article with no frills. He doesn't think it's worth a blow-up. And it isn't."

"Okay, Eddie." Paul walked to his desk, sat down and ran some copy paper into his typewriter.

Slowly, painfully, he began to write the story of Henry Thayer's death and to fill in the outline of the life that had gone before the suicide. The cold, dry words, the hard facts that gave no indication of the personality of a man who had been so warm and loving were pitifully inadequate, and Paul felt a growing sense of frustration.

He wanted to shout to the world that Uncle Henry had been one of the finest human beings Chicago had ever produced. And as a final tribute to someone who had meant so much to him, he longed to recapture on paper some reflection of the glowing humanity and zest for life that had made Uncle Henry what he had been.

But there was no place in modern journalism for such a tribute to someone who had never been prominent in the public eye. The Express would print only a straightforward account of the facts of the case and the readers of the newspaper would be mildly interested, at the most, in an unvarnished story of why an elderly business executive had chosen to kill himself.

Paul finished his article, handed it over to a copy boy and continued to sit at his desk, neither seeing nor hearing the activity around him. He remembered the impassioned story he had written about the boy with the broken leg, then he recalled the harried face of the small town editor in whose newspaper he had been interested. And now, after writing his callous and impersonal article about Henry Thayer, the scales of false sentiment began to fall away from his eyes and for the first time he examined himself and his career honestly.

Until now he had tried to persuade himself that the newspaper profession was more exalted and offered greater opportunities for service to the community than what he had always liked to think of as "ordinary" business endeavors. But he had been deluding himself. It was right that the Express could find no space for an emotional word portrait of Uncle Henry; by the same token there was no place in the business world for a facade of romantic sugar-coating, either.

Uncle Henry had been an ethical man, a decent man, an honest man, and as Paul thought of him he began to understand that no one line of endeavor held a monopoly on what was right and principled. There were newspaper editors who were good men and those who were bad, just as there were business executives who believed only in the survival of the rapacious, and others, like Uncle Henry, who spent their whole lives trying to be of service to their customers and clients, dealing fairly and justly with everyone.

In order to be of help to people, Paul realized, a man had to live up to his own obligations first. If he didn't at least try, he would be paying mere lip-service to his ideals, and in reality he would fail to achieve the basic principles that made life worth living.

Striking his desk with the palm of his right hand, he stood abruptly; he knew now what he had to do.

*   *   *

The dull stone of Whitmarket and Company's office building looked dirty in the clear sunlight of late afternoon, and Paul glanced at his wrist-watch. It was four-thirty, much later then he would have guessed. He had walked all the way up here from the Express office, yet he wasn't tired, and in spite of the fact that he had eaten so little for several days, he wasn't hungry. At this moment he felt stronger, more in command of himself than ever before in his life; straightening his necktie and squaring his shoulders, he pushed open the door and walked into the building.

His grandfather gazed down at him from the portrait on the wall, and Paul stared at him for a moment. The main floor receptionist, a girl he had never before seen, looked up at him expectantly, but he informed her, "I know where I'm going," and walked to the elevators. It was true, he thought: he did know where he was going.

"Hello, Mr. Dawson," the elevator operator said, and several people who were already in the elevator, most of them stenographers and file clerks, examined him surreptitiously. As recently as this morning Paul would have resented their curiosity, but he was able to accept it now as a normal and healthy interest, and he paid no further attention to them. His mind was occupied with matters of far greater consequence.

When he arrived at the executive floor, someone called a somber greeting to him, but by the time he turned, whoever the person was had disappeared into an office. Instead of poking his head into several nearby open doors, however, as he might have done at another time, he walked straight down the broad corridor to the Presidential suite, pausing for a moment before the door on which was nailed a bronze plaque bearing the inscription, *"Henry Thayer, Senior Vice President."*

As always, the door to Gordon's outer office was open, and Paul entered quietly. His father's secretary, in one of the grey tweed suits that she wore regardless of the season, was watering the row of plants lined up on the window sill, and Paul noted that her hand was trembling. Her eyes were red-rimmed, as though she had been crying.

"Hello, Miss Keebling," he said quietly.

"Oh! Paul."

"I'm so sorry. I didn't mean to startle you."

"No, it's my fault. I was—busy with my thoughts, and I didn't hear you."

"Is my father in, please?"

Miss Keebling hesitated for a fraction of a second. "He gave me strict instructions that he wasn't to be disturbed by anyone. So I think that includes you, Paul."

"But he is here?"

"Well, yes."

"Then would you tell him I'd like to see him, please?" He continued to speak gently, but there was a firmness in his voice, too.

And Martha Keebling, who had heard her employer use the same tone of authority for so many years, could not help but respond to it. "All right," she said uncertainly. "I just hate disobeying his orders, but everything is so dreadful and so mixed up that I—well, I'll tell him you're here."

She moved to the door of the inner sanctum, stood there in doubt for a moment, then went in. After what seemed like a very long time she came out and held the door ajar. Paul spoke before she had a chance. "Thank you, Miss Keebling," he said, and stepped past her.

Gordon was seated behind his desk, and the lines of exhaustion in his face were burned deep. There was nothing in front of him on his leather-bound blotter except a scratch pad, on which were some meaningless marks and smudges. Plainly he did not know what to make of this totally unexpected visit, but his surprise was tempered by the depletion of his energies.

"Hello, Paul," he said, rising.

"Hi, Dad."

They stared across the room at each other, then Gordon remembered that there were other things in the world than his business tragedy. "I've been intending to get hold of you. And Helga. I made a jackass out of myself, and if that's what you've come to hear, I hope you're satisfied. I'll repeat it for your wife."

"There's no need to do that," Paul said evenly. "Helga understands. She has all along, and she bears you no grudge. As for me, I wish you wouldn't apologize." It was difficult to catch his breath, but he continued doggedly. "That kind of thing is unnecessary—between you and me. Fathers and sons don't have to bother being formal with each other."

They met in the center of the office, their arms went around each other, but both turned their faces away. For several seconds they stood locked in an embrace, then at almost the same instant they were both overcome at this open display of their emotions and broke apart. Gordon returned to his swivel chair and Paul sat down opposite him.

"Thank you," Gordon said, looking straight at his son.

"If we start thanking each other for one thing or another, we could keep it up for hours." Paul tried to keep his voice light, but the emotions that welled up in him threatened to choke him. "I could spend the next twelve hours or so delivering a fancy monologue, thanking you for all sorts of things. Most of them, I imagine, you've forgotten. Like the tennis racquet you bought me when I was six. Or maybe I was only five."

[305]

The mention of tennis reminded them of what had been unsaid. "You've heard?" Gordon asked.

"I was there, Dad. I saw him. The Express sent me up to cover the story."

"I see," Gordon said, his voice compassionate.

Paul was not looking for sympathy, however; there were more vital matters on his mind. "How bad is it here, Dad?"

"Tough."

"How tough?"

"It couldn't be much worse." Gordon took a deep breath and began to draw on the scratch-pad. "I won't bore you with the details of how the company got into this mess. It's happened to hundreds of others, all over the country. Right now we're in an impossible jam, and that's what Henry couldn't face. If we're to have a chance of survival, we need refinancing on a big scale. I'm told the government will supply half if the rest comes from private sources. And of the remaining amount, I can get the banks to put up fifty percent if I'll put up the other fifty percent. It's a hefty bite."

"Too hefty, Dad? More than you have?" Paul persisted.

"If I throw in everything—my bonds and stocks, the property I own, cash in my life insurance, too, I can just about swing it. But it's a terrible gamble. There'd be no security of any kind left for your mother and the girls. And if the company didn't pull through after the refinancing, they'd be left clean as a bone."

"I see." Paul stared at the Venetian blinds and watched specks of dust drift in the sunlight. "I have about seven thousand dollars, Dad. I'll get it in the morning and throw it into the kitty."

"What about that newspaper you want to buy?" Gordon seemed to be developing a huskiness in his throat.

"Forget it. We're in trouble, aren't we?"

"Not quite that much trouble. Thanks, son, but your seven

[306]

thousand would be a drop in the bucket. What I've got to scrape together goes up into six figures."

Paul whistled soundlessly, stood and jammed his hands into his trouser pockets. "I hope," he said carefully, enunciating very slowly, "that you'll be going ahead."

Gordon could only look up at him, silently.

"You see, Dad, I don't have a job at the Express any more."

"You were fired?"

"No. I quit. About an hour ago."

"Why did you do that, Paul?"

"A few nights ago you said there was a need for me here." Paul looked at his father a trifle uncertainly. "I guess I should have checked with you first. Maybe you've decided to keep Fredericks after all."

"Fredericks isn't with us any more. I let him go yesterday. In fact, the way he handled his department is part of the reason for the mess the company is in. He wasn't honest. He made half-claims that sounded like one thing and were really another. As a result a lot of clients with whom we'd been doing business for a long time lost confidence in us and started going to our competitors."

"That's rough. And unprincipled."

"Very rough, Paul. And very unprincipled."

"Can those clients be won back, Dad?"

"That all depends. A hard-working promotion man—with ideals and integrity—might be able to restore the confidence that's been lost."

"I think I know the right fellow for the job, Dad. A guy who'll give it everything he's got and never stop trying."

Their eyes met and held; Paul could not see clearly, for everything was suddenly blurred, but he had the definite impression that his father was crying a little, too. Gordon pulled a handkerchief from his pocket, blew his nose vigorously, then picked up his telephone. "Miss Keebling," he said, "get me

George Franklin over at the bank. Right away. No, don't buzz me back. I'll hang on."

Paul lit a cigarette, and to his surprise his hands were steady. His tensions suddenly lessened and he grinned at his father. Gordon smiled back at him, then devoted his entire attention to the telephone.

"Hello, George ... Yes, I've come to a decision. I'm going ahead." He laughed, without bitterness. "Maybe I'm a brave man, or maybe I'm just a damn fool. We'll find out eventually. In any case, I'll have the full amount for you in cash and negotiable securities within forty-eight hours. And after you people have matched it, we'll get after Washington ... Oh? So much the better. We'll put through a call to him at the Mayflower Hotel first thing in the morning, then ... Right, George."

He hung up, looked down at the instrument for a moment, then crossed to the front of his desk. "That's it, Paul. And from the looks of things we'll have the Government loan set pretty fast, too." He gripped his son's shoulder. "In six months to a year, we'll have the answer. Either we'll weather this thing, or we'll be out in the street."

"If we are, we'll be out there together."

"I think we'll manage." In spite of Gordon's exhaustion, there was the beginning of a new note of confidence and strength in his voice.

"There's just one thing, Dad."

"Yes?"

"If it's all the same to you, I'd like to have the office—that was Uncle Henry's."

*   *   *

There was barely time, Helga thought, to prepare dinner before Paul came home. She had been delayed longer than she had bargained for on the South Side, but she couldn't have dashed away any sooner. After driving Molly home, it would have been impossible to avoid a talk with Betsy, and she just hoped she had done the right thing by advising her sister-in-law to return to college for the remainder of the school year. There was nothing Betsy could do here, her full tuition was already paid and it was senseless to give in to a sense of panic.

Helga was desperately sorry there had been no opportunity to discuss matters close to her own heart with Betsy, but Marcia had required attention when she had come home from school, and Molly had been too upset herself to soothe her younger daughter. In times of emergency, Helga had remembered, it was always best to give people something to do, so she had put Marcia to work in the kitchen, and had herself spent more than an hour with the child, helping her scrub vegetables, talking to her incessantly, soothing her.

But now that she was home again, her own problems loomed larger than ever before her. How Paul would react to the death of Henry Thayer, whether it would clarify things for him or make him even more bitter than before were questions she could not answer in advance. And it was useless to try.

She hastily changed into a white sweater and a pink linen skirt. Then, after running a comb through her hair, powdering her nose and freshening her lipstick, she started toward the kitchen. But as she approached it she heard a key in the front lock, and to her consternation Paul walked into the house.

"You're early," she said.

"Am I? Yes, I guess I am."

"I haven't even started to fix dinner yet." There was no time like the immediate present to let him know of her latest act of what he would consider disloyalty; she would bring it out into the open, and he would make of it what he would. "Your mother was here today. We had lunch, and then I drove her back out South, so I just got home a little while ago myself."

"I see."

She wasn't at all certain what it was that he saw, and her

sense of insecurity increased. As Paul moved toward the window, Helga was shocked at the appearance of his face. He was haggard and worn, and there was more than a hint in his features of what he would look like as an older man. He knew, then, about Henry Thayer.

"Your mother was dreadfully upset, and so were the girls."

"I imagine so."

"They were so worried about your father."

"They needn't be. I'll tell you about that. And later we can talk about Uncle Henry. Right now there are some other things I want to discuss with you."

"All right." Helga stood very still, looking at him. There was something different about Paul, she decided; in spite of whatever suffering he had undergone, his eyes were at peace now, and the lines of bitterness around his mouth had vanished. He was a man who had faced himself and his present, but whether his future included her was something she could not determine.

"I've left the Express—and the newspaper business. I'm a wholesale grocer now, as of about half an hour ago. How we're going to make out with the company we don't know. It'll be an uphill fight all the way, but we'll try."

"I'm sure you will." It would be disgraceful to weep, Helga told herself fiercely.

"I'm going to have my hands full, there's no mistake about that. The promotion man who had—my new job—did some pretty unethical things. So I'm going to have to convince Whitmarket's clients, and the public, too, that the company is honorable and that it's doing an honest job. There's a real principle at stake."

"I—I'm glad, Paul. You've exchanged the idealism of a boy for the principles of a man."

"I wouldn't put it that way. I've just discovered something that should have been obvious to me a long time ago, but I was too mixed up to see it. I don't have to be a newspaperman to be of service to people. The opportunity I have now is just as big and just as challenging. And what's more, Dad really needs me. That means something." He hesitated for an instant before continuing. "The feud with Dad is finished. He sends you his love."

"And I accept it very happily."

"So that settles just about everything, Helga. Except the one thing that's more important than all the rest put together. I mean—you and me."

"What about us, Paul?" Here at last was the moment she had been waiting for and yet dreading.

"If I'm turning into anything even vaguely resembling a human being, it's due to you. How you've put up with my—my adolescent stupidity is beyond me. So—if you feel you've played nursemaid long enough—I'll understand."

The tears came now, but Helga was laughing, too. "Oh, darling," was all she could say.

Paul went to her and took her into his arms. "Thank you for standing by. Thank you for being so patient—and wise—and—" Rather than finish the thought in words, he kissed her, with infinite tenderness.

When they finally moved apart, Helga was slightly breathless. "I haven't started to cook dinner yet."

"Never mind that just now. There's something I want to know first. Mrs. Dawson, will you marry me?"

"Mr. Dawson, I already have. For as long as we both shall live."